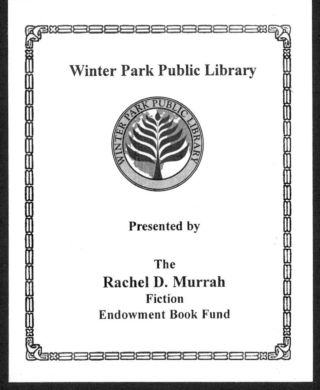

Sister's Choice

EMILIE RICHARDS

Sister's Choice

ISBN-13: 978-0-7783-2565-9
ISBN-10:   0-7783-2565-2

SISTER'S CHOICE

www.MIRABooks.com

Printed in U.S.A.

To all those quilt makers
who use their considerable needlework talents to help others,
particularly those who are working so hard to Quilt for a Cure.

8/08

ACKNOWLEDGMENT

When novels become alive for readers, new and interesting ideas can develop. One such idea was suggested to me by Pam Brown of Muscatine, Iowa, at a quilt-show book signing. So thanks to Pam, who wasn't shy about talking to me, for sending my own imagination in a brand-new and fruitful direction. Thanks, too, to the Brainstormers, Jasmine, Karen, Connie and Diane, for their energy and creativity.

Two sisters answered the call for a Sister's Choice quilt for this cover, one the quilt maker, one the recipient. Thanks to Kathy Rankin and Jeanne Prue for sharing their quilt. How appropriate that Jeanne's quilt, made to celebrate Kathy's brand-new master's degree, would inspire the cover art on a novel about the love between sisters.

PROLOGUE

Most of the time Kendra Taylor found that spending time with her nieces helped fill an empty space inside her. When Alison or Hannah wrapped their chubby arms around her neck or planted a sloppy kiss on her cheek, her primary feeling was gratitude that she and their mother, her younger sister, had finally built a bridge across the abyss of their dysfunctional childhood.

But "most of the time" also meant there were moments, like this one, when Kendra found herself wishing for more than a day, or even a week, when she and her husband, Isaac, could enjoy the high-voltage electricity of children in their lives. Now, as she watched four-year-old Alison shove a red-and-white Santa Claus hat over her copper Orphan Annie curls, she felt a pang she knew too well.

"They're something, aren't they?"

She turned at her husband's voice, and saw that Isaac had moved up beside her and was smiling at the little girls, who had woven their way into the crowd of onlookers enjoying the

National Christmas Tree on the Ellipse in Washington, D.C. In the background, the White House stood sentinel, as if to discourage snowflake intruders, but the air was chill and promising. Even the most powerful family in the nation might not be able to stop a light dusting later that evening.

"They are that," Kendra said, over the warbling of a high-school ensemble faithfully recounting "The Night Before Christmas" for everybody's enjoyment. "The girls know how to get what they want."

Without shoving or asking for favors, the girls had wormed themselves into front-row positions. Hannah, nearly eight, was instructing her sister on how close she was allowed, but Jamie, their mother, stood two rows behind, near enough to make a lunge in case the ebullient Alison decided to ignore her. There were model trains to tempt any little girl, and fifty additional trees, one for every state. Jamie was taking no chances.

"It's been a great visit," Isaac said.

Kendra linked arms with him and for just a moment rested her head against his shoulder. Jamie's arrival had been a surprise. They hadn't seen her since Labor Day, when she and her daughters had flown in to present the plans Jamie had drawn up for a small guest cabin on the property Kendra and Isaac owned in the Shenandoah Valley. Then, on the past Friday, after Kendra had casually mentioned on the phone that she and Isaac had nothing going on that weekend, Jamie and the girls had flown in to surprise them. Since they were scheduled to return in two weeks—on Christmas Eve—this additional trip was puzzling.

To their left, two laughing young couples were shouting down the seconds until five o'clock, when 75,000 lights would glow among the branches. Kendra watched Alison clap her hands as the lights finally came on and the magnificent blue spruce was magically transformed.

"I hate to see them leave, even though they'll be coming right back," Kendra said.

"Jamie's going to be looking for an internship as soon as she finishes her master's. Has she said where she plans to settle? Could this visit have anything to do with job hunting?"

"She's been surprisingly evasive."

Isaac glanced down at her. "What do you think that means?"

"Maybe she knows I'll disapprove?"

Isaac wasn't classically handsome, but he was easy to look at, tall and broad shouldered, hair and eyes a warm golden-brown, and these days wearing an expression of contentment that softened his strong features. Now he sent her the ghost of a smile as he touched her chin with a gloved finger.

"You don't think Jamie's beyond needing your approval, K.C.?"

When Isaac looked at her sister, Kendra knew he saw the redesigned Jamie, the only one he'd ever known. Sometimes she envied him that view. Yes, the Jamie she saw was at least partly that responsible adult, the excellent mother and fabulous cook, the talented student architect, the forthright young woman who never made self-serving excuses for wandering aimlessly, dangerously, through her young adulthood. This mature Jamie freely admitted to her failures and counseled others to avoid the same traps that had snared her. She was wise, forgiving and hungry to make amends.

But what about the other Jamie, the sister who had disappeared for years, who had given no thought to the pain she caused, who had brought two daughters into the world without allowing Kendra access to them? Unfortunately, *that* Jamie still lurked at the periphery of Kendra's vision. In Kendra's worst nightmares, *that* Jamie returned, and in an instant their newly established rapport vanished, her nieces were snatched from her life and she and Isaac were left alone again. Without Jamie, without the girls, without hope that children would ever be part of their days.

"I'm not sure she needs my approval," Kendra said. "But I do think she loves to avoid a hassle."

"A pretty common trait. I don't like hassles either, do you?"

She heard the gently veiled reminder to ease up. In the year and a half since Jamie had returned to Kendra's life, she had been difficult to fault. She was a spontaneous, freewheeling mother, with few stated rules and a tendency to overlook precise bedtimes. But under the thin veneer of "anything goes," the girls were learning a solid respect for others, a deep belief in their own abilities and the importance of making good decisions. Jamie seemed to be doing an excellent job.

"Worrying is deeply ingrained in me." Kendra squeezed his arm, then let her own fall free so she could wind her scarf tighter around her neck. "And right now I'm worried about Alison. She looks beat."

To her credit, apparently Jamie noticed that, too. As Kendra watched, Jamie stretched out her hand and rested it on Alison's drooping shoulder. Whatever she said did the trick, because Alison wiggled her way to her mother's side, and in a moment, dark-haired Hannah followed suit.

"Maybe she'll take a nap while we put dinner together," Isaac said.

Kendra doubted that, but she had squirreled away a couple of simple jigsaw puzzles and picture books for a quiet hour. In a moment, Jamie and the girls joined them. Kendra put her arm around Hannah's shoulder, and Isaac bundled Alison into his arms and out of the flow of the crowd.

"You two ready to go home?" Kendra asked.

Hannah leaned against her aunt's hip. She was blithely unaware that she shared her mother's fine-boned beauty, and today she had garbed herself in a faded denim skirt, an adult-size sweatshirt that displayed Harry Potter's Gryffindor crest, and olive-and-maroon-striped knee socks. For warmth the ensemble was covered by Kendra's faux fur jacket, which fell past her knees. Her shoulder-length hair was tied on top of her head with an elastic shoestring. No amount of coaxing on Kendra's part had convinced her that a barrette would be a better choice, or that a wool cap would be a welcome addition.

"Alison is ready. I would choose to stay, but there will be no living with her," Hannah said.

Quelling a smile, Kendra squeezed her niece's shoulder in commiseration. Hannah was an overly mature eight-year-old with a rich imagination, precise speech and a strong herding instinct. She kept Alison in line; sometimes Kendra suspected she kept Jamie in line, as well.

"This way we can beat the crowds to the Metro," Kendra said. "And I've got hummus and pita chips to snack on while Uncle Isaac and I make dinner."

With an expression of forbearance, Hannah ran ahead to catch up with Isaac and Alison, who were forging a path through the crowd. Kendra was left to pick her way with Jamie. They didn't speak until the crowd had thinned and they were walking side by side toward the nearest Metrorail stop at McPherson Square for the ride under the Potomac into Arlington.

Jamie glanced at a man who was giving her a visual once-over. She tossed her dark hair over one shoulder and gave him a small smile, just enough to let him know she'd noticed his attention, but not enough to encourage him to approach. Then she turned back to Kendra, who, despite herself, was impressed with her sister's easy confidence with men.

"I'm so glad we could make the trip," Jamie said. "It was such a luxury to just hop a plane. All kinds of opportunities have opened up for me, now that I have access to my trust fund."

Kendra had wondered how Jamie would deal with the unseemly amount of money she had recently inherited from their father's estate. When Kendra's share had been turned over to her eight years ago, she had left it where it was. She only used a fraction of the available interest for large purchases; most of the time she and Isaac lived within their means. Of course, knowing that they had no reason to save for a rainy day, no mortgage or car payments, meant that they could do almost anything they had the time to.

Until last year, when she had turned twenty-eight and her share had been turned over to her, Jamie had chosen to live on her own, without help or supervision from the estate. She had spent a lot of years counting pennies. The change had to be huge.

"I love being able to just get a ticket on the spur of the moment," Jamie said, as if she were reading her sister's thoughts. "But I still went to a broker for the cheapest deal. It's ingrained in me. I go to the consignment shop to look for clothes for the girls. I clip coupons." She gave a low, musical laugh. "I got three cans of creamed corn last week because the third one was free. I was halfway up the aisle before it hit me that none of us like creamed corn, and we don't have to eat it ever again."

"I tried to ignore the impact when the money came to me, but it's pretty hard. I wondered how you felt."

"I'm keeping most of the investments right where they are. Say what you will about Jimmy Dunkirk, but he knew the right people to watch over his money, and I don't see any reason to change that now."

Jimmy Dunkirk, their father, had died spectacularly—the way

he'd lived—in a skydiving accident. Although he had been a careless, absentee father, he had managed to nurture the multiple millions left to him and turn it over to them on his death. Kendra would have preferred love and affection, but she was fairly certain money was the best Jimmy had been capable of.

Now she saw an opening and took it. "If nothing else, the money'll help you get established after you graduate. I know you still have more than a year of graduate school. But have you made plans for what comes next?"

They had almost caught up to Isaac and the girls before Jamie answered. "Well, to some extent that depends."

"What depends on what?" Isaac asked, as if he had been part of the conversation all along.

"I was quizzing Jamie about her future," Kendra said.

They were interrupted by Alison, who pointed toward a shop across the sidewalk. A few minutes later the girls had to be prodded not to stand forever in front of the Santa display in the window. The moment to find out more about Jamie's plans was lost.

They reached the Metro stop at last, and Jamie took Hannah's hand for the escalator ride. Once they arrived at the proper platform, the girls took seats on a bench, and Isaac chatted with them. Kendra followed Jamie to the edge overlooking the rails. Somewhere, echoing in the distance, she could hear a lone violinist playing "Silent Night" for tips.

"Okay, I've been waiting for you to notice, and you haven't," Jamie said.

"Notice what?"

"What's different about me."

Kendra chewed her lip in concentration. "Since Labor Day?"

"Uh-huh."

Kendra gazed at her sister. Jamie's hair—one shade from

black—was still halfway down her back, falling in waves from a deep widow's peak. The body under a bright pink ski jacket wasn't visible, but Kendra hadn't noticed that Jamie had gained or lost weight. She still wore her jeans tight enough to showcase a small waist and narrow hips. She still attracted attention just by the way she carried herself and met the eyes of any man who cared to look her way.

Isaac joined them, turned slightly so he could still see the girls. "I haven't seen you smoke."

Kendra realized he was right. "Did you quit?" she asked Jamie. "You've always been so careful about smoking outside that I just didn't pay attention."

"I quit." Jamie nodded to Isaac. "Right after I got back to Michigan after Labor Day."

"Good for you." Kendra gently punched her sister's arm.

"Yeah, way to go," Isaac said.

Kendra heard the rumbling of a train heading their way. "What made you do it?"

"I never smoke when I'm pregnant."

For a moment Kendra thought she'd heard her sister wrong. Then, when she realized she hadn't, she searched for an explanation other than the obvious. Jamie was simply pointing out that she could stop and had already proved it twice. Now she was announcing that it was time to make that permanent.

But even as she ran through those possibilities in her mind, Kendra knew that wasn't what her sister had meant at all. In her own way, Jamie had been answering Kendra's question about her future. This was not a change of subject but an explanation. As that realization hit her, the void deep inside—the empty place that would never be filled with a child because she could never risk carrying one—throbbed in protest.

Jamie had already proven that she could get pregnant without making an effort. Double proof was sitting on the bench behind them. Hannah and Alison were the product of two casual relationships, and their arrival in the world had been unplanned.

"You're pregnant?" she asked, as the train, not yet in sight, grew louder.

Jamie rested her hand on Kendra's arm. "Not yet."

Kendra tried to make sense of this. They were standing on the edge of a subway platform; people streamed by on their way from holiday events downtown. Isaac was beside her, and they were going home for a quiet family evening before Jamie and the girls disappeared again. But there was something here she didn't understand, something large enough that Jamie had chosen this moment to play it down. She had needed the crowd, the rush, the noise, to make her announcement.

"I don't get it," Kendra said, and she heard the edge to her words. "You've decided to have another baby? While you're in grad school? Is there a man in the picture? Somebody you're in love with?"

"No, somebody else is in love with this man." Jamie searched her sister's face. Her smile was tentative. "You were asking about my plans for the future. Well, in the immediate future, I want to have another baby. *Your* baby, Ken. Yours and Isaac's."

Kendra stared speechlessly at her sister, but Jamie went on.

"I want to be your surrogate. I'm in perfect health, and my doctor's given me the go-ahead. You can conceive, and I can carry. There's nothing I want to do more, and I want to do it this summer, when I'll have some of my basic graduate work behind me. I can live in the guest cabin out in the Valley—if it's finished by then—and keep an eye on the crew building your new house and learn some things while I'm at it. You're getting *those* plans for Christmas, by the way."

"Jamie…"

Jamie held up her hand. "I can do some work on my own and take a break from formal classes until I'm sure what area I want to concentrate on. The timing's right for me, and I know it's right for you."

The train appeared, then slowed as it approached the platform, but Kendra might as well have been standing on a newly discovered planet. She didn't know the language to communicate what she was feeling. Somewhere deep inside she thought that the girls must have felt just this way as they waited, breaths held, for the Christmas tree to blaze into life.

Jamie rested her hand on Kendra's arm. "Don't make this hard, Ken. It's easy. All you have to do is say yes. Let me do this for you and Isaac. Let me do it for all of us."

1

Jamie Dunkirk could sell almost anything. Maybe her talents hadn't always been put to the best uses, but in her twenty-nine years, she had proven her ability to make quick connections and convince likely targets they had to have whatever she was peddling. Without conceit, she knew that nobody was better at building excitement until a buyer was ready to take the plunge.

Still, nothing she had sold in all her years had been as difficult as selling Kendra and Isaac on her offer to carry their baby.

In the end, her sister and brother-in-law's deep yearning for a child, not her own expert salesmanship, had prevailed. They hadn't been easily swayed by words. They had considered and re-considered all the things that could go wrong, then balanced them against the possibility of a baby, their very own baby, in their arms. The scales had been heavily tipped.

Now, if luck and Mother Nature did their part, one of the embryos a doctor had placed inside her three days ago was settling in for nine months of incredible changes. And when that baby emerged and she presented the squalling, sticky bundle to its rightful parents, Jamie knew she would finally have sold *herself* the most important commodity of all.

Forgiveness.

"Really!"

As so often happened, a living, breathing child interrupted Jamie's train of thought. "Really, we have to be there," Hannah said. "Are you sure we haven't passed it?"

Jamie glanced at the passenger seat of her minivan and saw that once again her older daughter was tracing their route on the Virginia map with her index finger. A callus was sure to develop before they arrived in Toms Brook.

"The exit is just ahead," Jamie said. "And Aunt Kendra's still following us. Right? Don't you think she would have called me on the cell phone if I passed the turn by mistake?"

Hannah looked frazzled, but Jamie couldn't blame her. Since the end of May, their lives had changed so drastically that even the adaptable Hannah hadn't been able to keep up. First they had terminated the lease on their house in Michigan—the only home Hannah really remembered—then they had packed their belongings and put most of them in storage. Finally Hannah and Alison had said goodbye to the friends and parents of friends who had peopled their little world. The future was a question mark, and even a whole week spent with Kendra and Isaac hadn't cured Hannah's anxiety about what was coming next.

Unfortunately that was just for starters. Hannah didn't know that her mother might be pregnant with her aunt and uncle's baby. There was plenty of time to tell her once the test was positive. The thought of explaining surrogacy to an eight-year-old, even one as mature and intelligent as Hannah, made Jamie long for the simplicity of the birds and the bees.

Hannah looked over her shoulder to see if Kendra really *was* following them. "I have to go to the bathroom."

"Which is why I suggested that you forgo that last juice box."

"Is there proof I wouldn't have to go now, if I had?" She sounded more interested than combative.

Hannah's analytical nature was Jamie's reward for sleeping with Hannah's father, a hotshot attorney. Larry Clousell wasn't often on the scene. He didn't like children and found parenting too complex to master in his brief interludes between high-profile court cases. Still, this little apple hadn't fallen far from the tree. More and more often Jamie saw flashes of Larry in their daughter, and she knew that before long, Hannah, too, would win every battle she engaged in. By the time Hannah was in college, no doubt Larry and Hannah would discover their similarities and become fast friends—after he apologized for more or less abandoning her as a child. Until then, this verbal sparring was Jamie's penance.

"Hannah, what goes in must come out. That's a general rule of physics, and it applies here. We'll be there soon. You can wait."

"You're sure of that?"

Jamie lightly poked her in the arm. "Stop giving me a hard time. I'm tired, too."

"I liked the old cabin."

"You remember it?"

"Of course." Hannah rarely pouted, but now she was doing a reasonable imitation. "It had *character.*"

Jamie tried not to smile. "Well, now the new cabin will have characters. Two of them. You and Alison. And your aunt and uncle say it's very inviting."

"Do we have to live there if we don't like it?"

Jamie considered. "No."

"You're certain?"

"Who could be more certain? I'm in charge. There are plenty of other places to live. It's just that this makes sense, don't you think? The contractors are going to start building Uncle Isaac and Aunt Kendra's new house using the plans I drew for them. We can live in the cabin, and I can be there to learn some things and watch it go up."

"Why did the old one have to burn down?"

"Because somebody was careless with a cigarette. Another reason not to smoke."

"You smoked."

"And I quit."

"Forever?"

"I hope so."

"Why would you start again?"

Jamie wished they were already at the new cabin and the questions were finished. "Some things have a very strong pull, even when we know they're bad for us. That's why it's a good idea not to start bad habits. Not starting is pretty easy. Quitting is not."

"Like the people at First Step? The ones who are trying to quit using drugs?"

"You got it."

"Is there a list of things I shouldn't start? So I will know?"

"You learn them along the way. And I'll be helping, so you don't have to worry."

"You might want to put them in writing. So I can check every once in a while."

"I'll take that under advisement."

"Alison is lucky. She can sleep anywhere. I want to sleep, too, only I have to go to the bathroom."

Jamie was delighted to see the Toms Brook exit sign. "Hold on, kiddo. We'll be there in a few minutes."

"That will be just about right." Hannah closed her eyes.

The trip down I-81 had been scenic enough to remind Jamie what was in store for her. But now, turning off the highway and pulling over to give Kendra the lead, she let the cool green of pastures and the rise of mist-shrouded mountains blunt the fears she hadn't shared with her daughter.

Jamie knew herself better than most people. She had spent a year as a client at First Step, a drug treatment program, then more years as a staff counselor. No professional played games with addicts, because nobody could ever beat one. Addicts were the ultimate gamesmen, so brutal truth was the rule of the day. Her fellow staff members had never been shy about ticking off a list of her faults. She was impulsive and idealistic. Her expectations, particularly of herself, were ridiculous. She was tactful when she should be forthright; she was too slow to give up on losers and too quick to forgive. She continually strove for absolution.

Ron Rosario, the director of First Step, had put it this way: "You're not ever going to be content, Jamie, not until you make some sacrifice so huge that even you'll feel you've made up for the bad times."

So, knowing what she did about herself, Jamie had considered, then reconsidered, the extraordinary idea of becoming Kendra and Isaac's surrogate.

She wasn't sure when the idea had taken root. In September, after visiting them and seeing how delighted they were to spend time with her daughters, she had caught an interview on a morning news show with a woman who had carried her infertile sister's baby.

The story hadn't shocked her. She'd felt as if a question had been answered, a miracle had been witnessed. Somewhere inside, she must have nurtured this possibility, even if the words hadn't surfaced. Because when she heard the woman recount the joys of giving her beloved sister a baby she could not bring into the world herself, Jamie had known, beyond the shadow of a doubt, that this was her mission, too.

But she was impulsive. She was prone to idealism. She knew it, had survived having it pounded into her psyche until she understood how she could be harmed by both. So she had researched. She had surfed Internet bulletin boards, spoken to a counselor at a local fertility clinic, consulted with her own doctor. She had scheduled a few personal sessions with Rosario—which were guaranteed to knock the stuffing out of any bad idea. And in the end, the resolve that had formed while she watched that morning news show had grown even stronger.

She would do for Kendra what Kendra could not do for herself because of childhood injuries. She would carry her child. And when she was done, she would hand over the baby to her sister and brother-in-law, knowing that no couple would be better parents or love it more. Selfishly, she would know that she had helped create a cousin for her own daughters, who would never have one otherwise. Together, she and Kendra would raise their beautiful children to be healthy, happy adults. This new generation would have the start that she and Kendra had not. This would be a rebirth of the Dunkirk family.

"So, okay, that last part's a little over-the-top."

Hannah opened her eyes. "What?"

Jamie realized she had been muttering out loud. "See, we're at the *top* of the hill leading down to your aunt and uncle's land. We'll be there any minute."

Alison shrieked, not an uncommon occurrence when she first awoke from a nap.

"You might want to drive faster," Hannah advised.

"I want to get out!" Alison shrieked.

"Hold on tight." Jamie made noises of sympathy to her youngest and leaned on the accelerator.

Fitch Crossing Road had a Toms Brook address, but the tiny Virginia town was some distance away. The road was narrow and windy. Houses dotted the borders. Some had the shady, inviting front porches of another age, where inhabitants met in the evening to chat or tell stories; others were brick boxes that relied on air-conditioners for relief from the heat and television for entertainment. But no matter which they preferred, neighbors here relied on each other for help and support, rarely on elected or paid officials. Two years before, Kendra had moved here for several months and had made a number of friends.

Although the cabin where Kendra had retreated no longer stood, plans to live permanently on the property had survived. Now Kendra and Isaac wanted to begin rebuilding, with an eye toward moving here in the near future. Kendra hoped to use her experience as an investigative reporter at the *Washington Post* to freelance or work on a book, and Isaac, who was the head of a fledgling environmental group that concentrated on the health of the nation's rivers, hoped to move his office here, to the doorstep of the Shenandoah River, one of the waterways that needed his assistance.

Kendra braked, and Jamie followed suit. Then she trailed her sister down a long drive and slowed to a crawl.

"The driveway's a lot better. I think they've widened it. They've certainly graded it, and this looks like brand-new gravel."

"Gravel will be hard to ride a bike on."

Hannah had learned the rudiments of bike riding, but she was still prone to the occasional spill. Jamie had to agree. Spills on gravel would be lethal.

"We'll find good places for you to ride," she promised.

"Will there be anybody to play with?"

"If there isn't, I'll pick up your friends and bring them here."

"How will I make friends when it's already summer?"

"The neighbors are nice. I wouldn't worry too much. We'll find friends."

But even as she spoke, Jamie wondered how she and the girls would be greeted. Unless Kendra was completely open with the locals about the surrogacy, Jamie would simply appear to be an unwed mother. Having twice earned that title the normal way, she knew that not everybody would accept her or her children. For some people, the way a child came into the world was far more important than the child itself.

But even if the truth was widely known, there would still be people who felt what she was doing was unnatural and therefore wrong. They would not see that the act of giving birth to her sister's child was an expression of love, a family miracle. She just hoped those people would keep to themselves and not upset her daughters.

Kendra pulled to a stop before Jamie expected. The ruins of the old cabin were gone, and Kendra parked in the clearing near where they'd been. To Jamie's surprise, the new cabin that she had designed for her sister was nowhere in sight, although she had envisioned it on the western edge of the Taylors' property.

She turned off the engine and got out, then opened a rear door to help Alison out of her seat. "Did you forget to tell me something?" she called to Kendra.

Kendra slammed her door and started toward the van. Sunlight picked out the subtle red highlights in a wealth of brown curls. She was poised and elegant, despite freckles and a generous mouth. Kendra would look equally at home on a polo pony or a yacht, but Jamie knew that what seemed to be an aloof sophistication was just a barrier she erected to keep trespassers away.

Now Kendra snapped her fingers. "Oh, darn, I forgot. We didn't build your cabin after all. I guess you and the girls will have to camp out."

Hannah's eyes were wide. "Is there a tent large enough?"

Kendra ruffled her niece's hair. "I was just teasing your mom. There is a cabin, but don't worry, if you want to sleep in a tent some night, I'll come down and camp with you."

"Alison will want to come, too, and she is often afraid of noises." Hannah eyed her sister, who was rubbing her eyes. "We could wait until she's asleep."

"Oh, I think I have a tent big and safe enough for all of us."

"So what did you do with the cabin?" Jamie's curiosity was simmering.

"I think you'll be pleased." Kendra pointed to a road winding through the woods that bordered the clearing. "We can drive right up to the front door, or we can walk and stretch our legs."

"Little House in the Big Woods," Hannah said. "Like the book."

"This is more like *Little House in the Tiny Woods.*" Kendra draped an arm over her niece's shoulders. "These woods were cleared sometime in recent history for timber, so there weren't a lot of big trees to worry about when we selected a site for the cabin. We cleared away the scrub and left the nicest trees in place. I think you'll love the view. You can see the river below."

"Hannah, you'll be okay?" Jamie asked, remembering their bathroom conversation. But Hannah nodded enthusiastically.

They didn't have to walk for long. The road wound to the right, and a clearing opened up in front of them. Perched in the center was the cabin.

"And here's your mommy's masterpiece," Kendra said.

Jamie stopped to take in the details. She had not envisioned her plan in this setting, yet it was picture-perfect. The cabin was simple, meant for an occasional weekend getaway until Kendra and Isaac's new home was ready. Then it would function as a guesthouse or even an office. She had designed it with nearly as much square footage on the wraparound porch as inside. A loft rose over what was essentially one large room with a fireplace. A kitchen, bathroom and bedroom lined up along one side.

"For sentiment's sake, we used a few of the logs we were able to save from Isaac's grandmother's cabin for the beams. And the stone from her foundation went into the fireplace. The new with the old." Kendra faced her sister. "But it was never meant for a family, Jamie. You know that best of all. Are you sure you want to stay here? You have so many other options."

Jamie had considered all of them. She'd thought about moving somewhere new to begin a job in an architectural firm. Staying in Michigan and finishing the last of her course work. Moving here. Moving to Arlington to be near Kendra and Isaac while she was pregnant with their baby. She knew if she did the latter Kendra could help with the girls and be active in every part of Jamie's prenatal care.

In the end, she had discounted most of them. The first two options had seemed cruel. Jamie wanted her sister and brother-in-law to witness and participate as their child grew. And trips to and from Michigan, or anywhere else, would tire all of them unnecessarily, particularly if the first in vitro procedure didn't work.

The last option, moving to Arlington, had presented a different set of problems. Jamie's relationship with Kendra held promise, but so many things could still go wrong. The phrase "nipped in the bud" had been coined for situations like this one. She wasn't sure their relationship would blossom if it was fussed over and cultivated with too much vigor. So in the end, she had chosen to be near, but not too near. She hoped she'd done the right thing.

Jamie shooed the girls in the direction of their new home, and they took off to explore, Alison's short legs working double-time to keep up with her sister's.

"We'll give it a try, Ken, but I think we'll be comfortable. You forget, at this age the girls don't take up much space. I'll take the loft, they can take the bedroom."

"That's what I thought you'd do. But you're not afraid that climbing stairs will be a problem if…" Kendra fell silent, as if she was afraid that by speaking her greatest desire out loud, it would never come true.

"You've got to trust me. I have the most amazing preg-nancies. A few steps up to a loft will mean nothing. And I wouldn't let Alison sleep upstairs with Hannah. She'd swing from the rafters."

"At least they're sturdy rafters."

Although Kendra was trying hard to make light of things, Jamie heard her sister's fears. Everything in her life was changing, and so much of it was out of her control. As children, Kendra had been Jamie's only reliable caretaker. Kendra, who was thirty-seven to Jamie's twenty-nine, had been forced to grow up too soon and assume responsibility for her little sister because nobody else in their unstable family had any interest in doing so. So after a lifetime of being in charge, letting go, when so much was at stake, was alien and frightening.

"I know you'd like to watch over me, and wait on my girls hand and foot," Jamie said. "I understand that. But we have to have our own life separate from yours and everything else that's happening. Just don't worry. I promise that you and Isaac will see lots of us over the next year. By the time this is finished and you're changing diapers, you may wish we'd stayed in Michigan."

"That's not remotely possible."

"When the baby comes, Ken, the girls and I need to have other things going for us. I want them to see this as a gift we gave you while we were going about our ordinary lives. I don't want the next months to be all about the pregnancy. If they are, it's going to be too hard for them—" she paused "—and me to move on the way we'll need to."

"I can see that." Kendra released a deep breath. "It's just that things could go wrong out here."

Jamie thought about all the things that had gone wrong when Kendra had lived on this property. "You should know."

"Touché."

"I promise we won't burn the place down. We'll scare away varmints, and if we have a problem with trespassers, I'll make sure to report them. I'll have a telephone. We have neighbors. I have a car. There's a hospital nearby, and a rescue squad. And being pregnant's not an illness. Maybe we'll move in with you for that last month or so. We'll see. But for the time being, you have to relax."

Hannah was up on the porch now, peering into the windows. "There's furniture! Can we go in?"

"Leave the door open for Alison."

Hannah disappeared. Jamie figured she would find the bathroom on her own, since the house was only about thirty-six by twenty-four feet without the porch.

"I hope you like what Isaac and I bought to put inside," Kendra said.

"Having you furnish it made it so easy to just put all our stuff in storage. I'm grateful."

"You know, anything you need, anything at all, you only have to pick up the telephone."

Jamie stopped just before the porch. From inside she heard squeals of delight. "I know you. This place may be small, but it'll have everything I could ever want."

Impulsively, she reached out and touched her sister's arm to stop her from going inside. "We haven't really had a chance to be alone and talk. But we'll need to along the way. I have no qualms about this. I know I'm going to carry a healthy baby to term for you and Isaac. And I know you're going to be wonderful parents. But there aren't any manuals for our situation. I'm pretty sure it's not in any of the guides I consulted when I was pregnant with the girls. So we have to feel our way, and we have to give each other space. Then, when the big payoff comes, we'll be ready. All of us."

Kendra didn't look at her. "It's *such* a big thing, Jamie. You know how big it is, right? And if *I'm* scared, how must you feel?"

"Well, if you come around to visit often enough, I'll tell you. That'll help us both."

"I wake up in the middle of the night now and wonder what we've forgotten to worry about. You're right, there aren't any manuals. What if we've forgotten something important, something so important we can't get around it or over it?"

"Then we'll ask somebody for a road map."

"What if this comes between us?"

Jamie put her arm around her sister's waist. "And what if it binds us together in a brand-new way? Let me do this. Let me give you this. Just have some faith, okay?"

"Maybe this is hormones?" Kendra and Jamie had both been subjected to months of strong hormones to regulate their menstrual cycles and prepare for the implantation. Kendra had provided the eggs and Jamie the perfect host environment and both of them had been poked and prodded almost beyond endurance. Neither had enjoyed the chemical part of the experience, and Jamie was still taking progesterone to improve the odds of implantation.

"Maybe you're just preparing for motherhood," Jamie said. "I can guarantee you'll worry all the time."

Alison threw the door open wide and stepped back out onto the porch. "Mommy, bunk beds!"

"Oh, good, something new for *me* to worry about," Jamie said. "Will Alison try to crawl up to the top bunk with Hannah and fall on her head?"

"It's the safest system money can buy. I did the research."

"See what a good mom you'll be? So you concentrate on that, and let me take care of the little stuff."

"Like having the baby?"

Jamie felt a rush of love for her sister and hoped they would stay this connected in the months to come. She squeezed. "Nothing to it, Ken. A piece of cake. I promise."

Silently, she prayed she was right.

2

Little lives were not always shaped by big decisions, by moves across country or physical upheavals. More often, the lives of children were shaped by the small decisions, the mundane inter-actions, the patience required just to avoid leaving footprints on a little girl's soul. That was when the true mettle of motherhood was tested. Jamie had told herself that from the moment she had become a parent. And from that very moment, she'd learned that following her own good advice wasn't always going to be easy.

Two adult-free days later, two days of hormones that made her skin crawl and her breasts ache, Jamie summoned a new shot of serenity as she listened to yet another in the barrage of Hannah's questions.

"Our stuff comes today? You're sure? Manny and Warren can find us?"

Busy trying to tame her youngest daughter's mop of curls, Jamie glanced up and forced herself to wink at her oldest. "I dropped a trail of bread crumbs. Don't you remember? And they promised they'd follow it here."

"If you dropped bread crumbs, the birds ate them. We have lived here almost forever."

"Two days, Hannah, and the guys just left Michigan yesterday. I promise they'll find us."

Jamie gently nudged Alison back into a sitting position, grabbed one last lock of hair and teased out the tangles with a wide-toothed comb. Alison, with her pink cheeks, green eyes and copper-colored hair, looked as if she'd just arrived as an exchange child from the Emerald Isle. Her father, Seamus Callahan, had bequeathed her everything except the curls. Those had come from Jamie's father, Jimmy, an inheritance that Alison shared with her aunt Kendra. Jamie wondered if Kendra's baby—if there was a baby—would emerge, as Alison had, with curls already plastered to its tiny head.

"I wish we had a big truck."

Jamie tried to envision a real moving van creeping up their gravel driveway instead of the Ford Econoline with the two college students she'd hired to bring their personal belongings. "We'll have a big van when we settle somewhere and they bring all our furniture."

"But you promise they will have our clothes and toys?"

"I promise. I promise!" Jamie released her hold on Alison, who sprang to her feet and tackled her sister. Hannah, who was habitually braced for this event, caught her and pushed her back toward her mother.

Alison had been as patient as she could manage. "I want to go outside!"

Jamie nabbed her youngest daughter for a big hug. "We can do that. But it's sunny today. You have to wear a hat." She looked up. "Both of you."

Hannah rolled her eyes, but retreated to the pegs beside the back door, where hats and raincoats were hung. Alison followed at a gallop.

Jamie waited where she was. The pegs were child-height. In fact, everything in the cabin had been planned with children in mind. The bedroom closet was sectioned so the girls could hang their clothes on the bottom rack and store more in cubbyholes on the side. The room had shelves along two walls, wide enough for toys and low and strong enough to perch on for play. The state-of-the-art bunk beds had a dresser and two cubbyholes for night treasures. On the porch, two rocking chairs scaled to a child's shorter legs held special places.

Jamie wasn't surprised at Kendra's attention to detail. The cabin was tiny, but Kendra had treated that as an asset. She had scaled down, carefully choosing just the right pieces to make the cabin feel like home. From the Egyptian cotton sheets to the All-Clad cookware, no effort had been spared to make staying there comfortable and easy. In the days since their arrival, Jamie hadn't needed one thing that Kendra hadn't provided.

The cabin itself was extraordinary. Jamie had designed it as a class project oriented toward using readily available materials and fixtures that were commonly stocked at lumberyards and big-box stores. In theory, the design was geared toward do-it-yourselfers planning to put up their own vacation nest.

Rosslyn and Rosslyn, Kendra's builders, had taken her basic plans to an entirely different level. Quality materials and workmanship had been the rule here. The natural cherry cabinets had custom detailing; the counters were desert-sand granite. The lone bathroom, though small, had an etched glass shower surround and slate tile. She was particularly fond of the copper sink mounted on a handcrafted iron pedestal.

She was sorry that she hadn't been able to participate in the construction of the cabin, but there wasn't much she would have done differently. Kendra and the Rosslyns had made the cabin their own with subtle modifications and creativity. In the big picture, that meant Jamie's plans were adaptable and therefore a success. Photos of the cabin, along with the blueprints, would take priority in her portfolio.

Someday—which seemed like a long stretch into the future at that moment—she really *would* need a bigger and better portfolio. She would hang on to that thought in the months to come.

The girls screeched to a halt in front of her. All morning, she had promised a walk to the old orchard at the edge of the property, and she knew if they waited much longer, they would end up dragging themselves home, moping and sweaty. Since she was counting on the walk to tire them out, not transform them into heat zombies, the time had come.

"Okay, let's scoot," she told them. "Let's see who can spot the first bluebird."

Outside, she drew in a deep breath and almost tasted the humidity. Maybe June had just established a foothold, but no matter what the calendar said, summer had arrived. Despite the heat, the excess of hormones and her unusually short supply of patience, the morning seemed almost idyllic, a long breath expelled after years of combining school, work and parenting.

Jamie was not by nature a worrier. She was sure she had done the right thing by volunteering to carry a child for her sister and by bringing the girls to Virginia. She had her whole life ahead of her, years in which she could do exactly what she wanted to. Nine months was not a long time in the scheme of things. The time at the cabin would be a transition, a chance to take stock, to look over possibilities and make the best choices for their future.

But the reality of what was in store was already beginning to set in. She adored her daughters, would walk barefoot up an erupting volcano for them, would swim the length of the Shenandoah. But the uninterrupted stretch of time alone with them, the confines of the cabin, a community where she and the girls were complete strangers? She just hoped that in addition to her daughters' eccentric, charming companionship, she could find an accepting adult or two to converse with from time to time. Over the next year, she and the girls were going to need all the friends they could muster.

The girls took off for the orchard willingly enough, watching for flashes of blue along the route.

"I'm going to run!" Alison ran ahead, and Hannah allowed her a head start, then took off after her. Jamie followed behind, hauling a mesh bag with a Frisbee, bottled water, a picnic blanket, granola bars and *The Marvelous Land of Oz,* which she was reading out loud.

The trip to the apple orchard was short. The small orchard might once have been productive enough to help feed Leah Spurlock Jackson, Isaac's grandmother, and his mother, Rachel. Now, however, the trees were in the final stages of decline. Some had died with their roots still planted in the earth; others had fallen. Here and there, a carpet of dried blossoms indicated that some had struggled to bloom in May, but Jamie saw no indication of fruit. Her knowledge of gardening was limited to a philodendron that the girls had watered to death, but she wondered if any of the old trees could be saved.

She spread a blanket on the grass, then took out the Frisbee, but the girls wanted to explore.

"I will collect flowers," Hannah announced. "There are enough to share with the animals who live here."

"I'm sure the squirrels and chipmunks will approve." Knowing where the flowers would go for the return trip, Jamie opened her water bottle and drank a couple of slugs to prepare.

"Do you think Black Beauty left when the cabin burned down?" Hannah asked.

Jamie remembered Black Beauty well, but she was impressed her daughter did, too. He—or possibly she—was a gargantuan black rat snake who had lived under the old cabin and nearly scared Jamie to death the first time he'd showed himself. The girls, on the other hand, had been fascinated.

"Aunt Kendra said she saw him slither off into the woods right before the fire," Jamie assured her. "So he's safe somewhere, and probably two feet longer by now."

"Do you think he will come to live under our cabin?"

Jamie wondered how fast she could pack if he did.

They meandered, stopping every two feet to look at something, discussing snakes and squirrels and the kinds of birds that lived nearby. Alison and Hannah spotted the same bluebird at the same moment, a perfect end to the contest, then followed it deeper into the woods. As they went, the girls collected rocks and oddly shaped twigs, trading them back and forth like legitimate currency.

"I bet the woodpeckers love the old apple trees," Jamie said. "Bugs like to live under the bark, and woodpeckers like to eat bugs."

"If I invented the world, I would not let one animal eat another," Hannah said.

"How about flies and mosquitoes?"

"I would not invent flies and mosquitoes."

"I don't like mosquitoes," Alison said, siding with her sister. "I like spiders."

"I would not invent spiders, either," Hannah told her.

"I'd be sad."

They were just about to turn around and head back for the blanket when Alison stopped. She pointed just beyond them, where the woods parted and eventually opened up to Fitch Crossing Road.

"I see something!"

They hadn't walked far, but even in the woods, the air was warm and humid. Already tired, Jamie was ready to finish her water and collapse for a while. She had been warned not to interpret unusual symptoms as in vitro success, but she remembered feeling exactly this way when she was pregnant with both girls.

"There's always something to see," she said, resting her hand on her daughter's back. "But let's head to the blanket, okay?"

Alison resisted. "It moved!"

"Maybe it was a squirrel. There are lots of them around here."

"Bigger." Alison spread her hands. Then, before Jamie could stop her, she plunged deeper into the woods, not in the direction Jamie wanted to go.

"Come back, Alison." Jamie knew better than to depend on instant obedience. With thoughts of Black Beauty or worse, she took after her daughter to corral her.

Alison stopped abruptly. "See?"

Jamie nearly tripped over Alison's compact body. Without thinking, she put an arm out to hold Hannah back and snatched Alison with the other to keep her from going any closer.

But the sight that greeted all of them was nothing to be afraid of. Not far from their feet was a fawn, curled up in a ball. Its coloring was perfect camouflage, and if it had been moving before, now it was as still as a log. Jamie wondered how her youngest daughter had spotted it.

"Oh, Mommy." Hannah tried to move forward, but Jamie held her back. "But it's all alone."

"I'm sure its mommy is nearby," Jamie said.

"How do you know?"

"See how perfectly it blends into the ground and the leaves? I bet its mommy left it here while she went off to find food. We have to go."

"But how do you know for sure?"

"Mommy animals know how to raise their young. If we move the baby, or maybe even if we touch it, the mommy will be afraid to come and take care of it. And it could die."

"But what if the mommy is gone? Then it *will* die."

Jamie pressed her lips together before she said something she regretted. She knew this was an argument she couldn't win. Her oldest daughter would not forget about the fawn. Hannah would worry and fret until she was sure the little deer was safe.

"Here's what we'll do. I'll hang my hat on this tree." She took off the Detroit Tigers baseball cap she'd worn to shield her face from the sun and hung it on the branch of a nearby sapling. "Then we'll come back in the morning and check. How's that?"

"I want to check sooner."

"That won't give the mommy enough time to know it's safe to move the baby. She'll be afraid we'll come back."

"It might be sad all night, and crying."

"I think it will be sadder if we interfere and scare off its mommy."

Hannah squatted. "Are you sad?" she asked the fawn. "Do you need help?"

"Hannah! The poor little thing is hoping you don't see it. Let's get out of here and let the mommy come back." Jamie urged Hannah up with a hand on her back.

"I saw it," Alison said. "Me!"

"Yes, you did. What wonderfully sharp eyes you have. I'm very proud of you."

Alison beamed.

Jamie managed to drag them away, but not until they had stopped for half a dozen peeks until they were too far from the fawn to see it anymore. Once they were out of sight, she knew their imaginations would set to work. The fawn would never be out of their minds.

Thirty minutes later, after snacks and wildflower selection, they were finally resting on the blanket when the rumble of an engine sounded from the direction of the cabin. Jamie hoped the movers had arrived although, knowing how much college students liked to sleep in, she had expected them much later in the afternoon.

She pushed herself to a sitting position. Hannah had been telling a story based on cloud shapes, but she had run out of steam and was recycling the plot. No surprise, the clouds had yielded a herd of deer and a mean wolf who wanted to eat them, until a little girl saved them.

"Somebody's here," Jamie said, hoping whoever it was might help the girls forget the fawn, at least temporarily. "Are you girls ready to go back?"

Alison bolted upright. "Lunch!"

Jamie got to her feet and offered her oldest daughter a hand. "Let's see who's here, then we can eat."

As they packed up and started down the hill toward the cabin, the girls argued about what kind of sandwich they preferred. Jamie had found a natural-foods market in Woodstock and a farm stand on the outskirts. She was looking forward to buying fresh produce, and cooking for Kendra and Isaac when they came to visit. Since it was a passion and something she could do at the cabin, she suspected she would be cooking a lot in the next months.

"We ought to plant some tomatoes," Jamie said as they neared the clearing. "And maybe some peppers. We can learn how. I don't think it's too late in the season. Aunt Kendra said there's space in the beds near the old cabin site."

"I want to grow M&M's." Alison shoved Hannah when she laughed. "I do! Stop it!"

Jamie started to scoop up her youngest daughter, then she re-membered that the doctor had warned her against lifting anything heavy while she waited to see if the in vitro was successful. Instead she pulled Alison close and admonished her softly.

"You can't grow M&M's in any garden," she explained after she'd delivered a mini-lecture on shoving. "They make them in factories. But I'll tell you what. If you help me plant tomatoes, I'll buy you a pack of M&M's. How's that?"

"I don't like it when Hannah laughs."

"It's a good thing to make people smile, isn't it? Better than making them cry."

"Well, *I* want to cry." Alison puckered up but was unsuccessful.

"I would like an older sister," Hannah said.

Eyes narrowed, Jamie sent her a warning glance.

"As well as Alison," Hannah said, shaking her head. "An older sister for both of us."

"Nice save," Jamie said.

They made the rest of the trip in silence, which was a relief. By the time they drew near enough to see a pickup parked outside their front door, Alison had forgotten she was angry.

"Not the movers." The truck looked vaguely familiar, and a man in a T-shirt and khaki shorts was unloading plywood. After a few seconds, Jamie realized who it was.

"That looks like Mr. Rosslyn. Cash. Remember Cash, Hannah? He fixed the stairs on the old cabin when we were here." She glanced at Hannah. "You liked him. He's a nice guy."

"What's he doing?"

"We'll find out." Jamie called to him as they rounded the last bend. "Cash, up here."

The man stopped and turned, watching as they drew closer. He didn't wave, then go back to work, as most would have. He watched them approach. Jamie saw a slow grin light his face.

"Boy, have they grown," he said when the three females reached him.

Jamie was delighted he remembered her daughters so well that he could catalog the changes. "Hey, it's nice to see you again. I was hoping you'd come by this week, so I could tell you how much I love the cabin."

"I had good plans to work with."

"I hope you'll say the same thing about the big house. I've been working on incorporating Kendra and Isaac's ideas with my own. Maybe you'll have a chance to look over my final drawings soon, so we can have your architect go over them and draft the blueprints? Kendra says you'd like to break ground in a month or so."

"I'll be glad to. It was a darned shame about that fire. I'm glad they're planning to get started again." He squatted and looked Alison in the eye. "You're Alison. I'm Cash. Remember?"

"We found a baby deer."

"You did?" He sounded properly enthused. "Did it run away?"

"No, it was little."

"Like you?"

"No! Little, like this." She threw her arms open. "With spots."

"Why are you throwing boards on the ground?" Hannah asked.

"You're Hannah, right? Somebody told me two little girls needed a playhouse. Do you think they were right?"

Alison whirled. "Mommy?"

"Kendra sent you?" Jamie asked.

"We both figured they'd need something to do out here this summer or go crazy as trout in a drought. A place of their own. And a way to give you a little more space."

Jamie wondered how *much* Kendra had told Cash about their reason for moving here. "I think it's a wonderful idea. Girls, what do you say?"

Hannah spoke first. "How big is it going to be, and where do you plan to put it?"

Cash got to his feet. "You're Hannah, all right, only bigger. I remember all those questions."

"I was hoping for a thank you, not an interrogation," Jamie told her daughter.

"I would like to know exactly what to thank him for."

Cash laughed. "Well now, I thought with your mommy's help we could figure out something together. What do you think? Would you have some ideas?"

Hannah's whole face glowed with excitement. "A pirate ship?"

"Too many showings of *Peter Pan*," Jamie explained.

"Or maybe a spaceship?" Hannah added

"*Lost in Space* and *Star Trek*. Why don't we let Mr. Rosslyn build you something that can be anything you want it to be. A castle, a ship, a fort."

Cash gave a low whistle. "You don't ask for much, do you?"

Jamie met his eyes and smiled a little. Cash was an attractive man, and she was aware he was thinking of more than a playhouse. She felt his interest and saw it in his eyes. She reminded herself that she was feeling lonely, that she'd been yearning for an adult to talk to and was therefore a tad too receptive to the warmth in his smile. But despite her better instincts, she heard herself playing along.

"Oh, you might be surprised what I could ask for."

He hesitated just long enough to make a point. "A man could have trouble keeping up."

She doubted this man would have trouble on any level. She studied him for a moment. Cash was taller than she was, although an inch or so shy of six feet. His hair was a warm brown, his skin deeply tanned. His eyes were most arresting of all, neither blue nor green but something in between, like a tropical ocean under dark brows and lashes. She guessed Cash was maybe four or five years older than she was, but like her, he had lived those years at warp speed. He was country-boy casual on the outside, but from the first time they'd met, she had thought there was probably something more simmering inside.

"I was thinking imagination ought to be the key component," she said, pulling herself back to the matter at hand. "The girls can supply that."

"Now that's funny, because that's exactly what I had in mind. A deck with a sandbox under it? Slanted railings at the sides, a roof, maybe a slide for Alison, and a knotted rope to climb up and down for Hannah. A good pirate would have a rope."

"But no plank to walk, okay? Alison would take that challenge in a heartbeat."

"I can see that. She looks like a pirate to me."

Alison beamed. "Cap'ain Hook!"

"Definitely a resemblance," Cash said, nodding. "I thought maybe you girls might like to help me figure out just what to do, then put in a nail or two when the time comes. Would you be willing?"

Jamie could see that lunch had been temporarily forgotten. The girls were thrilled. For however long this took, they had a project to occupy them. Then, hopefully, the playhouse itself would be good for many happy hours.

"This sounds like a lot of work to me," she warned. "If you ask for their input, you might end up building a McMansion."

"Oh, I'll take my chances."

"It all sounds great, but we'll owe you big-time for this."

"Your sister's footing this bill."

She felt a surge of affection for Kendra, who had thought so far ahead and seen the need. "Listen, money can't buy the peace the pair of you'll be giving me."

"The fawn wasn't moving," Hannah said, as if they had never changed the subject. "Do you know about fawns?"

Cash squatted down so they were eye to eye. "Yes, ma'am. I know that's how they protect themselves. Where did you see it?"

Jamie listened as Hannah tried to explain. Once her daughter had finished, she clarified. "Where the woods curl back toward Fitch Crossing."

"It wasn't moving. I think it will die," Hannah said.

"I tell you what. I think we should check on it tomorrow morning. Just to be sure. I'll come over, and we can go together, but we shouldn't go back any sooner."

Jamie was glad to have reinforcements. "I marked the place with a baseball cap."

He got to his feet. "Girls, I left something on the porch. My grandmother sent you a pie."

For the moment the deer was forgotten. Hannah's expression brightened, and Alison clapped her hands; then they took off together to see.

"This is all very nice of you," Jamie told him.

"No trouble. That's how we welcome people in the country. By fattening them up."

"I was afraid the whole day was going to be about the fawn. Now they'll spend at least some of it drawing up plans for the playhouse."

"And eating apple pie." His face grew serious. "I didn't want to alarm them, but I did see a dead doe up on Fitch Crossing not too far from where you're describing. I'll call one of my men to help me remove it on the way out of here, so the girls don't see it next time you leave, but we probably should keep an eye on that baby. Just in case that was the mother."

"Not hunters…"

"Not this time of year. No, a car. People aren't always good about cleaning up their own messes."

"And what should I do if that *was* the mother and the baby's alone?"

"That's why I volunteered to come with you. We'll see if we can figure out what's up."

"You're going down in my book as a helpful guy to know."

"I'd say just going down in your book is a good thing."

Despite the silent voice urging caution, she was enjoying herself. Talking to a man was a welcome change from the girls. Flirting with one was a welcome change from just being somebody's mother. And she liked Cash, had liked him the first time they met. Had even thought about him a time or two since.

"So you were serious about stopping by in the morning?" she asked.

"This is just my first load of materials. Maybe the girls can come up with an idea or two for the playhouse between now and then. We'll look for the fawn first, then see what we can do about starting on it."

"I'll show you what I've done on the house plans, and by then the girls will have thought of a hundred good ideas to share with—" She came to an abrupt halt. "I'm sorry. I'm assuming you're still single and don't have a wife who has the right to claim your Sundays. I wasn't thinking."

"How did you know I was single in the first place?"

"Oh, last time I was here, it came up in some conversation or other."

"I'm sorry I didn't get to hear that one."

They were back to flirting. Worse, she was back to liking it. "I doubt it was anywhere near as interesting as you're imagining."

"I'm not married. No woman in her right mind wants to be saddled with me, and of course this is strictly business, right?"

She thought of the baby that could well be growing inside her. "Oh, yeah. That's definitely what it is."

Alison gave a whoop, and Jamie turned to see Hannah holding up the pie. "I'd better go. I promised the girls some lunch. I'd be happy to feed you, too."

"Thanks, but I ate. I'm going to unload this truck, then head out. But I'll bring another load when I come back tomorrow."

"You'll thank your grandmother for me?"

"I'll tell her."

Jamie started toward the cabin, then she glanced over her shoulder. He was watching her, but she had known that. She'd almost felt his gaze. "See you then, and thanks again for everything."

"It will be my pleasure."

Jamie was just a little worried about the pleasure *she* felt.

3

Before moving into the old mobile home parked at the back of Cashel Orchards, Cash Rosslyn had reluctantly painted the exterior—but only because at the rate the trailer was rusting, he was afraid one morning he might wake up in his birthday suit with nothing sheltering him except gnarled apple trees and the shoulder-high weeds he called his front yard. With the same level of interest, he had hauled away all the junk in view: the graveyard of farm machinery, the 1943 Studebaker, the disintegrating hay bales complete with mouse housing developments and, last but best, the still pungent dog run where generations of retrievers and hounds had waited impatiently for hunting season to begin.

The inside of the mobile home was another matter. After the first trip inside he had bombed it for fleas and roaches and every other critter that had set up housekeeping. He had hauled out the remnants of the last farmworker's belongings, removed and replaced the old cheap paneling with new cheap paneling, then hired a neighbor woman to scrub the whole place from top to bottom.

That was the last time he had paid much attention to interior decorating.

This evening, of course, a woman decorated his interior, the only one who felt free to come and go as she pleased, who ignored his protests—if he even bothered. Grace Cashel sat on his secondhand sofa watching one of the three channels his malfunctioning satellite dish would part with. She didn't look up as he opened the door.

"Sandra was disappointed you didn't make it for Sunday supper," she said, eyes still trained on the fuzzy images flickering across the screen.

"I had a prior engagement. I told her way ahead of time I wouldn't be there."

"Your mother is easily hurt." Grace picked up the remote and turned down the volume a notch. "I hope this woman who intercepted you on the way to a family engagement was intelligent enough to chew with her mouth closed."

Cash plopped down next to his grandmother and put his arm around her. "Just somebody I know from high school. We went for a pizza, and she didn't stop talking long enough to chew, although she sure downed her share."

"You're lonely."

"I'm fine. And I'm not the one sitting here watching somebody's thirteen-inch TV set when she has a twenty-six-inch and a working satellite dish in her house up the hill."

"Whenever I turn that one on, I can almost hear Ben insisting I change the channel. I swear he's still living there. Some nights I just have to get away from him."

Cash squeezed her shoulder. "What does he want to watch?"

"He's prone to wrestling and anything with John Wayne. Oh, and cowboy movies. If he hadn't had so many responsibilities as a young man, he would have taken off for Wyoming and a home on the range."

"He never would have left you."

"You might be surprised. I'm not always the easiest woman to live with."

"No…" Cash let loose with a long, low whistle. "You, Granny Grace?"

"She uses cheap perfume." She finally glanced at him. "Your pizza-eating chatterbox. I can smell it on you."

"I told you, she's an old friend from high school, and she just got divorced. She spent the whole night sitting beside me in a booth swallowing eight slices to my two and telling me every rotten thing her husband ever did to her."

"Your mother made roast chicken, mashed potatoes and green beans. Not an herb or garnish in sight. Last week I gave her my recipe for jerk seasoning, but apparently she was unimpressed."

"I've got a job for you."

His grandmother groaned. "I could swear I retired. Didn't somebody somewhere give me a gold watch? I certainly deserved one."

"Did you keep up your permit for wildlife rehabilitation?"

"What have you gotten me into?"

"There's *another* woman…"

The fawn was not easily forgotten. When bedtime rolled around, the girls demanded Jamie tell them a story about a deer. Jamie discounted all the ones she knew—*Bambi* and *The Yearling* certainly weren't appropriate under the circumstances—and made up her own tale about a deer's happy life in the forest. She was fairly certain they didn't completely buy it, but by the time she had finished describing the many happy moments eating grass and leaves and destroying local vegetable gardens, they were fast asleep. Although she wanted to stay up and savor the quiet cabin, the chirping of crickets and a little time with the plans for Kendra and Isaac's new house, she wasn't far behind.

The next morning, the girls were up with the sun, demanding another trip into the forest. Dragging herself out of bed, she reminded them that Cash was coming later to help them look, so they had to wait. That did not make for peaceful conversation.

The telephone rang while she was getting eggs out of the refrigerator; Cash was on the other end. The call was brief. When she hung up, she recounted it to the girls.

"That was Mr. Rosslyn. He's coming over at nine with more wood for your playhouse. I told him we'd feed him breakfast." She went back to the eggs. "And he's bringing somebody to meet us."

"Who?"

"He said it was a surprise, and they'd be here by nine." Actually, what he had said was "I'd be happy to come, but would you mind if I brought somebody with me? I promise she eats like a bird."

Jamie was intrigued. She had decided not to prod, since that was probably exactly what he'd expected. But with the challenge issued, she rummaged through the refrigerator again to see what she could make that would be more festive than scrambled eggs.

She decided on mushroom omelets, a simple fruit salad and surprise muffins. The surprise was two teaspoons of jam buried in the center, which Hannah and Alison loved to help with. Once the muffins were in the oven, she put Hannah in charge of peeling bananas and Alison in charge of folding napkins.

The movers had come late yesterday afternoon, piling most of the boxes in the girls' room or on the back porch, and after dinner, Jamie had unpacked several and tidied the cabin. With some of their own things on display—framed finger paintings and photos, an afghan a First Step friend had crocheted and a carnival glass pitcher filled with wildflowers they had brought back from the orchard—the cabin seemed more like their own.

Once the muffins were out of the oven, she showered and changed while Hannah read to Alison. By age four, her daughter had gotten tired of waiting to be read to and had taught herself, with only the most perfunctory help. Now, at eight, Hannah read to her sister almost as often as Jamie did, although Alison was learning to figure out words, as well.

As she towel dried her flat abdomen, Jamie pondered how quickly her daughters were growing. Cash had seemed surprised at the differences, and she understood. Unless an onlooker was watching every moment, the changes could be startling. Sometimes, she mourned the loss of the cuddly, malleable infants and toddlers they had been.

She rested her hand on her belly for a moment, wondering how that belly would look after *three* babies had grown inside her. Would men still find her attractive? How about somebody like Cash?

Did she care?

She smiled at that. She wasn't even thirty, but her luck with men had been terrible. Of course, her ability to select men with an eye toward a stable future had been terrible, too. In her defense, early role models had been sorely lacking. As a child she had been a prime witness to her mother's destructive relationships; then, as a teenager, she had been educated on city streets where nothing wholesome could flourish. The men who had crossed her path had been as lost and angry as she was.

Even when she finally began to rebuild her life, she had not chosen well. Neither of her daughters' fathers were husband material. Imperfect birth control, not hopes for a loving family, had turned them into parents. Her heart had not broken when either man walked out of her life, although sometimes her heart broke for her girls, who needed more than financial support and their fathers' reluctant visits.

So did she really care if the time came when men no longer gave her a second glance? If they looked at her hugely expanded body, no longer as likely to spring back into form after this third pregnancy, and turned away? Did she care if Cash lost all interest when he found out *why* she was in Virginia?

She had no answer. She wasn't ready to give up on men. Just because she'd habitually chosen losers didn't mean that, somewhere, some man wasn't routinely crossing the finish line ahead of the pack. On the other hand, she wasn't sure she wanted any part of the race for a while, either.

Didn't she have her hands full already?

From the great room she heard the patter of bare feet, then Alison's loud giggles. She'd had her five minutes of contemplation. Both charmed and wary, she dressed quickly in a denim skirt and tank top, ran a brush through her hair and went to see what was up.

By nine o'clock Hannah was providing running commentary from the front door.

"It's nine and they are not here."

"That's called being fashionably late."

"When is it fashionable, and when is it rude?"

"When the muffins get stale it's rude. That's a long time yet."

"There are not always muffins."

"Hannah, when you host a meal, even breakfast, you plan to eat some time after your guests arrive, to give them time to sit and chat, have something to drink, enjoy your company."

"How long does that take?"

"Anywhere from half an hour to an hour, although shorter at breakfast time, and now I'm done with the entertainment tips."

"I think I hear a truck. They are only—" Hannah glanced at a clock on the mantel "—two minutes late. Does that mean they are unfashionable?"

"No, it just means that you're watching the clock. Why don't you go out and greet them?"

"Me, too!" Alison took off for the door after her sister.

Jamie shook her head and hoped that whoever Cash's guest was, she was up to the onslaught.

By the time the girls came racing back, the muffins were arranged on a stoneware platter, a pitcher of tea sat on the counter next to a carafe of coffee and the fruit salad was adorned with sprigs of mint.

"Cash and Granny Grace are here!" Hannah said.

Granny Grace? Of all the people Jamie had anticipated, Cash's grandmother hadn't been one of them. She stepped out from behind the breakfast bar just as one of the least grandmotherly-looking women she had ever seen crossed the threshold.

Granny Grace was tall, almost as tall as Cash, who entered behind her. She was willowy and slender, with iron-gray hair and sharp features. The features were belied by creases and folds around dancing dark eyes adorned with rectangular black-rimmed glasses. A wide mouth signaled decades of smiles and laughter.

The most extraordinary thing about the woman was her sense of style. Rarely had Jamie seen lime green and purple used together with such abandon. Harem pants billowed around her hips and tucked in at her ankle; a hip-length vest, sprinkled heavily with crystal beads, sparkled like a fireworks display. She wore gold tennis shoes, and her fingernails were a deep scarlet that matched her lipstick.

Judging by the wrinkles and the patches of scalp visible under spiky hair, this woman *could* well be someone's granny. But judging by her bouncing step, her flamboyance and obvious delight with life, she was a teenager.

What exactly did it say about a man when he brought his grandmother to visit?

"You must be Jamie." Granny Grace extended her hand. "Let the rest of them call me Granny Grace. You call me Grace."

Jamie shook, impressed by the strength of the narrow, age-spotted hand. "I'm so glad to have you here. Cash didn't tell me exactly who he was bringing. Now I can thank you for the pie."

"Cash is a rogue and a renegade. It skipped a generation. His mother is as tightly reined in as a carriage horse. Sandra's a good daughter, mind you, but I was thrilled to see the mischief emerge again in this one. Until he came along, I was afraid all my genes had been flushed down the eternal toilet." She nodded toward Cash. "Although he could do with some breaking in."

Jamie laughed. "I bet if anybody could do it, you'd be the one."

"Your oldest daughter has your dimples. She's your spitting image. Was there a father?" She waved away her own question. "Never mind. Clearly there had to be, but he didn't leave much of a footprint, did he? Now the other one? The leprechaun princess? Not a bit of you in the face, but I bet you had that same amount of energy and enthusiasm as a child."

"I'll have to ask my sister. She would know."

"Don't bother. I can see it in your eyes. I'm not fond of women who look like everything's been washed out of them."

Cash put his hand on his grandmother's shoulder. "Granny Grace has no real opinions about anything."

"There's no reason to keep what I've learned to myself, dear. I need to share, share, share while I can."

Jamie was enchanted. Normally she was suspicious of outrageous women. Her mother was all flash and dazzle, with little under the rhinestone exterior to anchor her to reality. But Grace had already paid close attention to Jamie's children and made connections. Jamie thought this was a woman who probably paid close attention to everything and everyone.

"So what do you think of the cabin?" Cash asked his grandmother.

"I think it's a lovely little postage stamp, and I think these girls are going to need that playhouse you're building for them, so their poor mother can breathe a little. I suggest turrets and portholes and places to hide secret messages."

Cash's gaze swung to Jamie's. "If I didn't know better, I'd say there's a conspiracy brewing."

"And we just met." Jamie flashed the dimples that were exactly like Hannah's. "Just think what kind of trouble we'll get into when we've known each other a week."

Grace did not eat like a bird. She ate the way she dressed, with gusto. Once she was seated at the table, she listened raptly as the girls explained how they had helped with the muffins. She asked for seconds on the omelet and stole more off Cash's plate when he wasn't looking. The fruit salad interested her most of all.

"There's not an apple anywhere," she said. "It's delicious just as it is, of course. And eye pleasing. Food that looks good is as important as food that tastes good. I can see you know that already, but where are the apples?"

"I don't like Red Delicious, and that's all they had at the grocery store. It's too early for the local apples at the fruit stand."

"I knew you had excellent taste. You have, after all, already become friends with my grandson, which means you can spot a diamond in the rough. But what apples do you like best?"

"Not too sweet. Firm and crisp."

"Jonathans, then, and Ida Reds, although I'm not sure you can find them easily. Yorks aren't so tangy, but you would like them, as well. At one time, we had five hundred or more. Nothing beats a York in the kitchen, although it's a funny-looking thing. The Pennsylvania Dutch—and we had some around here, you know, although I suppose by rights we'd have to call them Virginia Dutch. Anyway—" she waved her words away "—they called it a *schepabbel*. Crooked apple. And the cider we made? That pie was from last year's apple crop. But, of course, today people want apples that look like they're made out of wax, even if they taste like sawdust."

"Granny Grace and Grandpa Ben had an orchard," Cash explained.

"*Have*. Ben's gone, of course, God bless him, but the orchard still belongs to *me*."

"We know that," Cash said. "Nobody's disputing it."

"And nobody's helping, either." Her expression belied the words. She didn't look angry. Jamie characterized the set of her lips as determined.

Jamie didn't know what was going on, but she intervened, hoping to turn the conversational tide. "There's an orchard on this property, or at least the remnants of one. I wonder if any part of it can be saved."

"You could try pruning the trees over a period of years if the trunk is still firm. And I've seen trees topped, just lopped nearly in half, and brought back to life that way, but it takes years, too, and it's not always successful. Still, if they're old friends… You do whatever it takes for a friend, don't you?"

"They were somebody's old friends. My brother-in-law's grandmother Leah lived on this property. Did you know her? Leah Spurlock Jackson?"

"I don't recall. I was so busy with the orchard and my children…that's the way my life went. It races by, you know. Remember *that* if you have a boring day. Boring is the period at the end of a run-on sentence. Meant for a deep breath and a nap."

"We don't have many boring days around here."

As if to prove it, Alison jumped down from her chair. "Ready!"

"We'll wait until everybody's finished," Jamie told her daughter. "But after you've asked to be excused, you may put your shoes on."

"May I be excused?"

"You may," Jamie said with a grin.

"May I please be excused, too?" Hannah asked.

"Yes. And as soon as we've finished, we'll join you."

Cash caught Jamie's eye and flashed her a grin. "May I be excused, too, Miss Jamie? I'd like to unload the materials before we go for that walk."

"You bet. The sooner that playhouse is finished, the faster my life improves."

"Now, tell me about the fawn," Grace said, once the girls had gone into their bedroom to get ready and Cash was outside. "Exactly what did you see?"

The fawn was in the same place Jamie and the girls had left it yesterday. Today, though, it was bleating softly, like a baby lamb.

"Girls, you stay here with me," Jamie said, when they tried to follow Grace and Cash closer. "Too many people will scare the poor thing to death."

"It was in exactly the same spot yesterday?" Cash stood behind his grandmother, who got down on her knees.

"I don't think it's moved," Jamie said.

Grace was kneeling beside the fawn, examining it gently, and Cash backed away to join them, watching his grandmother as he did.

"She's really a wildlife rehabilitator?" Jamie asked. She'd hardly believed it when Grace had told her so at breakfast. "That's a stroke of luck."

Cash spoke softly. "She always says it's her life's work to take care of castaways."

"A good job, that one."

"Uh-huh, if what you're trying to bring back ought to be rescued. My mother says people who lived around the orchard and beyond always brought injured animals to Granny Grace. I know when I was a boy she let me help raise a trio of baby coons who'd lost their mother to a redbone hound. Eventually, the authorities caught up with her, if you can believe it. Told her unless she had a permit, it was against the law to do what she'd been doing for years."

"I guess they're just trying to protect wildlife from people who don't know how to help."

"She could have taught them a thing or two, but being Granny Grace, she did what she had to and got the training."

Grace stood and joined them. "We could leave the poor thing here another day or two, see if the mother comes back. But it's my opinion that this mother hasn't returned for some time. No need to go into why I think so—" she glanced at the girls "—but I'd say we'd be in our rights to take this little one up to my house and see what we can do with her. If we leave her, I don't think she'll fare well."

Cash turned to Jamie. "What do you think?"

"I was so afraid you were going to tell me I had to take care of her. I don't have a clue what to do."

Grace glanced at the girls again. "It's a delicate business. Best leave it to me. If things go well, the girls can come up and visit."

Hannah had been unusually quiet. "Is she going to die, Granny Grace?"

"Not if I can help it, Hannah. But truth be told, she might."

Hannah looked stricken. "I don't want her to die."

"Nor do I, which is why I'll do my level best to help. You can count on me. But you know, child, some things are simply out of our hands. So we can feel sad, but we can't feel responsible."

Jamie knew that was a lesson every child had to learn, but she was sorry.

"The fawn's very lucky good people found her," Jamie said, trying to make Hannah feel better. "First Alison spotted her, then Granny Grace came along. And Granny Grace knows how to help, when almost nobody else would. That's two times so far that fawn's been lucky."

"Lucky," Alison said. "Her name is Lucky."

Jamie knew naming an animal was the end of objectivity. But this time, objectivity had fled at first glance.

"Lucky is a good name," Grace said. "Good names are important. Cash?" Grace nodded to the fawn. "Let's get her home right away."

Cash bent over and picked up the little deer. She hardly struggled. Jamie knew this wasn't a good sign.

"Let Cash and Lucky go first," she said, holding the girls back.

"I'll have to visit your orchard another day," Grace said, walking with Jamie and the girls once Cash had strode ahead. The girls were abnormally subdued, as if only now had they realized the gravity of removing the fawn.

"I hope you'll come back as soon as you can," Jamie said.

"As soon as things stabilize, I'd like you and the girls to come and visit. Will you do that?"

"You won't be able to keep us away."

"I think we'll be friends. I've been away for some time, and a number of my old friends are gone. So I'll be happy to have you coming in and out as often as you please."

Jamie was surprised that somebody like Grace could ever be lonely, but she heard a hunger in her new friend's voice and recognized it. It matched her own. "You may not be so happy if we hit you on a day when the girls are hot, tired and cranky," she warned.

"Even children in fairy tales aren't always well-behaved."

"Why did Lucky's mother leave her?" Hannah asked, as if the question had just occurred to her. "What kind of mother leaves her baby for somebody else to take care of?"

"I'll let you answer that," Grace told Jamie. "I'll welcome your children into my home, dear, but I'll be equally thrilled to turn the difficult questions over to you."

Jamie shot her a smile, but as she fumbled through an explanation that didn't include the dead doe on Fitch Crossing Road, she wondered in how many ways and how often she would have to answer the same question and all its variations if indeed even now she was carrying her sister's child.

4

"She's clearly not here."

Kendra rounded the porch to the side of the Fitch Crossing cabin where her friend Elisa Kinkade was lounging in an oak swing. Almost two weeks had passed since Kendra left Jamie at the cabin. Now she and Isaac were back in Toms Brook to finalize the new house plans with Rosslyn and Rosslyn later that evening. Jamie had invited them to dinner, but Jamie wasn't home.

Elisa patted the seat and stopped midswing so Kendra could join her. Kendra had left Isaac and their car at the house Elisa shared with her husband Sam, who was the minister of the Shenandoah Community Church when Elisa had volunteered to drop her here.

"I'm not sure where she's gone," Kendra said. "Jamie knew we were coming."

"Maybe she's doing some last-minute grocery shopping."

"It probably gets lonely with only little girls to keep her

company. I guess she likes to get out at least part of every day, just to see grown-ups again."

"I hope I'll have the chance to meet her, so I can see her when I'm in town."

Elisa, an obstetrician in her home country of Guatemala, was completing a second residency across the mountains in Charlottesville so that she could practice in Virginia. Today was one of her infrequent days off. Kendra was glad for even this brief opportunity to catch up.

"We wanted to have a peaceful dinner together before Jamie goes back to the fertility clinic for the pregnancy test on Friday. We don't want her to think that everything hinges on whether the in vitro worked."

"Would she think such a thing?"

Kendra wondered. Until today, she hadn't checked on her sister. If there was any problem, Jamie knew how to reach her, and Kendra knew hovering was counterproductive. Still, she had spent every day worrying.

And about what? The list was so long, she could hardly keep track.

Kendra knew Elisa and Sam wanted children, too, although they were tabling it until Elisa was finished or nearly finished her residency. But even with Elisa's credentials, even though her friend yearned for a child, no one could understand the ache of infertility until she had experienced it herself.

"It's uncharted territory, this surrogacy thing," Kendra said, starting with the obvious.

"Surrogacy is not so uncommon anymore. Unfortunately, the problems make the newspapers but the success stories are less likely to."

"Have you had experience yourself? As an obstetrician?"

"My area of practice took me in other directions. But from observation, I know the most important marker for a positive outcome is a strong emotional and personal commitment by all parties. There is a sense of mission, of something meant to be. No one should feel coerced or desperate."

"Jamie's offer came out of the blue. It never occurred to me that anyone would do this for us. It's so huge…" Kendra glanced at her friend, who, with her shining black hair and slender figure, was pretty enough to walk a runway instead of a hospital corridor. "It's so overwhelming."

"Can you list your worries? Because I sense you have more than one."

After a nearly fatal carjacking two years ago, Kendra had come to this land, to Isaac's grandmother's long-abandoned cabin, in search of answers, and she had found them in the peaceful countryside and in her friendship with Elisa and Sam. She still had very few people with whom she felt comfortable sharing her innermost thoughts, but she knew she could be truthful with Elisa.

"Well, first and foremost—and not yet answered—is the big zinger. Is my sister pregnant with my child?" She put a finger to her lips. "It seems so odd even to say that out loud."

"And if she's not?"

Kendra shrugged. "Then it'll be up to her what we do next. I can't make her try again."

"And that worries you."

"I've trusted her with my dreams, Elisa. And I hardly know her, because we were estranged for so long. I'd given up hope of having a baby, and now I've opened myself up to heartbreak again."

"Or wonder. Wonder is the other side of that coin, isn't it? A baby of your own? The baby you and Isaac created together?"

Kendra tried to send her mind down a more productive path.

There were signs that Cash had been here. A nearly finished playhouse existed in the woods just beyond the cabin. He was building it where Jamie could keep an eye on the girls without appearing to, which Kendra approved of.

Alison was daring and imaginative. But what would happen if Jamie didn't keep her eye on her? The little girl might take it in her head to go down to the river on her own. Last summer, a child just about her age had fallen in near the bed-and-breakfast where Kendra and Isaac stayed now whenever they visited the Valley. Gayle, the innkeeper, had told her the story, which luckily had a happy ending. But now Kendra worried that history might repeat itself.

"I'm a mess." She turned back to Elisa. "Apparently I'm eaten up with anxiety. I look at that wonderful playhouse Cash Rosslyn is building the girls, and all of a sudden I'm worried that Jamie won't keep a good enough eye on Alison and she'll end up in the river."

"Why don't you just put all your fears out to air?"

Kendra didn't have to think long or hard. "Will the girls be happy enough here that Jamie will stay where I can share in the pregnancy? Will the neighbors understand and support what we're doing? Will Jamie's pregnancy—if there is one—be problem free? If we have to try in vitro again and again, will Jamie be willing? Or is this a one-time impulse, something she'll grow tired of quickly?"

"What makes you think the last might be true?"

"Jamie's always been flighty." Kendra shook her head at her own words. "But that's not really true. Jamie was flighty as a child, but aren't all children flighty? And after a disastrous adolescence and beyond, she did pull her life together."

"You don't say that like you believe it's true."

Kendra was ashamed, but she couldn't pretend otherwise. "Of course that's the real question, isn't it? Everything comes back to that. How much of what I see in my sister is really just the normal difference in our personalities, the kind sisters everywhere have to deal with? How much is my own unwillingness to believe that Jamie really cleaned up her act? And how much is my profession? Investigative reporters aren't trained to believe what we see on the surface. I've been suspicious since the moment she reentered my life. I know I have to trust her now—not just for the sake of the baby she might be carrying, but because trust's the only way to keep Jamie and the girls in my life."

"But if you do trust Jamie, how will you survive if your trust is betrayed?"

"You do know how to get to the heart of the matter." Kendra tried to smile, but it was a weak attempt. "But other than that, life is simple, huh?"

"You're making a start just by admitting your mind is running wild. That's a step. And I'm glad to see you can still smile about it."

"I think I'm going to need my sense of humor in the next months. Add it to a long list of things I have to do. Rein in my feelings. Concentrate on being logical." This time the smile was surer. "Rent a straitjacket."

Elisa squeezed her hand. "You might also consider letting go a little. Worrying never heads off a crisis, and it doesn't prepare you for one."

The sound of an engine halted their conversation. In a moment, Jamie's van came into sight, and in a few more, the girls were spilling out of it.

"Here they come," Kendra said, rising to greet her nieces.

"We have salmon and rice and lettuce that came right out of

a field!" Hannah ran up the steps to give Kendra a huge hug, then made way for Alison's smaller arms.

"And shortcake!" Alison shouted.

Kendra hugged them back, then stood to introduce her sister and the girls to Elisa.

"I am so glad I get to meet you at last," Elisa told Jamie. "I'm not around as much as I would like, but if you ever need anything, please call our house. If I'm at the hospital, Sam will help."

"I've heard so much about you. I feel like we're already friends."

Elisa rummaged through a fabric bag and pulled out two small gaily wrapped gifts, and handed one to each girl. "And for you, a welcome to Toms Brook."

Hannah thanked Elisa politely, as Alison forgot and tore into her gift. It was a small doll dressed in Guatemalan clothing. Hannah had received one, too, dressed in a different color.

"They are worry dolls," Elisa explained. "If you have something that is worrying you, you tell it to your doll, and then you put her under your pillow or right beside it. While you are sleeping, she will think of a way to help you. And if you aren't worried, then she will be glad just to play with you." Her gaze flicked to Kendra's, and she smiled.

"I like it!" Alison held hers up high.

"Maybe she will help us find friends," Hannah said.

"Hannah's concerned she's not going to meet anyone her age until she goes to school in the fall," Jamie explained. "So far, we haven't had much luck."

Elisa closed up her bag and slung it over her shoulder. "Our church will have a vacation bible school at the end of July. It's nondenominational. Some of the children from La Casa will be coming, too."

"La Casa Amarilla's a community center the church sponsors,"

Kendra said. "That would be a good way for the girls to make acquaintances."

"I will ask Sam if he knows anyone the girls can play with in the meantime. So many are in and out of town this time of year, but maybe we can find you some friends," Elisa promised Hannah.

"Then I can save my worry doll for something else."

Elisa extended her hand to Jamie. "I have to go. Sam has a meeting tonight, so we need to have an early dinner. Make sure Kendra gives you our phone number."

On her way to get the rest of the groceries, Jamie walked Elisa to her car. Kendra stood with an arm around each of her nieces and knew that the next time she saw Elisa, she was probably going to be the recipient of a worry doll herself, maybe even a set.

And it would be up to her to learn how to let them do their job.

While Kendra listened to a blow-by-blow description of everything the girls had done that day, Jamie retrieved two more bags to bring up to the house. She had hoped to have things ready by the time Kendra and Isaac arrived. Now she felt a sliver of annoyance. Kendra had arrived earlier than expected, with a guest in tow for Jamie to meet, and of course she hadn't even been home. She felt as if she'd failed some odd sort of test, as if she had proved once again that she couldn't be trusted to be on time or live up to her end of a bargain.

Of course ninety-nine percent of what she was feeling was probably caused by the hormones zinging through her system. But she was bigger than progesterone. Better than estrogen. More than chemicals. She told herself to shake this off, and by the time she got back to the house, she'd nearly convinced herself she had.

On the porch, Kendra took one of the bags and followed her inside.

"This looks like you're cooking a feast. I told you not to go to any trouble. We'd be happy to take the three of you out for dinner."

The sliver of annoyance widened. "I know *you* view cooking as a chore, but I've told you before, cooking is my joy. I do it because I love it. Always."

"Can I at least help?"

"You can slice the strawberries and sprinkle them with sugar while I unpack. And you can monitor Hannah. She's a strawberry sneak, and too many will make her sick."

"I will eat five," Hannah said. "Six will be a problem."

Inside, Kendra admired the personal touches that Jamie had added to the cabin. "I love those place mats. Did you bring them with you, or did you find them here?"

Jamie hoped the praise was real and not just her sister's way of apologizing for her early arrival. "They're great, aren't they? I found them in a shop in Strasburg. They're denim strips, hand woven on a loom. I wish I had time to work with my hands. I've always wanted to do something. Knit, crochet, paint."

"Be careful what you wish for, and keep your voice down."

Jamie turned. "What? Who's listening?"

Kendra lowered her voice. "They're everywhere."

"Are you nuts? Who's everywhere?"

Kendra lowered her voice even more. "The quilters."

"Quilters?"

"Now you've gone and done it. They'll be here momentarily. Bolt the doors."

Jamie was relieved to see this more playful side of her sister. "Explain yourself."

"I'm afraid you'll find out soon enough. Let's just say that if you ever had a yen to learn how to quilt, you're in the right place. Toms Brook is crawling with them."

"Does that have anything to do with the old quilts in your house?"

"I collect, they quilt, although I'll confess they've taught me a little. Call it survival."

"I'll keep my eyes open."

"They'll sniff you out."

In the kitchen, Jamie lifted a package from the bag. "Have you ever seen prettier salmon? If I marinate it and light the grill, do you think Isaac will do the honors? The grill's great, by the way. State-of-the-art, like everything else here."

"I want you to be happy."

"Why wouldn't I be?"

"Because you're in the middle of nowhere with two young children and a lot to think about."

Jamie wasn't sure she liked hearing her days characterized that way, as if she was serving some sort of prison sentence—even if her sister's words mirrored some of her own thoughts. But again, she managed to keep her voice light.

"So far, those two young children have been completely enchanted with a certain playhouse. I don't know if they can possibly like it as much once it's built as they've liked helping build it, but I can't thank you enough, Ken. That was absolutely brilliant."

"It sounds like that's been the center of everybody's days."

"That and the deer." Jamie told her about the fawn.

"So Cash and his grandmother took it home?" Kendra asked.

"Grace is licensed and trained. It was the right thing to do."

"And how has it fared?"

"Not well at first, apparently. She almost lost it. But the crisis seems to have passed. We're invited to see her tomorrow. The girls are beside themselves. They spent the day making collars out of ribbon for Lucky."

"Lucky?"

"Alison's idea. And apparently the fawn *was* lucky. I get the feeling Grace lost a lot of sleep until she was able to get her stabilized."

The kitchen had room for both of them, but just barely. Jamie rummaged through a plastic bag and handed Kendra a carton of perfectly ripe berries, then another. "Aren't these gorgeous? Roadside stand. I got enough for tomorrow's cereal, too, though I'll probably be down there every day to see what else they have."

"I'm glad the girls like the playhouse. I'm actually surprised Cash took it on. Rosslyn and Rosslyn's in demand all over the area. But he seemed to want to do this himself. Very enthused, our Cash."

Jamie stopped rummaging and looked at her sister. "Okay, what are you implying?"

"Me?"

"You can't just leave it there."

"I'm sure he simply likes the girls."

"Of course you're right."

"And maybe he thinks their mother is worth a trip or two."

"Oh, sure. I'm such a catch, or will be in a couple of months, or a couple more after that, or a couple after that." She put her hand on her tummy, then pretended it was growing.

"You're saying that after everything you've been through the past months, you would do this again?"

For a moment Jamie wasn't sure what Kendra meant; then the smile that had started to bloom died, and she felt a quick burst of anger. Real anger this time. She put her hand on her sister's arm and lowered her voice. "I've told you and told you, getting pregnant is my most outstanding talent. I'll be completely amazed if the first try didn't take. I'll be properly humbled if we have to go to three or four."

"You'll do that?"

"I told you I was in this for the long haul. That's what I meant. And you know, you and Isaac already did your part and made that possible."

Kendra seemed to be feeling her way. "I know it hasn't been fun so far."

Jamie kept her voice level. "Did I miss something? I'm not doing this for the fun of it, am I?"

"But I wouldn't blame you if you didn't want to keep on and on."

"That's good."

Kendra must have heard the change in Jamie's voice. "I guess I'm just trying to give you an out if you need one."

"And I guess I appreciate that. But honestly? Being the big girl I am, I more or less know I have an out if I have to take one."

"I'm sorry."

Jamie sighed and closed her eyes. As hard as it was, she tried to put herself in Kendra's place. She tried to imagine being the mother who waited and watched and hoped, not the mother who was bringing the baby into being. She tried to put herself into her sister's shoes, a mother for whom control of her child's fate was an illusion. Because when things came right down to it, Kendra was right to worry. Right now Jamie was the one with all the power.

Ninety-nine percent hormones. One percent well-deserved frustration.

She opened her eyes. "Did it blow up, or are we safe?"

"What are you talking about?"

"The first landmine in a minefield nine months long. Did we manage to avoid it, or did we step right on it?"

Kendra was silent a moment, then she shrugged, but her eyes

looked suspiciously moist. "We got close, but I think we're still intact."

Jamie went back to the contents of her plastic bag. "Plan for some injuries. You don't trust me yet, not completely."

"I'm asking you to carry my baby, Jamie. That sounds like trust to me."

"I think what it is…" Jamie faced her again. "I think that's you *wanting* to trust me. Making the effort. But you know, I don't think you're going to feel it right here—" she touched Kendra's chest with her fingertip "—until I place a baby in your arms. And I understand that. I really do. I understand your general trust issues and your specific issues with me and everything in between. I'm personally responsible for the latter and own up to it willingly. But we're walking along this road together now, so you have to let go of whatever you can and just keep your eyes open."

"And what about you?"

"Me? I've been psychoanalyzed and confronted and supported until not an atom inside me hasn't been thoroughly explored. I know why I'm doing this and what I can expect to feel along the way."

"Why *are* you doing it?" Kendra paused, but only for the briefest moment. "Before you go on, I know you're doing it for me, Jamie. I do know that. I know you love me. I believe that's the biggest part of it, I really do. But is there more?"

Jamie didn't hesitate. "Of course there is."

"Can you tell me?"

"Would it help? Would you stop worrying about everything if I told you in excruciating detail?"

Kendra considered. "I guess I don't really know."

"You know I love you. You know I want to give you something wonderful. Let's just say that the other piece of this is that I want to do something good, just because I can."

"You're raising two wonderful daughters. I hope you realize how much that counts."

"I am doing a bang-up job of it, don't you think?" Jamie handed her sister a cutting board. "Here you go. When you're done with those, let's take some tea out on the porch and admire the view. We have nine months to hash this out. Let's not do it in one fell swoop. What else will we have to talk about in the months ahead?"

Kendra took the cutting board, but she set it on the counter and pulled Jamie close for a quick hug.

5

Two years ago, when Leah Spurlock's old dogtrot cabin still stood, Kendra Taylor had planned to build on to the structure that already existed. Leah had moved to Toms Brook and the old cabin during the Depression, and sometime soon afterward another cabin had been built beside the first one, connected by one roof and common porches. The space between them had been narrow enough to act as a wind tunnel, sucking breezes from the river and serving as a place for the household pets to sleep, hence the name.

At first Cash, like his father, had wondered about trying to in-corporate this particular piece of the past into the future. Both Rosslyns believed in historical preservation and deeply appre-ciated the importance of restoring Virginia's heritage. The Valley wasn't the same place Cash had roamed as a boy. Farms were being sold and divided, agriculture was slowly giving way to tourism and the suburbs and strip malls of Northern Virginia were encroaching. He was committed—as much as he could commit to anything—to keeping the past alive between the Blue Ridge and the Alleghenies.

The Spurlock cabin hadn't been worth a lot, either histori-cally or structurally. Luckily there was nothing like sentiment to jump-start a project. Kendra had felt an attachment to the cabin and her husband's past, and with some creative design ideas from her kid sister, Cash's enthusiasm, along with his father's, had grown. They'd found an old barn and dismantled the logs to use in the addition. A foundation was dug, a skeletal structure begun. Then a fire destroyed almost everything except the logs, which were stacked at a safe distance.

Now, with nothing left to anchor the new house to the past, Jamie, clearly a promising architecture student, had taken on the task of drawing up plans that looked toward the future. But her efforts had turned up something unexpected. Last week, when he'd stopped by to work on the playhouse, she'd told him that, after questioning Kendra and Isaac at length and showing them plans and designs, rough sketches and sophisticated renderings, in the end, the concept they were most excited about used the same dogtrot design as Isaac's grandmother's cabin.

"Some ideas just take root," Jamie'd said, as she showed him what she'd done. "This one will not be shaken loose. I think we have to go with it."

And she had been so darned cute when she said it, so absorbed and serious, that right there on the spot he probably would have agreed to build the Taylors an igloo and chop the ice blocks from a glacier himself.

Tonight his father was going to look over the finished product and give his opinion. They were on the way to Jamie's right now, with Manning much too quiet beside him.

"I think you'll agree Jamie Dunkirk's got talent," Cash said, to break the silence. "A covered porch connects the two wings. The porch'll have a stone fireplace for warmth on cool nights and expansive square footage for entertaining. The second story covers the whole length of the house and makes use of window walls to bring home the views. The barn logs will find use as beams and posts in conjunction with stone."

"Well, talent's all well and good, but I'm not agreeing to anything until an experienced architect critiques and finalizes her ideas."

Cash hoped that Brady, the architect who sometimes worked with Rosslyn and Rosslyn, would let Jamie draft the blueprints and simply review them when she was finished. Still, even if he didn't, Jamie could certainly claim the design in her portfolio.

"I don't think there'll be much of a problem," he said. "I made a few suggestions, but she's got a great eye. And she's well on her way toward her master's degree and licensing."

"I'm not sure why I had to come tonight," Manning said. "You know I trust your judgment. If you and Brady say the plans will work, they'll work."

They had been over this before, but as he turned onto Fitch Crossing Road, Cash tried again.

"It's Rosslyn and *Rosslyn*, and the Taylors will expect you to at least make a brief appearance. Besides, Mrs. Taylor trusted you with the last house. She'll feel more comfortable if you give this one your stamp of approval."

"Really? I've been wondering if you just want me involved because you're not planning to see the project through to completion on your own. Maybe you're thinking about taking those horses of yours and hightailing it back to Kentucky, and you want me up to speed."

Cash felt a prick of irritation. "I want you involved because, I re*peat*, the name on the side of this pickup is Rosslyn and Rosslyn."

"Just remember that yourself."

"Are you wearing down, old man? Is that what this is about? All you have to do is say something if you're just getting too tired and cranky to keep up." Cash was careful not to smile.

"I can still run circles around any codger my age. I'm up and down ladders as often as you are."

"Then why drag your feet on the Taylor project? In case you don't remember, these folks want quality work. Nobody's asking us to cut corners. We can do some of our best detailing, make it a showplace."

"I put some fine work into the last one, too, and before we could see any results the whole place burned down because one of *our* men brought a careless buddy of his onto the property."

Cash heard a deep and unwelcome chagrin in his father's voice. The old cabin had burned when a troubled young man Manning had hired to work on the cabin had taken a buddy and gone back after hours and, worse, after too much liquor. A cigarette butt, a pile of debris and poof, Leah Spurlock's history had gone up in flames.

"I think if the Taylors held that against us, they would have hired somebody else to build this house," Cash said.

"I used to visit that cabin as a young man, you know. Rachel Spurlock, Leah's daughter, was a friend of mine."

Cash knew the basics. Rachel Spurlock was Isaac's mother. She and Manning had grown up together, but after high school, Rachel had left Toms Brook, never to return. Sometime in her thirties, she had given birth to her only child out of wedlock, then died in a tragic accident. By then, she had already given Isaac up for adoption.

Isaac had known nothing of his roots until the attorney in charge of his grandmother's estate presented him with the deed to the cabin and a quilt Leah had left him in her will. Isaac hadn't been interested in finding out about the family who had abandoned him at birth, but Kendra hadn't been able to let it go. The whole story of Leah and her husband, Jesse, had unfolded after a great deal of digging. Rachel's story was still something of a mystery to Cash, but at least Rachel Spurlock's youth lived on in his father's memories.

"Does being out here stir up the past?" Cash asked. "Is that the problem?"

"Why would it be?"

"You'd have to answer that."

"I just lost heart after the cabin burned. That's the sum total."

"You're not responsible, and they don't hold you responsible. They want you involved, and that's as clear a message as any I've ever heard."

Manning leaned back in his seat. "Let's just get it over with. But don't forget, I'm entrusting this one to you. We're going to be spread pretty thin in the next months. We're going to have to split up our responsibilities. That's the point of having two Rosslyns in the company."

Cash issued his usual warning. "Don't go taking on too many projects without my consent. I haven't made any promises about how long I intend to stay at this. You know that."

"Yeah, I know that and more. You're giving me ulcers. You and that grandmother of yours. I don't know why things always have to be in upheaval with you two."

"Granny Grace always says, the rougher the river, the better the fishing."

"Yeah, well, I don't recall your grandmother ever spent a lot of time on the banks of the North Fork with a fly rod in her hand."

"No, from what I've been told she was pretty well busy in that orchard everybody's so anxious to get rid of, making a go of it and holding her family together."

"Don't start with that. Don't we have enough going on tonight?"

Cash knew the subject of his grandmother and Cashel Orchard was a sore one right now. He slowed just before the drive that led to the new cabin and changed the subject. "Jamie Dunkirk's not only got talent, she's got two of the cutest little girls you've ever seen in your life."

"So I suppose that means there's nothing going on between the two of you."

"Why, because she has kids?"

"No, because she sounds like a responsible human being capable of taking care of herself and her daughters."

Cash laughed. "I'm just footloose and fancy free. You know what I always say…"

"Yeah, you go by Cash because then you won't have to take credit for anything."

Cash turned into the drive and slowed to a crawl. "But tonight I'll take credit for getting you out here, old man."

Manning gathered up a couple of file folders and tucked them under his arm. "Let's get this over with. Then I want you to take full credit for this job. I have enough on my plate. I want as little to do with it as possible."

With dinner a pleasant memory, the kitchen cleaned courtesy of Isaac and Kendra, and the girls playing with newly unpacked toys in the bedroom, Jamie served her sister and brother-in-law coffee. Manning and Cash were expected any minute, so she had brewed a full pot. She didn't pour herself any; instead she made a cup of apple tea with a little honey and pretended it was just as good.

Her annoyance with her sister had evaporated. They'd had a wonderful meal, pleasant conversation, a chance to be a family. And along the way there had been a revelation, too, that she was keeping to herself for the moment. If her brighter mood was caused by hormones, she hoped they remained for a while in exactly this proportion.

"You're looking forward to getting Manning's opinion, aren't you?" Kendra said.

"Cash likes the plans. I hope his dad will, too."

"I'm almost surprised Manning's making the trip," Kendra said, accepting her coffee. "Every time I've tried to pin him down, he's been evasive."

Jamie gave Isaac his cup, then settled on the largest sofa beside her sister. "I haven't met him yet. But he's probably old enough to retire if he wants to. Could be he just wants to turn more of the business over to Cash."

"Two years ago, Cash sounded like he wasn't committed to staying around here forever. Or even very long. To tell the truth, I'm kind of surprised he's still here. I don't think construction is his only love."

"What would be?"

"I seem to remember him mentioning he was involved in the Kentucky racing scene before he came back to Toms Brook."

Although this was news, Jamie could imagine Cash in the adrenaline-fueled world of horse racing. At the same time, she believed that his interest in historical preservation and quality construction was a genuine part of him, as well.

"He's a multifaceted guy," she said. "The most interesting kind. And it's all going to turn out just fine."

"You've been awfully positive since dinner ended," Kendra said. "Are you our official optimist?"

"If you'll listen to me."

The crunch of gravel signaled the Rosslyns' arrival. Jamie leaped up to answer the door. Beyond the porch, fireflies dotted the twilight. Darkness had brought cooler air and the sweet smell of the last wild roses and honeysuckle. She savored a deep breath.

Cash sprang down from the driver's side of a Rosslyn and Rosslyn pickup, and the passenger door opened. An older man stepped down. Not awkwardly, but not with the same ease as his son. Jamie saw that he was broad shouldered and tall, and in his prime had probably been formidable in fistfights or on a football field.

Cash waited for his father, and they walked up the path together. Cash raised his hand in salute, then introduced his dad.

Jamie held out her hand, and they shook. Up close, Manning's age was more apparent. She guessed he was in his early to mid-seventies. He was nearly bald on top and made no attempt to comb over the gray strands that were left. She liked his dark eyes, which warmed when he smiled a greeting. She saw no resemblance to his son.

"It was nice of you both to come out in the evening like this," she said.

Manning gave a short nod. "Sometimes that's the only way we can find time to talk to our customers."

"Kendra and Isaac are going back early in the morning, so this is one of those opportunities." Jamie stepped back to usher them in.

Cash lingered a moment. "Granny Grace says to come ahead tomorrow."

"Lucky's improving?"

"If she made it this far, I think she'll pull through."

"The girls can't wait to see her."

"If you come by nine, they can feed her. I brought directions. The house won't be hard to find."

"Will you be there?"

He grinned. "What makes you think I live there?"

"You live somewhere else?"

"No, I live on orchard property, but I'll probably be gone tomorrow. I'll show you where another time."

Jamie was aware that the others were waiting for them. Manning had seated himself across from Kendra on a straight-back chair. He motioned for Cash to join them, as if he was in a hurry to get started.

"He's had a long day," Cash said. "We'd better get moving."

At the end of an hour, they had all agreed on a final plan to send to Rosslyn and Rosslyn's architect. Even Manning, who impressed Jamie as a man who said little unless he had something big to say, told her the house was going to be magnificent.

"Cash said you were talented," he said, rolling up the plans. "This cabin's one thing. Nice and simple. Well thought out. But these plans are a different universe. Brady's going to be impressed. Probably unhappy, too, that he won't need to do much of anything to earn his keep. I want you to get together with him after he's had a chance to look, if you will. To answer any questions."

Jamie felt like she had the day the trustees of her father's estate had handed over her trust fund. Better, in fact, since she'd won this by hard work, not the genetic lottery. "I really appreciate hearing that from somebody who should know. Someone besides my professors."

Manning smiled, something he didn't seem to do very often. He stood and held out his hand to Isaac, giving it a perfunctory shake. Then he shook with Jamie and Kendra.

"First thing we'll have to do is find you more water," he told them. "You'll need a good well for a house this size, but Cash will get you what you need."

Manning nodded to the group and started toward the door. Jamie followed, as Cash said goodbye to the Taylors.

"I'll be here for most of the next year," she said. "I'll look forward to watching the house go up."

"Cash won't disappoint you."

"You won't be working on it?"

"He'll handle most of it." Manning looked back at Kendra and Isaac. "Isaac looks something like his mother. It jumped out at me first time I met him."

"I'd forgotten. Kendra said you and his mother were friends growing up here."

"Rachel Spurlock was nobody's friend, not the way you mean. She was always something of a loner, but we cared about each other."

Jamie thought that was a uniquely old-fashioned way of admitting to sexual attraction. She needed to get the complete scoop from Kendra.

Cash joined them, and the two men descended the steps. Jamie waited until they were gone before she rejoined the others.

The girls had gone to bed, and the house was quiet. Kendra and Isaac were getting ready to go to Daughter of the Stars, the bed-and-breakfast where they often spent the night, but Jamie held up a hand to stop them.

"Don't go yet. I have something for you."

Kendra brushed off her pants. "Don't you want some peace and quiet? You must be exhausted."

"Not yet." Jamie disappeared into the kitchen; then she came back with a package wrapped in blue and green foil. "I've been saving this for the right moment. It's for both of you."

Isaac took the package. "You don't think the house design was enough? You've already given us so much."

Jamie heard what he didn't say. Isaac rarely mentioned the sur-rogacy, as if by doing so he would jinx it, or perhaps admit how much it meant to him.

"This is just something you'll need to help you understand all the steps along the way," she said. "The more you know, the easier it will seem."

Isaac offered the package to Kendra, who took it and began to untie the ribbon. "We ought to celebrate what Manning said about the plans," Kendra said. "I knew it already, but it was great to hear Manning give his opinion tonight. You must feel wonderful."

"Actually, I do," Jamie said, "although you two have the wrong project in mind. You know how long it takes to build a house. I'm thinking about something shorter term."

She paused, and when they didn't try to guess, she broke into a grin. "Come on! Use your imaginations. Can't you guess what I was doing when you were stacking the dishwasher?"

Kendra stood very still, aware at last what Jamie was about to say, then she tore the remainder of the wrapping and stared at the cover of *What to Expect When You're Expecting*. "Exactly what are you trying to say?"

"I bought a home pregnancy kit at the drugstore today, even though I wasn't sure whether I should use it. I was trying to be good and wait for the official verdict from the clinic. But since it's been almost two weeks since the transfer, I decided to give it a try tonight. I've just had a feeling all day that something was going on inside me besides all the meds I've had to take. I realized the wait was killing you. I know the doctor said the home tests aren't always accurate after in vitro, but from everything I've read, that's mostly if you do them too early. So since you were here and we're all dying to know…"

She put an arm around each of them, pulling them closer. For a moment she couldn't speak. Her throat clogged, and she tightened her hold on them. Then she swallowed and said the words she'd been wanting to say all evening.

"Congratulations, Mom and Dad. We're going to have a baby."

6

Sometimes in the morning, before he went off to whatever job site he was working on, Cash stopped by for a cup of coffee, and Grace liked to be ready with something tasty and healthy enough to make it worth her while to do the work. When her grandson chose his own breakfast, he was prone to either black coffee or the full Southern heart-attack-on-a-platter. She had seen him slather enough butter on his grits to lubricate the chassis of Rosslyn and Rosslyn's entire fleet of pickups.

This morning she had whole-wheat coffee cake made with fresh blueberries picked from bushes Ben had planted not long before he died. That they were bearing so robustly was a sad reminder of how long Ben had been gone. Had she needed one.

She wasn't sure Cash would stop, but about seven, she heard the familiar rumble of a truck, then the dying of an engine and the slamming of a door. She had three grandsons, two grand-daughters and four great-grandchildren, and she didn't believe in favorites. From the beginning she had struggled to treat them all like the priceless works of God they were. But despite that struggle, she had always been a little closer to Cash. Not because he was Sandra's—her only daughter's—although most of the world would think that likely. Just because he was Cash.

This morning he came into the kitchen with his customary swagger. Cash moved as if he owned the world and didn't give a hoot. The confidence was innate, the indifference a product of too many tears he had swallowed as a young man. Of course, if she told him that, he would deny it. Cash had worked so hard to cultivate his good ol' boy persona that years ago he had begun to believe it himself.

"Still trying to fatten me up, huh?" He strolled over to kiss Grace's cheek, then grabbed the coffeepot and poured himself a cup. He held it up in question.

"Had mine," she said. "Piddling poor, too, if you want to know. Half a cup, mostly decaf, filled to the brim with skim milk. I do not recommend annual physicals, dear. No doctor has ever said, 'Oh, please, be sure to drink an extra cup of coffee every day, Mrs. Cashel. And don't forget to pour in the whipping cream.'"

"We could probably find you one like that if we looked hard enough and paid him under the table."

"Growing old is not for sissies."

"Good thing, because you're doing it so beautifully, Granny Grace."

Her heart warmed. She did love this boy.

She watched him stroll over to the crate where little Lucky was making herself right at home. He bent down and spoke soothingly to the fawn, who listened to every word. The last time he'd stopped by, he had taken Lucky out, and Grace had caught them sitting on the sofa, Lucky nestled in his lap. Manning had taught Cash to hunt, a rite of passage for boys in the Valley, but at the final moment, Cash, a crack shot, had somehow always missed every moving target. Manning had never shamed him for it.

Grace still thought Sandra had done well for herself when she batted her pretty green eyes in Manning Rosslyn's direction all those years ago, even if he was a good bit older than her daughter.

"I'm having visitors this morning," she told him.

Cash joined her as she cut the coffee cake, sliding a large piece on to a plate for him, then she helped herself to less. She hoped that the berries had been ripe enough to do their job. Squeezed between her thumb and index finger, they had seemed that way, but it wasn't the most reliable of tests.

"Who's visiting?" He cut a piece and popped it into his mouth. "It's great," he said. "Even if you probably sneaked wheat germ and flax seed and Lord knows what else into it."

"Glad it passes muster. And Jamie and the girls are coming up to see Lucky. You could stay and visit with us."

"Oh, I don't think so."

She wished she could read the expression hidden behind his coffee mug. "I like her. And those little girls? She's awfully young to have them, but she's a superior mother, isn't she? Just from the little I've seen, I can tell she lets them be who they are."

"Does she walk on water, too?"

She smiled. "Enthusiasm is a good trait, dear, not one to make fun of."

"I just saw her last night. Dad and I went over plans for the new house they're going to build down by the river."

"They?"

"Her sister and her husband. The property and the cabin belong to the Taylors."

"Do you know why Jamie's living way out here with the girls?"

"Kendra, that's Mrs. Taylor, said something about Jamie and the girls wanting to be nearby and enjoy family, now that she's finished with college. They're planning to stay for the next school year, I think. Maybe she's trying to find herself. I don't know."

Grace leaned forward. "You could find out."

Cash set down his cup and leaned forward until they were almost nose to nose. "How many projects do you need, Granny Grace? You've got your quilts, the orchard, this house, whipping the family into shape so they see eye to eye with you. And now you're playing matchmaker?"

"I said nothing about matches. I just worry about a stranger in our midst, living in the middle of nowhere with nobody to look in on her now and then."

"I'm going to be building a house right under her nose. I just put up a playhouse for her children. Do you want me to move in with her?"

Grace considered. "Let me give that some thought."

Cash grinned. "The devil's going to grab you and drag you down below, Grace Cashel."

"Your grandfather told me as much, you know. But I'm still here, and he isn't. What does that say?"

"It says Grandpa Ben is up in heaven playing his harp so loud that the devil's too annoyed to bother with you. That's why he went first."

She liked the sound of that. "If anybody could do that, it would be Ben."

Cash finished the last swigs of his coffee and stood. "I've got to be halfway to Winchester in twenty minutes. Mind if I take my coffee cake with me?"

"You do that, and don't you stop along the road for country ham and fried eggs."

He leaned over and kissed her cheek in farewell. "Don't go falling in love with those little girls. In a year or less they'll be out of here, and going off somewhere so their mama can finish her degree and get a job in some top-notch architect's firm. We'll probably never see them again."

"That should make Jamie Dunkirk the perfect woman for you."

He shook his head, plopped his coffee cake on a napkin and headed out the door.

Grace listened as his truck roared to life again a moment later.

"Score one for Grace Cashel. Tell *that* to your angel band, Ben." She cut herself another slice of cake and enjoyed every crumb.

Jamie stared at the skylight directly above her bed. Once Kendra and Isaac had gone last night, she had spent hours worrying that she'd sent their hopes soaring for nothing. The pregnancy test had been absolutely clear. According to Johnson & Johnson, she was pregnant, but what if she *had* jumped the gun? What if she went into the clinic on Thursday and discovered that under these peculiar circumstances, the home test still wasn't accurate? What if she wasn't really pregnant?

Then this morning, after an uneasy night's sleep, she'd sat up and a wave of dizziness had swept her. Immediately afterward, the dizziness had been followed by a surge of nausea so strong that she'd had to lie back and close her eyes or suffer the consequences.

Pregnant.

She smiled. Pregnant *again*.

Pregnant with somebody else's baby.

Before offering to carry this baby, she had considered and reconsidered whether she wanted another child of her own. She had known that, if she still yearned for more children to fill her life, perhaps even the son she'd never had, then turning over a baby she had carried for nine months would be doubly difficult. Even if the baby had been conceived outside her body and was technically only her niece or nephew.

That first round of soul searching hadn't turned up any latent desire to become a mother again, nor—she was relieved to find— had that changed now that she was in the throes of morning sickness. She adored her daughters. She looked forward to watching them grow and establish themselves in the world, but she had no wish to wind up her own child-rearing clock all over again. When all was said and done, Hannah and Alison were the only children she wanted, even if she married someday and had a husband to share the work of raising them.

Technically she was four weeks into the pregnancy, since weeks were calculated by the last menstrual period, whether it was simulated or not. If she carried full-term and not a day more or less, then she had thirty-six weeks ahead of her. The baby would come at the end of February, before the new house was finished, and Kendra and Isaac would take him or her home to Arlington. She would need a plan for herself and the girls.

But there was time for all that. Time to savor bringing a new life into the world.

"Mommy!"

But not much.

She sat up gingerly, hoping the nausea had diminished. The room didn't spin, and although she didn't feel like wolfing down the truck driver's special at the Milestone Restaurant beside the interstate, she thought she would probably be able to handle a cup of coffee.

Then she remembered that a nice cup of fruit tea would have to substitute. Between hormones and giving up cigarettes and coffee, she was surprised she hadn't already alienated everybody in Virginia.

When she peered over the railing, Alison was staring up at her, as if willing her to materialize. "What is it?" Jamie asked.

"I want strawberries on my cereal."

"That makes sense."

"Hannah said no."

"Why?"

"Dunno."

"I'll be right down." Jamie slid into the robe at the foot of her bed and made the trip to the bathroom without a significant return of the nausea. By the time she joined Alison in the kitchen, the strawberry crisis was readily apparent. Hannah sat at the table with her head in her hands. The green cardboard carton that had held the second quart of strawberries was empty. Last night it had been half-full.

"Apparently I have to stop buying fresh berries, Hannah." Jamie threw the carton in the trash. "The bathroom's empty. I suggest you go there immediately. And when you're done being sick, you can apologize to your sister."

Hannah took off at a trot.

"I'm sorry about the berries," Jamie told Alison. "I'll cut up a peach for your cereal."

"Hannah's sick."

The cabin was small enough that Jamie could affirm that just by sound. With her own stomach in rebellion, she was afraid to go into the bathroom to check on her oldest. Instead she fixed Alison's cereal and set it on the table. Alison climbed up on the booster seat and started eating. Jamie looked away, not at all sure she could watch her youngest eat while her oldest finished being sick. She went to boil water for tea and hoped for the best.

Two minutes later, a pale Hannah came out of the bathroom, drying her face on a hand towel.

"Feel better?" Jamie asked.

Hannah managed a nod.

"That's a tough way to learn not to be piggy."

"I was only going to eat five." Hannah looked like she was trying not to cry.

Jamie thought back on her own past. "Not everything we like's good for us. That's one of the hardest lessons you'll ever have to learn."

"Like cigarettes?"

"Like cigarettes. And like strawberries. You may have to stop eating berries altogether, unless you can learn to just eat a few at a time." She paused, then decided she had to add insult to injury. "Now apologize to Alison, please. You ate her share, not to mention mine."

Hannah burst into tears. Jamie's heartstrings were thoroughly tugged, but she stood resolute.

"I'm sorry," Hannah managed at last.

"I like peaches," Alison said, not quite understanding what all the fuss was about.

Jamie gave Hannah a casual hug. "That was the right thing to do. Now have a seat. Would you like a slice of toast, or would you rather wait a little while?"

Her daughter sniffed. "Can we still go see Lucky? I won't be sick anymore."

"Not until you get something in your stomach. I'll pour you some apple juice, but I suggest sipping slowly and waiting a little on the toast. You can have a slice right before we leave."

Forty-five minutes later, they were on the way to Granny Grace's. The orchard was a half-hour's drive away. Had Jamie been a bird, she could have gotten there in ten, but the road switched back and forth as they crossed the river at the first available bridge and climbed farther into the mountains.

She was quickly learning to love the Valley. She loved the vast array of greens, the blue-gray mist that rose from the ground in early morning, clouds veiling individual peaks, then falling away as the golden summer sun rose higher to meet them. She liked seeing horses in wildflower-strewn meadows, the glint of sunlight on creeks and river, the pragmatic simplicity of rural architecture. Clematis on mailbox posts. Pansies guarding doorsteps.

Now, as they came to the end of Grace's directions, she admired the farms set back from the road. Somebody's border collie came charging down a driveway, and the girls waved and called to it as Jamie shot past in hopes of avoiding a roundup. The dog, who clearly thought he'd done his duty, trotted back up the drive.

Jamie slowed and checked her directions one more time. "Will you help me watch out for the sign, Hannah? It should say Cashel Orchard, but Grace said it's small and easy to miss. Should be on your side."

"Cashel? Like Cash?"

"That's probably where his name comes from."

Jamie slowed even more until she was almost creeping. Even at that, they nearly missed the sign. Hannah spotted it just as they were pulling past.

"There!" She pointed.

Jamie leaned over to peer out Hannah's window. The sign hung by one hook when it should have been suspended from two. It was weathered gray, with an apple in the center that was so faded it was almost invisible. Equally faded letters were painted in script.

The sign might be dilapidated, but someone had recently bushhogged and graded the driveway. No limbs hung over the road, and in the distance, Jamie could hear the steady hum of a tractor. She took the turn and drove slowly, watching for rocks and potholes. An unkempt hedge choked with wild grapevines flanked the road, hiding most of what lay beyond it. The road wound to the right and seemed to climb gradually. When they finally came to a clearing, Jamie slowed to a halt and gazed at the farmhouse just ahead of them.

"It's a classic," she said out loud.

The house, painted a fading blue-gray, had a deep front porch that wrapped around the sides. A hipped roof rose above the second story, and twin chimneys were like bookends holding it all in place. Roses tumbled over arbors; evergreen shrubs nearly hid the porch railing. Two black walnuts stood as straight as soldiers, one on each side of the clearing. She was taken with the combination of graceful rural living and neglect. The porch needed painting, the flower beds needed tending. The house needed to be loved.

She had expected something very different. Contemporary, perhaps, with witty architectural details. At the very least, paint as bright as Grace's clothing. She loved the old house on sight, but it didn't look as if Grace should live there.

Grace did, though. As Jamie pulled up next to a Rosslyn and Rosslyn pickup, Grace, in a daffodil-yellow blouse and long pink broomstick skirt, came out to the porch and waved.

"Come on up," she called. "There's a hungry fawn waiting to be fed."

Jamie got out and retrieved Alison. Hannah, clearly feeling like her old self, ran ahead.

Someone had cut the grass recently, but grass was a misnomer.

What passed for a yard was mostly dandelions mowed into submission. Up close, the house was even shabbier.

"It's a wonderful old place," Jamie said, as she and Alison climbed up to the porch. Her mind began to whirl with changes she would make, a window enlarged here, a pergola there, a different sort of roof entirely over the front porch.

"Before I became mistress of the manor, Ben's family had lived here for five generations. They were talented carpenters, and when they decided to add on, they didn't throw it together higgledy-piggledy like some do. It's substantial and well-constructed. Of course, upkeep went by the wayside when I moved away. Renters and such. Cash should have moved in, but he claimed it was too big for a single man."

Jamie wondered why the family had been so willing to let the house deteriorate.

"They want to sell it," Grace said, as if she were reading Jamie's mind. "The family kept the house up, but only to the point that if somebody bought the land and wanted the house, too, it could be salvaged. But they don't believe that will happen."

Jamie didn't know what to say.

"I intend to live forever and keep them from selling anything," Grace said. "It belongs to me, lock, stock and acreage. In the unlikely chance that I die someday, I'm investigating the possibilities of a conservation easement. I don't ever want to see a housing development where these orchards stand."

Jamie felt her way through what seemed to be a loaded subject. "You don't sound angry."

"Oh, we understand each other. Everyone is trying to do what's right. So far, our paths just won't meet, that's all. But where there's love, there is, eventually, a solution."

Jamie liked that philosophy. She supposed a version of it had spurred her to volunteer as Kendra and Isaac's surrogate.

"But come in, come in, don't dawdle. Lucky's waiting for her friends." Grace threw open the screen door, which was sagging on its hinges, and let the girls inside.

The interior was in better condition than the exterior. Walls had been freshly painted, woodwork and floors polished. The house seemed to have fireplaces in every room, and each one was more interesting than the last. Jamie followed her children to the kitchen, admiring what looked like primitive antiques but were probably long-held family pieces. The walls had been painted light, bright colors that reflected the sunlight streaming through the un-curtained windows. Ripest apricot, exotic orchid, grassy green. And everywhere she looked, there were quilts. Not the old-fash-ioned quilts Jamie had investigated in the surrounding towns at antique and craft shops, but quilts like none Jamie had ever seen.

"Grace, the quilts! They're magnificent." Jamie stopped, although she knew her girls would disapprove, and pointed to one that hung from a wooden rod behind a sofa. "That one's incredible."

"I'm glad you like them. They're all mine. Except for the one in the front parlor. That was a swap with another quilter."

"Kendra *told* me there were quilters everywhere you look around here."

Grace gave a low laugh. "I doubt she meant me. I gave up tra-ditional quilts a while ago. I figured life was too short to redo what better quilt makers had done centuries before me. I never perfected my hand-quilting stitch, never got the hang of perfect piecing. I can do both well enough to get by, but this is my passion." She waved at the quilt that had stopped Jamie in her tracks.

All the quilts Jamie had noticed shared bright colors, interest-ing textures and items incorporated into the surface that she had never associated with quilts. Items like feathers, beads, old jewelry, branches, sprays of gilded wheat and ordinary nuts and bolts. Some had open spaces adorned by strips of ribbon or lace. Others were trapezoids or irregular hexagons. The one thing they all had in common? They brought the old farmhouse walls to life.

This quilt, almost double-bed size, was made of gold-and-red strips of every size and shape, sprinkled with crystal beads and what looked like gold nuggets encased in silvery thread. A parade of tiny rag dolls of every race and in various international costumes crisscrossed the center. Jamie was enchanted. The walls behind it were a pale metallic gold, and Grace had used the same bright red in the pillows strewn on a black plush sofa.

"I'll never think of quilts the same way again," Jamie said.

"I started these when I lived here with Ben. I'm not sure he ever truly understood what I was doing. Ben was traditional right down to his toenails, which nobody ever saw but me, of course, since a real man never wears sandals."

Jamie wondered about that marriage. But Grace spoke fondly of her husband, so Jamie preferred to believe it had been a happy one.

Grace continued until they were in a huge, sunny kitchen. Pine cabinets warmed the room under white tile counters. A conga line of fruits and vegetables adorned an eye-popping quilt on the wall beside the refrigerator. The walls were painted a deep peach.

Lucky was in a large dog crate beside the stove.

As one voice, the girls said, "Ah…"

"I have a bottle all ready to give her," Grace told Hannah. "She'll sit on your lap if you let her, and drink it all down. But Alison will need a turn holding the bottle, as well. You'll need to be the one to hold Lucky, Hannah, even when Alison has the bottle. Her hooves are sharp."

"We can do that."

Grace opened the door and reached inside for the fawn. Lucky seemed perfectly happy to leave the safety of the crate, but in no particular hurry.

Jamie echoed her daughters' sentiments. "Ah… Look at that. She's walking." The fawn was still as tiny as a stuffed toy, but her coat was shinier than it had been, and the darker spots now seemed to stand out in sharp relief against the tan. Her eyes were brighter, too. Jamie realized with a lump in her throat how close to losing her they had been.

"Still a bit weak in the pins, but she's coming along," Grace said. "We've graduated to goat's milk. A neighbor's supplying it. And she's going a full two hours between feedings now, sometimes three. Soon enough, she'll sleep through the night."

"It's been so much work for you. I feel badly—" she paused "—but not as badly as I'd feel if we hadn't moved her here."

"That's two of us. She's a dear little thing." Grace laughed at the pun when Jamie did. "She's kept me company. The nights are long up here."

She went to the refrigerator and got what looked like a soft-drink bottle half filled with milk and capped with a plastic nipple. She instructed the girls on how to get Lucky to drink, then she waved Jamie to an oak table. "Have a seat, and I'll get you some coffee if you like."

"No coffee, but a glass of water would be great."

"I have lemonade."

"Greater."

Grace poured four glasses and set them on a tray that she brought over to the table. In the corner, the girls squealed with delight as Lucky tried to grab the nipple.

Grace took the chair beside Jamie's and passed her a glass. "Would you like to see the orchard once the girls feed Lucky?"

"I would. Is it still producing?"

"Not the way it should. There are no farmers left in the family, I'm afraid. One of my sons works for the U.S. Mint out in San Francisco. The other teaches physics at a small college in Massachusetts. Their children are professionals with no interest in the land. My daughter—Cash's mother—loves the place, but she's not confident enough to save it. Sandra sees no way to continue production, pay the taxes, pay for labor, upkeep, machinery and everything that goes along with orchards. The crop's not worth as much as it should be. Americans expect their food at rock-bottom prices. Farmers go out of business every day, faster than you can blink your eyelids."

"There are other orchards around. I've seen signs on the roads. How do they keep going?"

"Pick your own. They bring families up from the cities to spend a day in the country, ride in a hay wagon, pick their own fruit, have picnics. But it takes dedication and a lot of hard work to make that happen. Mostly the ones who make it are family enterprises. That's true for most of the orchards that pick and ship the usual way, too. Or sometimes there's a family member or two who subsidize the cost of keeping the business going."

"I don't know a thing about it, but it does sounds like a huge amount of work."

"Yes, and pay regular wages for all of it and you go under right away."

"So what do you do? You said you were still producing."

"We sell for cider these days, and for sauce. No direct sales, no grocery-store sales. Apples aren't perfect enough. But even that crop's declined. You have to plant new trees and fuss over the old ones like they were your children. So that's why I'm here. To make sure that happens."

"You've figured out how to put it back together?"

Grace smiled. "Not yet. But I just got here."

"And we've kept you busy." But even as she said it, Jamie wondered how a woman Grace's age could fix such a vast problem. Although she was vivacious and energetic, Grace was probably in her eighties. It seemed obvious from the general disrepair Jamie had seen that Grace's children were just biding their time until they could take control. That seemed sad.

"Cash could turn it around if he chose." Grace refilled Jamie's lemonade. "He was born to do it. He's the most like me, of course. He just hasn't quite realized that staying here and making a go of it would be all the challenge he needs. Cure his restlessness."

Jamie was enjoying herself. Behind her, the girls were laughing, clearly thrilled with their task. And now she had a chance to learn more about Cash.

"You think he's restless?"

"No, *he* thinks he's restless. He thinks if he moves on, then moves on again, he'll find some peace. Only that's not going to help, of course."

"Peace can be elusive."

"He's had a hard road."

Jamie didn't want to be a busybody. She told herself that if Cash needed peace, the reason was his own business. But the question must have showed on her face.

Grace sat back. "What do you know about my grandson?"

"That he's a talented carpenter and a nice guy."

"And that he has his eye on you?"

Jamie could feel her dimples deepen. "I wouldn't go that far."

"I told you he was a rascal. Now I'll tell you that he hasn't had a serious relationship since he became a single man again."

Jamie was taken aback. "Oh."

"You didn't know he was married." It wasn't a question. "He's sure he never wants to be again."

Jamie thought of the baby growing inside her. "And if Cash doesn't want ties, I'd be the last person he'd want anything to do with," she warned. "My kids and I are a regular ball and chain."

"The girls? He loves children. All my great-grandchildren think Cash could raise the dead. No, you would be the obstacle. He's afraid to fall in love, and you'd be a short drop, you know. Slip an inch, and there he'd be."

Jamie almost spat out her lemonade. "Grace, that's a lovely thing to say, but really, you don't know a thing about me."

Grace peered intently at Jamie through her thick glasses. "Trouble in the past. I can see it in your face. Something to do with the men who fathered those girls, perhaps, or something older. But a strong determination to make things right, patience, intelligence, creativity. And you cook like a pro and design houses. What else is there to know, dear? He would be lucky to have you."

She stood before Jamie could say another word. "Girls, how is that silly fawn doing?" She walked over to supervise the feeding. Lucky seemed perfectly happy, but Alison had tired of trying to keep the bottle in the fawn's mouth, and now she came to sit on her mother's lap and drink lemonade. In a few minutes Hannah joined her.

"We'll take Lucky outside first," Grace told them, "then off we'll go for a drive. She needs a walk and some fresh air, and a place to poop."

The girls giggled at that. Jamie had to smile, too. Grace lifted the fawn into her arms and started toward the door. Halfway there, she stumbled over a footstool that rested against a cabinet and nearly fell.

Jamie was close enough to grab her arm.

"Was that silly?" Grace asked. "But it's hard to see over this little thing."

"I'll guide you," Jamie said. She kept her hand on Grace's arm.

"You're a woman who can be counted on," Grace said. "I can tell."

Jamie inadvertently put her other hand on her belly. "That's what I want to be," she said. "That's exactly what I want to be."

7

Kendra climbed the stairs to the second floor of her Arlington home; then, because she couldn't help herself, she stepped into the small bedroom that looked over the backyard. Ten, the tattered Garfield look-alike who shared their lives, ran between her legs, followed closely by lovable but clueless Dusty, a canine mixed breed that she—a talented wordsmith—had never been able to adequately describe. Used to this behavior, she moved to one side as soon as the second tail passed, so they would have a clear shot out the door for the return trip. They made it in record time.

In the nearly two years she and Isaac had lived in the house, this room had never been used by anyone except Jamie's girls. When Hannah and Alison visited, they slept on twin beds that Kendra had found at an estate sale. The beds were country-French in style, walnut, with hand-carved flowers on the head- and footboards and graceful cabriole legs. She had lovingly furnished the rest of the room with a dresser and rocking chair of the same period, taking her time to select the perfect items to go with them. A fluffy white rug and cheerful redwork quilts she had bought at the Shenandoah Community Church auction harmonized with pale yellow walls.

She had thought it would be the last time she furnished a room for children.

She heard footsteps behind her, and when Isaac slipped his arms around her waist, she leaned back against him.

"What are you thinking?" He nuzzled her ear.

"It's too early to be thinking what I'm thinking."

"You're planning a nursery, aren't you?"

She laughed softly, because of course he was right. This room was the closest to the master bedroom, and it would be the obvious place for a baby to sleep.

"I hate to displace the girls," she said, "but we won't be living in this house much longer. We'll make sure there's a room just for them in the Valley house."

"I'm thinking a sports theme here," he said. "Easy to put up and take down when we move. Baseball pennants, a basketball hoop."

"If it weren't sexist, I'd point out that the baby could be a girl."

"Who will then learn to pitch with the best of them," Isaac promised. "Hannah's already working on her curve ball."

"I can't believe this is really happening."

Isaac's arms tightened around her. "We'll see the proof in a little while."

If all was well, their baby was six and a half weeks old today. Jamie had been absolutely correct. She was pregnant, and she was scheduled to have an ultrasound at the fertility clinic in an hour. If this one went well, she would have another in a few weeks. At that point, if everything was fine, she would transfer her care to a regular obstetrician. They had decided on a practice in Front Royal, which was closer for Kendra and Isaac than Woodstock, and still easy for Jamie to reach. From the beginning, Jamie had insisted that she wanted Kendra and Isaac to attend any appointment they wanted to.

"There's still so much that can go wrong," Kendra said. Isaac was so quiet that she knew he was trying to frame his response.

"Just say it," she said. "Get it over with. I've got a pretty good guess anyway."

He tightened his arms around her. "I know you're just trying to protect yourself—and me—by holding back, but isn't it about time we started to enjoy this? Shouldn't we be able to talk about the baby without backtracking?"

"It's just all so new. And so tentative."

"So Rod Serling? So *Back to the Future?*"

She laughed again. She felt better with his arms around her. "Let's face it, this isn't something I trained for. Nobody ever prepared me to let my sister carry my child."

"Then we ought to just let go, don't you think? If we're not trained, we don't even know what to worry about."

"It doesn't seem to work that way. Instead, I just worry about everything."

"Try to stop, okay?"

She heard him loud and clear. The last thing in the world she wanted was to ruin this experience for Isaac.

She turned in his arms. "Of course you're right. Worrying about everything's not going to change the outcome. It's not like I can head it off by thinking about it first.. Jamie's been pregnant twice without my help, and she doesn't need a worrying section on the sidelines."

"Good. Now work on believing that, okay?" He squeezed

again, and kissed then released her. "Decorating the nursery might be a good first project in making the house a worry-free zone."

"No, it really is too early. But I'll make a list of ideas."

He was already at the door, but he turned. "As long as they revolve around blue."

"You don't really care what sex the baby is, do you?"

He smiled a little. "You know I don't."

"I guess you could use an ally. I've got my sister and the girls. We need more testosterone in the family."

"We need a healthy baby. Let's go see our first photo, shall we?"

She took one last look at the room they would bring their child home to. A wave of worry swept over her again. Resolutely, she pushed it as far away as she could, but she could still feel it lapping at the edges of her mind, waiting to wash over her. She was afraid that was the best she was going to be able to do.

"Please tell me you've finished all your questions," Jamie said.

The nurse who had brought her to the scanning room, a middle-aged woman with complicated trails of French braids zigzagging over her head, laughed. "When will anybody ever be this interested in every little symptom you have, honey? Nobody's ever going to get this excited about every little drop of pee again. You'll miss me."

"The questions? Not so much."

"We're going to start with an external scan today, but if it doesn't go just the way they want, we're going to do the vaginal one. You know that?"

Jamie had strongly suggested that she be allowed to try the external scan first, so that Isaac could be present. Their doctor had reluctantly agreed.

"I know. I'm just hoping we can hear the heartbeat," she said.

"That full bladder of yours will help."

"That full bladder of mine would like to get started."

Somebody knocked on the door, and the nurse let Kendra in.

"I'll get you settled," the nurse said. "Then the technician will come in. The father can join you then."

"How are you?" Kendra asked Jamie.

"Let's just say that after thirty-two ounces of water, I'm looking forward to a little rendezvous with the bathroom when we get done here."

Kendra watched as the nurse got Jamie into position on the examination table. Jamie undid her jeans, pulling them low on her hips.

"You've done this before, huh?" the nurse asked.

"I'm an old hand."

"You comfy?"

"More or less."

"You're set. Lori will be with you in a few minutes."

"Few being the operative word, right?" Kendra said. "If Jamie says she's uncomfortable, she's not kidding."

"I promise we won't let her float away." The nurse patted Jamie's hand; then she disappeared out the door.

Jamie shifted a little to make herself more comfortable. "I like it when you get all stern and demanding."

"I'm going to make absolutely sure everybody takes good care of you. That's my new job."

"New? That was always your job. We got beyond it for…what? About ten minutes, and now you'll have to take care of me all over again."

"That's not exactly what's happening. Aren't you taking care of me? Making sure I get my heart's desire, even at considerable expense to your freedom and muscle tone?"

"That's a nice way of thinking about it." Jamie reached for Kendra's hand and squeezed it.

Kendra smiled, then sobered. "Jamie, speaking of taking care of you and our happy childhood... Have you spoken to Riva? Does she know you're here, and why?"

Now Jamie understood why her sister had turned so serious. Riva Delacroix was not so much estranged from her daughters as she was oblivious to them. Her life was a high-speed train to nowhere, with frequent stops at watering holes for the rich and famous. Their childhood had been spent in the care of household servants and poorly chosen nannies, and Kendra had tried, for most of Jamie's childhood, to make up to her for the neglect of both parents. That, of course, had created a new set of problems.

Jamie remembered her last conversation with her mother. "Right before we moved, I called and told her we were going to spend some time in Virginia. She was somewhere in Tuscany at a house party, or would that be a villa party? Anyway, she regaled me for most of an hour with tales of a new man who was the answer to every prayer she'd ever prayed, every dream she'd ever dreamed, every—"

"I get it."

"I thought you might. She sounded even more Riva than usual. She said she had a vision just before this man appeared. A woman dressed in flowing robes told her that her suffering was over, and that she would attain heaven on earth. Then in he walked."

"Riva, our lady of perpetual confusion."

Jamie had been forced to deal with her feelings about their mother during her residency at First Step, but she wondered if Kendra ever really had. She hoped so. Putting a poor parent in perspective seemed like a prerequisite to becoming a good one. It certainly had been for her.

Someone knocked, and a woman with a lab coat over a gray skirt came in and introduced herself as Lori, the sonographer. She was young, blond and chirpy.

Kendra stepped to one side to give Lori room to set up. "May I get my husband now?"

"You're all right with that?" Lori asked Jamie.

"He's the daddy."

Lori didn't blink. This was a fertility clinic, and she had probably seen every combination and situation imaginable. "Go get 'im," she told Kendra. "We don't want Daddy to miss out, do we?"

Jamie thought she would probably like Lori under different circumstances. But she was tired, a little nauseous and anxious to make a break for the toilet. All this, plus the girls were waiting outside, wondering why Mommy and their aunt and uncle were all visiting a doctor's office together.

Isaac came in with Kendra, and they stood where the sonographer told them to.

"Are the girls doing okay?" Jamie asked.

"Alison is coloring cows lime-green, and Hannah is seeing how fast she can progress through crossword puzzles for much older children. They're wondering what's going on."

"I'll tell them soon. I wanted to get through this first."

Kendra took her hand. Lori warned Jamie that the gel she was going to spread on her abdomen was a little cold. Jamie was ready for it.

"This is the transducer," Lori explained, holding up her magic wand. "It picks up sound waves. You can watch on the screen."

Jamie had been introduced to this technology with Hannah, but even now, three pregnancies later, the idea that they could "see" the baby while it was forming amazed her.

Images flashed by on the screen as Lori moved the transducer across her belly, explaining a few. There was little definition to any of them. Even after witnessing a number of ultrasounds, Jamie still couldn't tell what she was seeing. If there was a baby there, it was invisible to her.

Lori fell silent, and Jamie actually missed her chirping. She had hoped Lori would explain everything as she went, but her demeanor now was completely professional.

After a while she stopped, removing the transducer. "Okay, I'm off to get the doctor," she said.

"Why?" Jamie demanded.

"It's routine. We'll let him tell you when he arrives."

"I'm pretty much ready to get up off this table and head out of here," Jamie warned.

"Back in a minute or two. Don't go anywhere."

"What do you suppose this is about?" Isaac asked, after she left.

"She didn't sound that concerned," Kendra said, sounding concerned herself. "But she's also the kind of person who would find something positive to say while a tornado was shredding her house."

Jamie had a pretty good idea what was up. She'd had enough ultrasounds to know that whatever Lori had seen had neither surprised nor worried her. She wondered why her brother-in-law hadn't figured it out. She supposed anxiety could block even Isaac's good sense.

She wished she was back in Michigan, where her young gynecologist, Dr. Chinn, would have been present at the ultrasound and more than willing to report everything right up front. They had become good friends when Suz Chinn's brother had needed First Step's outpatient clinic to help overcome a fondness for painkillers. She could use Suz now, to put Kendra and Isaac at ease.

"This is a medical clinic," she said, not wanting to spoil the surprise or jump to the wrong conclusion out loud. "If they tell you what's going on, they can't charge as much. They charge by the mysterious moment."

When the other two fell silent and she realized that they were still preparing for the worst, she added, "Listen, whatever it is, no matter what, we'll move on. If we have to do this again, that's what we'll do."

"Do you think that's what they're going to tell us?"

"No. I'm pretty sure I *know* what they're going to tell us," Jamie said.

Before they could demand she guess out loud, the door opened and one of the doctors strode in with Lori. He was short, completely bald, and his smile fed Jamie's certainty.

"Okay, let's look at this together," he said. "Did Lori tell you what she saw?"

Kendra moved closer to the screen. "No, but you don't seem concerned."

"My sister, the investigative reporter," Jamie said. "That's her way of getting info. Why don't you just come out and tell her?"

"We'll have a look see first," the doctor said. "Just to be sure, although Lori's the best sonographer I know, the real McCoy."

Jamie generally didn't trust people who used terms like "look-see" and "real McCoy," but she kind of liked this guy. He and perky little Lori were a team. Together they excelled at good news.

"Okay, Mommy," he told Jamie. "Let's take one more look."

"Mommy," Jamie asked Kendra, "is that okay with you?" She winked.

Kendra was pale. Her freckles seemed to have grown three shades darker. "Let's just get on with it, okay?"

Lori squirted more gel on Jamie's abdomen and began to move the transducer. A minute passed, then two. "There," she said at last.

The doctor was silent as Lori moved the transducer again, then again.

"Just tell them so I can go to the bathroom, okay?" Jamie said.

"We're going to let you go," the doctor said, "then, if you don't mind, we're going to put you back up here and finish with an internal ultrasound. Just to get more data."

"Only if you tell these poor people exactly what's going on," Jamie said. "Right this minute."

The doctor walked over to the screen and pointed his finger. "Congratulations, Mr. and Mrs. Taylor. Right there. See that? That's two heartbeats. Both embryos implanted. If everything continues to go the way we hope, it looks like you're going to be the parents of twins."

8

Jamie was glad to get home. Between the driving, the procedures themselves, the news that she was carrying twins and the nausea that had dogged her all morning, she was ready for a nap. Despite her fatigue, she was thrilled for Kendra and Isaac, who were in shock. Not only were they going to become parents, they were going to have the opportunity to do it big-time. From the beginning, everyone had known this was a possibility, but since the chances were higher that no pregnancy would result than that both embryos would implant, she supposed Kendra and Isaac had simply pushed the possibility aside.

Surprise, surprise.

Of course, it wasn't a complete delight. A dual pregnancy complicated things. After the second ultrasound, the doctor had warned them that, although things seemed fine at the moment, twins were harder to carry. She would need to take it easier. She might experience stronger symptoms, such as increased morning sickness and fatigue. Toward the end, she might well need to go on a regimen of bed rest, and even then, she would probably deliver early. The trick was to deliver as late as possible to give the babies the best chance.

The pregnancy would also become obvious earlier. It would be difficult to keep secret for long.

As she drove up to the house, she wondered how she was going to tell the girls, then how she would announce it to the other people in her life.

Not that she had many people or even much of a life right now.

She pulled into the clearing, and saw three trucks and more people than she'd seen since arriving in the Valley.

Cancel the part about no people in her life. The Rosslyn and Rosslyn workers had arrived.

Hannah had been tired and subdued on the trip home, but she perked up now. "Who are all those men?"

"I think they're here to start work on Aunt Kendra's house."

"Will Mr. Cash be here? I would like to show him the way we decorated the playhouse."

Cash had finished the playhouse two weeks ago, and it was both charming and sturdy enough for ten little girls. Jamie and the girls had been off shopping in Winchester and hadn't been able to thank him in person. She had left him a cell-phone message, but she'd never gotten a response. Then, on one of their visits to see Lucky, Grace had mentioned that Cash was in Kentucky visiting friends but would be home this week.

"I bet he will be here," Jamie said, as she released Alison from her seat and helped her down. "And he'll appreciate a thank-you, too."

The girls took off to see what was happening, and Jamie followed at a more sedate clip.

One group of men was pacing out the area of the new house

site. Another group was having a smoke by a pile of rocks and laughing. Closer by, a lone man was making notes on a clipboard.

She chose the guy with the clipboard and introduced herself. He was sixtyish, with ruddy skin and the pale blue eyes that often went with it. He told her his name was Gig, and that he was the project manager and foreman for this crew.

"Cash will be here shortly," he said. "He's going to find water today. You ought to get out of the sun for now, but you'll want to watch."

"Is he planning a geological survey?" Jamie knew professional hydrologists looked at rock formations, plant growth and other wells to help determine locations for new ones. She imagined the drilling company knew the area and what to look for. She was surprised Cash was the one slated to figure out where they should drill.

"You don't know, do you?"

"Know what?"

"Old Cash might look like a simple country boy, but he's really a witch. A water witch."

"You're kidding. Cash is a dowser?"

While the girls chased each other across the clearing, Gig escorted Jamie to the shade. Then, while they waited for Cash to appear, he regaled her with stories of his successes.

"He can just about tell you how many gallons a minute you'll get, too. He's not the only one who can do that, you understand, but he's the best I've seen. He found water for a neighbor of mine who thought he'd have to move out when his well ran dry. Everybody else said his land was as dry as a witch's—" He caught himself. "Dry as a desert."

"How do you think he does it?"

"A little science, a little inherited talent, a little luck, a little tuning in to heaven."

Jamie knew that people in the Valley took their religion seriously, but this surprised her. "You think God guides his hand?"

"No, ma'am, I don't think God has that kind of time, what
with the mess this world's in and all. I think there's all kinds of
stuff we'd know if we could just tune in. It's all right there. It's
just that most of the time we're not on the right frequency. Cash
now, he just seems to tune in to the right one to find water."

Jamie pictured heavenly radio waves pinging along the surface
of the earth. It was a comforting vision, even with no receivers
to pick them up. There was always the possibility somebody
would invent the right equipment. Or maybe all any person had
to do was stay quiet long enough to hear them.

"Ma'am?"

She pulled herself back to the conversation. "Sorry, I just liked
what you said."

"Me, I couldn't find water if I was standing on the banks of
the Shenandoah. But put me out in the woods, and I can just
about smell whatever animals are nearby."

"You make a good hunter, I guess."

"Did as a boy. Now I go off without my rifle, just to see the
animals."

Cash chose that moment to appear. The familiar pickup
stopped just in front of the site, and he got out. One group of
men was gone now. The others were still pacing and making
notes. Gig said he had finished what he needed to do for the day,
but he was going to stay and watch Cash work.

Cash got out of his pickup and started toward the men, but
when he saw the girls, he changed direction and crouched down
to say hello to them. He was carrying a black canvas bag with
what looked like coat-hanger wire peeking out the top.

Jamie joined them after a moment and waited her turn while

the girls thanked him for their playhouse. Cash promised to go over later and see what they'd done with it.

"Looks like the fun's starting," she said, after the girls ran off.

Cash's smile lit his eyes, which were more blue than green today. She hadn't forgotten what an attractive man he was, but she *had* forgotten just how much she liked looking at him.

"Miss Jamie." He removed his cap. "Long time no see."

"I've been up to your grandmother's house. I'm surprised we didn't run into you."

"Granny Grace told me she gave you a tour. So what did you think?"

She wasn't sure how to answer that. Cashel Orchard sat on spectacularly beautiful land, with distant views of river and mountains, green stretches of forest and neighboring farms, but everywhere neglect was obvious. She had been surprised and saddened by the sight of what had to be more than a thousand trees waiting for bulldozers to end their existence. Five minutes into Grace's tour, with its view of packing sheds, hay fields and tumbling barns, she had been fairly certain that Grace's quest to restore the land to its former glory was going to fail.

"I think it must be hard for all of you to see eye to eye on the orchard," she said carefully. "I almost got the feeling the trees know their fate's being decided."

"It's complicated."

"I'm sure."

He smiled to signal a change of subject. "I figured you were getting bored here all alone. I just told your girls I'll be putting some finishing touches on their playhouse tomorrow. But I've got a surprise for you. Some genuine recreation. Today we're going to find water."

"Gig told me…" She smiled. "*Mr.* Cash. You're really going to dowse?"

"Sure am."

"This should be interesting. I guess I don't believe in dowsing any more than I believe in knocking on wood."

"Then you'll have to watch and learn."

Jamie looked for the girls and saw that at the moment they were perfectly content collecting stones from the driveway.

She turned back to him. "How does this work? You figure out where the well should be drilled, and the drillers just take your word for it?"

He replaced his cap, bill turned to the back. "That's about right. Of course, if I told them to drill eight hundred feet through solid granite, they might give a second thought to the matter. But I won't tell them that."

"Are you ever wrong?"

"A time or two I've been off. They've had to go a little farther down, got a little more water than I expected or a little less. I don't make promises."

"I'm looking forward to seeing how you do it."

"I don't talk much while I'm working. I have to clear my mind and pay attention."

"I wouldn't dream of disturbing you."

"That's a good thing, I guess. In case you start disturbing me down the road a piece, I'll know it's not intentional."

She couldn't help but smile again. She was aware of just how much smiling she had done since he arrived. "So how do you start?"

"Well, first we'll go over to the area where we want to have a well, so we don't have to run pipe any farther than necessary. Sometimes we're lucky. Then I'll fan out a little, move back and forth until I find what I'm looking for."

"What if there's no water to find?"

"This close to the river? Not much chance of that, is there? This'll be like shooting fish in a barrel."

"I guess it wasn't that easy for Isaac's grandmother. Isaac told me there probably never was a lot of water in her well. The girls and I are conserving. Fewer baths. That appeals to them."

"Mrs. Spurlock probably didn't need a lot. People washed and they drank. They watered their animals but never their lawn. That was about it. No fancy showers or whirlpool bathtubs the way there are now. She probably pumped water for years and brought it inside, washed each night in a basin, filled the kettle and the tub for dishes. What would she have done with more?"

Jamie supposed he was right. The average modern family probably used at least twice as much water as their forbearers. "I know Kendra and Isaac will want to put safeguards in place no matter how much you find. I don't think they plan to drain the local aquifers."

"Always sound thinking."

They had been strolling as they chatted. Now Cash stopped on the edge of the clearing, to one side of the new site. It was near where the old cabin had been, but without that as a given anymore, they had chosen to move the new house farther west for better views.

"This would be a good place to start," Cash said. "We find water here, we'll be sitting pretty. We were lucky the land perked so well. It's a good omen."

Jamie knew that before they had originally removed even a teaspoon of dirt, Rosslyn and Rosslyn had done a perk test to be sure a large-enough septic field could be installed for the bathrooms. That had been successful—not always a given—as had the recent retest.

As Jamie watched, he opened the bag and removed two wires, which extended from something that looked like the plastic casing of a ballpoint pen. The wires were bent at a ninety-degree angle.

"Angle rods," Cash said, holding them up.

"Tell me that's not coat-hanger wire inside a gutted Bic."

"You got it exactly."

"I guess nobody's making money off dowsing supplies."

"My granny used a forked willow stick. Some folks use the tip of a fishing rod. I have better luck with these."

"Your granny? Grace?"

He laughed. "My other granny. My dad's mama. She's gone now. Probably dowsing in heaven, if she's not making drop biscuits and sausage gravy."

She envied his family ties. That kind of intimacy across generations was foreign to her. She and Kendra had grown up without grandparents. The Dunkirks had all died young, and the Delacroixes had lived in fear that their granddaughters would bring Riva back into their lives. Unfortunately Jamie understood that last too well.

She realized he was waiting for more questions. "What happens when you sense water?"

"The rods come together and cross."

"It's sounding very Ouija board to me. You don't think you make them react by the way you move them?"

"Well, if I just guessed where water was, how often would I be right?"

"Have they done studies about how often dowsers *are* on the mark?"

"Depends on what studies you want to believe. But if it'll make you feel better, Einstein thought there was something to dowsing.

He said we just don't understand enough yet to put our finger on what exactly's happening."

She liked that explanation. It covered almost every mystery. "Can you find anything besides water? Oil? Gold?"

"Oh, people dowse for all sorts of things. They even dowse for bodies, when somebody goes missing."

She winced. "I'm sorry I asked."

"I dowse for water. Period. Any bodies buried here, someone else'll have to find them for you."

"I am *really* sorry I asked."

Cash took the rods in both hands. "Okay, now I'm going to get quiet."

Jamie went to check on the girls, who were still happily piling up stones. Then she went over to stand beside Gig. As Cash stood silently for a few minutes, Gig folded his arms and rested them on his ample belly. Just as Jamie was starting to get bored, Cash began to move away from the house.

As he walked, Jamie watched the wires. They flopped a little with every step, but they remained pointed away from him. Then, after he'd moved perhaps ten yards, the wires turned slowly.

At first she thought she was imagining it. But Cash stopped, moved a little farther, stopped and turned a little, then moved forward again. The wires swung and crossed in front of him.

"Something there," Gig said, as if he wasn't surprised.

They waited. Cash moved away, then turned and came back. He did it several times from different angles. Each time the wires crossed in nearly the same place.

"There's water here," Cash said, looking up. "Pretty far down, though. I'd say about three hundred feet. And not as much as I'd like. Maybe ten gallons a minute tops. Not good enough."

He moved away, and after a moment Jamie and Gig followed.

He was roughly on a line with the old excavation now, but maybe thirty yards away, close to the edge of the clearing. The wires swung, and he repeated the steps he'd taken before, moving into the area from different directions until he finally stopped, rocking back and forth on his heels and the balls of his feet. He looked up at last.

"Still not as good as I want, but better. Maybe twelve gallons and a little closer to the surface."

"What now?" Jamie asked.

"We keep looking."

Cash tried three other places with mixed results. One was acceptable. He thought the water was probably about two hundred feet down, with perhaps as much as fifteen gallons a minute.

"I want twenty or more," he said. "All the problems with drought we've had, I want some insurance."

Jamie was into the spirit. She wasn't a true believer, but she was enjoying herself. The girls had joined her temporarily, but now they were off looking for crickets. "Where are you going to try next?"

"Where I ought to have right off the bat."

"And that would be?"

"The old well."

"But we already know it's not producing enough for a new house, right?"

He was standing beside her, his hip just brushing hers. She could smell the clean scent of his skin and clothes, a pleasant merger of laundry detergent and spicy aftershave. "Come on, let's try something."

The three of them started toward the area on the other side of the house where the well was situated. About twenty feet away, Cash stopped, took off his cap and pushed it down over Jamie's head, the bill forward to shade her face.

"You're going to give it a try," he said, offering the rods.

"I don't have an ounce of psychic ability. I never know what's going to happen until it's all over with. Even then, I'm not always sure."

"You don't sense things with those little girls of yours, follow up on ideas that just occur out of nowhere? You don't have hunches?"

She couldn't deny it, although she believed her "hunches" were simply clues that had gathered in her subconscious until she finally recognized them. "It's not the same thing."

"Sure it is. What are you afraid of?"

"Not a single thing. I'm just warning you this'll be a bust."

"Sure will, if you go into it with that attitude. Dowsing is like anything else. You're positive—your outcome is positive."

Despite her own warning, she thought this might be fun. She held out her hands. He gave her the rods, then slipped around behind her and put his arms around her, resting his hands on hers. "Like this."

She was surprised at the contact, which was perfectly justified. She was more surprised at the warmth suffusing her, which had nothing to do with the July sun.

"No, turn your hands," he said. "There. That's right. Not too hard. Just let them do the work. Now stand there and imagine the well you want. Ask for twenty gallons at least, no more than two hundred feet down. That's an average around here, so close to the river." He didn't move away. His breath, when he spoke, was soft against her ear.

"Who am I asking?"

"Doesn't matter who. Just ask with the idea you'll get an answer."

"To whom it may concern, I guess. Then what?"

"Then you start to move. Slowly. Let things happen." He moved away, as if to give her the space she needed. She was sorry he had.

She concentrated on following Cash's orders. Like Gig, she was afraid she could parade back and forth in the middle of the river, and the wires would never touch. Still, this was an experiment. She tried to clear her mind, and she tried to have faith.

When she was as centered and positive as she could manage, she began to walk slowly in the direction of the well. Nothing happened except that her arms felt heavy and rigid because of the way she was gripping the plastic pen casing. She moved slowly and tried to imagine water flowing in the ground beneath her.

Suddenly all her senses snapped into a single track, and she could almost hear a river flowing. At the same moment, the wires fell together.

"You all right?" Cash asked. Without her realizing it, he had come to stand beside her. He rested his hand lightly on her shoulder.

"I must be more tired than I thought. My arms and hands are weak. I guess I couldn't hold it right. And I was sort of fading out there. I need a nap."

He laughed. "Not likely. Come over here."

She followed him to a spot about twenty yards away. "What now?"

"You walk back the way we came. But first, remember what I told you before. Ask for what you want."

"I feel a little silly and a whole lot tired."

"Dowsing never killed anybody. Give it another try."

She shrugged. After a moment, she repeated the entire sequence. The centering, the slow amble, the effort to hold her arms steady.

Suddenly she could almost smell the water below her—just at the moment when the wires crossed again.

"Almost the same place," Cash said. "Only about six feet away. That probably means we'd want to dig right here." He stepped to a point between the first and the second spots where her wires had crossed.

She thrust the rods in his direction. "Don't trust me. *You* give it a try."

"You'd better believe it. But I know a dowser when I see one. Welcome to the trade."

She stepped back. He approached the spot from several angles, taking his time, rocking back and forth whenever he reached the place he had pinpointed. It was only about fifteen feet from the old well. When he seemed secure, he put the rods back in the bag.

"This is our spot," he said. He moved away, picked up a rock and brought it back to mark the location. "Gig'll put a few more here, right, Gig?"

Jamie still couldn't believe it, even after experiencing something herself when the rods were in her hands. "But the old well's funky. You told me so yourself. Why would we want a new one so close?"

"Because they didn't dig deep enough the first time. I'd say there are two springs here. They tapped into the first one pretty quick and stopped. Drilling deeper would have cost more, and Mrs. Spurlock was probably happy enough with what she got. But the big seam is another fifty feet down. You'll have a well you can be proud of."

"How many gallons?" Gig asked.

"I'm betting on forty, maybe more. And just two hundred feet down, at the most. Maybe a hundred or so that'll need casing, another hundred into the limestone."

"Casing's to keep the dirt out," Gig explained. "Don't need it once you go through rock. We could maybe drill the old well deeper, but I'm betting that pipe would need replacing anyway. Better to just start fresh."

Jamie was sorting through this extraordinary event, trying to figure out exactly how it had happened. "You're not kidding?" she asked at last. "You're not trying to make me think I succeeded when I didn't?"

"That would be a whole lot of kidding, wouldn't it? Asking the men to drill here just because you thought you got a reaction? No, there's water here, right where you found it."

"But I'm not a dowser. I can't do this."

Cash laughed. "Looks to me like you just did."

9

After that, Jamie had to invite Cash to dinner. This only made sense, since she hadn't properly thanked him for all the time he'd spent building the playhouse. Maybe Kendra had paid for his labor, but she doubted her sister had expected anything so creative and beautifully constructed. A lot more had gone into the play-house than had strictly needed to.

He accepted without hesitation and promised he would be back at seven.

The minute Jamie got to the cabin, she asked herself what she was doing. She was too savvy about her own motives not to know. She made a stab at pretending she had invited him to tell him she was pregnant. But even if that were true, the real reason was that she liked Cash. A lot. And although he hadn't exactly been knocking down the cabin door, she thought he liked her, too.

And darn it, she was lonely.

She reminded herself that she had been lonely when she

hooked up with Seamus Callahan, too. Loneliness had driven them together, and good sense had parted them. Her fling with Seamus had been short-lived and fertile. Loneliness could be downright dangerous.

"What shall we make for Cash?" she asked Hannah. "We could barbecue, or I could make the pasta with artichoke hearts that you like so much."

"Both." Hannah was trying to finish the book of crossword puzzles she had started at the clinic that morning.

She decided Hannah was right. That way, if he didn't like one, he could eat the other. She refused to ask herself why she was overachieving for this man.

The puzzles lost their glamour, and the girls went out to spruce up the playhouse. Jamie had taken them to the local discount store to pick out colorful cushions to sit on and fabric to thumbtack around the windows. They'd stored some of their favorite outdoor toys on the tiny porch, and underneath, bright plastic buckets and shovels, sieves, molds and watering cans to make their own sand castles.

While Jamie chopped and sautéed, she considered ways to explain her situation to Cash. Then the girls had to be next. On their way home, Hannah had quizzed her about the fertility clinic. So far, Jamie had explained the visit as a checkup, like Hannah's checkups at the pediatrician. But Hannah was too smart to buy that for long. Particularly when Kendra and Isaac had showed up at the clinic, as well.

Cash, of course, would understand the technicalities, but the emotions? How could she explain those?

Last week, she had marinated and frozen a pork tenderloin, so tonight she only had to defrost it for the grill. The pasta recipe was simple. She made a salad with farmers' market tomatoes and basil, topped with smoked mozzarella and a dash of balsamic vinegar. Dessert was fresh peach cobbler. By the time she heard his pickup arrive, everything was nearly ready.

Cash didn't come right up to the house. She heard him talking to the girls, then heard their laughter. By the time he climbed the steps, the table on the front porch was set. The girls had remained at least temporarily in their playhouse.

"I brought them a little something," Cash explained. "It might be a while before they can be coaxed out again."

"You already spoiled them with the house." She smiled to belie her words. She saw that he had changed into something slightly more formal. Gone were the Rosslyn and Rosslyn shirt and shorts. He wore khakis and a dark red dress shirt. She had changed, too, and wondered about the meaning of his crisply pleated pants and her own thigh-high sundress.

"Can they be spoiled? They seem refreshingly down-to-earth to me," he said.

She thought of the money she had inherited. "I have to work at that and always will. What was the present?"

"I made them a little table and stools to fit in one corner."

"That is so nice. That's just what the house needed."

Cash held out a wine bottle. "I brought this. You don't need to serve it tonight, but it was a very good year."

Although he made a point of being a six-pack kind of guy, it didn't surprise her that Cash knew "a very good year" when he came across one. She was pretty sure that what you see was not what you got with this man.

"I'll save it for my next dinner party," she said, keeping her voice light. "I don't drink, but I love to serve good wine to my friends and family." She hesitated, then forged ahead. "I've had problems with substance abuse. Alcohol wasn't my drug of choice, but I don't see any point in doing a survey to see what I can handle and what I can't."

"You didn't have to tell me all that."

"It saves a lot of time, don't you think?" She looked up from straightening the napkins. He didn't look distressed or turned off.

"It takes courage to admit you aren't perfect."

"Oh, did you think I was?"

"Verging in that direction. Although since the girls' daddies aren't on the scene, I'd say you haven't been lucky in love."

"I'm not sure I've ever been in love. And I never set out to have children by the girls' fathers. I was as surprised as they were. Luckily, both times, once the shock passed, I was thrilled."

"It's a lot of work, raising two little girls alone."

"I can't think of better work."

"They're lucky to have you."

He sounded sincere. She felt the compliment blooming inside her. A smile bloomed, too. "That's a nice thing to say."

"Is that why you're here? To spend a quiet summer with them, away from everything else?"

He had opened the door; now all she had to do was walk through it. But before she could tell him about the pregnancy, Hannah and Alison came screeching up the steps to rhapsodize about his wonderful present.

"I have a pork tenderloin," she said, over the noise. "And the grill should be hot. How do you feel about doing the honors? I will, if you don't want to, but it might take a while before I can get to it."

"No problem. I'll do it, and the girls can help. Just tell me how you want it."

Once they sat down to eat, she was proud of the food and delighted by the response. Cash ate like a starving man, and even the girls found nothing to complain about. The conversation was geared to their level, and by the time she went into the kitchen to pile the dishes in the small but efficient dishwasher, Cash was in the midst of a game of chess with Hannah and Alison was demonstrating somersaults.

She didn't get to talk to him again until the girls went off to brush their teeth. She made a pot of coffee and poured him a cup, setting it in front of him on the table, where he was boxing up the plastic chess pieces.

"I should have warned you," she said, "you not being a father. They take up a lot of space. Can you stay a little longer, so we can chat after I put them to bed?"

"That would be a pleasure."

"It's cool on the porch, and you can still count the stars."

"I'll wait for you out there."

The girls came to say good night to Cash. Traveling back and forth to Arlington had tired them out, and Jamie was surprised when they went to their room without a fuss. With Cash waiting, she hoped to avoid story time, but that was not to be.

Hannah settled herself on the top bunk, and Jamie leaned over to kiss her good night.

"What's a surrogate?" Hannah asked.

Jamie knew she'd waited too long to talk to her daughters. Hannah picked up on everything. "Where did you hear the word?"

"At the clinic today. A nurse said you are a surrogate. Are you sick, Mommy?"

While Alison always called her Mommy, Hannah rarely used the title. Jamie wasn't certain why. Sometimes she thought Hannah was reluctant to admit that they were somehow unequal. Hannah certainly understood that Jamie was in charge, but most of the time, she preferred not to make a point of it. When she did call her Mommy, it meant she was especially worried about something.

Jamie smoothed back her daughter's dark hair. "If you were worried, why didn't you ask me earlier, when you were asking about the clinic?"

Hannah shrugged.

Jamie guessed Hannah had feared the answer and had delayed the question until the pressure built too high. She leaned over and kissed her again. "I'm absolutely not sick. I promise. Being a surrogate is a good thing."

She peeked at Alison, whose eyes were still wide open, and decided the time had come.

"Let me tell you a story," Jamie said, "so you'll understand. Can you both stay awake?"

She'd been wondering how to tell them about the babies, and this idea had occurred to her on the way home. She hoped it would be a beginning.

"Once there was a mommy duck. She wanted baby ducks more than she wanted anything else in the world. Every day she would see other mommies with their newly hatched ducklings swimming in the pond, and she'd feel so sad."

"Why was she sad?" Alison asked.

"Because this mommy duck could lay eggs. Lots of eggs. But she was such a little duck, so light, that when she sat on her eggs, they couldn't hatch. You see, she couldn't keep them warm enough, or cover them exactly the right way. And year after year, her eggs didn't turn into baby ducklings."

"I don't like sad stories," Hannah said. "I sometimes cry."

"Don't cry, because this isn't a sad story. You see, this mommy had a sister. And her sister saw how sad the mommy duck was and how much she wanted to swim in the pond with her very own ducklings. So she told the mommy duck, 'If you lay eggs in your nest, then I will come and sit on them until they hatch. I am larger and I can keep them warm. Then you'll have your very own ducklings, and soon you'll be swimming in the pond with your baby ducklings floating along right behind you.'"

"Did she?"

"Well, at first the mommy duck had to think about this. If she didn't hatch the eggs herself, then whose babies would the ducklings really be? Would they really be hers, or would they be her sister's? Who should teach them how to float along on the pond, paddling their little duckling feet? But the sister duck promised that the ducklings would not belong to her. They would belong to the mommy who laid the eggs. She was only going to help them hatch."

"So did they?"

"Yes, that's exactly what they did. The mommy duck laid two beautiful eggs, and when they were all shiny and warm in the nest, the sister duck waddled over and sat on them. The mommy duck brought her sister food, and took care of her while she sat and sat. And while she sat, they talked about the things ducks talk about whenever they have the time. They were surprised to find that after a while they were even better friends."

"Like Hannah and me," Alison said sleepily.

"That's exactly right. Friends just like you and Hannah. Then one day there was a peeping noise, and then a cracking noise, and the sister duck moved away so she could see. And sure enough, two little ducklings were hatching from the two beautiful eggs. And before long, they were large enough and strong enough to follow their mommy into the pond and learn how to swim."

"But what about Sister Duck?"

"Well, every day Sister Duck saw the lovely little ducklings on the pond with their mother, and she felt so good that she had helped them hatch, because if she hadn't, they wouldn't be alive. But you see, even though she felt very good, she knew they weren't hers. She was only the duck who had helped them hatch. She was a surrogate duck. That's what the word surrogate means. Somebody who takes the place of somebody else to help them."

"I'm glad it does not mean sick," Hannah said.

Jamie smoothed the top sheet over Hannah's favorite red nightgown and straightened the rest of her covers. "No, nobody was sick. The sister duck only sat on the nest to help. Still, because she was their aunt, she loved the ducklings, too. And she saved fine bits of corn for them, and made sure that they stayed away from the edges of the pond where dogs might chase them. And in little ways, she helped Mommy Duck raise them."

"But wasn't she sad? I think she did all the work," Hannah said.

"Well, no. You see, she only did part of the work. Laying eggs is very difficult indeed. And here's the other part of the story that I didn't tell you. Sister Duck already had ducklings all her own, older ducklings, and she loved them, and they still needed her. So she was busy with her own family, and all she really felt was happy that she had helped her sister achieve her heart's desire."

"You are too large to hatch an egg," Hannah said. "You would crush it. So how can *you* be a surrogate?"

"People make babies in a different way than ducks. But this is important for you to understand. Your aunt Kendra can make babies, just like Mommy Duck could lay eggs. But your aunt can't keep the baby inside her because of a problem from many years ago. So I asked her if I could carry a baby for her, the way I carried you and Alison. Only when I was pregnant with *you,* you were mine from the very beginning. This baby, or I should say these babies, because there are two—just like Mommy Duck's two eggs—will belong to your aunt Kendra and uncle Isaac. They won't be your brothers or sisters, even though they're growing inside me, but they will be your cousins. And I won't be their mother, but I will be their aunt. So I'll love them the way an aunt loves her nieces and nephews, and you'll love them like cousins, but not quite the same way you love Alison."

Hannah was silent for a moment, her mind clearly whirling with this news. "How did the babies get there?"

It was an age-old question. This time, surrogacy actually saved the day, making the explanation simpler and to the point. "The doctors at the clinic helped your aunt and uncle make them, then they put them inside me," Jamie said. "And that's why we were there today, to make sure they were all right. And they are."

"You're going to have babies?" Alison asked, still a bit behind.

"Yes, sweetie. But they'll be Aunt Kendra's."

"Will you get fat?"

"I'm afraid I'll get very, very fat."

"Do we have to give them both to Aunt Kendra?" Hannah asked. "We might want to keep one and give her one. We could share."

"No, I have two wonderful little girls, and that's all I need. And remember, they aren't really mine to keep. I'm just Sister Duck, sitting on the nest."

"Will dogs try to chase them?" Alison asked.

For a moment Jamie didn't understand; then she realized she'd thrown dogs into the story. "No, but if they do, I promise I'll shoo them away."

She leaned over and kissed both girls again. "When the weather gets cold, sometime after Christmas, in fact, you two will have cousins. Won't that be cool?"

"They will need to learn things," Hannah said. "We might need a list."

"You can start one tomorrow."

She said good night again, and this time nobody stopped her. By the time Jamie got to the door, Alison's eyes were closed and Hannah was staring at the ceiling, trying to put everything into some sort of framework. Jamie knew her daughter well. By morning Hannah would have sorted out at least some of it.

She switched on the night light and turned off the lamp, closing the door softly behind her. Then she stood with her back to it and closed her eyes.

"I don't want to scare you, but when you open those eyes, you're going to see me standing here," Cash said.

Her eyelids flew open. "Thanks for the warning."

"I came in to get some more coffee. That was a while ago."

She knew what he was telling her. "You heard the story?"

"I'm sorry. I wasn't really eavesdropping. I didn't know it was going to be a lesson on the birds and the bees."

"Ducks and eggs and hatching." She was suddenly tired. She wondered if it was the long day, the pregnancy or simply knowing that Cash was probably going to walk out the door in a minute and not return. She had no plans for a fling. She was past wanting that with anyone, and was not exactly in the best of shape for one, anyway. But having a friend would have been great.

"I'll assume you're not drinking coffee with me, considering everything," he said.

"You're probably ready to leave."

He smiled. His eyes were warm. "I *meant* that you're not drinking coffee because of the babies. Not because I'm leaving. I saw lemonade in the refrigerator. There's a breeze on the porch, but you might like something cool to take out there with you."

"That would be nice. I would."

"Sounds like you've had a long day. You go sit, and I'll get it and be out in a minute."

She did just that. The moment she felt the seat under her, she felt as if she was dissolving, melting into the plaid seat cushion to be scraped off like candle wax. She knew better than to close her eyes. She kept them open but was still afraid she was going to fall asleep.

She must have, too, because she didn't hear Cash return, only felt him slide onto the seat beside her. She turned to smile at him, taking the lemonade out of his hand. "This is nice. Thanks."

"Were you going to tell me about the pregnancy before you got as big as a house?"

"That was one of the reasons I invited you tonight. We had the first ultrasound today and saw two babies. Now it's real. Up until now, it's been black magic."

"Whew." He shook his head. "That's exactly what I was thinking."

The lemonade was real, and now she was glad she'd taken the time to squeeze lemons and sweeten it to her taste. She drank half of it before she spoke again.

"Have you ever seen the way Kendra and Isaac look at my girls?"

Cash sat back, shifting so he could see her better. "Not so I've noticed."

"It's a little like somebody who's never had enough to eat watching guests at a banquet. They adore Hannah and Alison and always will. But there's more to it than that. They're so hungry for more than just nieces. They want children in their lives. Every day. *Their children.*"

"I don't mean to be nosy, but aren't there easier ways that don't involve *you* spending nine months of morning sickness and what all? I'm under the impression there are a lot of children in the world who need a home and family."

"Isaac's an adopted child. Most adoptions work out great, but his experience was gruesome. Even though he knows things would be different if *he* adopted, the baggage he would bring to it worries him too much."

"I suppose that make sense."

"These aren't my babies in any way. We did in vitro. The babies were conceived without me. I'm simply the carrier."

"Not so simply, I wouldn't think. Complicated to the extreme."

"I'm just glad I can do it. It's only nine months of my life, and it's not like I'm giving up everything else. Maybe I'm pregnant, but I'll continue taking care of my girls, working on some projects for my degree, figuring out what I want to do and where I want to go when I graduate. I won't be sitting around counting the days and the kicks."

"Sister Duck felt real good about those little ducklings swimming off after their mama."

"Okay, that's a fairy tale, and this is real life. I know the difference."

"It was a good way to tell your girls."

Until she relaxed, she hadn't realized she was tense. Cash had accepted her decision for what it was. If anything, he was just worried about the way it would affect her.

"I haven't told Grace—or anybody, for that matter," she said. "Things can still go wrong, although I generally have easy pregnancies."

"Twins will be harder."

"That's what I'm told."

"I can't think of any woman I know being willing to do something like this."

"None of your girlfriends are hanging out Womb for Rent signs, huh?"

"Not a one. I'd say you're a pretty special lady. Me, I can never figure out why anybody would want to put up with pregnancy. If it were up to men, it wouldn't happen."

"Well, some part of it is up to men. That's how it works."

"Not up to them to have morning sickness or stretch marks. You do all that work, lose your figure, and what do you get in the end? Little critters who can't do a blessed thing for themselves. Poop machines, milk guzzlers, screaming little red-faced monsters."

"Well, put like that, you're right, but have you ever seen a baby asleep?"

"You'd do all that work just to watch one snoring away?"

She slapped his knee. "But you forget, I don't have to put up with any of that. I have the babies and turn them over."

"And you're all right with that?"

"I'm all right with it."

"Someday I want to hear why. There has to be a story there." He glanced at his watch; then he stretched and stood. "But not tonight. You're beat. Dowsing will do that to you, even without all the extraneous stuff like being a surrogate mother, carrying twins, raising two lively little sweethearts and living out in the middle of nowhere without anybody to help."

She stood, too. "Wow, put that way, I ought to do a Rip Van Winkle."

"I'll be seeing you around, Miss Jamie. And I'm going to keep an eye on you. You need to take care of yourself."

"Let's drop the Miss Jamie stuff, okay? Just Jamie. I'm not your Sunday school teacher."

He smiled; then, almost as if he were acting against his own will, he rested his hands on her shoulders, leaned down and kissed her. The kiss was light and sweet, almost—but not quite— the kiss one friend gives another.

"Not my Sunday-school teacher, all right. Jamie." He touched her hair, wound one lock around his finger and tugged. Then he stepped back.

"Tell Grace we'll be up soon to see Lucky."

"I will."

She watched as he walked down the steps. In a moment she heard his pickup start. Then he was gone.

"A nice guy." And somehow more than that. She had no idea if tonight had ended a promising friendship, but she hoped not. She thought that Cash Rosslyn, along with his grandmother, was going to make the next few months a lot easier.

10

Four weeks later, Hannah was wearing blue jeans straight from the local thrift shop, a ragged Valvoline T-shirt that Jamie generally used to wash the minivan and sneakers one size too small, although it didn't matter, since she had cut out the ends so her toes could peek through. Alison looked every bit as grubby.

"What if somebody wears a party dress?" Hannah asked. "They could, you know. Some of the girls are Alison's age, and they do read."

Jamie glanced up from adjusting the sprinkler. Getting a decent spray was harder than she'd expected. Water pressure from the old well was just barely strong enough to make the sprinkler turn, and she was glad she had started on the mud puddle early. Although the August afternoon sky was dark with clouds, a lack of rain had turned the soil in the clearing to dust. The ground needed a thorough soaking to achieve their purposes. She hoped the well was up to it.

Once she was satisfied with the sprinkler placement, she dried her hands on her pants. "The invitations are perfectly clear, Hannah. And I've talked to all the moms. They know it's a Dirty Day party and everyone's supposed to wear their oldest clothes. I told them to send the girls in whatever they'd dress a scarecrow in for Halloween." She didn't point out that she'd bought a pile of old things when she'd bought Hannah's jeans, just in case. Hannah liked to obsess, and Jamie didn't want to spoil her fun.

"What if they don't like to get dirty?" Hannah skipped off as she spoke, since the question was purely rhetorical. Jamie had never met a child who, given half a chance, didn't like to roll in the mud.

Over the past month Jamie had discovered that days in the country *could* pass quickly, even when she had no job to go to or classes to attend. Every morning she woke up with a list of things she wanted to do, and by the end of the day, the list was only half complete.

Part of the problem was an overwhelming need for a nap each afternoon. Alison cooperated by taking a short one, curled up next to her mother, and Hannah was trustworthy enough that Jamie could leave her with some project to work on for the half hour Jamie was dead to the world. But nap time and waking up from nap time took up a large part of her day.

One of the ways she had occupied her waking hours was to find other children for her daughters to play with. Sam Kinkade had come through, introducing the girls to several children their age, although with family vacations and other commitments, those friendships had gotten a slow start. Then, at the end of July, as Elisa had suggested, she'd sent the girls to the vacation bible school at Shenandoah Community Church.

As predicted, some of the children from La Casa Amarilla had attended the church summer program, as well, and Hannah had made firm friends with two. The girls had spent a worthwhile week—learning the story of the good samaritan, the Lord's Prayer in Spanish and the importance of reaching out to help others—pepped up by a Mexican fiesta at the conclusion, complete with a donkey *piñata*.

Now, not only did they understand a bit more about the New Testament, they were no longer lonely. And today her girls were throwing a party.

The August heat and dry spell had inspired the theme. Hannah had wanted to play in the sprinkler, and Alison had suggested mud pies. Together the three of them had come up with Dirty Day. Alison had invited five-year-olds Reese Claiborne, a neighbor's daughter, and Bridget Brogan, whose mother was a mainstay of the church's quilting bee. Seven-year-old Maria Garcia and eight-year-old Carmen Sanchez from La Casa were Hannah's guests.

To finish off the afternoon, Jamie had made "dirt" cakes in individual flower pots, with ground-up chocolate sandwich cookies, vanilla pudding and gummy worms. Each pot had an artificial daisy poking out of the top, and there were "garbage" bags of Dirty Day goodies, such as bubble makers and sweet-smelling soaps, to take home. As children's parties went, it was bound to be a winner.

Jamie dusted off her hands and turned at the sound of a car. Cissy Claiborne, Reese's mother, had volunteered to bring all the little girls, and Adoncia Garcia, Maria's mother, was going to take them home. Adoncia and Elisa Kinkade were close friends, and Adoncia worked in a local medical practice learning everything she needed to so that when the time came for Elisa to open her own office, Adoncia could be Elisa's practice manager. Although Jamie had only chatted briefly with the two women as they brought and picked up their children from bible school, she liked them both.

The eighties station wagon arrived, and in a moment, the older girls piled out. Cissy, a pretty young woman with a cloud of strawberry-blond hair, unhooked booster seats and belts, and the whole crew started toward them. Reese, her daughter, had the same blond hair and was easy to pick out from the three brunettes. Jamie was pleased to see that the mothers had taken her seriously and sent their daughters in what looked like hand-me-downs on their third go-round.

Hannah corralled the girls right away, and everybody ran off to see the playhouse.

"Oh, you're going to have your hands full," Cissy said. "Reese is so excited, she hasn't talked about anything else for days."

Jamie was delighted to see another woman close to her own age. The girls had made friends, but *she* hadn't really had a chance yet. In the past weeks a couple of neighbors had stopped by with casseroles or desserts to welcome her, but they were all older and, she suspected, busy with their own families and pursuits.

"It's just so hot," she told Cissy, "and I couldn't see them getting sweaty and grouchy and picking fights with each other. This way they'll stay cool. And filthy, but who cares?"

"Is this a family tradition?"

Jamie had to laugh. "I'm afraid I didn't grow up with a single tradition I would dare pass on. The girls and I are making our own."

"Well, neither did I, but this is a good one. I might add it to ours. Of course, it's hard to keep Reese clean even on a normal day. Every day is Dirty Day."

Cissy took out a card and handed it to Jamie. "I wish I could stay and help, but I'm assistant innkeeper over at Daughter of the Stars. I promised I'd work this afternoon while Reese is here. If anything comes up and you need me, that's the number at the inn."

Laughter and squeals came from the direction of the playhouse.

Jamie knew she had to check on things. She said goodbye to Cissy and went to see what the girls were doing. When it was clear she wasn't needed, she went back to the house to finish arranging things on the porch table, setting out plastic place mats and paper cups, then headed off to check on her mud pit.

The next two hours passed like lightning—or, more accurately, as if she'd been struck by it. The girls got hot quickly, and after they'd done a quick tour of the playhouse and Hannah and Alison's room, they were ready for the sprinkler. Sprinkler play quickly turned to mud play. They made up contests. Prettiest mud pie, biggest mud pie…nothing that a network scout would pick up for the next big reality show, but the girls didn't care.

They played in the sprinkler again, went on a supervised hike down to the river, came back up and delved into the mud, and then, after another sprinkler round, the thorough washing of hands and their dirt-cake dessert, they went back to the playhouse for a meeting. Somewhere along the way, a club had formed. Jamie was fairly sure she knew who would be the first president.

She was digging in the dirt with muddy hands to reposition the sprinkler when she heard another car drive into the clearing. She turned and saw her sister's Lexus. She hadn't expected Kendra, and she felt a surge of gratitude. Maybe if she pleaded, Kendra would help with the party finale. Even better, maybe she'd stay for a conversation.

She wiped her muddy hands on her oldest pair of jeans—she'd had a private Dirty Day whether she'd planned one or not—and prepared to greet her sister, who was dressed, as usual, in beautifully tailored sportswear. Flawlessly clean sportswear.

"Hey, Ken!" Jamie lifted a hand as Kendra approached. "What are you doing here?"

Kendra was alone. She got out of the car slowly and took stock of everything. Jamie, the new house foundation, the screeching of little girls in the distance. "What have I interrupted?"

"The girls are having a Dirty Day party." Jamie held up her hands and inclined her head toward the sprinkler. "I'm afraid I'm having the grown-up version. Please tell me you can stay and help me get them out the door."

Kendra's smile was a weaker version of her usual. "Cash is going to meet me over here with some information on heating and air-conditioning systems, then I've got a couple of appointments on the way home to look at tile and fixtures. It gave me an excuse to see how things were going with the house. And you and the girls. But that part goes without saying."

Kendra hadn't been to the cabin to visit since the night she and Isaac had come to dinner. The sisters had seen each other at Jamie's first doctor's appointment with the obstetrician in Front Royal. They'd had a brief lunch together afterward, but Jamie had expected Kendra to show more enthusiasm for the pregnancy. She'd been surprised and, she admitted, hurt, by Kendra's absence.

"They've got the foundation and the basement on the way, started the framing, worked on the drainage. The well company's been out to drill, and they got what amounts to a gusher." Jamie saw that her sister didn't look surprised. "But you must know that. I guess you've been in touch with Cash."

"We've arranged to talk every Friday afternoon. He keeps me up to date, but it's not the same as seeing it."

Jamie felt a twinge of irritation. Kendra called *her* every week, too. She wondered if she was simply on the list of people Kendra knew she ought to talk to. *Jamie at five on Thursdays.*

Jamie kept her voice even. "Well, take a good look. You'll like what they've done. Cash is in and out. I haven't seen much of him, but he seems to keep things moving."

"I thought you'd see a lot of him."

"Not as much as you'd think." She didn't say that when she and Cash saw each other now he was friendly, sometimes spilling over into charming. She enjoyed their banter, his genuine warmth, his enthusiasm for her daughters' welfare. But nothing had come of it. Since that one dinner, they hadn't seen each other after hours. Even her trips up to Grace's to see Lucky had been Cash poor, as she'd begun to think of them.

"So the girls are having a Dirty Day party?" Kendra's gaze flicked down to Jamie's hands. "And what kind of party is that?"

"Mud pies, running through sprinklers. Come see the cute dessert I made, or what's left of it. I have to check on everybody in a minute. They're in the playhouse, but I'm sure there'll be one more run through the sprinkler before they change to go home. It's a good way to stay cool." She paused, then decided it didn't hurt to beg. "You can help if you want. You could use some mud under that manicure."

"Maybe I should do it, and you should rest."

"Don't worry. I'm a little tired, but it means so much to the girls that it pumps me up. Cash's guys cleared a little hole for us with their backhoe and dumped in some topsoil they'd scraped off when they dug the foundation. They'll replace it for your yard when everything's all done, but I had to water it to make mud. I was just moving the sprinkler to a drier spot so this time they'll stay cleaner."

"Jamie..." Kendra looked as if she didn't know whether to continue or not.

Jamie was suddenly alert. True, she and Kendra had not spent much time together as adults, but she still knew her sister well enough to realize that something was wrong. And Kendra was trying to figure out how to tell her.

"You know, you could just come right out and say whatever this is," Jamie said. "Give it a try. I might surprise you."

"I'm not trying to upset you."

"Well, that's a good start. Mind telling me what you're not trying to upset me about?"

Kendra looked uncomfortable. "I don't have any right to tell you how to live your life..."

"But?"

"It's just that I've been reading a lot about pregnancy. I mean, I guess that's inevitable, even though you're the one who's pregnant."

"Something tells me this is one of those times when too much knowledge isn't a good thing."

"Maybe so, but do you know about toxoplasmosis? It's a parasite that can cause all kinds of birth defects. Most people think it's only something you have to worry about if you have a cat, so pregnant women aren't supposed to change the cat litter. But it can also live in soil. You're not supposed to dig in a garden, for instance, unless you're wearing gloves."

Jamie took a moment to frame her answer. "Well, you're thorough, I'll give you that. But that's what I'd expect. Researching the hot topics is in the genes. I mean, the Dunkirk fortune started with newspapers. I guess you can hardly be blamed for doing what comes naturally. Or for assuming, considering everything, that I'm clueless."

Kendra winced. "Your hands are covered in mud."

"And a million little parasites? I mean, do you have any idea how unlikely it is that I would get toxoplasmosis from moving a sprinkler?" She realized her voice had risen. "And just for the record, what gives you the right to practically ignore me for a month, then show up here and start criticizing me?"

"You know what gives me the right. And I've stayed away because I was afraid this very thing would happen."

"What? That maybe you'd find me smoking or drinking or taking up sky diving like Daddy? Or maybe extreme skateboarding, more the style of an irresponsible Gen Xer, huh?"

"No…" Kendra took a deep breath. "No. Afraid I might overreact. I'm sorry. But there you are, covered in mud, and I know that can be a problem, and…"

"Ken, I'm *immune* to toxoplasmosis. I was tested when I was pregnant with Hannah. I must have had it at some point as a child or in my teens. Now I can change kitty litter with the best of them, or dig my way to China with my fingernails. I might even buy a cat just to show off how immune I am. Just one more example of what a perfect surrogate I make."

Kendra was silent.

"I have had two children," Jamie said, a little calmer now. "I know all the ins and outs, and I've always had excellent prenatal care, which included lots of advice. I could probably deliver these babies by myself, I'm such an old hand at it. So you don't have to worry. I know the rules, and I go out of my way to pay attention. I'm no more careless with your children than I was with my own."

"I didn't think you were being careless because they're *my* children. I just thought that maybe you weren't thinking."

"Because you still haven't caught on that I think quite well and quite often, now that I'm an adult. I'm not that cute little baby you tried to raise all by yourself when the nanny was passed out at the kitchen table and Riva was jetting off to St. Barts."

"You never told me you were immune."

"No, and I never told you that all my shots are up to date, my blood pressure's on the low side of normal, I got chicken pox right after I ran away from home and I'm badly allergic to poison ivy. And there's a lot of poison ivy around here, but so far I've had the good sense to avoid it."

"I should go."

Jamie put her hand on her sister's arm. "Oh, no you don't! You're not going anywhere. You're going to stay and help me finish this party. I have six little girls who spent the afternoon making mud pies. And you can darn well stay here and help me get them into some kind of shape to send home."

"You're probably leaving a handprint on my arm."

"Then you'll need to stick it under the sprinkler, won't you?"

Kendra stared at her. "I'm not really into mud."

"Well, you'd better learn, then. You're going to have two children who'll be into it big-time. Kids don't just go to museums and concerts in the park. They dig up worms and try to eat them. They hang upside down from tree limbs and vomit in the car and wipe their noses on their T-shirts. Time to get used to it."

"Your grip's getting tighter."

Jamie let go of her sister; then, without thinking—which had gotten her into trouble a number of times—she shoved. Just a tiny shove. Not a full-fledged Sumo wrestler shove. More a shove to make a point. But Kendra was off balance, and the next thing Jamie knew, her sister was sitting in the mud pit.

Torn between apology and laughter, Jamie just stood there, trying not to give in to either. She backed away, but not quickly enough.

"Oh, no you don't!" Kendra grabbed her by the wrist and pulled her into the mud, too.

Jamie fell to her knees and started to laugh. "At least I'm not wearing Ralph Lauren. Look at you!"

"You were always a nasty, grubby little kid."

"And you were always so perfect!"

"Was not!" Kendra scooped up a handful of mud and tossed it at her sister."

"Were, too!" Jamie scooped up mud with both hands and went on the attack. "The nannies loved you more than they loved me!"

They were both laughing now. Kendra tried to get away, but Jamie pulled her down again.

"Consider this your parenthood training program," Jamie said, rolling to one side and scrambling to get up.

"You're not going anywhere."

They heard screeching, and looked up to see a swarm of little girls heading their way.

"Their mothers are going to kill me," Jamie said.

"Head them off!" Kendra got up, but it was too late. In moments the girls were flailing around in the mud with them.

"Enough! Enough!" Jamie shrieked.

But it wasn't enough. From somewhere behind them, a door slammed. Jamie was pinned beneath her daughters, who were decorating her T-shirt and hair with grass and gunk.

"I'll be drummed out of Toms Brook," Jamie told Kendra, as she tried to pick off her daughters and scramble out of the pit. "Exactly what are we going to do now?"

"It looks to me like that's pretty simple," a familiar male voice answered.

Jamie had managed to get to her feet. She glared at Cash, who just turned up his hands and waited.

"Help," she said.

He grinned; then he stepped into the mud, as well. "Don't worry, sweetcakes. I'm on it."

11

"Well, you don't have to grin like you're the only guy in the world who ever peeled six filthy little girls out of a mud puddle." Jamie glanced at Cash, who was lounging comfortably on her front porch, and saw that he was still grinning. He hadn't stopped since his first sight of her in the mud with Kendra and the girls.

"Kuk..kuk...kuk...kuk..."

She stopped braiding her wet hair and glared at him. "What's that about?"

"The call of a mud hen. Not sure why it just popped into my head like that..."

"Falling into the mud was just the tiniest lapse on my part."

"And your sister's?"

"It seemed like a nice way to cool off. If you've never had a conversation in a mud pit, don't knock it."

"Today I had plenty. With the girls, with you and Kendra. With Mrs. Garcia."

Jamie relented. "I don't know what we would have done without you."

Cash had hauled all the little girls out of the mud and sent them over to the repositioned sprinkler to hose down. By then Jamie and Kendra had righted themselves and joined the party until they were all soaking wet but no longer mud pies on legs. Inside, the girls dried off and changed into the extra clothes they'd brought along, while Cash unhooked the sprinkler and firmly steered them away from the mud when they went back outside. When Adoncia Garcia arrived to pick them up, they were still passably clean.

They left clutching their garbage bags of goodies and chattering excitedly about everything they'd done.

"It was a little unruly," a still grimy Jamie had told Adoncia, a widow who had a young son in addition to Maria.

"You are one brave woman. Me, I told my boyfriend, Diego, what you were doing, and he said someone should give you a medal."

"Someone should examine my head. But they had fun."

"By the looks of it, so did you."

"I always say we shouldn't ask our children to do anything we aren't willing to do ourselves."

"And me? I always say '*a la occasion la pintan calva.*'"

"My Spanish is pretty rusty."

"Make the most of your chances," Adoncia had translated with a wink.

Kendra was now showered and gone, and Hannah and Alison were inside trying to unwind. Jamie could feel herself drooping with fatigue.

"I was more than glad to help," Cash said. "But that was a sight I won't soon forget."

"I'm sorry you didn't get much of a chance to talk to Kendra. I guess neither of you were quite expecting the day to go the way it did."

"While you were in the shower, we had time to talk over the basics. Then she hightailed it out of here. Oh, you look better in that hot-pink scooped-neck thing of yours than she does. It's not her style."

"She'll probably never come back."

"I think she was having a pretty good time, but she had to get to Front Royal before the tile place closes. She told me to tell you she owes you."

"I hate to think what she owes me. I might need to change the locks." Jamie finished the braid and began to twist an elastic band over the end. "You're still here."

"I thought you and the girls might like to go up to the orchard, have a peek in at Lucky and maybe see my place. A good way to calm them down."

From inside the house, Hannah was singing at the top of her lungs, and Alison might have been attempting harmony, considering that she wasn't within a mile of the same notes.

"They might not calm down for a century," Jamie warned. "A millennium."

"I'm not planning to be there quite that long."

Part of her knew she ought to refuse. Cash kept showing up, backing away, showing up again. Maybe that only bothered her because she was still lonely for adult company. She was slowly meeting people, but none of those relationships had graduated to any real conversation.

Unfortunately, she had been trained by the best to be honest with herself. Truthfully, Cash's on-again, off-again behavior bothered her because she found him intriguing.

She tested the waters. "You seem to be a very busy guy. Are you sure we won't be taking up too much of your time?"

"Not any more than you already take up in my head."

Jamie's hand paused midtwist. He had surprised her. "We're a handful. You might want to just leave us right here."

"I've been trying. Apparently that's one of those things I'm not real good at." He got up. "Granny Grace showed you the orchard through her eyes. You ought to see it through mine."

He'd switched the topic so suddenly that she had to scurry to follow along behind. "Why is that?"

"Because it's a good excuse to spend some time with me."

"And I need an excuse?"

He examined her a moment. "Looks like you might. And this is a good one. The girls'll enjoy a look at my new mare. You can lecture me about the way I live. Granny Grace can fuss over everybody, which makes her as happy as a crow in a cornfield and gives you a little rest. It's what they call a win–win."

"And what do you get?"

"Another dinner with you and the girls. Granny Grace is baking a ham, just in case you say yes."

"How can I say no?"

"With a lot more effort than you'd want to put into it."

"I always vote for easy, if nobody's going to get hurt."

He lifted the end of her braid, then dropped it against her breast. "Let's just keep tabs on that to make sure."

The girls bounced on the rear seat of Cash's pickup, but by the time they reached the orchard, Alison was wearing down and Hannah only made an occasional comment about the scenery.

"All the mailboxes are smashed," Hannah said.

"Country baseball." Cash slowed as they neared the orchard

drive. "Nothing to do on a summer night except get together with a couple of friends, go out armed with a baseball bat and smash mailboxes out the old truck window."

"You sound like you know what you're talking about," Jamie said.

"Only tried it once. Went for one of those boxes a nuclear bomb would bounce right off of. You know, the kind they sell in fancy mail-order catalogs? Cost the moon, but some farmer knew what he was doing. Hit it once, that box jerked the bat right out of my hand and nearly jerked my arm right out of its socket. I figured that was enough of a warning, so I switched to the other side. Now I'm a mailbox vigilante. Been known to sit by Granny Grace's mailbox on a summer night with a six-pack and a shotgun filled with rock salt, just waiting for the next Ranger or Silverado that slows down on our road when it ought to be speeding up."

"*I* know you're making that up. Now tell my girls."

"Hannah and Alison, I'm just kidding about the shotgun." Cash glanced at Jamie and winked. "And the six-pack."

"And the baseball bat?"

"Not kidding about that. One of the problems with country life. High-spirited teenagers with nothing much to do. Basically, there are two kinds of kids around here. One kind excels in school or sports and has a family that insists on church and scouting and family events. Then there's the other kind—average students at best, parents too busy or too clueless to understand that they have to take their kids in hand and give them something better to do than just cleaning the chicken house or spraying the apple trees."

"This is beginning to sound personal."

"I was somewhere in between. Good enough in school to get accepted to Tech, family that knew they had to program a portion of my free time and enough high spirits to send me off looking for trouble when I got bored."

"Do you still go off looking for trouble?"

Cash turned into the drive. "You tell me."

She wondered if *she* was trouble for him. That would depend entirely on what he was trying to avoid, and why. She really knew next to nothing about him. He had been married and no longer was. He was restless, had spent some time in Kentucky around racetracks and still liked horses. He lived somewhere on orchard property, although her tour with Grace had not included his house. He was a talented contractor, with a keen eye and an engaging way of managing others. She knew from the little she had seen that his men liked and respected him. And Rosslyn and Rosslyn was a going concern, most likely with a bright future if he wanted to be part of it.

Despite the easygoing, country-boy persona, Cash was educated, insightful and witty—which was true of a lot of easygoing country boys, now that she thought about it.

They passed the driveway up to the house and continued down the road.

"Used to be, when Grandpa Ben was alive, these fields were all planted. Some in hay, some in vegetables for market. He trucked a lot of those into D.C. for the restaurant trade, grew things nobody else around here had ever heard of back then for restaurants in Dupont Circle or Georgetown. But the apples were his love. To this day, I think he had names for the trees, and I don't mean York or Delicious. They were like his kids. When one of them lost a limb or developed some disease, I think he felt it, too. Like it happened to him."

"Grace talks about him fondly."

"There's a story there, if you can get her to tell you. My

mother was the youngest of the three kids by a lot, and I think most of what's interesting happened before she was born."

Jamie filed that away to ask Grace about when they were alone.

Now they were threading through the orchard, acres and acres of apple trees flanking the road.

"We used to have peaches, too," Cash said. "But most of them are gone now. A couple of unusual freezes, the drought, a season of workers who took advantage of Grandpa Ben's final illness. The peaches bore the brunt of all that, and now we just have half a dozen or so trees for family and friends. Granny Grace will probably be making peach butter before too long. I'll get her to open a jar to go with the rolls she's making."

"My mouth is watering."

"Good practice for the real thing."

He kept driving. As before, Jamie could see fabulous vistas through the orchard rows. Not only was there a lot of land here, it was magnificent land.

"I know Grace is afraid the orchard will be sold the moment she drops the reins," she said, feeling her way. "I'm sure it's worth a small fortune."

"Large fortune. Picture the next crop of McMansions out here. City people looking across driveways into each other's kitchen windows, hiring the local boys to cut the grass and trim the evergreens, buying their apples over at the Food Lion, because these trees will be wood chips by then, mulching somebody's flower beds."

"I'm shuddering."

"Nobody wants to see it end like that. My uncles are good men. Granny Grace raised them, after all. But they're profession-als, and their children are heading down that track, as well. Not a money-grubber in the bunch, but practical to the core. They feel like they can do some negotiating at this point, while the taxes are still being paid and the sheriff's not at the door with an eviction notice. But down the road, that might not be the case."

"Hard decisions."

The road wound around a pond and over a dirt dam. She saw what looked like a riding ring, with a three-rail fence circling it, and freshly whitewashed stables beyond that. Cash slowed and pulled in to park beside a mobile home that more closely resembled a Dumpster than somebody's living quarters.

"Home sweet home," he said.

"This is a high price to pay for independence."

"You mean for not sleeping where generations before have laid their heads?"

"I can't believe Grace wants the family home all to herself. I bet she'd give you a bedroom if you asked nicely."

"I like my privacy. And I'm closer to my horses out here."

"I'd say you're closer to everything, like the sky and the grass and whatever else you can see through the holes in that thing. Bet it saves on air-conditioning."

"You're making fun of home sweet home."

"Cash, I wouldn't say a word, but quite clearly you don't have to live this way. So it's interesting, that's all."

"Women. There's a training manual somewhere. I'd like to get my hands on it."

"I'll save you the trouble. You're on page three-oh-two. Cash Rosslyn, a wild mustang who will not be broken, a—" she looked at him and bit her lip in contemplation "—a bluetick hound who will not be housetrained."

"What do you know about bluetick hounds, city girl?"

"What your men have told me. Gig was trying to convince me to take one from his next litter."

He snagged her braid in his finger and wiggled it. "They like you, you know. They're a little afraid of your sister, but you've wrapped them around that little finger of yours. And they all want to do their best work and make you happy."

She was delighted to hear it. "That will serve me well in years to come when I'm out on job sites. Do you think they'll be half so accommodating when I start looking like the mother of twins?"

"Granny Grace hasn't said a word to me about that, by the way. Does she know?"

"It just hasn't come up. And I guess you haven't told her."

"Your business."

"I'll tell her soon. It's going to be obvious before long."

Cash got down and let the girls out the rear door. Then he stopped them before they could go running toward the stables.

"Okay, we have to have rules here. One, these horses aren't pets. They're easily frightened, and a frightened horse is something you don't ever want to see. So we'll speak softly, and we won't make any sudden movements around them, okay?"

"You train racehorses?" Jamie thought it was a rhetorical question. She'd certainly been left with that impression. "Is this a large enough facility for something like that? Do you have enough help?"

"Sweetcakes, this isn't a facility at all. And I do more or less train racehorses, but I train them not to be. Or at least that's what it looks like I'm going to be doing for a while. Somehow that's the way things have turned out."

"You lost me."

"Come on, I'll show you." He scooped a giggling Alison off the ground and swung her around so she was riding piggyback before she knew what was happening. "Hannah, you'll take your mother's hand, okay?"

"Who's going to protect whom?" Jamie asked her daughter.

"I'm not afraid of horses," Hannah said.

"Caution's a good thing, though, wouldn't you say? They're definitely larger than you are."

"You can hold my hand tighter if you need to."

Once they walked in through the wide entrance that bisected the stable, Jamie stopped for a moment, gently hauling Hannah up beside her to wait until her eyes adjusted to the dimmer light.

"Do you ride?" Cash asked.

"I had lessons as a child. My mother went through a Princess Diana period. She was briefly determined I should join the British royal family so she could attend all the best parties. I took deportment lessons, too. Riding went better."

"I don't know whether you're kidding."

"Sadly, I'm not." She joined him, shushing Alison and reminding her that Cash had explained she would need to keep her voice down.

There were twelve stalls, six on each side, but one side was completely empty. The other held three horses.

Cash walked to the first occupied stall. "This is Sanction's Folly. My first mistake. He's the gentlest of the three."

Sanction's Folly was a huge bay, his coat a reddish brown with the traditional black mane and tail. He thrust his head over the stall door and waited for Cash to rub his forehead.

"I've always loved horse racing." Cash stroked the horse's head, then moved up to his ears as he spoke. "Not the gambling, I'm glad to say, but the horses. So after college I took off for Kentucky and got a job at one of the big racing stables in Lexington. Sanction's one of the first horses I had the opportunity to work with. Then some years passed, and Sanction's best season at the track passed, too. He wasn't winning big enough or fast enough, and he wasn't accomplished enough to be bred. He also had a reputation as a handful, and nobody wanted anything to do with him."

He glanced at Jamie. "Let's just say that by the time the word got to me, his options weren't good."

She knew he was protecting the girls from the sad fact that many former racehorses ended up at the slaughterhouse. "I understand."

"I was his best chance. So I bought him for what he would have brought on the hoof and set about retraining him to be a horse, not a racehorse. Then I was going to sell him to some lucky family who knew their way around and could handle him. Only it took longer than I expected. There was a lot I didn't know. And by the time he improved enough, I couldn't seem to part with him."

She was touched. "Who could blame you? He's a sweetheart."

"Now, yes." He swung Alison around so she was resting on his hip, and he explained how to pat Sanction's muzzle. Alison was thrilled, and not one bit afraid.

"Hannah…" He set Alison down, holding her hand out to Jamie, and then let Hannah have her turn, lifting her so she could more easily reach the Thoroughbred.

"The other two can't be petted yet," he warned the girls. "They're new here. And I'm just starting to work with them."

"Same kind of stories?" Jamie asked.

"Czar Bright, that's the chestnut, sustained an injury, a bowed tendon. I've been nursing him through it for about four months. He's doing better than expected. It's nearly healed. Pretty soon I'll be able to pasture him. Then we'll see an amazing change in his personality. There's a good horse in there, just waiting for his chance, and he'll make a good ride for an experienced horseman someday. In the meantime, we'll stay back from his stall. He's probably never seen a child up close."

"He's a beauty."

"Let me show you the mare."

With Cash carrying Hannah—who didn't protest—they walked toward the last horse, a light bay with a golden-beige coat and dark stockings to match her mane. "This is Lady's Choice and the reason I was back in Kentucky a couple of weeks ago. Isn't she a beaut?"

"She is that." Lady's Choice was slender, with a long neck and proud head, and her coat gleamed. "Why is she here?"

"She had a good career on the track, then they retired her to be a broodmare, but she has problems now that prohibit her from breeding again. She's been shunted around ever since, no training at all, no patience from anybody who's worked with her. It's nearly ruined her. But when I'm done, she'll be as gentle as a lamb. I'm thinking about training her as a therapy horse. If she works out the way I think she will, she can be a mount for children. I know some people that work in a good program, and they're interested in her, if I can just get her in shape. Right now she's just resting, getting used to the surroundings. Then we'll see."

"I'm so impressed."

He turned to look at her. "Of course, that's why I brought you here. To show you what a great guy I am."

"No, you brought me here because this is your real love, and like most of us, that's what you really enjoy talking about. It's got to be a big venture. Life here's a lot different than life on the track, I'm sure."

"You wouldn't believe how tough the transition is, and how much they have to learn. They aren't used to flies or socializing with other horses, or even something as simple as getting their own food and water and not having it served up to them. People think all you have to do to one of these retirees is throw them out in a pasture with some friends for company and make sure food and water's available, and they'll adjust. Not so."

"So they have to learn the basics."

"They're fed differently on the track, ridden differently. Most racehorses are only what we call green broke, which means they more or less just accept the saddle, bridle and rider, but aren't all that excited about it. They have to be trained to see differently, which is why I have that round pen out there and not the usual oval riding ring. They have to learn not take off the moment they feel a rider on their backs. Sometimes it takes months for the hormones and other drugs they've been fed to wear out of their systems."

He turned and smiled. "But don't get me started."

"How much time do you spend here with them?"

"I have a good guy who helps and fills in when I'm away. But I spend a couple of hours a day, at the least. Three horses has to be my limit. I probably should have stopped at two, but Lady was too much of a temptation."

"Do you ride Sanction now? For pleasure? It sounds like he's all yours."

"Every chance I can. Raoul, my helper, rides him, too, to make sure he gets enough exercise. He's *my* therapy horse."

She felt as if she'd been given a peek into his heart. "Do you ever want to go back to turning Thoroughbreds into racehorses? Or are you content now to turn racehorses back into Thoroughbreds?"

"Content seems to perpetually elude me. I'm never real sure where I'll be or what I'll be doing next week." He set Hannah down. "Girls, if you go out that way, you might be lucky enough to see a new family of kittens. The mama moved in from who knows where and had them under the shed out to the side a couple of weeks ago. Stay back, but if you crouch down on the ground a few feet away, you might get a peek without upsetting her."

"Remember, walk slowly and be quiet," Jamie said, holding the girls back until she was finished cautioning them.

They took off, but to their credit, managed to keep their pace to a fast walk.

"They're good kids," Cash said.

"We aren't taking a kitten."

"I didn't ask you to."

"No, but *they'll* be asking. You and I need a united front."

"They're cute as the dickens. The mother was a scraggly mess until Granny Grace started feeding her."

"Not just Granny Grace, I bet."

He didn't deny it. "We'll get her spayed once the kittens are weaned. We could use a good barn cat out here. My wife—" He stopped abruptly and didn't go on.

When he didn't continue, she touched his arm. "Grace told me you were married. You've been divorced a while?"

"Kary died not quite two years after the wedding." He didn't look at her. "It was a long time ago. We met in college, got married before we graduated. She was gone before she could ever use her education. We were Cash and Kary, although everyone had always called her Karen until she met me. How's that for young and foolish?"

"I'm sorry, Cash."

"Yeah, me, too. But she's been gone for years."

"She loved cats?"

"Had a pair of Siamese purebreds. They were spoiled beyond belief. They went to her mother after Kary died and I left for Kentucky, but Siamese darlings or not, she would have taken in that mama cat out there and made sure those kittens got good homes."

"And so will you, I bet. Used-up racehorses and homeless kittens. Not to mention a fawn named Lucky. There's a connection."

"Yeah, there's a theme going on here." For the briefest moment he rested the back of his hand against her abdomen. "The pair of us. What did that old commercial say? We bring good things to life?"

He was bringing *her* to life. She could feel blood rushing from every part of her body to the place where he had so gently laid his hand. She was sorry when he lifted it.

"We'd better go check on the girls," she said. "Or Alison will be running in here to tell us what she saw, and she'll scare your horses to death."

"I might have overplayed that a bit, but better safe than sorry. A racehorse in rebellion's not a pretty sight."

"Thanks for bringing me here."

"My pleasure." He paused. "Thanks for listening."

"That was *my* pleasure." She wanted to say more but knew he wouldn't appreciate it and settled for reaching for his hand instead, giving it a quick squeeze. "Five'll get you ten that Hannah's already named the kittens."

"I wouldn't take that one even if I was a betting man." He draped his arm over her shoulders, and they walked out that way together.

12

Jamie saw Grace standing on the porch, waiting for her to trudge up the steps. It was Wednesday, just four days since she and the girls had come with Cash to eat baked ham, spoon bread and an array of fresh vegetables from Grace's little kitchen garden. This morning Cissy Claiborne had invited both Alison and Hannah to spend part of the day with Reese in a plastic wading pool, beating a harsh August heat wave, and Jamie had quickly agreed. Time by herself was precious, and she'd had almost none since moving to the cabin.

But no sooner had she dropped the girls off at the old farmhouse where Cissy, her husband, Zeke, and Reese lived, than she abandoned her plans to spend the morning with her feet up and headed to Cashel Orchard instead. She still hadn't told Grace she was pregnant, and now, without the girls to eavesdrop, she thought she'd take the opportunity.

And while she was here, coming clean about her personal life, she hoped Grace would tell her a bit more about Cash's, as well.

At the sound of her van, Grace had come out to the porch. Since she hadn't called ahead, Jamie was relieved that Grace appeared pleased.

"I'm sorry I came without checking," Jamie called. "But you're not programmed into my cell phone. I'll come another time if this is a problem."

"You're always welcome. When I was a young woman nobody ever called ahead, so every moment had potential for a surprise. I liked that. Made me keep the house a great deal cleaner. Not an easy feat with three children and orchard chores."

Jamie joined her, fanning herself with an open hand. "I don't know how you managed."

"Where are the girls?"

"They're playing at a friend's house. She doesn't live far away, which is nice for all of us. Just farther down on Fitch Crossing. Cissy Claiborne's the mom, maybe you know the family?"

"Oh, I know the Claiborne house. I went to school with one of the Claibornes, although not one of their most law-abiding members."

"Actually, I think Cissy and her family live with a neighbor." Jamie tried to remember the name of the woman she'd met briefly when she dropped off the girls. "Helen Henry? Old white farmhouse? I think Cissy said her husband's family owns the next farm down."

"Oh, my. Yes, Helen Henry. It's been a long time since I've seen Helen. We were girls together."

"Friends?"

"Not by a long shot." Grace smiled, but she also changed the subject. "It's good you're getting a bit of a holiday. I've never met more engaging children, but I'm sure a little breathing space appeals to you."

"Two can be a handful."

"More than two before long, I think."

Jamie felt her shoulders sag. "Cash already talked to you."

"No, dear. No one has to say a thing. I know a pregnant woman when I see one. There's a certain glow, a certain blooming of the complexion, that has nothing to do with temperatures close to a hundred. A certain refusal to drink a glass of wine or a cup of coffee, too. And usually a snap undone at the waist and a zipper inched down. I'm tired of waiting for you to tell me, so I'll just take that bull by the horns."

"That was the big reason I came up today. To explain how it happened."

Grace had a bubbling chuckle of a laugh, and now it lightened the oppressively hot air. "If you had to explain how it happened, I would be a sorry excuse for a grandmother."

"Well, believe it or not, this didn't happen the usual way."

"Come in, come in. I'm intrigued. Does this mean an even Newer Testament? A miraculous birth in the twenty-first century?" Grace opened the door and ushered Jamie inside. "I would worry it was something too hard to talk about, but you don't seem upset."

Jamie stepped in and whistled in relief. "Wow, the air-conditioning feels great."

"That unit is as old as Cash. I could swear Ben had it installed when he was born so Sandra would bring him up here to see us in the summer. I wait for it to breathe its last, but while it's still working, I'm making good use of it. Come in the kitchen and have some lemonade."

Jamie followed her, admiring Grace's quilts again as they went. "How's Lucky?"

"Happy in the pen Cash made for her outside, and growing like a weed. We'll go and see her later, if you'd like. Three mornings ago I looked out the window and saw two does not far beyond it. I don't know what they thought of each other, but that'll be her new family, I think, when it's time for her to be released."

In the kitchen, Jamie flopped in a chair while Grace filled glasses with ice and lemonade. She added sprigs of mint and brought them to the table, along with a platter of cinnamon rolls, plates and napkins.

"I don't know why I even turned on the oven for these. I could have put them in the sun and let Mother Nature bake them." Grace sprawled in her chair and nudged the platter in Jamie's direction. "Eat. You're eating for two."

"Three." Out of habit, Jamie cut one of the rolls in half and lifted it to a plate. Then, shrugging, she took the other.

"You're pregnant with *twins?* Oh, my dear. Do they run in your family?"

"No, but they do run in the laboratory. In vitro fertilization is such an inexact science that when you opt for it, the doctors want to give you every opportunity to get pregnant. So we opted to try for two, hoping for at least one. More gets iffy." She looked up and silently enjoyed the expression on Grace's face. "Three or more create problems if they all make themselves at home in the womb. Triple pregnancies are harder on everybody, and not as safe for the babies. I don't think my sister and her husband were ready for three babies at once, either."

"They're your sister's children?"

"In every way." Jamie gave a short rundown of the situation. "And that's why I haven't been forthcoming about it. At first I just wanted to be sure everything was a go. Then I wasn't sure how to explain. I'm absolutely thrilled to be doing this, but not everybody's going to understand. And I guess I'm not ready to face criticism."

"I hope you didn't think I would be critical."

"Oh, no, but it's still hard to explain, especially with the girls around. Cash knows. But I guess the cat's about to leap out of that bag. I just bought larger jeans. I'll show a lot quicker with two than I did with one."

Grace reached over and put a second cinnamon roll on Jamie's plate. "Eat up. You're going to need it. And not eating won't keep you thin."

"My appetite was flagging for a while, but everything's settled down. Now the heat makes it hard to eat, but I'm still gaining steadily."

"You know, I'm just stunned." Grace sat back and watched Jamie eat. "You're a levelheaded young woman and a compassionate sister. You must have considered your part in this carefully."

"I needed to do it."

"That's a strong statement."

"Have you ever been presented with a choice so clear you knew you had to go forward? This was one of those. Kendra and Isaac would never hire a surrogate. I don't think that idea ever crossed their minds. I wasn't even sure they would agree to let me do it. They had to think it over and discuss it endlessly."

"Of course they did."

Jamie looked up from her rapidly disappearing roll. "When all was said and done, I knew I was their only chance to be parents. And I owe Kendra everything."

"Why do you think so?"

Jamie couldn't seem to stop talking. "She more or less raised me, and gave up her own childhood to do it. Then I took off when I was seventeen and didn't see her for years. I was putting my life together after some serious false starts, and I was afraid if I sought her out, she'd try to put it back together for me. By then

I knew it had to be up to me and nobody else. Sink or swim with no life preserver."

Grace was silent for a moment; then she nodded. "Because she's your *sister*, not your mother."

Jamie was grateful Grace understood. "That's the biggest part of it. I needed to get my life to a place where we could be equals, where we wouldn't fall back into a situation that was never right or wise to begin with."

"But you feel guilty about it."

Jamie smiled. "You're good at this."

"I'm not sure it's a natural talent. I learned to be over the years."

"Kendra was hurt and worried all those years. When I finally felt ready for a reunion, she wasn't sure she could trust me. Now I can give her the thing she wants most."

"And in the process prove yourself?"

"I hope so. And forgive myself for hurting her."

"The things we do—and don't do—for love." Grace reached for her glass and it tipped over, spilling ice cubes but little lemonade on the table.

Jamie grabbed napkins out of the holder in the center and mopped up what had spilled.

"I'm always clumsy when I'm thinking," Grace said. "Thank you for taking care of me."

"Thank you for listening." Jamie rested her hand on Grace's for a moment. "But since you brought up the things we do for love... When he was showing me his horses on Saturday, Cash told me about Kary."

"Two for the price of one. He doesn't show the horses to just anybody, and he never talks about Kary. For that matter, he never brings anybody here for dinner, so that makes three."

Before romantic notions got too entrenched, Jamie had to issue a warning. "Surely you can see I'm no bargain. Cash and I are becoming friends. But I'm more or less off the market these days, wouldn't you say?"

"You young people do have a way of saying things."

"It must have been terrible to lose somebody he loved so young."

"They *were* young. Married in college, as he probably told you. Neither of them knew it, of course, but Karen was already living on borrowed time. She had a rare disease, something like multiple sclerosis, only this one takes you quickly. They had two years together, but Karen was very ill for most of them. He stayed by her side, but once she was gone, he was a changed man, our Cash. He doesn't trust the universe anymore. If something like that can happen once, that's all he needs to know."

Jamie didn't know what to say or whom to feel sorrier for. Cash, who had watched his young wife slip away, or Karen herself.

"You had to know," Grace said. "It'll help you understand him."

"What was she like?"

"Funny, pretty, smart. She hailed from Radford, farther south of here. She wanted to be a teacher. I don't remember now of what. We were just getting to know her when she got sick, and then everything became about that. I think that was the hardest part for her, that in the end, she was a patient, not a person. Cash tried his best to keep that from happening, and if it hadn't been for him, those last months would have been terrible. But he wouldn't let her family or the doctors prolong the inevitable. He made sure Karen had the last word. He listened to her when nobody else would and let her die as peacefully as he knew how. But that took its toll, as well."

Jamie felt tears sting her eyes. Her voice was husky. "He should be proud."

"Pride disappears in the face of hardship, Jamie. I can tell you that from experience. But we can't keep this up. This is all too sad for a hot summer day. I have something a lot more cheerful to show you."

Jamie got to her feet when Grace did. She needed something to erase the picture of Cash's all-too-short marriage. "Something to do with Lucky?"

"Nothing so hot as going outside. No, I want you to see my sewing room."

"Wonderful. Do you have a quilt in progress?"

"Yes, indeed. That's a question you never have to ask a quilter. There are quilts in our heads, quilts in the way we pile fabric on our shelves, quilts on our design walls, under the needles on our sewing machines. Quilts waiting to be bound. Always quilts. Some of us will die planning the next one. We won't even notice that final breath."

They were wending their way through the house now, heading up the stairs. Grace turned right and went to the end of the hallway, then into the last room. It was large and airy, with cross ventilation and good light. One entire wall was crisscrossed by built-in shelves and cubbyholes filled with rolled-up fabric and what looked to Jamie like quilt batting. Pegboard covered another wall, with lots of things Jamie recognized, such as scissors and rulers, and many more she didn't, hanging from hooks.

"Oh, no wonder you do this." Jamie was entranced. Grace was clearly in the process of cutting fabric for another quilt. A high table was covered by a large rectangle in a bold floral print. Jamie lifted one edge and counted eight different colors in the nearest flower, a bloom that *had* never and *would* never appear in nature.

"Do you like to work with your hands?" Grace asked.

"I haven't had much time to. Of course I draw passably."

"Cash showed me your plans for your sister's house, and I've seen the cabin. You're very talented, and you have a good eye and imagination. Have you thought about making quilts for the babies?"

Jamie continued to look at the fabric on the table, running her fingers along the edge of one piece. "Isn't that a little like laying claim to them?"

"I can see you're being careful, and that's commendable. But you *are* their aunt, correct? As well as their bed-and-breakfast for the next few months?"

"Yes to both."

"Then you have a perfect right, and won't they treasure the quilts in later years, knowing their life story, as they will? I know just the pattern for you, dear. Do you know anything about quilts?"

"My sister collects them. She has some lovely old ones, mostly signature quilts."

"There's a pattern, an old traditional pattern, called Sister's Choice. Doesn't that seem appropriate for your situation? And it makes lovely baby quilts. Lovely large quilts, as well. Depending on how many colors you use and how you place them, you get completely different effects, which is one of the beauties of the pattern. You could do two quilts, using different fabrics and colors, and the novice won't even realize they're the same blocks."

"I've done a little sewing. But very little."

"Good, then you don't have much to unlearn, do you?"

"I don't have a machine, or much room." Jamie paused, because it sounded as if she was trying to wiggle out of making the quilts, and the idea was already growing on her.

"But I can buy a machine if you tell me what to look for. That's no problem, and if I'm making baby quilts, I could just use our great-room table, couldn't I? The girls might even like to help."

"Oh, you won't need a machine. I think we should work on them here, and you can use mine. That way I can teach you as you go."

"That seems like a lot of work, Grace. Are you sure?"

"I tell you what. You'll be working on quilts for the babies, but why don't I make quilts for your girls, *with* your girls, while we're at it? That way they won't have hurt feelings. You can always make quilts for them, too, when they're a little older."

Jamie could just imagine how much her daughters would love that. "They're very opinionated," she warned.

"Children should be, you know. You're raising them to know what they like and not be at all insecure about making it known. They'll need those skills as they grow."

Grace wandered over to the fabric shelves. "I have enough fabric here to start my own shop. I imagine Hannah and Alison will find things they like, and if not, we'll visit a store. Children love to sew. Adults just don't love to let them."

Jamie sensed that the project excited her new friend. She had suspected Grace was lonely, and this reinforced the feeling. She was delighted that both of them were going to benefit from something that, on the surface, looked to be so one-sided.

"Do you have pictures of a Sister's Choice quilt?" Jamie asked. "I'd love to see one."

"Oh, even better. I have one on my bed. An old one. I'll show you."

Jamie followed her back to the other end of the hallway, past multiple doors and bedrooms. The house was larger than she'd thought from the outside.

Grace opened the door. This room was half the size of the sewing room, which seemed more the room to use as a master bedroom. There was an old walnut sleigh bed, a dresser of the same walnut and a mirror that needed to be resilvered. One wall sported a chest of drawers, but that was all the room could hold.

The quilt on the bed was lovely, but nothing like the ones that Grace made. This was composed of multiple sedate florals, in lavenders, blues and greens, with the occasional punch of red. The pattern formed an unusual star with a cross intersecting it. The blocks were connected by the same dark green corners, which, when linked, made smaller stars in between. The background was white, although it had mellowed to ivory.

"It's charming," Jamie said. "And completely unlike you. Is it an heirloom?"

Grace lifted the edge and held it up for Jamie to see. "Yes and no, but I made it. By hand. One of the few quilts I ever did that way."

Jamie saw neat little stitches holding the quilt together. "When?"

"I finished it in 1943. This is what I did in the evenings after I put the children to bed. Ben was gone, of course, at war, like all the other men who had joined up or been drafted. Late at night this house was very quiet. The whole Valley seemed quiet during those years. Breaths held, prayers prayed silently."

"I'm sure this was better than worrying."

"No, at first the quilt was simply the way I dealt with my past and future. And I had a lot to deal with. But that's a long story."

Jamie sensed that Grace was asking if she wanted to hear it. Cash had told her that Grace had an interesting tale about life with his grandfather. Now her curiosity was piqued. Grace wasn't a woman who talked endlessly about herself. She was a listener and a doer. Whatever she had to tell would surely be fascinating.

"I have time," Jamie said. "I don't have to pick up the girls for another hour. And this sounds like a story worth listening to."

"You might be sorry you got me started."

"I feel the need for another glass of lemonade. And another cinnamon roll."

"All right. I might have time to begin. Even Sandra doesn't know every bit of this, nor Cash, of course. But I think you, of all people, might like to hear it."

Jamie was touched, and honored. "I would."

"I'll tell you a little over that lemonade." Grace smoothed the quilt back over the sheets. "But really, we're going to need to find something else you can drink. I'm beginning to pucker up, dear. You will, too, and it's not a pretty look."

"So bring on the apple juice."

Grace fluffed a pillow. "Now those are words that warm my heart. But you may need to drink a lot, because this story is long and complicated. And like your own, it begins with a choice I made for my own sister. I was Grace Fedley in those days, and my sister was Anna. She was more than ten years older than me, so I understand all too well how powerful an older sister can be. Then, one day, everything I'd ever known about myself and my sister changed."

13

1941

Grace Fedley didn't like the hulking farmhouse at Cashel Orchard, and she despised the steep road up the mountain to get there, a trip her father's elderly Chevrolet stake bed truck was, in the best of weather, reluctant to complete. This evening, as January sleet silvered the new permanent wave in her chestnut hair, dislike turned to revulsion. One mile back, the truck was steaming by the roadside, and somewhere below that, her father was stumbling wearily down the mountain, hoping to find a neighbor to help get it started again. She had elected to continue by foot.

Now, as Grace trudged up the orchard drive, ice water from the melt-off river gushing along the roadside seeped through the soles of her shoes and bled up her stockings. Brambles reached out to grab and imprison her, and shrubs long denied pruning leered from above, spurred to a macabre dance by the winter wind.

She could have remained in the truck with her mother. But a message brought by a neighbor who housed the local telephone switchboard had claimed Anna needed Grace, and needed her immediately. She was to proceed to the orchard without further delay. And she was to bring the family Bible.

Now, as then, Grace wondered what reason her sister could have for this summons. Anna was pregnant with her second child, but if Anna was in early labor, Grace certainly had no skills to assist. Nor were she and Anna close. Grace was, in fact, one of the last people Anna would turn to in an emergency.

Halfway up the drive, two German shepherds appeared, snarling and snapping until—to her relief—they recognized her and trotted back to the house. She could see lights in the windows, and a stranger's car parked at the side. Frowning, she summoned what speed she could, and in a minute she had climbed to the porch.

The fact that she couldn't simply walk into her sister's house was a sad commentary on their relationship. Instead, she shifted from foot to foot while she rapped on the door. When nobody came, she banged with the side of a fist, and finally, when that brought no results, she let herself in. What point was there in trying not to invite criticism, when nothing she did would please Anna anyway?

The entry hall was dreary, with wallpaper that had been old decades ago curling in strips at the ceiling. One lamp tried to fight off the January gloom but couldn't succeed. She registered these things, but vaguely. The man at the top of the steps invited most of her attention.

"Well, you took your time getting here, didn't you?"

Grace stared up at Ben Cashel and thought she probably liked him even less than usual. She had never liked Ben one iota more than she liked his gloomy house, the winding road that led to it or the woman he'd married. Anna might be her sister, but Grace couldn't call forth one happy memory of Anna's years as a Fedley. Her own life had improved immeasurably the day Anna married Ben and moved away. And now Grace believed that these two people, so perfectly suited to each other, should enjoy eternal and solitary companionship and not force anyone else to watch.

She reminded herself that soon, very soon, she would be so far away that Anna would never again be able to order her to appear again. She wasn't even sure Anna would be able to find her.

"The truck broke down," Grace said without apology. "Mama stayed inside, and Papa went to find help. I walked the last mile."

Grace was not one to complain or argue. But when Ben's expression didn't change, she was goaded to do both. "Through the sleet, which you would notice, if you weren't so busy passing judgment."

Ben was a tall man, and he seemed taller now because of his position so far above her. A shock of brown hair hung over his forehead, and he was wearing overalls that faded against his tan skin. He had a handsome face—straight nose, high cheekbones, Rudolph Valentino lips—handsome enough that at first Grace had thought he could do a lot better for a helpmate than Anna. But that was before she'd gotten to know him. Before she discovered Ben was as somber, as hidebound, as judgmental, as her sister.

His voice was flat and emotionless. "Your sister is dying."

For a moment Grace wasn't sure she'd understood him.

Anna had been in top form on Christmas afternoon, the last time Grace had seen her. Grace had listened to criticism of everything, from the round-toed shoes she had purchased with her first paycheck at the rayon factory to the length of her hair. Grace had cuddled her sober two-year-old nephew on her lap, while his mother insisted she was teaching the boy things Anna would only have to discipline him for later. When Grace protested, Anna had turned to her husband. In silent agreement, Ben had whisked the disappointed Charlie off for a nap.

Anna had been cold. Anna had been critical. But Anna had been well.

Now Grace protested. "Dying? She can't be. She was fine Christmas day."

"She is *not* fine now. Why would we have called you if she was? The baby came at noon, and Anna hasn't stopped bleeding. It's just a matter of time."

He might have been reciting the story of an unfortunate mare or cow. He sounded tired, but not unduly upset. He sounded as if he just wanted this day to end.

Grace steadied herself with a hand on the newel post. "And the baby?"

"Another boy. Too small. I doubt he'll make it, either."

She wanted to tell him she was sorry, but something inside her rebelled. She *was* sorry. Desperately sorry. But Ben probably wouldn't believe it, and even if he did, he certainly wouldn't care.

"I saw a car," she said instead.

"The doctor. He's done what he can."

"Where's little Charlie?"

"A neighbor came and took him home for the night."

Grace was glad Charlie wasn't here, but she hoped they'd had enough sense to let him say goodbye to his mother. "I'm sorry about Mama. Anna will be wanting her."

He shrugged. "No, for some reason it's you she wants."

Grace couldn't understand this. "Now?"

"In a few minutes. Dry yourself. I'll call you when it's time." Without another word, he left her standing there.

She went into the kitchen and found feedsack towels, and without even thinking, she began to do as he'd ordered, stripping off her coat and shoes, and doing what she could to sop up the moisture.

Grace felt numb. Numb from the cold. Numb from the news. Numb from Ben's delivery of it. Her sister was dying, and although Grace truly was dismayed and sorry, she knew she didn't feel everything she should. Anna might be her sister, but the two of them were so different that their shared origins were hard to believe.

Shared they were, though. Grace and Anna were the only two girls in a family of eight children. By the time Grace had finally made an appearance, her parents had been exhausted from child rearing. Perhaps the death of three young sons had made them reluctant to take a chance on loving another child, or perhaps the couple had just despaired that, so late in life, Grace's mother, Mina, had conceived again. Whatever the cause, Grace received little supervision. The sunny disposition and high spirits she exhibited from infancy were left to blossom freely. Curbing natural inclinations was a job her parents no longer had the energy for.

While the other Fedley children toiled in Fedley fields and worked in the family sawmill, Grace was left to her own devices. Although neither her mother nor father thought much education was valuable for girls, she finished high school without obstacles, since school was a way to keep her busy and out of sight. As she matured, her frequent absences from home went largely unnoticed by anyone except her older sister. But Anna, who was still living at home, *did* notice, appointing herself Grace's guardian, conscience and personal Simon Legree.

Although the somber, perpetually exhausted Fedleys were not an ideal family, were it not for Anna, Grace might have considered her childhood good enough. At school, at church and recently at her first real job, she discovered friends who, like her, had no use for the restrictions of rural life when the country was finally coming out of the Depression, and factories and offices were clamoring for help. She discovered laughter, dancing and parties, pretty clothes, radio shows and older boys who smelled of Brylcreem and Old Spice. Only Anna stood between her and total freedom, Anna who chastised and questioned her whenever she came home, Anna who locked the doors to keep Grace inside and her hands busy with mending or ironing.

Grace had counted the days until Anna married and left. Now, at seventeen and finally finished with school, Grace was counting the days until she could escape the Valley prison she was forced to call home. The world beckoned. She planned to accept that invitation.

Her parents didn't know yet. The family farm and sawmill had been heavily mortgaged to pay Depression-driven debts, and now they were planning to sell to avoid foreclosure. As soon as they could, her father and mother would move to Delaware to live with their oldest son and his family. They expected Grace to continue her new job as a spinner at the rayon plant in Front Royal and find lodging with the family of one of her brothers, where she could help keep house or care for their children in addition to her factory hours.

But Grace had other plans.

On the trip up the mountain, she had told herself that whatever Anna intended for this evening, Grace's own intention was to tell her sister goodbye once and for all.

Sadly, she hadn't realized how true that would be.

At last tears filled her eyes. Anna was dying, and the two of them would never have an opportunity to solve the problems between them.

She stopped blotting and straightened, suddenly aware of a new possibility. Maybe forgiveness was the reason Anna had asked for her. Maybe Anna wanted to confess that she had always been jealous of her prettier little sister, of Grace's relative freedom and lack of supervision, and that had colored their relationship. Anna might well ask Grace to forgive her, which of course Grace would do. Their past seemed childish now in the face of what was to come.

Even if Anna was too exhausted to voice any of these thoughts, Grace could tell her that she forgave her anyway. She would promise to look in on Charlie whenever she could. This would mean coming back to the Valley occasionally, but she could do that for Anna. They were, after all was said and done, sisters. That had to mean something.

She went back to the bottom of the stairs and waited to be called. She could hear people talking above her; then the midwife, a gap-toothed old woman Anna recognized from church, came down the stairs shaking her head.

"She fought good," she said, admiration in her voice. "She's a stubborn one, that sister of yours. She pushed that baby out with everything she had left in her. But it took all she had. Ain't nothing left in her now. She won't last long."

"The baby?"

"He's all wrapped up in his cradle. I saw to that. Gotta keep him warm. That's the way of things. Might make it, might not. I'd expect the latter, I were you. Oughta have a box ready to put him in the ground. Sensible thing to have one done and ready, and a good hole dug. That last part'll be hard, the ground's so froze up."

Grace wondered how the woman, whose name she couldn't remember, could think ahead to mundane details like a coffin for the baby before the poor little thing had even passed on.

The midwife gave a humorless smile. "Don't look so surprised, Missy. I bury 'bout one baby to every dozen or so I save. Nothing to be done about it. You ask that doctor. He'll tell you I do the best I can, but your sister had no call to have another child. Doctor and I both told her so after the last baby came. But she paid us no mind. Now look what she's gone and done."

Grace hadn't known this. Anger filled her. She wondered if Ben had forced himself on her sister, demanded she share his bed, even though the results could be fatal. She wasn't clear on all the details, but she had heard from some of her friends that there were ways to prevent pregnancy, even when a bed was shared. She wondered if her sister had known any of them.

"Best milk to try for that baby would be goat milk, 'less you can find somebody to nurse him. I told Mr. Cashel such. When your sister's gone, you remind him now. I think the Lindemuths down the mountain a piece have some goats, and they'll likely sell or even give him the milk, he just asks."

"I'll remind him." Grace put her hand on the old woman's arm. "Did Anna mention me? She called and asked for me."

"She didn't mention nobody, but I know she sent a neighbor out on an errand jist as soon as the doctor told her she needed to get right with God."

Grace tried to imagine how Anna felt. Her sister had never seemed excited about having another baby, but Anna never seemed excited about anything. Still, to be told that a child you might have wanted, at least in some part of your heart, was stealing your life away...? She felt another wave of sympathy for her sister and wished she could go upstairs to comfort her.

"Can I go up now?" she asked.

"The doctor's finishing, though there's nothing much to be done now. And she's saying goodbye to that husband of hers."

Grace looked up as more footsteps sounded and saw Dr. Flint, the white-haired gentleman who had brought her into the world, at the top of the stairs, adjusting the handle of his black bag. He came down and joined them.

"She's asking for you," he said. "Time to go up in a moment. Don't upset her. Nothing you say will matter much to her, since her time is short, but you'll remember whatever it is all the days of your life. Better to let things drop right here, before you see her."

Grace realized the doctor must have heard that she and Anna had never been close, that there was, in fact, bad blood between them. "I don't want to upset her. I just want to say goodbye."

"Make sure that's all you say, then." He pulled the midwife to one side, and they conversed in hushed tones.

Grace wondered if she *should* tell Anna she forgave her. What if that was what the doctor was warning against? She tried to think of a way to phrase her last words to her sister. Should she tell Anna she loved her, even if Anna would know it wasn't exactly true? *Did* she love her, simply because Anna was her sister? It seemed possible, but the question might take a lot more time to answer truthfully than she had.

Ben appeared and motioned for her to join him. She wished the stairs were longer, steeper. She wished this day had never begun.

When she reached the top, he wrapped his fingers around her wrist, and not gently. "She wants to see you alone. Don't you say anything to her that will make her go faster, you hear me?"

Grace shook off his hand, her eyes narrowed. "If you hadn't gotten her pregnant again, Ben Cashel, then none of this would be happening. So don't you bully me."

He looked as if she had struck him, and his hand dropped to his side. Grace felt a stab of remorse, but it was too late to take back her words.

"I'm going in," she said in a softer tone. "You stay nearby, in case you're needed."

"I never wanted this."

She didn't know if that was an explanation or a plea for understanding. Whatever it was, it was unlike the Ben Cashel she knew. Since she didn't know what he meant, she didn't know how to answer. She just shrugged, took a deep breath and went to stand in the doorway.

The room was nearly dark, and her eyes adjusted slowly. A walnut four-poster bed took up the entire middle of the room, which was sparsely furnished. There was plenty of empty space for more, since the room was expansive and airy. A feed-store calendar was the only adornment on the walls, which, like the hallway, were covered in fading wallpaper from another era.

The room was spotlessly clean. That didn't surprise Grace, since Anna was one to put cleanliness above godliness, without a thought for the eternal ramifications. She stepped inside, then closer to the bed. Anna was huddled under quilts, lying flat, with her knees raised, most likely propped on pillows. Grace suspected that was meant to slow the bleeding. She felt such a rush of sympathy for her sister that she could barely breathe. Nobody deserved this.

"Oh, Anna." She went to the bedside and leaned over so that her sister could see her. "Oh, Anna, I'm so very sorry."

Anna's eyelids opened. Slowly, as if this was a sacrifice beyond measure. "Are you?"

Grace perched on the edge of the feather mattress. Dark-haired Anna had always had rosy, almost feverishly flushed skin, but now her cheeks were drained of all color. She was scarecrow thin; her two pregnancies had seemed invasive, as if the child inside her was at war with her long, prominent bones. Now Anna looked almost skeletal, and her eyes were the only things that still seemed alive.

"Of course I'm sorry," Grace said. "I've never wished you harm, even if we haven't always gotten along."

"Always?" Anna made a sound that was almost a laugh, although not a pleasant one. "You always hated…everything I tried to do. Selfish…never cared for anybody…but yourself."

Grace wondered if her sister had really called her to her death-bed to deliver yet another lecture in the series she'd begun in Grace's early childhood.

"Let's put that behind us," Grace said carefully, remembering the doctor's words. She wondered how she could have been foolish enough to think maybe Anna wanted forgiveness.

"Oh…I'll be putting it…behind me soon enough."

"Is this the baby?" Grace slipped off the bed to view the tiny bundle wrapped and motionless in the old wooden cradle by the window.

"Never mind him. I got some…thing to say to you…and not much time."

"Anna, don't let go yet. Mama and Papa are on their way. You got to hang on."

"Don't care…about them. You got to listen…now."

Grace went back to the bedside, having seen nothing of her new nephew except the tiniest upturned nose. "What? Just tell me."

"You got to do something. Got to, you under…stand?" Anna wheezed, and if possible, grew paler.

Grace saw a cloth in the washing bowl on a nightstand and wrung it out to wipe her sister's brow. "Whatever you need, Anna. Take a moment. Breathe deep."

Somehow Anna found the strength to push Grace's hand away. "Listen to me! Ben…can't raise these boys alone. Not and keep the land. You saw…what happened to Papa. That'll…happen to Ben, too. He'll lose it all." She coughed, and for a moment, she was silent.

Grace knew better than to speak. Clearly there was nothing she could say that her sister wanted to hear.

"You've got to marry him."

Anna's words had been so soft, Grace thought she must have misunderstood. "Anna, what did you say?"

"You…got to marry Ben. I know…you're sweet on that… Tom Stoneburner. But this…it's the only way. Ben can't keep the boys and the orchard. His family's all gone. He's got nobody. And Mama can't take the boys. She's too old, and…there won't be room…where they're going. Ben wouldn't…just give them… away. He'll hang on, but there's…nobody else can help. Just you. And you can't…be staying up here with him. Not without a wedding."

Grace stared at her sister, who was growing paler by the moment. "No, Anna. Mama and Papa can move up here and take over. Papa can help Ben, Mama can raise the boys. I'm sure they'll want to—"

"No!" Anna coughed, but continued muttering through it. "They couldn't even raise you! Too old. Don't care…Papa let the farm go. Could save it, but he doesn't…want to work that hard. In Delaware, he'll help Luther a little…in his garage, Mama will do a little helping out at Luther's house…but that's all they'll want. They'd be no help…here. Won't come…even if Ben asks. And he won't."

Grace realized Anna was right. Her parents *had* given up a long time ago. They were old, exhausted, beaten down. The hard work here would finish them off quickly. That was why they had chosen to live out their final years at their oldest son's home in

Delaware. Luther, who owned his own garage, was the most pros-
perous of their children, the most likely to give them some ease.

"I can stay a while, and help Ben," she said. "Until he finds
somebody to live in and care for the boys."

"Nobody…will. You know that. Anybody young enough…
to do it…wouldn't be up here alone…with a young man like
Ben. You know…what people will say? And besides…they've all
gone out to work. Anybody strong enough to do this work,
they're…already working somewhere better. It's Tom…isn't it?"

"Anna, this doesn't have anything to do with Tom. I can't
marry Ben any which way. You can't expect me to give up my
whole life. If Ben loses the orchard, so be it. He can find work
somewhere. He's strong and able. And the boys will be—"

"Are you…so selfish…you don't see what's coming? There's
going…to be a war!" Anna fell silent, breathing hard, and her
eyelids closed. Grace leaped to her feet, but before she could get
the doctor, Anna recovered enough to open them a little. "You
think what's happening…in Europe won't come here? What…
will happen to my babies…their daddy's called to fight? There's
only one way to fix this…you have to do what I say. You have
to marry Ben. Stay up here with him, 'til the boys are old enough
not to need you. Then you…can leave. I don't…expect you to
stay forever. You're not that kind of…woman. But are you the
kind…that can do what she has to…even if it's not…what she
wants?"

Grace heard the door creak, and in a moment Ben was beside
her. By his expression, she knew he had heard Anna's plea. He
looked like a man being torn in two.

"Anna, you don't have to worry about me and the boys," he
said, bending low to make sure she heard him. Anna's eyes were
closed again, but her eyelids fluttered when he spoke to her. "I

can take care of things. There's always a way. I swear to you the boys will be well looked after, and this orchard will still be ours when it's time for them to take over."

"Grace…you bring that Bible?" Anna whispered.

Grace wondered if Anna wanted her to read from it. "I'm sorry. It's down the road in the truck. The truck broke down and I had to walk up here, and I was afraid it would be ruined."

"Get our Bible, Ben…" Anna's eyes opened. "Now, 'fore it's too late."

Ben glanced at Grace. She shrugged, and he left the room, returning quickly with a worn Bible that had clearly been in his family for many years.

"Do you want me to read something to you?" he asked.

"Grace…put your hand on that Bible. Ben, you, too. Both of you swear…to me that you will do…what I ask. Swear it…right now…so I can die in peace."

Grace looked at him. Ben said nothing, but his expression said everything. She had never seen real emotion in his eyes until today—nor had she looked for any. But now she saw torment. His wife was dying, and despite what Grace thought of this marriage, clearly he loved her sister. He was about to lose her, and probably the baby she had just brought into the world. There was only one thing he could do to help her before she died.

Grace wondered if God would strike her dead, too, if she put her hand on his Holy Word and told a lie. But which was worse? Telling the truth and watching her sister die in turmoil? Or lying, and hoping that God would understand why she had done it?

"For once…think of somebody but yourself…." Anna's gaze locked with Grace's. "I tried…to teach you what I could… Grace. I know…I didn't do it right. But Mama and Papa…they weren't going…to teach you a thing. It was my duty. And now… this is yours."

I know I didn't do it right. For a moment Grace wondered if this was the apology she had hoped for. She was sure this was as close as her sister would ever come, yet her own sense of relief was out of proportion to the simple words. Still, for a moment nothing mattered except that Anna knew she had made mistakes.

No, something else mattered, too. Anna had tried to teach Grace right from wrong, because in her own rigid and limited way, she'd cared what happened to her. When their parents had given up caring about anything, Anna had still cared enough to try.

"Ben…" Anna turned her head to look at him. "You got to do what I ask."

Grace watched him struggle for the right thing to say. In that agonizing moment, she knew what she had to do. No matter the consequence.

"Give me the Bible, Ben." She held out her hand.

When he didn't immediately hand it over, she took it from him. Then she set it on the bed beside her sister, and she put her hand on top of it.

"Ben, you put your hand here, too," Grace said. "Do it now."

He looked at her to see if she was serious. She wondered if he could tell this was only a motion she was going through to ease her sister's journey into the hereafter. But whether he did or not, after a long hesitation, he put his hand beside hers.

"Anna," Grace said. "Can you hear me?"

Anna gave a slight nod.

"I swear to you I'll marry Ben and make sure your boys are brought up to be healthy, Godfearing and strong. Ben?"

His voice was low. "I swear I'll marry Grace, if that's what you want."

"It...is..."

Grace snatched back her hand, as if the flames of hell resided between the book's tattered leather covers.

"Leave us now," Ben said, his eyes fixed on his wife's face.

Grace didn't know exactly what to do, so she did the one thing that seemed right. She leaned over, and she kissed Anna's cheek. She could not remember ever kissing her sister before.

Anna's eyes opened. "You'd...better...mean what you said."

"Or you'll come back to haunt me?"

"You never...did take...anything serious enough."

Grace thought it was appropriate that her sister's last words to her were an indictment of her character. "God be with you, Anna."

Outside the bedroom, she leaned against the wall and closed her eyes. She didn't open them until she heard the door open and close downstairs, and her parents appeared. Even now, they moved slowly, as if each step was weighted by a lifetime of labor and cares. But no matter how fast they might have moved, it was already too late. By the time they went in to see their oldest daughter for the last time, Ben was sitting on a chair beside Anna's bed, his head in his hands, weeping.

14

According to Hannah, this morning was going to be as exciting as Christmas. Last night she had tossed and turned on the top bunk as she tried to fall asleep. And when Jamie's own eyes finally closed, she could still hear her oldest daughter trying hard to make morning come faster.

Now the moment had arrived and they were on their way to Grace's house, where they were going to choose fabric for their very own quilts. Then, after they had settled on colors and prints, they were going to take Grace to the Shenandoah Community Church Wednesday morning quilting bee, where the girls could play with Bridget, Reese and Bridget's brother Rory while the women quilted. Jamie had warned them that, yes, while it was going to be a wonderful morning, there was a lot entailed in finishing a quilt. This was just the very beginning, and they weren't to expect much progress. It would be enough in the hour before they all drove to the church together if they could just pick out some fabric they liked.

"I am partial to green," Hannah mused out loud. "And purple. Queens wear purple, and sometimes I am a princess."

"Granny Grace loves purple and green together," Jamie said. "She'll help you."

"I like blue!" Alison shouted. "Very, very, very blue! Like the sky. Like stars."

"Stars aren't blue," Hannah said. "What makes you think stars are blue?"

"Blue bright! I see them at night."

"That rhymes," Jamie said, hoping to avoid an argument. "Alison's writing a poem. 'Blue bright, I see them at night.' Let's see what else goes with that."

They worked on the poem for the rest of the trip to Grace's. By the time they arrived they had six stanzas, none of which made any more sense than the first but all of which were lilting on the tongue.

Attending the church quilting bee this morning had been Jamie's idea. Elisa Kinkade had stopped by on Sunday, and when Jamie told her that she was going to make each twin a baby quilt, Elisa had urged Jamie to give the bee a try.

"I wish I'd thought of it before," she'd said, "but I didn't know you were interested in quilting. It's a social occasion, and you need to meet some people." She had carefully refrained from inviting Jamie to attend church services, for which Jamie was grateful. She wasn't sure yet she was ready for *that* step, but the quilting bee would be perfect. And once she'd discovered there were children there who played together while their mothers worked, she had been hooked.

Hooking Grace had been a little harder.

"I've heard Helen Henry is their star member," Grace said. "I think that means I won't be welcomed."

"How can you say that? It's a church group. I'm not much acquainted with religion, but isn't everybody welcome in a church?"

"You're not from here, dear. You have no idea how long memories are. They stretch to the farthest star and back again, and then only as a warm-up. Helen and I were not friends as girls. That means we won't be friends now."

Jamie hadn't been able to restrain her curiosity. "Did she hold your marriage to Ben against you? Was she a friend of your sister's and angry that he married you so quickly after she died?"

"No, it had nothing to do with Ben. Let's just say that Helen never quite saw things that were right under her nose, and she's still never realized it, either. She's one of those women who is sure of everything, even when the facts she's based her opinions on are completely wrong."

"Maybe she's changed. Cissy and her family live with her now, and they seem perfectly happy. Could be this is the right moment to let bygones be bygones."

"My gones went by a long time ago. Life's too short to hold grudges. But not everyone shares that attitude."

Jamie smiled sympathetically, just a shade *too* sympathetically. "Okay, I see your point. We certainly don't want you to feel uncomfortable. If Mrs. Henry makes you feel unwelcome, then I can understand why you would back off and let her win the day."

"I am perfectly aware what you're up to."

"Is it working?"

"We'll give the bee a try."

"We need more friends, and the girls will have a wonderful time."

Now, as she pulled to a stop in front of the old blue farmhouse, Jamie hoped Grace hadn't changed her mind. And when Grace stepped out on the porch to greet them, it was clear she hadn't. She was dressed in one of her more outrageous outfits—bright red capris, a hip-length purple T-shirt with a glittery fruit salad sprinkled across it, what looked like a pound of gold-and-silver charm bracelets and matching earrings that nearly grazed her shoulders. At least her spiky hair wasn't as visible as usual. It was covered in a platinum beret set at a jaunty angle.

"I see you're all ready to quilt," Jamie said.

"If they tar and feather me, they'll have to do it in style."

"I'm sure they'll only use peacock feathers." Jamie kissed Grace's cheek, then stepped back as Grace welcomed the girls. Of course, the first thing they had to do was visit Lucky, who was no longer a tiny, fragile fawn but was sturdy now, sporting a brand-new red collar and acting curious about everything.

"I limit her visitors," Grace said, as the girls stepped into the pen where Lucky seemed perfectly contented. "I really don't want her to feel she's one of us. But the local deer are curious. She'll fit in nicely when the time comes. Of course, if my family develops every inch of this property as they're planning to one day, then there won't be a bit of room for anything on four legs, will there?"

"How's the orchard going?"

"I'm well beyond the age when I can drive a tractor or prune a tree, but I've been able to keep tabs on our workers and make a few improvements. They're good men, but they have no incentive to do their best. They've been left on their own too long and have fallen into sloppy habits. We need a better manager, but so far, I've yet to find the right person. And, of course, my children are unwilling to commit to anybody long-term, which makes it harder."

"I don't think Cash wants to see the land developed."

"None of them do, not really. But they're aware that even if somebody buys the property and says they'll continue growing apples, their word won't be enough. We've all seen shady deals go down that way. Developers are not above using shills to get what they want."

The girls finished their visit and said goodbye to Lucky. Grace promised they could take her for a walk next time, and that was good enough for them.

Inside, Grace started right in, since they wanted to be at the church at ten when the bee started. Elisa was planning to introduce them to the others, so for now they only had an hour at the house, and the girls were ready to go.

Forty-five minutes later, every scrap of Grace's fabric had been examined and a fair amount of it had been sorted into new piles. Alison had, as promised, stuck to blue, although Grace had convinced her that prints that were "mostly blue" were blue enough, so she had a rich assortment of shades and patterns. Hannah had ranged further, immediately falling in love with a bright print of wizard children casting spells. Grace had showed her how to match colors in the print with other fabrics. Her pile might glow in the dark, but Grace promised that when the prints were toned down with a neutral background, the quilt would be lovely.

Jamie had let Grace take the lead with the girls, but she, too, had browsed through fabric looking for ideas. Kendra was coming up for the afternoon to visit the doctor with her, and Jamie and the girls were invited for lunch beforehand. Maybe she could shop for fabric in Front Royal after the appointment, or later on the Internet, so as not to diminish Grace's stash too heavily. The girls were working with scraps, but she needed larger pieces.

"Finding anything you like?" Grace asked.

"I found the Sister's Choice pattern online, like you said I probably would, and even found a layout I could print and color to work out fabric placement."

"Good. I have a computer program that will tell you how much of each piece of fabric you'll need."

"Wow, high tech. The Web site gave some estimates, too."

"You'll be safe enough buying what you think you'll need and some extra just in case. And sometimes, when you run out of fabric, substitutions make the quilt come alive."

Jamie refolded a fabric with what looked like fifties housewives washing dishes. "I think Kendra and Isaac are going to want to know the sex of the babies, although they're arguing over that. But that won't happen for a couple of months, so I want something unisex, something that'll pop and make the babies take notice."

"Now you're thinking like a quilter. What colors were you drawn to?"

"One quilt in red, black and white, I think. Something graphic. Then I saw a quilt in one of the magazines you loaned me made out of bright citrus prints. Lime green, lemon yellow, orange…orange."

"I love both ideas. And not at all alike."

"No, I'm going to use different color strategies, too, to make the patterns look different. The babies are individuals. The quilts should be individual, as well."

"They'll be wonderful. I'm impressed you've done so much thinking about this."

Jamie glanced at the sewing-room clock, a sassy Betty Boop who swiveled her hips as the pendulum swung back and forth. "We'd better go." She finished helping the girls pile their fabric into two cubbyholes that Grace had cleared just for them. While she did, Grace gathered up a small quilt she was working on to take to the bee with her. It was many shades of yellow and gold pieced into fractured sunflowers Picasso would have understood perfectly.

"You're sure you want to do this?" Grace asked. "Aren't you spending enough time with old ladies?"

"Nice try. Elisa's going to be there, and Kate Brogan, and maybe Cissy. There'll be an assortment of ages."

"I hope you'll be willing to throw your body into the fray if Helen Stoneburner Henry goes after me."

"Someday you'll tell me what this is about, won't you?"

"It's quite basic. Helen thinks I broke her brother Tom's heart. And she's never forgiven me."

"You were in love?"

"Helen is convinced he was in love with me and that I led him on."

"And he never got over you?"

"Poor Tom never had time to do much of anything. He died in the war, and so did their older brother, Obed. I think Helen held that against me, too. Ben came home, they didn't, and unfortunately, neither did her husband. I can't remember his name. Ray? No, Fate, which was short for something, I suppose. I didn't know him well, but I do remember he died at Pearl Harbor. She lost so many of the men she loved, and I went on to have a full life with Ben."

Jamie guided both daughters toward the door. "A lot of years have passed, Grace. Just give her a chance."

"Jamie, dear. You're young enough to think giving chances can work a miracle. I'm afraid I'm not so confident anymore. But we'll go and see. Just don't say I didn't warn you."

The women were just finishing their business meeting when Grace and crew walked in. The circle was small, and moving chairs to join them would have been a disruption. They stood in the back and waited until the minutes had been read, but Grace did an assessment to pass the time.

The room was a generous size. Beams across the ceiling indicated that walls had fallen to a sledgehammer and several smaller
rooms had been combined. She could see that the group was
trying to encourage young mothers. There was an area at one
end with shelves stocked with children's books and toys, and a
glass door led outside to a fenced-in play area with some low-
key climbing equipment. The other side of the room was reserved
for serious quilting. A flannel-backed design wall where quilters
could put up blocks or tops for better viewing covered one
smaller wall. A large quilt frame rested to one side of a wall of
deep cabinets. Small quilts, one a large design of a beehive,
brightened the walls.

Grace had been a regular at the large guild in Northern California where she had gone to live after Ben's death. She had
chaired committees and once the annual quilt show that had
brought in so many attendees they'd been forced to hire additional security to protect the quilts from enthusiastic viewers. She
had won prizes in competitions, done trunk shows of her own
creations and taught classes in technique. She'd been blithely
unaware of herself throughout all those events, secure in what
she knew and how she was regarded. But here at home? Where
she had been raised and raised her own brood?

She felt like a stranger.

Once the minutes—surprisingly short—had been read, a
lovely Latina woman stood and came back to greet them. Grace
knew from Jamie's description that this had to be Elisa Kinkade,
wife of the church's pastor. Manning and Sandra attended this
church, and Grace had attended a few times herself, but Sam
Kinkade had come after her years here and married Elisa several
years after settling in. In a community as small as this one, everything the new minister had done since then was fodder for gossip.

"We have first-time visitors," Elisa told the group of twelve women. Grace listened as Elisa warmly introduced Jamie and her daughters, explaining that she was Kendra Taylor's sister and now lived on the Taylors' property in a brand-new cabin.

Then she smiled at Grace. "And some of you already know Grace Cashel, I'm sure. She lived here for many years, well before I did. She's a long-time quilter, and I've heard she's well-known on the West Coast for her beautiful art quilts. I hope she'll bring some to show us. I can't wait to see them."

Grace's gaze flicked to Helen Henry, who had turned in her chair right away to see what the fuss was all about. Helen had aged in the years Grace had been away—just as Grace herself had—but now she was less relentlessly dowdy. Her thin white hair was nicely cut to give it a little bulk, and she appeared to have lost enough weight to make a difference in her health. She wore a pink-and-gray knit jogging suit that didn't look as if it had come straight from a resale shop and glasses set in gold frames that actually suited her square face.

As she watched, Helen's eyes narrowed, then she turned to face front again. So much for bygones.

Jamie and Elisa took the girls out to the play yard to meet their friends, and Grace pulled a chair into a space two women made for her.

She nodded and chatted as they welcomed her. The woman on her right had retired to Toms Brook from Washington, D.C., and the woman to her left, Kate Brogan, had grown up here, moved away, then come back to raise her family away from city life. Two of the children outside belonged to her.

"It's funny," Grace told her, "that what I took for granted and never really appreciated when I was young is worth searching for now."

"Did you want a different life when you were growing up here?" Kate asked.

"Oh, I wanted to be anywhere but here."

"You finally got your wish, didn't you?" Helen was three chairs down, but that didn't stop her from responding. "Lit out of here like you'd been let out of a cage." She didn't add "once that husband of yours died," but she might as well have.

"How have you been, Helen?" Grace smiled sweetly. "Still living in the old Stoneburner place?" She restrained herself from asking if Helen had been any farther away than Mauertown— just a few miles down the road—in all the years since they'd last seen each other.

"Who, me? I'm not like some folks. I know a good thing when it's right in front of my nose."

"Of course, if it's the only thing in front of your nose, it's hard to say whether it's good or not, isn't it?"

If Kate Brogan picked up on the tension, she didn't let on. "So you went off to see the world a little." She directed this to Grace. "How did you like California?"

"It's breathtaking. Amazing. I had no idea there could be so much to do in one place."

"I'm surprised you're not still back there doing it," Helen said.

"It was time to come home. I'm needed here."

Helen looked as if she had a lot of responses she was sifting through. Grace could almost hear them. *Not by us, you're not* was undoubtedly at the head of a long list.

A middle-aged woman with tightly curled gray hair and a softly padded body stood and introduced herself to the newcomers as Cathy Adams, the bee chairman.

"We have several projects to work on this morning," she said. "Some of us are making baby quilts for the staff at La Casa to give to the new mothers who use the center. We have our bear's paw quilt in the frame for the fall bazaar. We pieced it as a group, but Helen Henry did the wonderful appliquéd bear scenes on the border. We expect this one to make a lot of money, so we're asking only our experienced hand quilters to finish working on it. You know who you are, and I won't be with you."

A pleasant ripple, not quite a giggle, went around the circle.

"And I know some of you brought your own projects to work on, so feel free to do whatever you want," Cathy continued. "First, though, we'll have show-and-tell. We'll start over here with Dovey and go around the circle. If you brought something to show, that's fine. If you have a project you're in the midst of, hold that up and tell us what it is. And don't be shy.... Not that anybody here ever has been."

This time the ripple was louder.

Jamie came in from the play yard with Elisa, and before the door closed again, Grace heard children laughing. She smiled at the sound.

Jamie and Elisa settled on the other side, and show-and-tell began. Not everyone produced something to share, but by the time it was Grace's turn the group had been treated to a beginner's first log cabin in patriotic shades of red, white and blue; a sweatshirt turned jacket covered with ragged-edged flannel patches; and a baby quilt with appliquéd figures of the major characters from Peter Rabbit. Everyone clapped politely, but the baby quilt got an extra couple of seconds, since it was clearly destined to become an heirloom.

Grace debated, but in the end pride won the day. She lifted out her sunflower quilt and unfolded it to hold it in front of her. "My daughter always loved the sunflower garden at our orchard. We never had the variety that's available today, but we grew every kind we could. So this wall hanging is meant for her bedroom."

"Wow, that's awesome," one of the younger women said.

"Where are the sunflowers?" Helen asked.

"Try to imagine a bouquet. But you're close-up, so you can't necessarily see the whole thing. You see a petal here, a piece of a leaf there." Grace pointed to each. "The larger picture is the sum of the parts. But the smaller picture, this quilt, is a different sort of look at the parts. A close-up. You can see the drops of dew, the tiniest ladybug."

"Me, I expect a sunflower to look like a sunflower," Helen said. "But I guess that's just an old woman's fancy."

"I suppose you need imagination to be able to put this together in your mind," Grace said, not looking at her nemesis to see how that response affected her. "But to me, that's what's left out of so many traditional quilts. They're predictable. We know what they are and what we're supposed to think about them. With an art quilt, the viewer has to do some of the work that the quilter sets up for her. So when anybody looks at this quilt, they'll have to think about it, examine it closely. They'll find little surprises, which will make that worth their while." She smiled. "Or we quilt makers hope it will."

"I'd like to learn to think about quilts that way," Kate said. "Can you teach people to see differently?"

"You can go a long way if they're willing." Grace folded the quilt and set it on her lap.

Kate pulled out a nursery-rhyme block she was embroidering in red embroidery floss and held it up. Show-and-tell continued around the circle and stopped at Helen.

"Well, I have one of those boring traditional quilts to show you all. I guess you don't need much imagination, 'cause I made sure you could tell what it is." She unfolded what looked to be a twin-size quilt. "Little Reese Claiborne is awful fond of snakes, which concerns me no end, just the way you'd expect. Anyway, I decided to make her a snake-in-the-hollow quilt. And that girl likes bright colors, so that's what she's getting."

Jewel-toned snakes slithered across a pale green background. The quilt was made of fan blocks with a fan in opposing corners of each block. When set together, the fans did indeed look like snakes side-winding their way across the quilt. There was nothing imaginative about the pattern. Grace remembered seeing it on an uncle's bed as a child, although certainly not with these animated fabrics. But Helen's placement of colors and her use of many child-pleasing prints set this quilt apart. Any child worth her salt would adore it.

As one voice everybody oohed. Helen looked pleased.

"I'll quilt bugs in the background," she said, as she folded it up. "Reese likes bugs, too. She makes houses for daddy longlegs. Condos, more likely, since she piles them up, one top of another. Never saw a child so attracted to things she shouldn't be."

"She sounds like a child who can see things the rest of us can't," Grace said. "If all of us could go back to being children for just one day, just think of what we could bring back to our quilting."

"Dirt, scabby knees, bubblegum." Helen shook her head. "Me, I'll stay a grown-up and see the world just the way it is."

"Or isn't," Grace said, fully aware she was stoking this blaze but suddenly powerless not to. "And that, of course, is always the problem, isn't it?"

The circle continued, but the two women's eyes met. If Grace hadn't known better, she would have thought war had just been declared in Shenandoah County. And it looked to her as if Sheridan's historic march through the Valley, burning everything that might feed the Confederacy, was going to look like a minor skirmish when she and Helen were finished.

★ ★ ★

Attending the SCC Bee had been a great way for Jamie to spend her morning. She liked the women, both old and young. The quilts and all the different techniques had whetted her interest. She knew she would never have time to turn out the abundance of quilts that Helen, Grace and some of the others had made in their lifetimes. But she could see herself working on a quilt in the quiet evenings after the girls had gone to sleep. She could imagine herself listening to music as she stitched, or watching *Mystery* on PBS as the needle rocked in and out of blocks she had made. She had taken drawing classes at the university, but she had always wanted to try her hand at crafts. And now she had the opportunity. She would be back.

"So what did you think of it, dear?" Grace asked. She was waiting for Cash to pick her up. Jamie and the girls were heading to Front Royal for a doctor's appointment, and Jamie was waiting with her while the girls finished a game in the play yard.

"I think you and Helen Henry probably aren't going to indulge in any senior citizen sleepovers." She punched Grace lightly on the arm. "I hope she didn't scare you off."

"On the contrary, I like the others quite a lot. Several of them asked me to do a program on art quilts sometime in the upcoming months. We can safely guess that Helen won't be attending."

"All this because you weren't in love with her brother?"

"Feelings fester over time. I wouldn't be too surprised if she blamed me for Tom enlisting so early in the war. She intimated as much once, although she never said so outright."

"Loss can be a profound shaper of personality."

"It has shaped many a man and woman." Grace nodded toward the pickup that was pulling into the church lot. "Although *that* man never speaks of it."

Cash pulled up and opened his door, greeted both women, then helped his grandmother around the truck and into the passenger seat. Jamie could hear country music on the radio, something mellow and sad. Somebody had been done wrong and wasn't afraid to tell the world their side of the story.

She turned to go back inside, but a hand gripped her shoulder, and she reversed to face Cash again.

"It's awfully hot out here," she warned. "Grace is going to roast."

"The cab's nice and cool, sweetcakes. I've had the air conditioner blowing full tilt all the way here."

"So how are you?"

"Looking for a date for a dinner dance. Are you interested?"

She was surprised, and for a moment she didn't know what to say. "Have you taken a good look at me?"

He stepped away, his hand still on her shoulder, and looked her up and down. "Always a pleasure."

"I'm pregnant with twins. I've already gained nine pounds. I'm holding these pants together with a safety pin. When is this dance?"

"Labor Day. You have a couple of weeks to get used to the idea of being seen in public with me."

"Do you know what I'll look like in a couple of weeks?"

"No, but I can't wait to find out."

"Well, I won't be wearing anything tight and slinky."

"I'll do my part for your sister and brother-in-law and suck it up like a man."

She laughed. "What kind of dinner dance? Do we have to impress anybody?"

"It's the local homebuilders' association. An annual event at a nearby lodge. The food's good. They always hire a band. It's a rowdy bunch. There might be a bunny hop if they're really feeling wild."

She debated, but only for show. "I'd like to come. Thanks for inviting me."

"I'll ask Granny Grace if she'll take the girls for the night, so you don't have to worry about them."

He had thought of everything. She was impressed. "Just let me know the details."

"Wear something sparkly. That's about it. Now I'd better rescue Granny Grace. She's turning the music up. That's a signal she's ready to boogie." He rubbed his thumb across her cheek, gently and so quickly that for a moment she wasn't sure he had. Then he was gone.

"Sparkly." At the rate her belly was expanding, Jamie knew she wouldn't look like Cinderella at the ball, she would look like Cinderella's pumpkin.

"I need a fairy godmother, too." Unfortunately not even magic could turn her into a slender, sexy young woman, not until the babies had been born. Cash knew it, and he had still invited her.

Jamie was smiling when she went back into the church to get her daughters.

15

Hours later, Jamie leaned back against the passenger seat of Kendra's car and closed her eyes. "Pregnancy used to be simple. You slept with the guy in the next cave, you threw up a few times so you knew something was going on, you got fat, you had a baby and then to feed it you just unbuttoned your blouse—"

"When it was that simple, nobody had to worry about buttons." Kendra pulled out into Front Royal traffic. "If they wore clothes at all, they were made from dinosaur skins and were held together by mammoth teeth."

"Dinosaurs and people never walked the earth at the same time."

"Old moldy dinosaur skins, then. And don't be so literal, college girl. I was just making a point."

"I feel like I'm in some high-tech drama."

"Forget it. Let's go have some fun."

Jamie was surprised that for once *she* was the worried sister. After the quilting bee she had met Isaac and Kendra for lunch;

then, at the doctor's office, they had listened to baby heartbeats, enjoyed reassurances that everything seemed fine, then sat through a lecture about the hardships of providing trustworthy screening for chromosomal abnormalities in twin pregnancies. And apparently surrogate pregnancies were the least fun of all.

"You don't want to talk about this?" Jamie asked.

"My head's spinning. Nuchal translucency, trisomy 21, maternal serum biochemistry? I need a snack. You must be starving."

"Where are you taking me?"

"Well, nowhere close by, unfortunately. Did you get enough lunch to keep you going?"

"If I start to eat the upholstery, pull over to the side of the road." Lunch seemed like something Jamie had indulged in during a different century.

"There are crackers in the glove compartment to help you resist."

Jamie peered behind her and just caught a glimpse of Isaac shepherding her daughters into her minivan. "Are you sure Isaac's up to babysitting the girls until we get back to Toms Brook?"

"It'll be good for him. You know he's nuts about them, but he's a novice at child care. Think of it as a practice session."

"Well, that kind of parenting—the kind where they talk you to death—is down the road a piece for you two, but the girls will soften him up. Are you preparing for the stress of having two babies at once?"

"How do you prepare for that?"

"I have no idea. I was so young when I had Hannah, I didn't know enough to prepare. When I had Alison, I pretty well knew what I was getting myself into, but I was already so busy with Hannah I didn't have much time to think."

"I'm just taking it one step at a time. Close your eyes and take a nap. You probably need one."

Jamie did as she was told, fully expecting to open them again in a minute. The next thing she knew she was waking by stages as Kendra's car slowed to a halt. She looked around and saw the unmistakable signs of a mall parking lot. No matter what developers did, a mall looked like a mall anywhere in America.

"Where are we? Tucson? Providence?"

"Winchester. You were snoring before your eyes closed." Kendra unhooked her seat belt. "Are you getting enough sleep?"

"I am."

"I'm sorry. I'm not trying to pry, and I'd be asking even if this was a regular old pregnancy. I just wondered if you might need some help with the girls, maybe somebody to come in and take them in the afternoons once in a while so you can nap."

"Alison and I manage to steal a little nap most days. We're okay."

"It's a big assault on a slender body."

"Only going to get bigger." Jamie sat up and unhooked her own seat belt. "Why are we here?"

"Your jeans."

Jamie looked down. Okay, so the outline of the safety pin at her waist was visible through her oversize T-shirt, and the jeans— the largest she owned—were more or less ready for the rag bag.

"They're clean. And I have another pair at home I can still wear, but I need to buy larger pins."

"There's a Belk here, and a maternity store. They're bound to have some nice clothes. I'm assuming you don't have any left from Alison?"

"When I was pregnant with Alison, I was shopping at Goodwill, and by the time I gave birth, Goodwill wouldn't have taken any of my clothes back for another round." She waited for Kendra to make the point that Jamie hadn't needed to live that way, that the trustees of their father's estate would have gladly helped her. But Kendra just arched a brow, and looked her up and down.

"This time you don't have to look like the Little Match Girl, kiddo. Let's go do some serious shopping."

Jamie felt a warm glow that had nothing to do with two babies increasing her blood volume or August's sunshine. "We haven't shopped for clothes together since I was a teenager."

"I don't think we got much shopping done then. I was too busy trying to convince you not to pierce body parts or cover yourself with tattoos."

"I have a great tattoo. Want to see?"

"The orchid at the base of your spine? Yep, seen it. Every time your shirt rides up or your pants ride down."

"So what do you think?"

"I kind of like it." Kendra opened her door and got out.

Jamie was waiting by the time she came around. "You're kidding? You like my tattoo?"

"I need one, don't you think?"

"How about a heart with Double Trouble inscribed inside?"

"Yikes."

They wove their way through a sea of cars and into the cool pleasures of air-conditioning.

"I've been reading about twin pregnancies," Kendra said. "And you're going to get as big as a house."

Jamie sidestepped a mother with two little boys and a shopping bag on each arm. "Well, that's something to look forward to. I've already had the nausea, my breasts are lumpy and swollen and I'm spending way too much time on the john. Now you tell me I'm going to look like a blimp."

"Some of the bulletin boards recommend that you just buy up a size or two to start with, until you really need maternity clothes."

"We could do that, but they'll be too large in the thighs and hips."

"Let's just do a blitz and try on everything in the mall. What do you need for starters?"

"Food. Let's find the food court."

"Good, because I could use a cup of coffee."

"That's not nice. You should be drinking apple juice with me, out of sympathy. You should gain weight."

"I know this sounds impossible, but I envy every change you're going through."

Jamie was pierced by regret. "Oh, Ken, I'm sorry."

"And I hate that you're suffering."

Jamie rested her hand on Kendra's forearm. "I'm not suffering. Pregnancy can be uncomfortable, and sometimes it's hang-your-head-over-the-toilet-bowl grim, but it's not suffering. I want to do this. I'm ecstatic you agreed to let me."

"You knew I would, didn't you?"

"No such thing."

"We thought there were no solutions. Then along you came, with the only one we could both live with. How could we say no?"

"By pursing your lips, touching your tongue to your top front teeth, expelling air. I was offering you an option. But it's been your show right from the top."

Kendra faced her. People were streaming by. Overhead, somebody was crooning a song Jamie recognized from her unfortunate childhood.

"If it's my show, then do I get to decide whether you'll have the nucal translucency testing?"

For a moment Jamie couldn't put this together. Nucal translucency testing was one of the options the doctor had mentioned. "What are you talking about? Of course it's your decision. What do I have to do with it?"

"You're carrying the babies."

"They're *your* babies."

"And what if we do the testing, as uncertain as it is, and find out we need amniocentesis? Then we do that and find out the babies—or one of them—have Down's and I want you to have an abortion?"

Jamie just stared at her. "I never thought about abortion," she said at last.

"Me, either."

Kendra started toward the food court, and Jamie strode to keep up with her.

"So that's what you've been thinking about," she said. "While I was napping. That's what you didn't want to talk about."

"Did you ever think about this when you offered to be our surrogate? Who makes these awful decisions? The egg-and-sperm duo, or the woman who's nurturing the babies inside her? Maybe if we were doing this through an agency, that would have been in the paperwork. But this is complicated. This is us. This is family."

Jamie was silent until they were seated. Kendra had a cup of coffee in front of her, and Jamie had a hot pretzel and a bottle of cold water.

"Okay, I see what's going on here. This isn't about Down's or abortion," Jamie said. "It's about whose babies these are, isn't it?"

"Not so simple. It's also about the woman who's carrying them. Could you have an abortion?"

Jamie unscrewed the top of her water and poured it into a paper cup filled with ice. The familiar movements gave her time to think.

"Could you ask me to?" she said.

"I don't know."

"That was going to be my answer." She took a sip, then another. "For the record, I believe in a woman's right to choose.

But when I was pregnant with both girls, I opted not to do any screening for birth defects. The tests are too inconclusive, and I was pretty sure if I got bad news it would simply ruin the pregnancy but not change what I did about it."

"I can understand that."

"And you have that option. The tests under these circumstances are even less certain."

"The biggest problem? We don't know a thing about Isaac's father." Kendra looked up from her coffee. "We don't know who he is or was, if he had serious health problems, nothing."

"Do you need a wee reminder, Ken? You know a lot about our side of the family, and you might be better off not knowing it."

"Riva..."

"She's bipolar. It can run in families."

"I know. I know."

"We don't know if she's an anomaly or if there's an entire wing of the Delacroix family who buy sixty pairs of the same shoes in one shopping blitz and have nightly conversations with saints who even the best Catholics can't identify."

"Didn't that worry you when you had your girls? Weren't you afraid they might turn out like our mother?"

"Didn't that worry you when you were raising *me?*"

Kendra put down her coffee cup. "Weren't we talking about something else? How did we get here?"

"One thing led to another. But that *was* your big concern, wasn't it? That I was turning out like Riva. That the drugs, sex and rock and roll were all symptomatic."

Kendra was quiet for a long time. She finally shrugged. "I was just barely an adult. What did I know? We had a mother with serious problems. You were desperately unhappy, and nothing I did made it better. You seemed happiest when you were out whooping it up."

"And of course you were concerned and tried too hard to rein me in. I was lucky to have you. But my problems didn't sift down through the family genetics. They were all about our crazy background, and one older sister couldn't save me completely from the impact."

When Kendra didn't answer, Jamie pointed at herself. "But look at me now, Ken. I am who I am because, despite those little blips called our mother and father, I came through. And I'm sure it's because in our background somewhere there were good, strong people who were able to overcome adversity and move forward. Those are the people we have to remember and count on to pass on their genes to our kids. Every family has something in their background to worry about. If you knew Isaac's background, that's what you'd discover. Some things to worry about, some things you hope get passed on. Look at *him*. He's a great guy who got through his own difficult childhood because he's strong. Look at you. Taking care of me when you needed to be taken care of yourself. These are great genes you're sending down through the centuries."

"The tests we're talking about don't turn up any of that, you know."

"These are your babies, Ken. You and Isaac have to make your decision without thinking about me. Then I'll have to decide if I can do whatever you ask."

Kendra lifted her eyes. "You know, for somebody who was a huge pain in my neck all those years, you've more or less turned out well."

Jamie laughed. She saw that her sister's eyes were moist. "Now to the important stuff. Can we buy something besides jeans?"

"This is my treat. You can buy the whole darned mall."

"I probably could afford it. That's weird, isn't it? So Paris Hilton. Anyway..." Jamie leaned forward. "I have a date over Labor Day. And I need a dress."

"Cash."

"That was my line. I hate to be scooped. Yes, Cash."

"A maternity dress?"

"Maybe not that drastic yet, but we can look. Something that doesn't show the expanded waistline and the bump."

"Bump?"

Jamie grasped Kendra's hand and guided it to her belly. "*Your* bump."

Kendra nodded, message clearly received. "Black. With your hair, definitely black."

Jamie was glad they were done with the hard part. "Cash said sparkly."

"Black with a discreet number of rhinestones or sequins. Or maybe some really wonderful costume jewelry. I have some of Riva's that she tossed out the window on a bad day."

"How about something cut way down in back so my tattoo shows?"

"How about something that won't get us banned from the Valley?"

"I probably should have ordered two pretzels, one for each twin." Jamie took a big bite, then another, before she stood. "While we're at it, I'm thinking some new underwear might be appropriate."

"Should I be in on that?"

"Nothing to worry about. Less Victoria's Secret, more Granny's red flannel drawers. Something loose at the waist and nonbinding."

"I'm assuming this is not for Cash's consumption."

Jamie finished the last bite of pretzel. "You always were too nosy about my personal life."

"Well, I've got spies this time." Kendra stood and tapped Jamie's belly. "Just remember. My bump, my spies."

"I'll bribe the little darlings into silence with a passion-fruit smoothie. Can we stop for one on the way out?"

"It's going to be a long pregnancy, isn't it?"

"You don't know the half of it, Sis. We're both going to be very glad the day it's over."

16

With the unshakable determination of a flock of geese heading south, the remainder of the summer flew by. Between registering the girls for school and preschool, buying supplies and school clothes, and making sure all their paperwork, immunizations and checkups were in order, the last few weeks passed quickly. Those hours when the summer had stretched endlessly had transformed into busy days filled with purpose, new friends and pleasurable visits to Cashel Orchard to see Lucky and Granny Grace.

The word was out, too, about the pregnancy, since at nearly fifteen weeks Jamie was displaying the evidence for all to see. She wasn't sure how the details had become known. She suspected Elisa Kinkade had, in her gentle, reasoned way, explained the situation to key members of the Shenandoah Community Church, and they had passed the word.

Although some people purposely ignored the pregnancy, as if it were a missing nose or ear at which they were afraid to be caught staring, others found ways of showing quiet support. Helen Henry, who was still waging an underground war with Grace, arrived with fresh eggs and half a bushel of produce from the vegetable garden she kept with the help of Cissy Claiborne. Cissy added a dozen of the best biscuits Jamie had ever eaten and a chocolate meringue pie. The bee had begun work on a large crazy quilt made from different types of fabrics, so that the babies could lie on the floor and investigate the bright colors and varied textures with their tiny fingers.

Somehow, though, in all the flurry of preparation, Jamie had hardly seen Cash for more than a word or two. The Rosslyn and Rosslyn crew was working hard on the house, and more than a few times she and the girls had spent their days elsewhere to avoid the relentless beeping of heavy machinery and the whine of stone saws. When they were at home, Cash came and went quickly, since this wasn't the company's only project. Once he'd stopped by the cabin for a cup of coffee, but had been forced to drink it on her front porch when a subcontractor arrived to hash out the eventual placement of fixtures in a guest bathroom.

On the Friday morning before Labor Day, Jamie pulled out the dress she and Kendra had bought for the home builders' association dance that night. Unfortunately, they had hit the stores between the summer clearance sales and the arrival of new fall merchandise. The fall dresses had seemed stodgy and plain, roomier than she needed and not dressy enough. The summer dresses had been largely picked over. She'd settled on a taupe jersey A-line with a nice drape to it, hoping that between her jewelry and scarves and Kendra's, she could find something that would vault it from ordinary to wonderful. Now, staring at the dress, she knew she had her work cut out for her. So far, Kendra hadn't brought her any appropriate jewelry, and her own was fairly tame.

Cash had said sparkly. With the distance of a few weeks she could see that she should have kept searching, perhaps taking a day in Northern Virginia at one of the larger malls. This dress would be fine if she ever went to church. It would be fine for dinner out. It was not and never would be fine for a dance.

Hannah and Alison were sitting on the bed watching with interest. "What color is that dress?" Hannah asked. "What do you call it?"

Hannah and Alison were both fascinated by color now. Grace was working with them on their quilts, helping them arrange the blocks they had cut into pleasing arrangements. It was "art camp" Grace style, and the girls had learned a lot— and quickly.

"Taupe," Jamie said. "Which is what you call something that's not gray or brown or beige. It's a word that covers a lot of territory."

"It's Dirty Day color," Alison said. "Like my pants on Dirty Day."

"Out of the mouths of babes." Jamie held the dress at arm's length and screwed up her face. Alison's opinion was too close to the truth.

She slid the dress back into the wardrobe, and one at a time lifted out the three other dresses hanging there. One might serve if she wasn't pregnant, but she was fairly sure she could no longer zip it. The other two were simple cotton sundresses. She took out the taupe jersey again. She was stuck with it.

"I have a pretty lace scarf thingie," she said. "And some good pearls. I'll pretend I'm Grace Kelly."

"Who's Grace Kelly?"

"She was a princess and a movie star. Very classy lady." The problem was that tonight Jamie wanted to look like Penelope Cruz or Scarlett Johansson. Not just classy, but daring, and definitely glamorous.

The cabin door opened, and a voice drifted upstairs. "Anybody home?"

The girls squealed and ran down the steps. Jamie went to the railing and peeked down at her sister.

"What are you doing here?"

"I'm supposed to pick out kitchen cabinets, and I brought you something."

Jamie hoped that Kendra had finally located Riva's discarded rhinestones, and that they would work a miracle.

She joined the crew downstairs and gave her sister a hug. Kendra rested her hand on Jamie's belly. "Definitely bigger."

"When I was this far along with Hannah, nobody knew it."

"How are you feeling?"

"Like I'm going to set a world's record for weight gain if I'm not careful. Morning sickness disappeared, and I can't seem to get enough to eat."

Kendra held up a shopping bag. "I brought you Lebanese deli food from our local market and fresh croissants from my favorite bakery."

Jamie's mouth watered. Middle Eastern food was a weakness of hers, one of those rare weaknesses that were actually good for her. And Kendra knew she would do almost anything legal for fresh croissants.

"If men only realized the real way to a woman's heart. Yum! What's in the other bag?"

"A couple of things I found at Nordstrom. You don't have to wear either of them. I can take them back. But just in case you're having regrets about that dress…"

Jamie closed her eyes. "Please, let it be true."

When she opened them, Kendra looked pleased. "I thought you might. I went scrounging through old boxes looking for Riva's rhinestones or something to pep it up, and it finally hit me that it's the dress that's the problem. So I did a little power shopping."

Jamie was already reaching for the bag. "Whatever you have there, I'll wear it. I'll wear them both, one on top of the other."

Kendra snatched back the bag. "Actually, there are a couple more things in here for later. Do you know how cute maternity clothes are these days?"

Jamie felt a pang. She knew Kendra had shopped for her because she really wanted Jamie to feel pretty on what was the closest thing to a date she'd had in her months in Virginia. But she also imagined that Kendra had felt some genuine conflict looking through the racks of pretty dresses. Kendra should be the one wearing maternity clothes, not Jamie. And no matter how grateful she was that Jamie was carrying her children, no matter how excited she was that soon she would be a mother, Kendra had to feel sad that the clothes were never going to belong to her.

"Thanks, sis," Jamie said, putting her hand over Kendra's. "Your taste is wonderful. I know I'll love whatever you got me."

"Then let's have a fashion show. What do you say, girls? Do you want to see your mommy all dressed up?"

Half an hour later Jamie redonned the first new dress she'd tried on for her fashion consultants and studied herself again in the full-length mirror in the girls' room. "This is the one. This is definitely the one I'm going to wear tonight."

Kendra gave a wolf whistle. "Hard decision, since both the dressy dresses look great on you. Shall I take the other one back?"

"Over my dead body. I'll find a use for it or die trying." Jamie admired herself in the mirror one last time. This dress was black, with a velvet bodice, narrow rhinestone-studded straps and a long taffeta skirt. It tied in the front, so it would expand as she did, and although the "bump" was visible for anyone paying attention, she still looked feminine and sexy.

Decision made, the girls wandered off to play on the porch. Kendra got up and retied the bow at the waist, fussing with it as she spoke.

"I do have Riva's jewelry with me, but I'm thinking nothing around your neck. The line is so pretty as is, and you have just the right tan for it. But dangly earrings. I brought some for you to choose from. And maybe one of her more discreet pins at the heart of this bow. You can try some and see."

"I'll wear my hair up." Jamie paused. "I was just going to let it hang. I should have made an appointment somewhere."

"Beat you to it. I made one for you in Woodstock—for a manicure and pedicure, too." Kendra checked her watch. "In one hour. Will that work? I'll stay with the girls."

Jamie hugged her. Besides the black dress, Kendra had bought a short red cocktail dress with a discreet lacy overlay that would have made a hit tonight, too. And with them were three tops, a far more sedate green wrap dress for everyday and a pair of corduroy jeans for the chilly weather to come. Jamie liked them all.

"You're awfully good to me," she said.

"I want you to have fun. Now, do you need me to stay and take care of the girls tonight, too?"

"Grace is going to keep them at her house. I'll go home with Cash afterward and spend the night, too." She realized how that sounded. "With Grace and the girls."

Kendra smiled. "I knew what you meant. That'll work fine. I'm on a pretty tight deadline after the weekend. But anytime you need me to stay, just let me know." She paused, then smiled more broadly. "Maybe this will turn into a habit?"

Jamie pretended to misunderstand. "I don't think the home builders' association has that many dances."

"You know what I mean. Going out with Cash."

"I'll settle for just seeing him a little more often. He's one busy guy." Jamie glanced at Kendra to make sure she understood. "I'm not in this for keeps, you know. It's nice to have a guy around to flirt with and talk to. It does get a little lonely here from time to time."

"You're not looking for someone to be serious about?"

"Would it matter? Look at me. Single mother of two active girls, pregnant with two more that aren't my own. A long, time-consuming internship ahead of me. A terrible track record with men. A life history that points out serious flaws in my reasoning. What kind of bargain would I be?"

"Come on, you're intelligent, talented, resourceful, cued in to your own shortcomings, a wonderful mother, beautiful and rich. Sounds like a great package to me."

Jamie enjoyed her sister's praise, but she was caught short by that final adjective. "I wonder if Cash knows I'm rich."

"He knows Isaac and I can do almost anything we want with the new house. I've never discussed the details."

"You know, I don't think that would make one bit of difference to him."

"I'd say that's a mark in his favor. And I hope you're right. I'm not sure what Cash is about, but he doesn't seem to be about living off anybody else."

"Do you think I should tell him?"

"Why? You said yourself you're not in this for keeps."

Jamie wasn't sure, but she thought she heard the faintest taunt in her sister's voice. "Well, I guess if we start trading portfolio advice, I'll mention it."

"Or maybe just trading the stories of your lives."

Cash had already said a lot about his own past. Maybe it was time to come clean and tell him everything about herself. Maybe it would be good practice for the future.

Or maybe it was simply time to stop pretending that what he thought didn't really matter.

Cash brought Jamie orchids. One was an old-fashioned pale lavender wrist corsage. According to the tag, the other one, with its bright pink bloom, was a Phalaenopsis orchid in a wicker basket to set outside on the porch or on the window ledge behind the sink.

"They're not as hard to grow as you think," he said when she didn't respond immediately. "Just water it when it gets dry, add a little orchid fertilizer to the water and it'll bloom every year."

"It's not that. I'll take great care of it." She looked up. "It's just that I'm a big orchid fan. How did you know?"

"You've got the cutest orchid in the world at the base of your spine. More or less an advertisement, wouldn't you say?"

She wasn't given to blushing, but she felt her cheeks grow warm. "And what are you doing looking at the base of my spine?"

"Where else would a man look when your shirt rides up? Not that it has lately. That's the thing about maternity clothes."

"This is a maternity dress. How bad is it?" She spread her arms wide.

"You look like an angel. Well, maybe not an angel, exactly." He grinned. "You look beautiful."

"And you don't look bad yourself. Dress clothes suit you." The dark jacket made his hair seem even darker, and the blue in the tie brought out the unusual hue of his eyes.

Grace came out to the porch. Jamie had brought the girls up

to the farmhouse in the late afternoon, then changed into her dress and done her makeup in the guest room where she would sleep tonight. Grace and the girls had already told her she looked gorgeous, but it was doubly nice to hear it from Cash.

"It's cooled off so much today, I'm afraid you're going to be cold later," Grace told Jamie. "Would you like this?"

Jamie took the loosely knit shawl of black-and-silver yarn with just an occasional red nub. "It's lovely. I brought a sweater, but this is much nicer. You're sure?"

"There are half a dozen more where that came from. They go fast. I knit when I'm not quilting. More portable. Sandra's begged me to quit giving her scarves and socks."

Jamie rested her cheek against the soft wool. "Thanks. I'll enjoy it tonight."

"It's yours to keep, dear. It suits you perfectly."

Jamie gave her a hug as another thank-you.

"If we're all done with the oohs and ahs, I think we'd better scoot," Cash said.

"Shall I say goodbye to the girls again?" Jamie asked Grace.

"It would require a trip upstairs to my sewing room. I'd advise against it. When I left, they were fully occupied sorting darks and lights with a bit of friendly disagreement."

"Thanks for taking them. They've been so excited all day."

Grace kissed her cheek, then wiped off the lipstick smear. "Lucky and I agree it's our pleasure."

Cash escorted her to his car, a black Honda sedan. "It's my mama's. She lets me borrow the car keys if I'm a good boy."

"I like your pickup just fine."

He opened the door. "Mama says she'll know I've grown up for good when I buy a real car. But there's no point I can see in that. The pickup gets me wherever I have to go and then some."

Once she slid inside, she could tell the car didn't belong to Cash. The upholstery was clean enough to do surgery on. There were no tools, no empty soft-drink cans or fast-food wrappers. Plus, the car had a navigation system. She knew Cash well enough to be sure he might spring for mud tires or heavy-duty woofers and tweeters, but he would no more admit to needing a navigator than a map.

"Your mother's a very tidy person," she said when he got in.

"Not as much as you think. I cleaned out the car just for you."

"I'm impressed."

He started the engine and pulled out to the drive. "Didn't all your boyfriends clean out their mamas' cars?"

"That sounds like a normal adolescence, and mine was anything but. My boyfriends were more likely to clean out their mamas' purses—even bank accounts, if they could get to them."

He glanced at her. "Lived on the wild side, did you?"

She sidestepped that for a moment, although Kendra's suggestion that she tell Cash about herself was on her mind. "You must have had some pretty wild times yourself."

"More so in Kentucky. I spent the first couple of years doing the party circuit. Not the mint-julep circuit, mind you. The *down and dirty, drink yourself into oblivion with anybody who comes along* circuit."

"I can understand that."

"From everything you've slipped into our conversations, I think you probably can."

"You had a good reason. Better than mine." She decided to take the plunge, or at least dip her toes into the confessional stream. "I was just miserably unhappy and immature. I didn't like the only person who had ever loved me, and I made sure she knew it. I made her life a living nightmare, then I disappeared and left my future to her imagination."

"You're talking about Kendra?"

"The one and only. We moved out of the family home when I was just eleven. Our father was dead. Our mother showed up occasionally. Basically Riva—my mother—spent her good days charming every available man with a seven-figure-or-better income. She spent her bad days with us or in recovery of one sort or another. Kendra decided to break that cycle, so she went off to college at Northwestern with me in tow. Only I didn't want a different life. I wanted the only one I'd ever known, as crazy as it was."

Jamie knew how to gauge whether a man was interested in what she had to say. Had Cash looked uncomfortable or bored, she would have stopped there. Probably for good. Because she didn't owe anybody the story of her past. But Cash was neither. He was listening carefully, and he reached over and lightly covered her hand.

"Seems to me you're making up for that now," he asked. "That's at least some of what this pregnancy is about, right?"

"I owe her more than I can ever give her. She tried her darnedest to give me a real childhood and adolescence. But she was my sister, not my mother."

"And you resented her for that?"

"I was a kid."

"What happened after you left?"

"I learned the hard way how much Kendra loved me and exactly what she'd tried to save me from."

"Bad times."

"I didn't just walk on the wild side. I wallowed in the gutter. Then I got arrested. I was guilty, by the way. I was caught with a guy who stole a car, and I didn't do a thing to try to stop him. I was too high to care. But we got caught, and the court appointed me an attorney. His name was Larry Clousell."

"Hannah's father?" He sounded surprised.

"Larry's firm required pro bono work, so he was an associate doing some time as a public defender. He got me off on a technicality, and got me pregnant while he was at it. He's not nearly as bad as that makes him sound, by the way. He was young and pretty sure he could handle anything. I turned on the charm—and him while I was at it—and for a while he was so head over heels, he forgot to worry about scruples. When he found out I was pregnant, he came to his senses and gave me an ultimatum. Either I cleaned up my act in rehab, or he would make sure I never held the baby."

Cash gave a low whistle.

She went on. "You've heard the expression 'scared straight'? That's what I was. But Larry did something else for me. He made me believe I could turn my life around. He gave me that chance, and got me into the best program he knew. And once I got into therapy, I realized I had a choice. I could be all the things my mother never was—responsible, loving, involved—or I could be exactly like her. And by then, sober and terrified and already in love with the baby inside me, I knew which I wanted to be."

She was silent a moment, and so was he. "Not exactly a cheerful start to our evening, was that?" she said at last.

He glanced at her; then he grinned. "I'd say you were just laying it out, making sure I understood who was in my car. Or maybe you were giving me a chance to drop you off by the side of the road. You have mad money in that cute little purse?"

"Will I need it?"

"You know what I like about that story? Not the details, because my imagination's working on those, and I'm getting mad at a world that put you through that."

"I put myself through that, Cash. Nobody else was responsible."

"You're saying if you'd grown up in a good home, with loving, caring parents, you'd have done the same?"

"A lot of people grow up in worse circumstances than I did and go on to live exemplary lives."

"And a lot more don't. How you grow up matters, which is why you're such a good mother to those little girls. But let me tell you what I like about that story."

"Go on."

"You're not ashamed of yourself. It's just part of who you were. Who you are. You've accepted it, put it in perspective, owned up to it. All that. And you can lay out that tale to a man who's more or less a stranger. Not to get attention. Not to impress me. But just to be clear. So I'll understand."

"I do spend a lot of time looking for absolution. I'm not quite as put together as you make me sound."

"I'd say that's a good thing, too. We could all use some absolution. Just tell me. If you have these babies and give them to Kendra, will you be able to move on once and for all? Will you be able to say, 'my debt is paid'?"

She wondered. "I'd rather just say, 'I love you, sis. I'm glad I could do this. I'm glad I could give you something wonderful.'"

"You're a special kind of lady, Jamie Dunkirk."

And despite herself, she was beginning to think Cash Rosslyn was a special kind of man.

17

Cash normally stayed away from the Valleywide Home Builders' social events. Most of the members were closer to his father's age than his. When his colleagues were in each other's company, many of them felt it was their sacred duty to flaunt whatever wealth they had achieved. Out on a job site, they weren't so bad. He would run into them from time to time, dressed informally, caps set firmly on graying heads, clipboards and portfolios in one hand while they tapped out the next cigarette with their other. Too busy to prove anything, they were good for a chat or a laugh or a beer. But more than beer flowed at these gatherings, and as Cash pulled to a stop at the lodge, he warned Jamie.

"There's a couple of guys who'll try to hit on you. You'll be the prettiest thing they've seen in years, and they'll have had too much to drink. A friend calls this the annual Home Wreckers' dinner dance."

"Any lecher in particular?"

"Yeah, Orel Jensen, the guy who owns O'Jensen Homes, Inc. He thinks of himself as a real mover and shaker. They've been sniffing around Cashel Orchard. He wants to make an offer, but we've discouraged him for now."

"An offer? To do what?"

"Develop the place. He thinks he can get the county board to go along with a planned community there. High-density housing. Maybe a little undeveloped land in the middle and along the edges as a sop to the environmentalists and neighbors. Of course, it's not zoned for anything like that, but he has time, contacts and patience."

"Grace would have a fit."

"He's willing to wait until she's gone."

Jamie stopped. "Don't tell me you're talking to him about it? Without her knowledge?"

"Our family doesn't operate like that."

She looked relieved. "Good."

He ushered her out of the car and put his hand on her back, a pleasurable experience. He splayed his fingers wider so he could feel her flesh ripple as she walked. "He's not the only one interested, but he's the most vocal. Personally, I'd rather sell to the Devil and Sons, but Orel is successful at what he does, and he has the resources to show for it. Unfortunately his houses are cheaply built. The place'll start to look run-down in fewer years than it takes to finish all the houses."

"Grace said something about a conservation easement."

"That's possible. But Granny Grace knows that, unless somebody's really taking care of the orchard, the trees are just going to die anyway, and the whole place will become one huge brush pile. The land has been farmland or orchard since the 1700s, and we know that's how it should remain. But right now, nobody's stepping up to the plate."

"What about you?" She stopped and faced him. "Could you? *Would* you?"

"That's a lifetime responsibility." He paused. With Jamie in high heels, they were eye to eye. He grinned, because her eyes were so serious. "I don't do responsibility."

"Then I'd better tell Kendra. She's expecting you to build a house."

"I do short spurts of responsibility. And I finish what I agree to start."

"I guess the land's not in your blood."

The only thing in his blood right now was the smell and sight of this woman. He wasn't sure he'd ever seen anyone so lovely. Pregnancy certainly didn't detract from Jamie's sensuality. Her cheeks were tinged with rose; her skin was nearly translucent; her eyes seemed even larger and more luminous. And in that dress? She carried herself like royalty.

"Let's just go and have a good time," he said, brushing his knuckles over her cheek. "This is a problem we can't solve tonight."

She nodded reluctantly, and he took her hand and tucked it under his arm.

The lodge was really an old bank barn that had been converted years before into a social hall, used largely for gatherings like this one, or wedding receptions and reunions. Although the building's origins were clearly visible on the outside, inside a huge stone fireplace rose to the vaulted ceiling, and a full wall of windows made good use of the outside light and views. Round tables adorned with white linen and chrysanthemums hugged the paneled walls. A band was set up in front of the fireplace—synthesizer, two guitars, a drummer and a vocalist crooning "You've Lost that Loving Feeling" into a sound system that was better than they deserved. Waiters in white jackets carried silver trays of ap-

petizers and glasses of champagne, circulating throughout the cav-
ernous space. Above them, on both sides, narrow second-floor
mezzanines provided more room for tables.

"Cozy, huh?" Cash joked. "I like the place because it's impossible to have a real conversation. Especially if the band's loud
enough. That way I don't have to hear how well everybody's
doing, and how surprised they are that Rosslyn and Rosslyn is
still in business."

"Why do you come?"

"Because my father refuses to. And we need to remind these
guys we're still going strong. Let's get you something to drink.
Can you have a soft drink?"

"Something fruity, if they have it. Or tomato juice."

He led her to a bar across from the band, and she settled on a
Virgin Mary. He got a beer for himself, and they wandered across
the room to where a display had been set up of some of the
projects the members had completed in the past year.

"What's the drill?" she asked. "I'm pretty much starving."

"Sounds chronic for a woman carrying twins."

"Afraid so. I'll try not to eat your dinner, too."

He flagged down a waiter and got her a chicken wing. Then,
while she worked on that, he made the rounds, returning with
a small plate filled with a variety of finger foods.

"Spring rolls, chicken pinwheels, a cheese puff, two stuffed
mushrooms—don't you dare eat them both—and a barbecue
pork sandwich."

"It can't be a real sandwich, can it? It's only one bite." She
popped it into her mouth. "I bet there were more where that came
from, right?" Then she winked to let him know she was kidding.

"If we move closer to the middle of the room, we can just steal
food from people's plates as they walk by."

"You would do that for me?" She licked her fingers. "If you're going to take up a life of crime, go big-time. Get me another chicken wing."

He took his mushroom off the plate before it disappeared into her mouth, and watched her eat everything else. "How was it?" he asked when she was finished. "Did you take the time to taste anything?"

"Not bad. I used to be a cook, you know. While I was straightening out my life. Feeding people makes me happy. If I wasn't planning to be an architect, I'd be a chef."

"You're a good woman to know. I like being fed."

"I bet you've had women feeding you all your life." She stopped, and her eyes suddenly looked troubled. "I'm sorry. I wasn't talking about your marriage. I meant—"

"You meant my mother and my grandmother. They fight over me. Granny Grace couldn't cook a meal without adding something new. That ham she baked you and the girls? She glazed it with—"

"Root beer," Jamie said. "Tabasco sauce and orange rind. She told me. I copied the recipe, or what there was of one. She makes things up as she goes along."

"My mother likes things plain. She says she wants to savor every flavor all by itself. The result of a childhood of Granny Grace's cooking, no doubt."

"So which do you prefer?"

"I prefer to eat everything they give me with no complaints."

"Smart man."

The band stopped playing, and a man in a pastel blue suit, ruffled shirt and a string tie announced it was time to serve dinner. The music would resume at the conclusion.

"We should have staked our claim to a table," Cash said.

"There are a couple of smaller businesses, like ours, with good men and women running them. We try to stick together, but it might be too late now." He looked up just in time to see a man bearing down on them. He snatched Jamie's plate and tried to put himself between them, but it was already too late.

"Cash, my man." The man was dressed in a double-breasted striped suit that looked like an Italian knockoff. He had more black hair than a man pushing sixty had a right to, and a Rolex that he'd either gotten from a street vendor or an ultraexpensive jewelry store. Cash prided himself on not being able to tell the difference.

"I've saved you a place at my table," he said. Then he stuck out his hand in Jamie's direction. "Orel Jensen. Cash and I are old, old friends."

Jamie slipped hers into his. "Jamie Dunkirk. Cash and I are new, new friends."

"Cash, I sure admire your taste. In women, if not in houses." His laugh was hearty and counterfeit.

"Only the best of both," Cash said, but Orel wasn't listening. His gaze was sweeping Jamie from head to toe. Finally it came to rest on the just-visible mound that was slowly expanding her waistline.

"Well, you sly fox." He glanced at Cash. "I thought you said new, new friends?" He looked back at Jamie and grinned.

"Oh, the babies?" she asked with a dismissive laugh. "Oh, these aren't Cash's babies. They're my brother-in-law's."

Cash nearly choked, but Jamie wasn't finished yet. She watched Orel's eyes widen and timed her follow-up perfectly. "I can see you're worrying about my sister. You don't have to. She was right there with us when I got pregnant. She's all in favor. We're that kind of family."

★ ★ ★

Hours later, in the car on their way back up the mountain to the orchard, Cash was still grinning, and not because of the emcee's jokes over dessert and coffee.

"I can't believe you didn't tell the poor guy what was really going on," he said, looking fondly at Jamie. "Now I'll be the talk of the association. I'll be the swinger with the gorgeous, willing girlfriend."

"You can call him tomorrow and explain. I swear, though, he was sweating so hard just thinking about it, I thought he was going to fan himself with his toupee. And do people still use words like *swinger*?"

"The sexual revolution might have come to the Valley, but we're probably pretty far behind in the language department."

"Might have come?"

He smiled at her. "Are we talking about sex, Miss Jamie?"

"I seem to be."

"So if we're talking about sex, go ahead and tell me about Alison's father. So we'll be all caught up."

"You mean because I clearly had sex with him?"

"That's the connection."

"He was a mistake. Professional gambler. Good enough at it to pay adequate child support, too. Seamus is as Irish as a shamrock, a sweet talker and a nice guy. I'm better at getting pregnant than I am at making birth control work, and he was better at getting me there than at being a father. He offered to marry me, but his heart wasn't in it, and neither was mine, although he did come to the delivery and hold my hand."

He pretended to shudder. "He can't be all bad. That's more than I could ever do, even for you."

She punched him lightly on the arm. "Anyway, if I ever tie

the knot, I don't intend to drag my girls around from one high-stakes poker game to another."

"The girls' fathers don't see much of them?"

"A couple of times a year. If I'd chosen them, I'd say I hadn't chosen well. But I really didn't go into those relationships with motherhood on my mind. I probably didn't think about babies much before Hannah, but when I did, I saw myself settled, madly in love, tying climbing roses to a picket fence. The whole unrealistic fairy tale. Of course, I wasn't doing anything to get myself there. I wasn't picket-fence material, that's for sure."

"And now that you are?"

She laughed. "Not counting on it, not counting it out. The girls and I have so much to look forward to, whether I meet the right person or not."

"What would the right person look like?"

"I guess he'd know how to prune my roses. And be a father to my girls. And show up in the delivery room if he was needed."

He grinned at the last. "All in all, that's a pretty small order."

"Maybe one with a chance of being filled, maybe not. I really don't think about it. I think more about preventing another dead-end relationship. I'm not lonely."

"And you don't have trouble finding men if you get that way."

"Truthfully, no. But I'm not into casual sex."

"There's that word again."

"A perfectly good word, but for such a little one, it's fraught with meaning and anxiety, isn't it?"

"Sure is." Cashel Orchard was just ahead, and he made the final turn. "Was that a warning?"

She phrased her answer carefully. "Not meant to be. Let's face it, I'm not at my most ravishing, and unless I saw a complete health report on a man, with test results for any number of possibilities, I wouldn't get near him. I'm not risking the health of these babies for anything."

"Makes sense to me. Where do I take my physical?" He looked over and grinned at her expression. "Just kidding."

"We're taking care of business very efficiently, aren't we?"

"You're making your will known, and that's your right. But for the record, you *are* at your most ravishing. Maybe a few more months will turn that tide. But right now, you're a knockout."

She put her hand on his arm. It had already rested there earlier tonight. After dinner they had danced three slow dances before he suggested that they leave, because cigarette smoke was drifting in from the entrance, and she was starting to wear down. Cash was a good dancer. Not flashy. Not pushy. He'd held her just right, not too close but definitely not too far away. She had enjoyed the feel of his body against hers, moving slowly and sinuously. In fact, she had enjoyed it just a bit too much for someone who had months of celibacy ahead of her.

And that was intriguing in its own way. She really wasn't into casual sex, but now her definition of casual went deeper and further. Sex really was out of the question until after the twins were born. If she were in a committed relationship with a safe partner, things might be different. But she wasn't, and she wasn't willing to begin one now.

"I'm not the best bargain out there, am I?" She dropped her hand. "I really will understand if you'd like to let me off at Grace's and forget you ever knew me."

"But I *do* know you. And I like what I know, though I'm not some kid who's keeping score."

"Don't all guys keep score?"

"What, you think there's a smoky room hidden in the back

of some bar in Woodstock where bookies are taking bets and laying odds?"

"Pretty much."

He laughed as he pulled up in front of Grace's house. "Come on. There's a sky full of stars and the most comfortable porch swing you'll ever sit in over there. You've set up the ground rules, and I'll be a good sport. But I've been looking forward to this part all night long."

"What part is that?"

"Where we don't have to watch Orel leer at you or listen to old Pete Sutter's jokes about his mother-in-law's pet pig. Just you, me, the moon and my arm around you."

That sounded good. In fact, it sounded spectacular. She wasn't ready for a final good-night. Maybe the dinner and dance hadn't been a remarkable venue for a date. Maybe she would rather have gone to some quiet little restaurant where they could be alone and cover her life story somewhere other than in his mother's Honda. Or maybe they could have taken a walk on some mountain ridge, where they could watch the sun sinking in a blaze of glory, or the moon rising in a Shenandoah sky.

But none of that really mattered. They'd had fun together. Cash was easy to be with, smart, clever, entertaining and just distant enough to make her comfortable. He knew everything he needed to know—except that she was worth more money than anyone had a right to be—and he seemed comfortable enough with her past and even her foggy view of the future.

He came around and helped her out of the car, as old-fashioned a gesture as the orchid corsage. She let him, since it was that kind of night. She had missed out on proms and homecoming dances, substituting nights of rummaging in Dumpsters and scoring bad dope on street corners. Now she reveled in the simplicity, the ritual, the man himself.

Up on the porch, he fell into the swing and pulled her down beside him, positioning her so that she was resting against his chest.

"So here's what I want to know," he said, once she was settled against him, his arm around her, his hand resting casually on her belly where the twins slept away. "Did you give me more than a passing thought in the months since I saw you last?"

She leaned back against him, enjoying the intimacy. "That was two years ago. You're asking if at any time in those two years I thought about you once or twice?"

"Uh-huh."

"It's been a busy couple of years."

"Meaning no."

"Afraid I can't say no. I liked you right off the bat. I thought maybe if I'd had more time here, things could have developed between us. So every once in a while, there you were in my mind. How about you?"

"Well, you kind of spoil a man."

She thought that was one of the nicest things any man had ever said to her. "I like being the standard you hold other women to."

"I didn't think you'd be back. Funny how things work out, isn't it?"

"Yeah, funny. I didn't expect to be sitting on my sister's nest here in the Valley, that's for sure."

"I don't know where this is going. You've got the babies, then a life somewhere else. I have baggage I drag around."

"Karen. You still miss her, don't you?"

"You want the truth?"

"Let's make a point of it."

"I hardly remember the Karen who wasn't sick. I know I loved her, that I expected us to grow old together. But we never even started down that path. It's like I knew one percent of the woman she was, and nothing of the woman she would have been."

"I'm sorry. Life can be rotten."

"What I'm left with is memories of sickrooms, and decisions about what to do and how to do it, and a woman who wasn't old enough or well enough to know what to do for herself. So I had to make decisions for her, then watch the consequences. And that's baggage I'll be dragging into eternity."

"And you feel bad that those are the only memories you have."

"She deserves better."

She turned. She wanted to see his face in the lamplight shining through the living room window. "She was lucky to have you, Cash. I'm sure she knew it. I'm sure she was grateful you were right there helping her through it all. She probably had days when she was sure *she* didn't deserve *you.*"

"Sometimes I wonder, if I'd known what we had in store for us, I'd just have turned tail and run."

She touched his cheek. "Maybe that's why so few of us have the gift for seeing into the future. So we aren't tested that way. I'm afraid a lot of us would turn tail and run if we knew what was in store."

"You believe some people can see the future?"

She smiled. "I can see into yours. The hard times are over. You'll have a long life, filled with happiness and good things and people who love you again."

"And where do you see all that taking place?"

"Right here, on this land."

"Granny Grace put you up to that?"

She saw no alternative. She raised her head a little and kissed him. His arms tightened around her. She lay across him, her breasts pressing against his chest, her arms draped over his shoulders. The position couldn't have been more awkward, and yet it felt completely natural, as if they had always relaxed in each other's arms just this way.

The kiss deepened, and he ran his hands over her bare skin, tasted her lips at one angle, then another. She felt her hair cascading over her shoulders as he removed the pins a few at a time, and still he kissed her.

He was the first to move away, to position her so she was no longer so firmly against him, to brush her hair back from her face, and finally to set her away from him.

"Well," he said.

"I suppose that's been coming."

"We fell into it pretty naturally, wouldn't you say?"

"I should probably go inside."

"You probably should."

She smiled at him. He kissed her again.

Sometime later, she pushed herself off the swing and stood. "I really ought to go inside now."

"I'm thinking that's a good idea." He stood and put his arms around her, pulling her close for a moment. "When I'm gone and you're upstairs, open your window and look out at the stars. Every star in the universe clusters over this orchard. You'll never see so many in one place again."

"Will you be looking at them, too?"

"That's what I do every blessed night."

She took his hand and rubbed the back of it against her cheek. Then she kissed it. "See you soon."

"Yeah. I'll look forward to it."

He turned and started toward the sedan. She watched him go; then she went into the house, locking the door behind her, in case Grace cared about such things out here.

Upstairs, she watched her daughters sleeping on the double bed in the room Grace had given them; then she undressed silently and pulled on an oversize T-shirt she'd brought to sleep in. Back from the bathroom, she stood at the hallway window and looked out over the orchard. She was still standing there sometime later when Grace's door creaked open and she came out to join her.

"Not ready to sleep?"

"Not quite. Why are you awake?"

"You don't sleep much or well at my age. Remember that, so when it happens to you, you'll think of me."

Jamie laughed softly. "Things go okay here?"

"The girls wore me out. Poor Lucky will be glad to find a herd in the days ahead and abandon us all."

"I'm sorry. But you sound happy."

"We had a wonderful time. I miss my great-grandchildren. I need to go see them soon." Grace rested her hand on Jamie's shoulder. "I used to stand right there and look out at the land, and wonder what I was doing in this place. Eventually, of course, I knew what I was doing here, but by then I had other questions."

Jamie wasn't ready to sleep. "Why don't you tell me some more, if you're up to it? I want to know the rest. Do you feel like a cup of tea? I'll make it, if you tell me where to find everything."

"You're sure? You're up to it after a long evening?"

"It will help me relax." She put her arm around Grace. "It might even help you."

"It's nice to have you here, Jamie dear. Very nice indeed."

Jamie couldn't think of anyplace she'd rather be.

18

1941

Grace had always dreamed of a June wedding in her family's church. She'd imagined magnolias and peonies scenting the air, her arms filled with irises and pink roses. She would wear a simple long white dress with a sweetheart neckline, and cover her hair with a veil of ribbon-embroidered net. The groom would wear a dark suit and an expression of adoration. Her many friends would crowd both sides of the aisle to issue good wishes to the happy couple.

She had not expected to be married by a justice of the peace between Ben's tractor trips down orchard rows. June on a Virginia farm was ruled by wild garlic and thistle; every renegade weed stole the vigor from promising apple trees. In Ben's mind, their eradication was only slightly less important than the wedding vows that would reunite him with his sons.

"My long-awaited wedding day," Grace told her mother, who looked at least a decade older than her sixty years, stooped and sallow and shrinking. "I almost wish it was raining."

"Well, you knew there weren't gonna be nothing romantic about this," Mina Fedley said.

Grace had to agree. The past six months had been hard for everybody. Although Grace was not close to her family, she had been gratified by the way they tried to pull together after Anna's death. While her father went back to their farm and tried to find a way to hang on to the property for a few more months, Mina stayed on at the orchard to care for Charlie and tiny Adam, who, despite all odds, had survived and was now a passably healthy baby cutting his first tooth.

Mina was not able to manage the workload, of course. The damp old farmhouse, the premature newborn, the grieving toddler, the widower whose life was in ruins… Only days after Anna's death, she moved the children back home, hoping familiar surroundings might help her manage the boys. The family farm was close enough that Ben could see his sons when he had time and inclination. But even at home, the workload had been too heavy. There was no money for domestic help, and all the daughters-in-law had children and responsibilities of their own. Little Adam had to be fed hourly, and Charlie was inconsolable, having effectively lost both parents. There were animals to tend and household chores to manage. Not surprisingly, Mina quickly developed a hacking cough that threatened to infect the infant who was struggling for his life.

When she wasn't at work, Grace had done what she could, but in a matter of days, with no other choice, she quit her job at the factory. Only two weeks after her sister's death, she took over full care of her nephews. Now she was about to marry their father.

"I'm not interested in romance with Ben Cashel," Grace told her mother. "I'm marrying him because I made a promise."

"Didn't spur you on none. Not at first."

Grace fell to the bed. She was dressing for the ceremony in one of the farmhouse bedrooms, one that was slightly less gloomy than the others only because she had asked that Ben wash the windows and peel off the paper. This would be the bedroom that replaced the one where Anna had died. She knew she would never be able to sleep in that room or Anna would be sure to haunt her forever.

Grace gazed at her fingernails and shook her head sadly. As a spinner at the rayon plant, she had been required to keep her hands soft, her nails carefully manicured. Any nick, any hangnail, could snag the fibers. She had been so proud. Now her nails were cut to the quick, and her fingers were callused and rough. Of course, her nails were the least of the changes she'd made.

"I put my hand on that Bible, and I lied." She looked up at her mother. "I wanted Anna to die in peace. I thought we'd find another way to work things out."

"Maybe the good Lord is just making sure you do what you swore to. Better than burning in hell."

"If Hell's full of people with good intentions, then that's exactly where I want to be. In good company."

Mina slipped over to the window, as slight as a shadow. She couldn't eat when she was unhappy, and lately she'd taken to eating nothing but corn bread dipped in coffee. Grace was afraid that before too many months passed, her mother would follow her sister to the grave.

"No matter what was said, if there was another way, I'd be in favor." Mina looked down at the sunlit garden below, a garden choked with the very weeds Ben was trying to eradicate in the orchard. Anna had thought flowers were frivolous, and she had ignored the yard so joyfully tended by Ben's late mother. At one time, the air here had been scented by cinnamon roses and the clovelike fragrance of pinks. Grace remembered them from Anna's wedding day, a day that had been as sunny as this one.

"I'd be in favor, too," Grace said. "But how else can we keep the boys with their daddy?"

"Mebbe Ben should just have sold off what he had to. Stayed here, tended a few trees and worked in town."

"Doing what? And how, with the boys needing full-time care for years to come? Who would come up here to do it? Nobody willing to was reliable."

Mina turned. "You might as well tell the truth as a lie, girl. You don't want anybody else caring for those young 'uns. You love that baby boy now like he was your own. And little Charlie's got you wrapped around his finger. You came up here to marry their daddy just because of them and nothing else. You think I'm so beat down I can't see?"

Grace didn't know if that was true. Had she been able to find somebody willing to move up to the orchard—an older matron with stamina and patience who was able to survive on the pittance Ben could afford to pay—would she have been willing to leave the boys in another woman's hands? She thought so. She was almost sure of it. But that woman didn't exist. With her parents unable to make a living on the family farm, the bank nipping at their heels, and Ben increasingly pulled between his sons and his apple trees, the only solution had been clear.

Anna, of course, had seen all this on that night in January when she had demanded that, for once, Grace do her duty.

"I almost left." Grace got up again and began to unbutton the calico dress she had donned that morning. She looked up when her mother didn't say anything. "I was going to run away, take my last chance to see the world and let the rest of you work out a different way to deal with all this. Did you know?"

"I figured you might be thinking that way. But I knew you wouldn't do it."

"How? How did you know I wouldn't?"

"'Cause your sister was always wrong about you. What she saw as sassy and silly was just high spirits. I knew as much and told her so. *I* knew you were nothing but good inside, even if I never much got around to telling you."

Grace was stunned. "You never much got around to telling me anything, Mama."

Mina shrugged, as if to say that was true and there was not a lot she could have done about it. "I never had it in me to be much of a mother. You're like your grandma, though. You never knew her. But she was just like you. Pretty, smart, and always looking for a way to make life twice as much fun. Always taking care of things, making them grow. It was like she came back to us when you was born. That's why I named you Grace. It was grace that sent you when your papa and me were all done and all tuckered out. And you were so easy, I could just sit back and watch you grow and not worry overmuch." She paused. "Anna, now, she never did see that."

"I'll say." Grace was moved by her mother's words. They were the kindest Mina had ever spoken to her, and this was certainly the longest speech Mina had ever given in her presence.

"I just want you to know, what you're doing today, it's a good thing."

Grace wanted to hug her mother in thanks, but Mina would be embarrassed if she tried. In fact, Mina had gone back to staring out the window, and Grace didn't want to spoil the moment with either a hug or the truth.

Maybe marrying Ben was a good thing, but right now she was tempted again to make a run for it. She wasn't at all sure she could go through with this wedding.

"Mr. Foxhall's coming." Mina pointed out the window. "Driving that old Dodge of his. Can't blame you for not getting the preacher instead. Seems wrong to make a fuss so soon after Anna passed. Better to just get things done and over with."

"Mama, I'm going to finish changing now. Will you go and see how Charlie and Adam are faring?"

"I'm gonna find me some flowers to pick. You deserve some flowers, if nothing else."

"If you happen to see Ben, would you ask him to take a few minutes to marry me? Before he starts on the next row?"

Mina was silent for a moment, her lips tightly drawn. Then, as if she had dug up one more thing to say from a lifetime's unspoken store, she nodded.

"You listen to me, Grace. I know what you think of Ben Cashel. You think you know who he is. But there's two kinds of men in the world. Some are like a piece of glass. There's nothing to them but you can't see it. Everything's right there, and half the time there's not much scenery worth looking at. Then there's the other kind, like Ben. Ben's like a room with all the curtains drawn. You don't know what you're getting into when you walk through that door, but sometimes the best things are waiting— things you never dreamed of."

"Mama, Ben's marrying me because it's the only thing he knows to do. He's glad I'm willing, maybe even the teeniest bit grateful—though he'd never take the time to say so. But Ben knows if I'm willing, it's because of those boys and because I'm afraid Anna will find a way to make my life miserable from the great beyond."

"You don't believe that. Not for a minute. You can make a life here, Grace. A life for those boys, mebbe even a life for you and Ben, if you just put your mind to it."

"It might not be forever, Mama. I'm warning you. I'm not thinking about forever. Even Anna said I could move on soon as the boys were old enough not to need me."

"Don't talk like that. You'll bring the Lord's wrath on this family. You take those vows and mean them."

Grace turned her hands palms up and let her mother interpret that as she would.

Mina left, and Grace pondered her mother's parting words. She couldn't tell Mina that the only way she could stand in front of the justice of the peace today was if she was certain there was freedom at the end of this prison sentence. She had no idea if Ben knew that—or cared. They had engaged in very little conversation since Anna had died.

She heard a car door close and, in a little while, birdsong where there had only been the whine of a tractor's engine. Ben was probably on his way up to the house to change for the ceremony. It was time she got ready, too.

The dress she donned was nothing like the one she had imagined for herself; still, it wasn't anything to be ashamed of, either. Her brothers' wives had gone together and bought the fabric. She knew it was their way of thanking her for this sacrifice. Had she not been willing to marry Ben, most likely the boys would have been sent from one of Grace's brothers to the other, adding a burden at a time when even the smallest trial could sink a family. Their wives were grateful.

The fabric was cream-colored rayon sprinkled with tiny sprays of pink roses tied with cornflower-blue ribbons. She had treated herself to a pattern from the money she'd saved for her escape from the Valley, and made a dress with a keyhole neckline and batwing sleeves. It was stylish and feminine, but she doubted Ben would notice. Not that his attention mattered. She had made it for herself, not for him.

Once the dress was on, she fiddled with her hair. She had set it in pincurls last night and this morning, she had parted it on the side, combed the waves back into a loose pageboy and rolled the sides away from her face, covering the bobby pins with careful curls. Now she adorned the curls with the small white rosebuds she had plucked from her mother's sad little rose bed that morning.

She stood back from the oval mirror and viewed herself. Then she moved closer, reapplied her lipstick and powdered her nose. She looked fresh-faced and youthful, and, if she did say so herself, pretty enough to entice any man. Any man except Ben, of course. Her smile faltered, and for a moment, she was tempted yet again to leave. What kind of woman married the only man in the world who clearly disliked her?

Someone knocked on the door, and Sylvie, her brother Ethan's wife, appeared. She was chubby, with natural dark curls she usually tied back in a kerchief. But today they were combed into a semblance of order, and she was wearing her best print dress.

"You look pretty." Sylvie smiled, although clearly her heart wasn't in it. She knew, as did everyone else, that this wedding was for show. "Charlie and Adam are napping. I got them both to sleep, and my Lulie's going to watch them 'til everything's finished. That little Adam has grown like a weed. You've done a good thing taking care of him. We all thought he'd be in the ground next to his ma by now."

"I guess it wasn't his time."

Grace had made certain of that with round-the-clock feedings. With hot water bottles and quilts and little wool caps. With hours spent with Adam tucked in her arms against her chest so he wouldn't cry and tire himself.

Now, picturing baby Adam asleep with his favorite quilt, she knew she wasn't going to run. Not when the baby smiled every time he caught sight of her. Not when he held up his arms so she would pick him up whenever she came near. Not when his brother was finally beginning to laugh like a normal little boy.

She had to go through with the wedding.

"I guess everything's all ready." Grace straightened her hem and the seam of one stocking. "I guess we'd better just do it."

Sylvie cleared her throat. "I bet Ben won't bother you tonight, Grace. Not for a while. He's not a man who would push a woman. You'll have some time to get used to this."

Grace glanced at Sylvie, whose cheeks were flaming. The words had been delivered in a rush. Grace wondered if Sylvie had been appointed by the other women to speak frankly. She had certainly thought about what might happen tonight. She'd been raised on a farm and was well aware what a man and woman did together. She'd managed some of the preliminaries after parties and dances, and hadn't found them half-bad. But doing them with Ben? She suppressed a shudder.

"He'd better not." She finished straightening her hem. "I'm not taking any man into my bed who's grieving for another woman. This marriage is for show."

"Now, you oughtn't to go into it quite like that." Sylvie was looking at the floor. "He's a man, for all he's grieving poor Anna. One day he's going to stop and notice what he's gone and done."

"I'll worry about that when the time comes." Grace threw back her shoulders. "Let's go, Sylvie. Everybody's waiting."

Sylvie, who looked relieved, followed Grace downstairs.

Grace had made few requests when she'd agreed to this

marriage, but her one demand had been that the ceremony be held outdoors. The house seemed increasingly oppressive to her. At least when Anna was alive the house was clean, if dreary. Now, with no one to clean it but Ben, cobwebs highlighted the curling wallpaper, and dust balls lurked in dark corners. She had announced that she would not be married within its walls, and she had stood firm. A tight-lipped Ben had agreed they could say their vows out in the orchard, where apples were beginning to form. She just hoped he wouldn't stray from one row to the other and thin fruit from the branches when he was supposed to be saying "I do."

Now she walked down the front steps with Sylvie and shaded her eyes to see if the others had started toward the orchard. Her mother appeared from the side of the house, with a sparse bouquet plucked from the smothering flower beds.

"I got what I could," she said, handing over the bouquet, which she'd tied with a fragment of ribbon. "Not sure what all of them are, but it's a crying shame they're all just a-dying out there."

Grace thought it was a crying shame, too, that Anna had cared so little for the gardens left to her. Then she realized that Anna's wishes no longer mattered, that soon, the house, the gardens— Anna's life—would belong to her.

A life she did not want.

"I think you ought to stay here and walk down with Ben," Mina said. "Sylvie and I'll go out yonder with the others and wait for you there."

"Ben?" Grace had been sniffing her bouquet. Now her head snapped up.

"Only fitting. You should walk down there together."

Grace couldn't imagine why. But she realized if she couldn't do that much, couldn't walk side by side with Ben for seventy yards or so, then there was no sense in going to the orchard at all.

She thought of Sylvie's words in the bedroom. How much more was she going to be asked to do?

"I'll wait here. You go on." She managed a smile. "Thanks for the flowers, Mama."

"Ben's in no kind of shape to be thinking of it," Mina said, as if in apology.

"I know."

Mina and Sylvie took off, as if they felt their roles in this drama had ended. Afraid she would ruin her dress on the steps, Grace stood in the shade of a black walnut and waited.

Ben appeared at last. She wondered if he had been with his sons, although she doubted that, since they were asleep. Then she wondered if, like her, he'd been wracked with doubt and scrambling for another way, any way, to fix his life. If so, he hadn't found one. Because Ben was dressed in a suit and ready for the formalities.

Despite everything, she had to admire him. Ben in overalls was one thing, but Ben dressed up, even in a threadbare suit, was a sight. His shoulders were broad enough to strain the dark fabric. The white shirt made his tanned skin glow.

"Mama thought we should walk out together," Grace said. "Maybe she thinks it will give each of us a chance to bolt, if that's what we need to do."

He didn't smile. She supposed that if she'd ever cared to, she could have numbered the smiles she'd seen on Ben's face on the petals of a daisy. And those had all been before Anna's death.

"I'm not going to bolt." He looked down at the flowers she carried. "Who gave you those?"

"Mama picked them for me."

"There used to be more."

"I remember. There were more the last time you got married."

He looked away, and she realized he hadn't wanted that reminder.

"This wedding is what Anna wanted," she said. "If she's somewhere she can see what's happening, she'll be glad."

"There's no place like that. She's gone, and that's all there is to it."

She lifted one recently plucked brow. "Is that what you think? Then you're not doing this for her?"

"I'm doing this because there's no other way I can see." He seemed to realize how that must have sounded. "And I'm grateful that you agreed."

That last sentence was stilted, as if he was reciting a line from a poem memorized in school.

She was curious now. How much of what Anna had believed about her character had really rubbed off on Ben? "You didn't think I'd go through with this, did you? You thought I'd just abandon you and the children."

"Doesn't matter, does it? If I did, then I guess I was wrong."

"I'm not going to speak ill of my sister, but I am a better person than she led you to believe."

"Anna was a good wife and a hard worker, and whatever she thought, she was too busy to spend time talking about it."

She heard what he didn't add. *The way you're talking about it right now.*

"I'm going to do my best here," she said. "But just so you understand, I know this won't be a real marriage. It's a convenience, a way to help those two little boys up there. I'm not expecting more from you."

She paused, then forged ahead. "And I don't want more, Ben. You'd better understand that now, before we take any vows. I'm honoring my promise to Anna. I'm helping Charlie and Adam, but only because there's no other way. When the time comes those little boys don't need me anymore, I'm gone. I hope you're not planning on anything else."

He studied her a moment, as if she were a fish he had just caught and didn't know whether to keep or toss back into the muddy waters.

"I'm planning on getting through this day today, and tomorrow's tomorrow," he said at last. "I'm planning on thinning my fruit and spraying my trees and listening to Charlie say his bedtime prayers. I'm planning on placing flowers on Anna's grave every spring, because she was my wife and tried hard to be a good one. And I'm planning to leave you be, if that's what's worrying you. You can have that bedroom where you got dressed today. I've moved my things in with Charlie, anyway, and closed off the room where Anna died. You won't be sharing my bed, and you won't need to share my life, either."

"I see. I'll be the hired woman."

"No, you'll be Anna's sister, who's doing what she can to help out."

She didn't know what else she could ask for. She had already told him she didn't want a real marriage, and he was making it clear he would comply. It all seemed so sad to her, though. That the day that should have been the happiest of her life was the gloomiest.

She had one last thing to settle. "Then, as Anna's sister, there will be some changes. I'm not Anna. I'm Grace. And I'll do what needs to be done my way."

"Just don't interfere in what doesn't concern you."

"And once we're married what would that be, Ben? Because everything here will concern me as long as I'm living in this house."

He looked as if he wanted to answer but knew that if he

answered honestly, she might change her mind and leave. At last he shrugged.

"Then we understand each other." Grace gestured toward the orchard. "Shall we go and get this over with?"

He looked as if he dreaded the long walk with her as much as he dreaded the ceremony to come. But he stepped up and offered his arm.

Surprised, she had no choice but to take it. His arm was solid and heavy, and although she was a tall woman and strong herself, she felt oddly insubstantial. So close to Ben, she was aware of the heat from his body against hers and the not unpleasant scent of his skin. She would rather not have noticed either.

They walked that way until they had joined the others, but afterward, after the joyless, perfunctory ceremony when Ben wasn't even invited to kiss the bride, Grace knew that their walk side by side into the orchard had been the longest, hardest walk either of them would ever be called on to take.

19

Grace enjoyed attending the Shenandoah Community Church bee. The quilters had quietly rallied around Jamie and Kendra, and they were making a play quilt for the babies, as if this was the most normal pregnancy in the world. Not a negative word had been said, and that immediately endeared the group to Grace, who despite her advanced age would have taken on anyone who engaged in even the slightest sniping at her young friend. As it was, Jamie had enough on her plate.

Of course, Grace herself hadn't received exactly the same reception. Although most of the group had welcomed her warmly, Helen Henry—as expected—had not. The barbs still flew thick and fast, and although at first Grace found them somewhat humorous, now she was growing annoyed. In her opinion, backbiting was the biggest thing wrong with small towns and country life, the very thing she had hoped to escape when she was young, single and ready to see the world.

Before Ben.

Of course, all that had changed, and although she wouldn't trade a day of her life for anybody else's, she still wished that memories in Shenandoah County weren't so long, and that forgiveness, at least in some quarters, was more the norm than the exception.

Today *she* was the bee's monthly program, and she was excited about it. She explained her enthusiasm to Jamie, who, in the seventeenth week of her pregnancy and wearing real maternity clothes, was helping her gather demonstration quilts from the van. Hannah was at the elementary school, Alison in preschool until noon. The bee would seem quieter without them.

"I know it probably seems silly to you, dear. But the truth is, home is always the final testing ground. You know what Jesus said about prophets in their home country? Well, the same can be said for quilters. As hard as it is for me to admit, I'm not sure I'll feel like I've arrived as an artist until I'm validated here."

"That's hard for me to imagine. But then, I don't have that kind of connection anywhere."

"Do you want that kind of connection?" Grace piled more quilts into Jamie's waiting arms.

"Absolutely. When the girls and I settle in the next time, I want to buy a house and make it their forever home. There's still time to work on their roots before we work on their wings."

"I've more or less hoped you'd settle here, you know. That you'd fall in love with the Valley and decide to make this your home. Your sister and her family will be living here soon, and there must be opportunities for you, as well. Are we too rural? Too parochial for a girl raised in New York City?"

"Wow, where did that come from?" Jamie closed her arms around her bundle. "Staying here? That's right out of the blue."

"I just don't like to think about losing you."

"But you'll see lots of us. You can come and visit, and we'll be coming back to see Kendra and Isaac—and the twins, of course. I'm not going to let those kids grow up without me. I have a special stake in their lives."

"So you're not planning to distance yourself on purpose?"

"At first, sure. Kendra and Isaac don't need me looking over their shoulders. But after that? Unless I've miscalculated badly, I'll love the babies like an aunt with a head start. And Kendra and Isaac will want us to be close."

"I'm glad you intend to at least visit." But Grace realized she didn't sound properly enthused. She tried harder, even though at her advanced age, she wished she could have all the people she loved close by. "I really am."

"I love this area," Jamie said. "But is it the right place for a single mother with a career?"

Personally, Grace hoped Jamie wouldn't stay a single mother very long, and she knew the ideal candidate to make certain of it. But she knew talking about that would be too forward. Pushing Cash at Jamie was a surefire guarantee the two would never figure out how perfect they were for each other. To her knowledge, the Labor Day dance was the last time they had gone out together. And that had been almost three weeks ago.

She answered as best she could. "Only you can decide if the Valley's right for you, of course. But it's a good place to raise children, if you keep them busy enough." Grace retrieved the last of her quilts and closed the car door. "Okay, let's beard the lions in their den."

"You don't have a thing to worry about. Everybody's thrilled you're doing this." Jamie paused. "Almost everybody."

"I'm hoping Helen stays home in protest."

"Cissy said Helen wouldn't miss it."

"I'll need body armor."

"She's not that bad."

"I suspect I'm the only one who recognizes all her stray bullets for what they are."

"She's been awfully nice to me. She seems good-hearted under that crusty exterior. I can't help thinking the two of you would be great friends if you could ever get past whatever it is."

"There's more chance of peace in the Middle East, dear."

"Seems to me there's a chance for that, as well, if people would just listen to each other and see how much they actually have in common. It's really pretty simple."

Grace tried not to sigh over youthful innocence. "Please *don't* consider a career as a diplomat. Besides, it would take you farther from us, and we can't have that."

They were at the door now, and when Jamie opened it, a group of women scurried over to relieve them of their burdens.

Grace chatted with the attendees. There were more than normal, almost two dozen. Regulars had brought friends, and some members of a guild from Winchester introduced themselves and told her they'd heard about the talk at their last meeting. Cathy, the president, called everyone to order, and after a reasonable amount of time, people found seats and the business meeting began.

Grace settled next to Jamie. Helen hadn't arrived, so she was hoping for the best. Halfway through the treasurer's report—there was money enough to buy batting and backing for the bee's Christmas quilt, plus some to replace the slide in the children's playground—Helen walked in with Cissy Claiborne.

The only two empty seats were directly across from Grace and Jamie. Grace was careful not to roll her aging eyes, although the impulse was nearly overwhelming.

"And that concludes my report." Dovey Lanning, Grace's age and given to wearing her white hair in a bun as tight as her pursed lips, looked up from her papers. "I'm glad to tell you things are fine, and even gladder that I get to keep the books now and don't have to take notes at these meetings anymore. I'm planning to run off with the bee's money if we ever get enough."

"Anybody have questions?" Cathy asked.

"Not a question," Helen said, settling herself across from Grace. "But I've got an idea for that Christmas quilt. We need to get started right away, you know, now that the bear's paw is all done. These things take some time."

"We'll make that new business and take it up then."

Despite interruptions, Cathy went through the rest of the business quickly, which Grace admired, having once been the president of a similar organization. Then, when she got to old business, Cissy Claiborne raised her hand.

"I know Ms. Henry won't tell you herself, but just so everybody knows, she entered her Delilah's Dream quilt in the Houston International Quilt Festival competition, and she's a finalist. So her quilt's going to be there, and Ms. Henry and Mrs. Whitlock—you all know that's her daughter—are going to go and see the show."

Everybody applauded, Grace among them.

"And she's known for a while now, and wouldn't tell a soul if I didn't tell you for her," Cissy added.

"We're all so proud of you, Helen," Cathy said. "Delilah's Dream *is* a dream of a quilt, that's for sure."

"Just so everybody knows, it was my daughter entered that quilt. Not me. Nancy's always put on airs."

"I think Nancy just wants your talent to be shared," Cathy said. "And she's right. Somebody here would have done it eventually if she didn't."

Helen looked embarrassed but pleased, although Grace could see she was trying not to. This was an accomplishment to be proud of, since the competition was unbelievably stiff. Had Helen been one iota nicer to Grace at any of the meetings, Grace would have been thrilled for her.

They progressed to new business, and Cathy turned to Helen again.

"Would you like to tell us your idea?" She looked out at the group. "Of course, not all of you know what we're talking about, do you? We make a Christmas quilt every year and raffle it off before the holidays. Then whoever is lucky enough to win it can keep it or give it as a gift to somebody they love. It always makes a lot of money for the church."

"My idea," Helen said, "is to make a traditional red-and-green appliqué, maybe a coxcomb or something similar. Not too big, because we don't have that much time if we're going to put it in the frame and quilt it. But the colors would be right, and anybody with any taste at all would like it. Those who can appliqué could each do a block."

Nobody spoke, although Cathy gave them time. "So are we in agreement? Or does anybody else have an idea?"

"I did see a fun Advent quilt at a guild meeting in California," Grace said. "It's fun, because everybody has a chance to be creative. Each member makes a small pieced or appliquéd stocking of their own design. Maybe even a couple for a group this small, since we'd need a total of twenty-five to make this work. Each stocking can be a unique pattern but needs to be the same general size. Then we piece a simple background with five blocks up and down, add bright borders and sashing and attach the stockings with snaps or Velcro, one in each block. No fancy quilting needed, just some machine work. Parents can put little gifts in each one for their children, or wives for husbands, or if somebody is having lots of Christmas company, cute little toiletries for guests. It can be used for years and years in different ways."

"That sounds like fun," Cathy said. "Everybody has too much Christmas fabric. That would be a great way to use it."

A couple of other people agreed. Somebody volunteered to pass around a tablet for people to sign up to make one or more stockings. Grace agreed to draw up a pattern so they would all be the same size.

"So we're agreed. If enough people agree to make stockings, this is what we'll do?" Cathy asked.

They voted yes. Helen didn't vote at all, Grace noted. She told herself she wasn't gloating, then felt bad that "gloating" had even entered her head. She hadn't set out to thwart Helen, but since her return, Helen had been so openly hostile about Grace's own talent, it was nice to feel her idea had been vindicated.

With no further business, Cathy introduced Grace, then turned the program over to her. She stood and greeted everybody. The group looked eager to hear what she had to say. Then she glanced at Helen, whose eyes were narrowed. Some of the pleasure of showing her quilts drifted away. She remembered a slogan from the 1960s, when she had been a peacenik in a state devoted—at least for a time—to sending its native sons to Vietnam.

What if they gave a war and nobody came?

It was a slogan she vowed to remember when Helen Henry was in the same room.

"You wowed them, Grace. Don't think you didn't. And they asked you to teach a class, too."

Jamie turned into the cabin's driveway. She had insisted on bringing Grace home for lunch as a celebration, and had gotten up early to wash greens and chop vegetables to make a Greek salad to go with Alison's specialty, peanut butter sandwiches. There was a half gallon of cold fruit tea, and a peach cobbler made with local fruit.

"I shouldn't have pushed my idea for the Advent quilt. Now Helen will never forgive me."

"Grace, you suggested. You didn't push. They were just ready to try something a little different. Both ideas were great."

"Maybe diplomacy wouldn't be such a bad choice for a career for you after all, dear."

Jamie grinned, braked and, when the minivan shuddered to a halt, turned off the engine.

"Aunt Kendra's here," Alison said.

Jamie hadn't noticed the Lexus, because her sister's SUV was tucked into a space between a Rosslyn and Rosslyn pickup and one of the workers' old jalopies.

"She said she and Uncle Isaac were coming up sometime this week to check on things. I guess that's why they're here. Luckily we have lots for lunch."

While Grace disembarked, Jamie helped Alison out of her seat, then looked around for her sister and brother-in-law, and spied them talking to Cash. Her heart did the tiniest jig. Cash seemed to be around more lately, as if this project had suddenly assumed even greater importance. They hadn't gone out again, but sometimes he stopped by the cabin after work to sit on the porch with her girls and listen to them talk about their days at their new schools. He'd stayed for dinner once, and once he'd bundled all of them into his pickup to go out and buy ice cream for sloppy, decadent, child-pleasing sundaes. She wondered if he planned these darting forays into her life, or if the impulse just overcame him occasionally.

"Alison is going to show me how to make her special

sandwich," Grace said. "I believe we'll go on ahead. You come and join us when you're ready."

Jamie picked her way through rubble, around machinery and along the edge of the foundation. The house was framed in now. The workers were moving quicker than she'd expected, although anything could happen along the way to throw a kink into their schedule. Too much rain, delayed deliveries, immediate action needed on another project. For the most part, though, she was encouraged. And every evening, when she walked over to take stock of the work done and visualize the finished project, she was prouder and prouder.

"Hey, sis, Isaac..." She kissed Isaac's cheek and gave Kendra a one-armed hug. "Can you stay for lunch? We have plenty."

"I brought Indian food from my favorite restaurant. Lots of it, so you'll have enough for dinner, too."

Jamie's mouth watered. She turned to Cash. "Will you have lunch with us? Your grandmother's here."

"If I'm not in the way."

She smiled at him, he smiled at her, and for a moment nobody said anything.

"Well," she said at last, her gaze still locked with his, "I was probably interrupting. I'll let you finish..." Suddenly she felt just the slightest flutter inside her. For a moment she thought she was imagining it. She'd felt the same thing last night as she was going to sleep, but before she could give it any credence, it had stopped. Now she waited for a repeat. She wasn't disappointed.

"Are you all right?" Kendra asked.

"Here." Jamie grabbed her sister's hand and rested it against her belly. She was wearing stretchy pants, and she was glad she wasn't wearing jeans, since Kendra wouldn't have had enough access through the heavy fabric. "Do you feel anything?"

Kendra frowned. "Isn't it a little early?"

"There are two in there, you know. I'm getting as big as a house."

Kendra concentrated. The two men looked faintly ill at ease, as if they were witnessing something that wasn't meant for their eyes.

"Nothing," Kendra said at last.

"Whatever it was, it stopped." Jamie patted her sister's hand. "Maybe the Indian food will jump-start it. I'd better eat some for lunch."

Cash and Isaac started toward the cabin, discussing some green building techniques that Isaac wanted to incorporate. Kendra walked behind them with Jamie.

"It must be amazing to feel a baby moving inside you," Kendra said. "Like nothing else."

"Actually, it feels a little like too much chili on a hot summer night." Jamie slipped her arm through her sister's. "But it *is* amazing. I'm sorry it's not you feeling it."

"Me, too. But this is close."

"Once the babies are moving around, you can sit all day with your hand on my belly. They'll give it a workout."

"It's beginning to seem real to me."

"It seems real to me every time I look down."

"You're feeling better though, now that you're further along?"

"Like a million bucks. There's the occasional rush to find the nearest toilet. My breasts still feel lumpy. I sleep like the dead at night. But it's all small stuff." She stopped. "Okay, try again."

Kendra looked doubtful. "Maybe you're just hungry and your stomach's growling."

Jamie grabbed her hand and placed it on her belly again. "Right there. Now."

Kendra frowned as she concentrated. Then she looked startled. "Oh, I felt that."

"Probably as much as I did."

"It's gone now."

"Just wait another second or two."

They stood there, the September sun beating down on them. Jamie thought of the day she'd driven up to the clearing for the first time, that day more than two years before when she hadn't been sure her sister would even want to see her again.

Now, here they were, Kendra's children growing inside her. The world could be a funny place.

"Oh, I felt that, too," Kendra said in wonder. "Hello, little ones."

Jamie blinked back sudden tears.

Cash liked watching Jamie with her family. She and Kendra couldn't be more different. Jamie had told him once that she looked like their mother, while Kendra took after their father. They were both easy to look at, Jamie more Vivien Leigh in *Gone with the Wind*, Kendra more Katharine Hepburn in *The African Queen*. He supposed his enthusiasm for classic movies was bound to invite those kinds of comparisons.

Jamie loved to cook and entertain. Kendra went through the motions, concentrating on setting tableware precisely the same distance from each edge of the place mat while Jamie experimented with tossing fresh herbs into the salad. Kendra's dinner parties would probably include interesting conversationalists high at the top of praiseworthy professions, with quality food either catered or purchased from gourmet groceries. Jamie's parties would include colorful locals mixed with close friends, and everything on the table would be created by her own hands from recipes she'd probably developed on the spot.

"Alison is cutting the sandwiches into stars," Grace announced. "She has decided to make a quilt sandwich for you to enjoy."

Cash wasn't surprised his grandmother got along so well with Jamie Dunkirk.

"Jamie tells me you provided the program at the bee this morning," Kendra told Grace. "I'm sorry I missed it."

As they laid out the food, the women chatted about Grace's quilts. Cash went to wash his hands, and when he came back, he saw his father in the doorway.

Isaac had seen Manning first. By the time Cash reentered the room, the two men had already stepped out to the porch.

"I just need to see Cash a moment," Manning was saying loud enough for Cash to hear. "Something's come up on another site I want to check with him about."

"I'll let you two talk," Isaac said. "But sometime when you're not in a hurry, Manning, I'd like to have a little time alone with you. You're one of the few people who seems to remember my mother."

"We were friends, yes, but it was a long time ago."

"I know so little about her. I'd kind of enjoy hearing whatever you can tell me."

Cash knew his father well. And from Manning's tone, Cash could tell he was uncomfortable. He paused, not sure whether to rescue him or let this continue. Then his father began to speak, slowly at first, then gaining momentum.

"One thing I can tell you is that she'd be proud of what you're doing. You know, that work on the health of rivers? She loved that river out there. She was the only person I knew who even loved it when it was rising high. She always said flooding was the way the river got rid of all the bad things people put into it. Once we were walking together and somebody dumped some trash in the water from a truck. She threw herself in front of that pickup so he couldn't get out without running her down, and she screamed at him until I was afraid he was going to take his shotgun off the gun rack behind him and silence her for good. She wasn't afraid of anything or anybody."

"Well, that's a story," Isaac said. "My temper's a little more even."

"She *was* a little wild. Never quite fit in here. I always thought it was partly that Rachel needed more than our schools offered back then, especially for a girl. If she wanted to know something, she figured it out without half trying. These days, we call those kids gifted, but back then, teachers just called them troublemakers."

"Until Kendra started digging around a couple of years ago, the only thing I knew about Rachel Spurlock was that she didn't want to raise a baby."

"Couldn't, more likely. She never really found her way. And she wouldn't raise a baby alone and poor, not after her own childhood. She had a mother, sure, but she yearned, like nobody I've ever known, for a father, too. She wanted two parents, a normal life, something other than scraping along in that cabin that burned down over there, hoping her mother would get another job taking care of some sick person so they could buy what they needed. They were poor. Not dirt poor, you understand, but poor enough she felt it right here."

Cash could envision his father touching his chest with his fist, a longstanding habit. He had eavesdropped long enough, and he couldn't retreat without someone noticing, so he crossed the distance to the door and pushed it all the way open.

"Hey, you wanted to see me?" he asked Manning.

Manning looked as if he'd been pulled from another time and place, then relieved—so relieved, in fact, that Cash thought it was odd.

"Ran into some issues on the Sanford place we need to go over," Manning said. "Nothing big, but timely."

Isaac put his hand out to shake Manning's. "I appreciate your time. If you think of anything else you'd like me to know, I'd like to hear it. It's nice having somebody to talk to who knew Rachel. It's a little like piecing together half a puzzle. I'm afraid my father will always be a mystery."

Manning gave a curt nod. "I'll do that."

Isaac went back inside, and left Cash and his father alone.

"He seems like a good man," Manning said, almost to himself.

"I like what I know about him," Cash said.

"His mama would be proud."

"I'm glad you told him so."

Manning shook his head. "Little enough." He took a deep breath; then he looked at his son. "You're getting awful comfortable over here, Cash. What's going on between you and Miss Dunkirk?"

Cash raised a brow. "Let's talk about what's going on at the Sanford place."

Manning seemed to debate his answer. Then he shrugged. "It's that sunroom they keep insisting they want us to build."

Kendra and Isaac went off to do more shopping for the house, and Alison, tired from preschool, went into her room for a nap. While Grace told Alison a story in the bedroom, Cash helped Jamie put the remains of lunch away.

"There's a refrigerator filled with Indian food," she told him. "You could come back tonight and help me eat it."

"I've got to be down in Richmond for a meeting with some folks who want to build a house on the other side of the county. But I appreciate the invitation."

"Kendra was able to feel the babies moving. Just a ripple, but something. It was a holy moment, like we were in church together."

"How do you feel about it? Them moving and you knowing they're not yours?"

"It's nice of you to ask." She stretched plastic wrap over the leftover salad and put it next to the take-out cartons of chicken korma and basmati rice. "It feels odd, if you want the truth. It was such a special moment when it was one of my girls. A bonding moment."

"And not so much now."

"That part's in my head. I guess it's always in our heads."

"Hormones help."

"Well, I've got those coming and going. But there's this voice inside me that says not to get too impressed with what's going on here, that this is for Kendra and Isaac to enjoy and for me to keep a distance from."

"Probably smart." He looked up. "Probably hard."

"One day at a time." She smiled at him, then she put her hand on her midriff. "Oh. Wow."

"Moving again?"

She didn't think about what to do next. She just reached for his hand and guided it to her belly. "There. Can you feel it? Just a little ping, a little shake."

She released his hand, but he didn't move it away. He frowned, as if in concentration. Then he looked up at her and grinned. "This is as personal as I've been allowed to get so far. I'm making headway."

She slapped his hand playfully, but he didn't move it.

"There," he said at last. "Was that it?"

"That was probably the Indian food. I feel a burp coming on."

He moved closer, put his arm around her to turn her and pulled her so she was standing with her back against him, leaning into him. He circled her waist with his arm and splayed his hand across her belly, covering more of it.

"This way, if I don't feel a baby, I still get to feel something good," he said.

"Spoken like a man."

He kissed the top of her head. She could feel it, the slight warmth, the pressure. She smiled.

And then a baby moved again, and this time Cash laughed. "Well, I'll be. That was the real thing, right?"

"The real thing."

"This is good work you're doing. You bringing these babies into the world. Pro soccer players, I'm guessing by all this activity."

But she heard the catch in his voice, and she smiled and put her hand over his.

"Thank you, Cash."

"For what?"

"For making this special for me, too."

20

Jamie enjoyed working on the baby quilts with Grace. She had shopped for hours online and at two different quilt shops until she found what she wanted. For one quilt she had chosen three fabrics. Black with the white silhouettes of puppies and kittens, white with tiny red umbrellas and yellow ducklings in rain slickers, and finally bright red with cheerful one-word inscriptions such as "love" and "kindness" and "laughter" printed in white and black. The fabric made her smile, and the Sister's Choice design was graphic enough to show it to perfection.

She'd started on that quilt first, since she was only using three fabrics instead of four, so it was a little simpler. But she had bought the fabrics for the second quilt, as well, choosing bright tone-on-tone prints of lime, orange and yellow, and for the background, a snowy-white cotton sprinkled with small citrus polka dots in the other three colors. Both the fabric and its placement guaranteed that the quilts would be so different that only a sharp eye or another quilt maker would recognize that the pattern was the same.

"Building a quilt is a lot like building a house," she told Grace one morning when the two were stitching together in Grace's sewing room.

Grace was working on stockings for the bee's Advent quilt. Three weeks had passed since the meeting when the design had been decided on, and Grace had agreed to make four of the stockings herself. So far, she had covered one with appliquéd stars adorned with seed pearls and silver beads. A second was a crazy patch made with satins and velvets, and adorned with bits of old lace and a little jeweled mouse. Today she was cutting a stocking shape out of a quilt block she had patched together from sixteen homespun fabrics in muted country colors. She planned to stitch "Naughty or Nice" from top to toe in primitive black lettering.

"Quilting is much cooler on a hot day than building a house," Grace said.

"You have to have a plan. That's the pattern—or the blueprint, in the case of a house. Then you have to have a foundation, choose your materials carefully, measure very, very accurately—" Jamie knew this part from sad experience having ruined her first two blocks by forgetting to add the proper seam allowance "—and you have to put your best workmanship into it, or the end result is something nobody will want to live with or in."

"Spoken like an architect."

Jamie had ten out of twelve acceptable blocks now, and she loved putting them side by side and envisioning the finished quilt. She couldn't imagine putting the same kind of devotion and passion into quilting that Grace did, but she had found that piecing a quilt met some basic need inside her to work with her hands and create something useful, but something smaller than a church or an apartment building.

With Grace's help, her daughters had stitched together quilts in their chosen fabrics and were now learning how to tie them, making knots to hold the quilt "sandwich" together. It was easier for Hannah, of course, but with everybody's help, Alison was making headway, too. Jamie thought it looked like quilting might turn out to be an interest she could share with her girls.

She checked Grace's Betty Boop clock, then stood, put her hands against the small of her back and leaned into them. She was halfway through the pregnancy. She felt the babies move regularly now, and nobody looking at her could fail to notice what her body was up to. Her belly button had gone from an innie to an outie, and she had an itchy rash where her skin was stretching to accommodate her little guests.

The babies themselves should be almost a pound each and longer than her hand. She was scheduled for another ultrasound soon. Kendra and Isaac were still trying to figure out if they wanted to know the sexes of the twins. She hoped they could decide before she was up on the table.

"Are you okay, dear?" Grace asked. "Did you sit there too long?"

"My back's a little achy. And my stomach's a little rumbly. Maybe I didn't eat enough breakfast."

"I'll go right down and get you a snack. Why don't you come along, and you can recline in comfort on my sofa?"

"Oh, you don't have to fuss. I'm fine. I ought to just go. I have to pick up Alison in a little while, and I'll take her out to lunch on the way home. If I'm lucky, I can eat her leftov—" She stopped, because suddenly she realized she wasn't fine at all. Something was definitely not right.

"I need to use your bathroom," she said.

"You don't look well."

Jamie was sure she didn't. Fear was draining the color from her cheeks. "I'll be back."

"I'm coming with you. I'll stand in the hallway."

Jamie didn't object. She was already halfway there. Inside, she took a deep breath, then began to undress.

A few minutes later she came out.

"I'm spotting," she said, after she had swallowed hard. "And not just a little."

"Okay, it could be worse. You were afraid your water had broken, weren't you?"

Jamie gave a short nod.

"Can you make it downstairs?"

"I think so. I feel shaky, but mostly from—" She burst into tears.

Grace put her arms around her. "There, there. We'll get you looked at right away. You're an experienced mother. You know this could be many things, some of them not so serious."

"I can't lose these babies." Jamie tried to stop crying, and that made her cry harder. She dissolved in Grace's arms, wailing.

"You don't know you're losing them," Grace said, patting her back. "Let's get you downstairs and get your feet up, okay? I'll call Cash to get you into your doctor's office. Or Sandra, if I can't reach him. You haven't met Cash's mother yet. You'll like her. She's good in a crisis."

"My sister—"

"I'll call her, too. You can tell me how to reach her. She can meet us there."

"Alison—"

"Cissy Claiborne can pick up Alison when she picks up Reese. She's told you she'll do that anytime you need her, right? I'll call *her*, too."

Jamie felt as if the world was ending. She could not imagine what she would do if she miscarried. How had she thought she could pull this off, that she, of all people, with all the mistakes she had made in her life, could make a miracle happen? How could she tell Kendra and Isaac she hadn't been able to give them this gift?

"Stop it," Grace said. "Whatever you're thinking, stop it right now!"

"Let's do this quickly, okay?"

"Exactly what we'll do," Grace said. "Exactly."

Dr. Raille wasn't a hand-holder. A woman in her fifties, she was olive-skinned and sharp-featured, with hair that was more silver than brown. She was well educated and too busy to mince words with her patients. She had probably always been blunt, but now she had the excuse she needed.

She finished her examination of Jamie and told her to stay flat on the table. Kendra was there, holding her sister's hand. Unlike Jamie, she hadn't shed a tear. Instead, she looked like somebody who had just been through a hurricane or an earthquake. She was in shock and going through the motions, but clearly she was waiting for reality to hit.

"We'll do an ultrasound to be sure," Dr. Raille told them. "But I'm inclined to think this is not as serious as it seems. I think this may well be a partial previa. The last ultrasound bears that out. We sometimes see bleeding about now when that happens, and it's certainly more common with twins. It's nothing to be too alarmed about."

"Exactly what does that mean?" Kendra asked.

Dr. Raille seemed glad to lecture. "A low-lying placenta, one too close to the cervix, nothing more. If we're lucky, and I'm assuming we will be, it's marginal and will correct itself as the uterus continues to stretch. We'll know more when we take a look. Miss Dunkirk, you just rest until we're ready for you." She patted Jamie's hand awkwardly, then disappeared out the door.

"Is she just saying that to make me feel better?" Jamie asked.

"Does she seem like a woman who would say anything if it weren't true?"

"You're right." For the first time since she'd seen the blood, Jamie felt hope stirring.

"I'm so sorry—" They had spoken the words simultaneously. Jamie couldn't even force a laugh. "Why would *you* apologize?"

"Because I let you take this on. Because you have so much pressure to succeed, you must feel like you're being torn in two."

"I feel awful, but not for me." Jamie hesitated. "Well, that's not quite true." Then she started to cry again. "Darn hormones," she sputtered.

"Under the circumstances, makes sense to me." Kendra's eyes finally filled with tears. "Of course you feel bad, too. You're trying so hard. You want to make me happy, and it's been working really well."

"If something happens…"

"We aren't going to talk about that. Nothing's going to happen. This pregnancy is going to continue, and you're going to be fine."

"Grace and Cash's mother—did you meet her?—they got me here so fast, I haven't even had time to think."

"Isaac drove like the wind."

"How is he?"

"Quiet. That's how he gets when he's worried."

"I want to do this for you!" The words were a wail.

"You don't know how much that means to me." Kendra squeezed her hand.

"Not as much as having these babies!"

The nurse, much more maternal in nature than her employer, bustled in. "We'll get you set up in the next room, Miss Dunkirk. I'm so sorry about this, but you're in the best of hands."

Jamie looked at Kendra. "Do you want Isaac to see this?"

Kendra nodded. "He'll want to."

"If they're okay…the technician might be able to tell the sex."

"Doesn't that seem like the most ordinary question in the world now?" Kendra's eyes glistened. "And to think at one point it seemed so important."

Sandra Rosslyn probably wasn't quite sixty. Her hair was blond, although it had probably once been darker. She was slender and tall, and she moved with Grace's sense of purpose, but without her considerable energy. She seemed genuinely warmhearted, fond of her mother, although a little wary of Grace's eccentricities, and willing to take charge when it was clear she was needed.

She had appeared at Grace's door twenty minutes after Grace phoned her, driving the same comfortable sedan Jamie remembered from her date with Cash. She'd settled Jamie flat on the backseat and her mother in the passenger seat up front, and then taken off like a NASCAR driver with something to prove. Now she patted Jamie on the hand as she helped her out of the backseat after the trip home.

"I'm so glad the news is good. I hadn't even met you yet, but I've been praying for you and those babies since I heard about them from Mother and Cash."

"It was so kind of you to just drop everything and come for us. I can't thank you enough."

"I'm available anytime you need me. Cash told me enough about you to know I'd like you. And I do. Anything you need now, you call. Anyway, you'll be right here, and I'll be coming to check on all of you, whether Mother approves of that or not."

Sandra flashed her mother a smile and lowered her voice, although obviously Grace could still hear her. "She hates for me to fuss, but now I have an excuse."

Jamie couldn't believe she was going to be anybody's excuse for anything. But there it was. The pregnancy was not in immediate jeopardy, probably not in jeopardy at all, but just in case, Jamie was assigned to bed rest. No arguments, no time to make plans. Bed rest starting immediately or sooner. To be discontinued later if the spotting stopped.

After the ultrasound and in full view of the waiting room, she and Kendra had gone round and round about the alternatives. Kendra and Isaac had wanted Jamie to come to Arlington and stay with them until she delivered. But Jamie had rebelled. The girls were happily settled in school and enjoying their new lives in Toms Brook. Jamie didn't want to leave, either. She had Grace and the bee. She wanted to watch the new house being built using her plans. She wasn't ready to give up her independence. And she didn't want to say goodbye to Cash. Not yet.

Then Grace had set everybody straight.

"Jamie will come to my house and stay with me, of course," she told them. "I'm an old woman who could use the company, and she and the girls will get the best of care. The girls can finish school right where they are. Sandra will help me get ready—" she didn't even bother to ask her daughter, but luckily Sandra was nodding "—and so will Cash. When the doctor says Jamie can get back on her feet, she can move back into the cabin if she chooses. But as far as I'm concerned, she can stay until those babies come popping out. Now, how shall we get her moved in?"

So here she was. Sandra and Grace had brought her back to

Grace's house, and now they settled her on the living room sofa. She knew they were about to make sure that the two downstairs bedrooms were ready for guests. Kendra and Isaac had left the doctor's office to go straight to the cabin. Kendra was going to pack up what Jamie and the girls would need for a few weeks, and while she did, Isaac was going to the school to pick up Hannah, then over to Cissy's to get Alison. In a matter of hours, Jamie's whole life had changed.

"It must have been reassuring to see those little ones bouncing around on that screen," Grace said. "But I can't believe your sister and brother-in-law decided they didn't want to know the sexes."

"After they left the room, the technician asked me if I wanted to know, since I was carrying them."

"Now that would be something, wouldn't it?" Sandra said. "Trying to keep that from slipping out in conversation."

Jamie liked Sandra's practical bent. She thought that what Grace saw as a lack of imagination was really just old-fashioned horse sense. Sandra's personality was different from her mother's, but they complemented each other perfectly. Maybe the way Ben and Grace had complemented each other.

"That's what I told her," Jamie said. "When they drove away, Kendra and Isaac were still arguing about whether they wanted to know."

Sandra turned her attention to Grace. "Mother, I think we should put Jamie in the room that overlooks Daddy's old pumpkin patch. It's covered with wildflowers now, and the view of the mountains and the orchard in the distance is really lovely."

She turned to explain. "The room's a little smaller than the other downstairs bedroom, but that one looks over the parking area."

"If Jamie approves, then the girls can have the larger room and more space," Grace said.

Jamie propped another pillow under her head so she could see them better. "I approve without seeing it. I approve of anything you want to do with us. I just can't thank you enough for suggesting this. Hannah likes her new school, and she's feeling at home here. And Alison loves preschool with Reese."

"And I'll love having the three of you for company," Grace said. "This house is too large and too lonely. It needs a family in it."

"But I'm not going to be able to lift a finger to do anything for a while, and that's going to make so much work for you."

"Oh, I'll get the church to bring meals," Sandra said. "And I'll come up and help Mother clean and cook, plus your sister will be out to help whenever she can. We'll all make sure it's not too big a burden on Mother. Everybody likes to fuss when babies are on the way."

"You're both so kind. And together you can really get things done, can't you?"

The two older women looked at each other; then they laughed.

Not all the countryside had cell-phone coverage. By the time Cash got the first message from his grandmother, Jamie was back home from Front Royal, setting up housekeeping downstairs in Granny Grace's house. Grace put him through to her, and he'd chatted long enough to be sure she really was okay.

His stomach felt as if somebody had turned it inside out and sideways. No matter how hard he tried to tell himself Jamie and the girls were just a diversion, moments like this one kept cropping up to belie the story.

Jamie came with so much baggage attached, she shouldn't even be able to move about freely. He didn't need the mother of small children in his life, particularly children who were so easy to grow fond of. He certainly didn't need a woman who was pregnant again, even if she wasn't keeping the babies. And how about one who had worked so hard to prepare herself for a career that was not particularly portable and was likely to be short-lived? Jamie, for all her checkered past, for all her denials about needing a permanent relationship, was a forever kind of woman in search of roots.

He needed none of those things, but now, realizing how terrified she must have been, knowing that for a while it might not have been clear if her own health was in jeopardy as well as the babies', he realized he was already in over his head. A man didn't worry like this about a "diversion." A man felt this way about a woman he was falling in love with.

And nobody could tell him this was just sexual attraction. Circumstances had made certain that sex was the least of it.

He had to do something to quiet his mind, so with Jamie asleep at his grandmother's house, he drove over to the Taylor place to see if anyone there needed help packing her things. The Taylors' SUV was parked up by the cabin when he arrived, so he parked beside it and went up on the porch to rap on the door.

Before he got the chance, Isaac came out, his arms filled with boxes. "Hey, you must have heard what's going on."

"Just a little while ago. I'm sorry I wasn't around to get her to the doctor's. What can I do?"

"If you'd like to help me take some of this stuff up to your grandmother's, maybe you can lead the way, so we don't get lost. Kendra and the girls are boxing up what they'll need right away. There's a pile in the living room, if you're willing."

"That's why I came."

Cash waited until Isaac passed; then he went inside. Alison and Hannah came running, and he squatted so he could see eye to eye with Alison. "I just talked to your mommy," he said. "She's doing fine. She's taking a nap right now so she'll be awake when you get there."

"We're going to Granny Grace's!" Alison said, eyes shining. "For a long time."

"I know. And I'll be over every single day to see you and to find out if you need anything."

"Will you eat with us?"

Cash could feel the noose tightening. "Sometimes. You bet."

"Will you read us stories?"

"That, too."

Alison threw herself at him and almost knocked him over. He wrapped his arms around her and held her close while he glanced up at Hannah. "Are you doing okay, Hannah Banana?"

"I will miss the playhouse."

"Tell you what. On weekends, if I'm over here working on the new house, I'll bring you two back with me so you can play in it. Sound good?"

"That might work." She didn't look sure.

He wondered what would worry him if he were Hannah, and he thought he might know. "Now that you'll be living with Granny Grace, I'm sure she'll be happy to let you bring your friends up to the orchard to play. I bet they'd like to meet Lucky."

Her eyes lit up. "But that will be a lot of children, and Granny Grace is not young."

"Not to worry. Granny Grace thinks the more children the better. She wants you to feel right at home while you're there. I can absolutely promise that."

"Lucky will be glad we're nearby."

"That's true."

"And I can keep Alison a little quiet, although she *is* young."

He wanted to put his arms around her, too, but he thought

she might consider that a sign of weakness. "Honey, you don't have to keep anybody quiet, including yourself. It's a big house, and Granny Grace raised three children there. And she has grand-children and great-grandchildren, and she'll be disappointed if there's no noise. She'll think something's wrong."

"Really?"

"I'm not kidding."

Hannah smiled, looking in that moment exactly like her mother. He was glad he'd taken the time to make those dimples flash.

Alison bounded off to see what was happening with her toys, and Cash got to his feet. "Now pack up whatever you want to take with you. I don't care how many trips we have to make. Bring anything you think you might need."

"I would like the bunk beds."

Cash was sorry he hadn't exempted furniture. He chewed his lip. Hannah waited; then, when he nodded, trapped by his own generosity, she smiled her Jamie smile again.

"Not really," she said. "Granny Grace has comfortable beds. I just wanted to see if you meant it. And you did." Then she ran off to find her sister.

Cash filled the back of his pickup with Jamie's things, and Isaac and Kendra loaded their SUV. They left together, Hannah with him, Alison riding with her aunt and uncle. After asking permis-sion, Hannah turned on the radio and listened for a while.

"What is this song about?"

Brad Paisley was singing his old hit "All Because Two People Fell in Love" on one of the many country stations available in the Valley. Cash pondered the question.

"I guess it's about all the ways love keeps going through the years and changes lives. People fall in love, they have children who can make the world a better place, that kind of thing."

"Do you like it?"

In truth, he liked it a lot, but that wasn't the kind of thing a real man wanted to admit. "It's kind of sappy."

"What is sappy?"

"Sentimental." He wondered if she knew what that meant. "A song that's meant to make you feel mushy inside, maybe bring a tear or two to your eyes. Like songs about pets who die, and angels watching over us, and people growing old together."

She listened a bit longer; then she looked at him again. "How can hearts get connected? That would hurt."

He supposed even an especially bright eight-year-old might have problems with a metaphor now and then. "He doesn't mean connected that way, not by surgery or anything. He means when two people fall in love, their hearts—and hearts are where you're supposed to feel things, even if that's not exactly true—anyway, their hearts are connected, and they feel each other's emotions."

"I would rather not. That would mean if someone was crying, you would feel like crying, too. That's twice as much crying, and that does not sound good." She paused. "Do you think?"

He couldn't believe he was talking about love with Jamie's oldest daughter. "Yes, but it also means that if they were happy, you would feel that person's joy. Wouldn't that make up for the tears?"

"You would have to try to make sure they were happy all the time." She wrinkled her nose. "That would be a lot of work."

"They say love is a lot of work."

"Don't you know? Aren't you old enough yet?"

"Love *is* a lot of work. There, is that better?"

"I love Alison, and she *is* a lot of work," Hannah said. "Mommy is less so, although I suppose she will be more work now."

He struggled not to laugh out loud. He imagined what a hoot it would be to watch this child grow up. She was completely unpredictable. Her little brain was a circus act.

And there he was, thinking about watching Hannah grow into adulthood. Wondering what it would be like to witness her first clumsy attempts to snare a boyfriend, to sit with her mother when Hannah gave the valedictorian speech at the local high school, to celebrate proudly when she cured cancer. Just like the song.

He reached over and switched to another station, but it was too late. The song was already in his head, and so were the sentiments that went with it.

By the time they arrived and Hannah was running up to the porch and into the house to see Jamie, he found himself whistling as he began to unload boxes and plastic bags from the back of his truck.

Isaac pulled up and got out, and he and Kendra began to unload. Suddenly the air was filled with whistling. Cash stopped and realized that Isaac had been whistling, too. And he was good. He had a clear, warbling whistle that sounded a lot like Cash's own—something he was quietly proud of. And odder still? Isaac was whistling the same Brad Paisley tune.

"Guess you were listening to the same station we were," Cash said.

Isaac grinned and whistled a few bars. In less time than it took to think about it, Cash was whistling harmony.

When they had finished the song, Kendra applauded. "A concert, right here at Cashel Orchard," she said. "You two are great. You ought to go on the road. You're a perfect match."

"What do you think?" Isaac asked. "Want to give up your day job?"

Cash considered. "Let's just file it away in case we're both laid off."

Isaac smiled, and together they began to carry Jamie's things into Grace's house.

21

The girls settled right into the bedroom just down the hall from Jamie's. Grace gave them a pile of old quilts, then reported to Jamie that they had draped them over every surface, making a quilt city to play in before bedtime. Grace promised they could leave it in place while they slept, although she suggested a night-light, so if they woke up before dawn they could see what the strange shapes between dressers and night tables really were.

A dinner of fried chicken and biscuits with milk gravy was practically inhaled; Lucky was fed and walked through the fall twilight on a leash. Hannah and Alison finally came to say good-night smelling of toothpaste and lilac bath powder they had wheedled from Grace. Reassured by Jamie that she was fine and so were their unborn cousins, they were thrilled to be spending the night in the old farmhouse, with the promise of more to come.

The house grew quiet. Cash had set up a small TV with a remote in Jamie's room, and Grace had brought her the baby quilt to finish, insisting that learning to piece by hand would simply increase her skills. According to Grace, with all this time to herself, Jamie should be able to make excellent headway. Sandra had returned home to select a pile of her favorite novels and came back an hour later with books, a portable CD player with an eclectic mix of CDs, the newest edition of every women's magazine at the local Food Lion and a book of *New York Times* crossword puzzles. Jamie wasn't going to be short on things to do.

Unfortunately, there was nothing on television that interested her. She was too tired to sew or do crossword puzzles, and although Sandra's books looked worth diving into, the required concentration just wasn't there. It was too early to go to sleep, and too late to begin something new.

A soft rapping on the door gave her hope, and when Grace poked her head in, Jamie smiled her welcome.

"The girls are sleeping. Alison is snoring away."

"Good. Hannah will feel right at home. Are you on your way to bed?"

"Me? I'm a night owl. I'll probably go upstairs in a little while and finish that Christmas stocking. You don't look comfortable."

"I'm more comfortable than I have a right to be. I mean, one minute I had a million plans, the next I was flat on my back."

"Adjusting, I see. You'll feel more resigned tomorrow."

"Dr. Raille said I may only have to spend two weeks like this. Then I can extend my activities a little at a time until I'm back to normal, or as normal as it ever gets in a twin pregnancy."

"Then I'll make sure I relish every second with you here. Unless, of course, I can convince you to stay until the end of the school year. The girls love being in this house. I love having all of you. I'll make an excellent babysitter when you go off with my grandson."

"You're the kindest woman I know, but let's have that conversation in a couple of weeks, okay? You may be ready to boot us out by then."

"At my age, dear, one knows one's own mind."

"At what age does that happen? The young Grace seemed awfully torn to me."

"Torn? I suppose, as far as you've heard." Grace stepped inside. "But at a certain point, I realized I'd made a commitment and had to make the best of it, no matter what I felt. Ben came to that slower."

"I'd love to hear more. You could pretend it's a bedtime story." Jamie patted the mattress in invitation.

"I would hope it wouldn't put you to sleep."

"I can guarantee my eyes will stay wide open."

Grace perched on the edge, then she leaned back against the headboard, lifting her legs to rest on the quilt. "Then 'Once upon a time before the war…'"

22

1941

At three, Charlie had his mother's dark hair and rosy cheeks, but his eyes were the deep blue-green of Ben's. Like his father's, they were set off by thick, dark lashes. Now they looked like a storm-tossed sea—or at least Grace's best guess as to what one might look like.

"Where is my daddy?" Charlie demanded.

The morning was only half gone, but Grace was already tired. She had awakened just after dawn, all too aware that somehow she had stolen her mother's life—as if it were a prize worth having—and made it her own. She possessed everything that Mina had left behind when she'd followed her husband to Delaware two months ago. Backbreaking work. A lack of recognition. A lack of gratitude. Loneliness. Fatigue. And days that began too soon and lasted too long.

She'd not even had time to ponder that thought, not with breakfast to prepare and children to care for. She had gotten up and, once downstairs, had added kindling to the carefully banked fire in the wood stove, then, when that was hot enough, made coffee, following it with beaten biscuits and fried tomatoes from the last of the season's crop, which she had stored in brown paper in the fruit cellar. Minutes later, she had nodded a greeting to Ben, who arrived in time to split several biscuits, put the tomatoes inside them, then tuck them in a napkin before he disappeared out the door with a cup of coffee in his other hand.

That done, she had gone upstairs for the boys, dressed them, then gone downstairs again, set little Adam in the high chair and fed him applesauce and cooked cereal. Charlie had sat beside her, picking at a breakfast that was a mixture of the adults' and Adam's, as if he wasn't quite certain yet which category he fit into in this strange little family.

The day had progressed in that vein. Now it was ten, and she was finished with the basic chores. Adam was taking his morning nap, and until a moment before, Charlie had been playing quietly in the corner with blocks and three toy soldiers his grandfather had carved for him. But now he was standing at her knee, gazing up at her with the stubborn expression she had seen too often on his father's face.

"Where is my daddy?"

Grace sighed and lifted the little boy to her lap. "He's working, Charlie. Outside. Probably in the barn. Or the apple shed."

"I am tired of his working."

For a moment Grace was tempted to tell Charlie to be grateful, that things were even worse when his father was home. The strained silences punctuated by occasional angry outbursts were harder to take than Ben's absence. But she knew that even if that was true for her, it was not true for Ben's son.

"He'll probably be home for dinner." She glanced up at the clock. "In just two or three hours."

"But then he will leave and work more," Charlie said glumly.

She couldn't argue with the little boy's logic. Ben was rarely home for long. When the weather had been better and the busiest part of harvest season still months away, he had sometimes taken his son along to do chores. There had been rides on the tractor or Buddy, the old gelding who had once pulled the orchard plow and was now living out his days in the pasture. But as fall ended, and the last of the apples were harvested and stored, Charlie had been left at home more frequently. Now he rarely saw his father, and then only when Ben was so tired he had no patience or energy to spare.

Grace opened her mouth to defend him, but no words formed. How did you tell a little boy that his father didn't want to be in the same house with his new wife? That she, too, was happy with that arrangement, even if it meant she had no help with his children? That they were not a real family, as Charlie believed they were, but in fact were no better than strangers occupying different parts of the same life?

December was a fickle month. Yesterday had been lovely and clear, though the ground had crunched under her boots. Today the sky was as dark as her mood. The clouds above the orchard were dense and impenetrable, and the afternoon threatened to be worse. Other men might use the weather as an excuse to listen to a football game on the radio, or play checkers with a small child. Sunday was a day of rest. Sunday was a day for families. But Ben took time for neither.

She wondered if that had been true when he and Anna were married. Had Anna encouraged him to work seven days a week? In her months as Ben's wife, Grace certainly had. She had spent every waking hour caring for the boys and transforming the old farmhouse. Not because she wanted to make a home here, but because she wanted to stay so busy that she wouldn't have to think about what her promise to Anna had done to a life once filled with hope.

"Mommy, I want Daddy!"

Grace wrapped her arms tighter around the little boy and rested her cheek against his sleek dark hair. A month ago, Charlie had begun to call her Mommy. Usually it only happened in the evening, after she told him a story or kissed him good-night. But recently he had begun to use the endearment more frequently, although never in front of his father. She wondered if, in Charlie's childish mind, she and Anna had merged, and now the woman who had claimed that title until a year ago was fading in his memory. At first she had reminded Charlie that she was his aunt, but, stubbornly, he refused to acknowledge that. In his heart he had decided differently. Now she simply let it pass.

What was life going to be like for Charlie and Adam in the coming years? The tension in the house was palpable. How long could any of them go on this way? This was not a life; this was a marking of days. In a world as uncertain and tumultuous as this one, didn't they deserve whatever measure of happiness they could salvage?

Adam took that moment to wake, bleating like a baby lamb from the downstairs bedroom where he liked to nap in an old crib Sylvie had passed on to her, pushed close to the window so he could see what was happening outdoors. He seemed particularly perceptive to Grace—a baby who was fascinated by everything—and contented enough, if he had sights and sounds to occupy his thoughts as he fell asleep.

Charlie's little face puckered, as if he knew that with his brother awake, the discussion had come to a close. Grace made a decision.

"I tell you what, Charlie boy, we'll get Adam, then we'll all bundle up and go look for your daddy. Let's go see what he's doing today."

Charlie's face smoothed, and he grinned. She was sorry that it had taken so little to make him happy, and that she hadn't thought of it before now.

Half an hour passed before they were all ready, but even bundled against the cold, the wind was an icy blast when they opened the door. Luckily the boys didn't seem to mind, and she knew there was no harm in it. She perched Adam on one hip, and Charlie ran ahead, picking up sticks and tossing them to one of the dogs, who came to escort them.

She wondered what Ben might do on a day like this one. He could finish the morning farm chores in an hour. Judging by the droves of men, wagons and trucks that had come and gone during the harvest, she knew the apples were all stored or sold now, although she and Ben rarely discussed his work in the orchard. Weeks had gone by when the first thing she'd heard each morning was the rumble of the tractor moving up and down rows, and the shouts of men as more and more apples found homes in crates inside the trailer.

She had cooked a substantial dinner for their hired help each day and added that to her many other responsibilities. But that was as close as she had come to taking part.

Now she debated where best to find Ben and headed for the packing shed.

The shed was a distance to the west of the barn, bordering the beginning of the orchard. Whatever could be said about the morning's weather, at least the ice that had formed under brighter skies had melted, so walking wasn't treacherous. The walk was slow, though, with Adam choosing to toddle some of the distance and Charlie circling them excitedly. They arrived in about triple the time it would have taken her to make the walk alone, and by the time they did, the chill was seeping into her bones.

She opened the office door and poked her head inside. She knew this was where the orchard records were kept and thought she might find Ben here. But the battered wooden desk was empty, the filing cabinets locked tight. With the boys trailing behind, she opened the door into the shed proper and saw her husband at the far end.

She had been here, of course, but only once, when the place was teeming with local men and women who'd been hired to pick, sort, wash and pack the yearly crop. It was so different now, a long, narrow corridor, divided in a couple of places by partitions that only extended part way to the opposite wall.

At the end where she stood, a stone trough for washing the apples ran along the side, carrying spring water that flowed into a drain and out to a cornfield for irrigation. And beneath it all was the storage cellar, where the apples were held until sold.

At the far end she saw Ben, where some of the equipment and supplies were stored. Wooden apple crates were piled to the ceiling, and at least some of the ladders used during harvest hung from pegs on the wall. Canisters of spray, bags of fertilizer, she noted them all as she and the children drew closer. Ben appeared to be taking notes, and he continued, even after he saw them approaching. She lifted Adam into her arms to cross the room faster.

"Charlie was missing you," she said, after she drew close enough to explain herself. "I told him we'd visit to see what you're doing."

She waited for a surly response, an unfair criticism of her decision to bring his sons out into the cold, where they might catch one of the fatal childhood illnesses that took so many little lives. She waited for a protest that he was too busy for his children, that the boys were her job now, whether she liked it or not.

Instead he set the accounts book on a shelf and held out his arms. Charlie ran to him, and Ben lifted him high.

"Charlie boy, did you miss your daddy?"

"You work and work!"

Ben grinned, and Grace couldn't fail to notice how fetching that sight was. The big man and the little boy who looked so much like him, a different Ben, cares forgotten and pleasure radiating from every pore.

This man loved his children. She had never seen it more clearly. *This man was lonely. She had never seen that at all.*

"Da…" Adam struggled to leap out of her arms. She set him down, and he toddled to Ben, who squatted and gathered him close, as well.

"We had a lovely walk over," Grace said. "But it's not going to be lovely at all this afternoon. I think it's going to snow, or worse."

"Worse?"

"Sleet, ice. It just feels that way. Wet and nasty."

He was still smiling, transparently happy to have his sons in his arms. Perhaps that was what motivated her next sentences, or perhaps she had known for some time that their little family just couldn't go on this way. Ben needed to be part of their circle. He was the children's father. He was, for whatever it was worth, her husband.

"Ben, take the afternoon off. I'll make a real Sunday dinner, and you can listen to a football game, maybe teach Charlie to play checkers. We have that old set of my father's. He would love that." She paused. "And you could use a little time away from hard work. So could I. What do you say?"

The smile died slowly, and her heart sank. She had pushed too hard, too fast. He was thinking of Anna, feeling regret his real wife was gone and instead Sunday dinner would be eaten with her sister sitting at the other end of the table. He was feeling guilty that, for a moment, his children's visit had brought him pleasure when he should still be mourning. She couldn't guess what else he was feeling, but she suspected none of it was happiness at her suggestion.

"You're sure?" he said at last.

She was so surprised that for a moment, she couldn't answer.

"You're not," he said, looking down at his sons. "You don't have to be kind to me, Grace. That wasn't in the bargain we made."

"No, Ben…" She reached out and touched his arm, surprising them both. "You… I… Oh, dang, you just surprised me, that's all. You looked like you were going to say no. Of course I want you to spend the afternoon with the boys." She smiled. "Happy children are easier to take care of, right?"

"I'm not sure I would know."

She thought that was an odd thing to say. "Well, come and see. You'll certainly make them happy, then we can judge."

"There's not a lot I'll be able to do outside."

"All the more reason. But for the record, I think we ought to make Sunday afternoons a tradition." She glanced at Charlie to make her point. "Certain people need to have more time with you."

He set Charlie on the ground and handed Adam back to her. "We'll see."

That was plenty good enough for her, since it gave her a way out, as well. "We'll see you for dinner, then. About one."

Grace was a good cook, because cooking was an art. So many traditional chores were wretchedly boring. She would never keep house as well as her sister, although the house she was keeping was brighter and definitely cheerier since she had taken over the job.

The kitchen was a good example. When she'd moved in, dingy wallpaper had covered the walls and nothing brightened the counters. A scarred linoleum rug had covered the central portion of the floor, and a much-laundered gray tablecloth, the table. She had set about remedying the situation immediately. If she was going to spend a portion of every day cooking and serving meals in this room, she was going to make it a place where she could be happy.

Now the walls and cabinets were a clean, bright white, the cornices and trim a deep lipstick red, the windows outlined by fresh new curtains in a cheerful cherry print. She had traded one of the many serviceable quilts in her sister's linen cupboard for a neighbor's handwoven rag rug in red, white and green, and made a tablecloth of the same color plaid for the table. Until the freeze had robbed her of fresh flowers, she had made sure there were bouquets at the table's center every day, even if they were only wildflowers. She hoped for better next year. Before she had even tackled the kitchen, she had carefully weeded all Ben's mother's old beds, hoping to clear the way for any flowers that had survived or their seedlings.

Now she kept a bowl of polished apples in a yellowware bowl on the counter, and the metal canisters that Anna had hidden on shelves were painted and their contents labeled in colorful script. Cookie cutters hung from a wire strung across the window.

Ben had not been as pleased as she at the transformation. He had questioned her use of time when there was still canning to do. He had faulted her for preferring appearance to substance. At first Grace had been furious that her attempts to bring life and beauty to the house had been met with resistance. But later, as she fumed, she had realized that Ben saw everything she accomplished as a criticism of Anna. That had lessened her fury a notch.

Whether Ben liked the new look or not, Grace was happier working in the kitchen now, and today that translated into working harder on dinner. She sliced generous pieces of salt-cured ham, rinsed them well, then set them to sizzling in the frying pan. When they were browned the way she liked them, she added handfuls of sliced apples, put the top on the pan and set it on a back burner. She simmered purple hull peas she had been soaking since early morning, then opened a jar of collard greens and cooked them with a piece of fatback, and some onion, dried hot pepper and chopped garlic. The morning's biscuits had been quickly made, but there were enough that she didn't need to make more. Instead, she mixed up some corn bread and put it in the oven to go with them.

Then, as a treat, she counted out eggs and decided to make a sponge cake to eat with peaches canned from Ben's own trees and cream from their milk cow. She set Charlie up on a stool as a helper, and once the ingredients were combined, she gave him a wooden spoon. With enthusiasm, she crowed over the strength of his tiny arm and his attention to every little speck on the side of the bowl. Once he tired, she took over and briskly finished the beating.

By the time the dinner was done and the cake was cooling on the counter, the kitchen was fragrant and inviting, and her mouth began to water.

At one—exactly—Ben came back to the house and went to wash up. By the time he arrived to take his seat, she had dinner on the table. She poured hot coffee, got milk for Adam and Charlie, then untied her apron and took her place across from him.

Ben said grace, with Charlie bowing his head in imitation and Adam walloping his highchair tray with a spoon.

"We've got our own Gene Krupa," she said when Ben had finished, inclining her head toward Adam.

He paused in the midst of reaching for the platter of ham and apples. She realized what she had said and how it had sounded. *Our own.* As if Adam belonged to them both. She met his eyes and waited.

"Better watch for visitors. Benny Goodman may come calling." He lifted the platter off the table and offered it to her first.

Relieved, she took a slice, then helped the boys to their dinner from the platters and bowls closest to her. By the time they were all eating, the knots in her stomach were smoothing out. This had been a good idea after all.

She expected Charlie to babble through the meal, asking a thousand questions of the father he too rarely saw. But Charlie, despite his obvious excitement, was mute, even though, when she ate alone with the boys, he talked the entire time.

Finally she set her fork on her plate. "Charlie, why don't you tell your daddy about the fox we saw on our walk yesterday?"

Charlie's eyes shone, then clouded, and he looked down at his plate, only peeking once at his father's face.

"I guess I'll have to tell him," she teased. "You'll lose your chance if you don't speak up fast."

"Not s'posed to," he said so softly she nearly couldn't hear him.

She frowned at Ben, who looked away.

"You're not supposed to do what, honey?" She touched Charlie's elbow. "Be outside?"

He shook his head, then sneaked a quick glance at his father before he shook it again.

"I think Charlie's trying to tell you he's not supposed to talk at the dinner table," Ben said.

She tried to imagine why. Did Charlie talk with his mouth so full that he choked? If he talked too much, did he forget to eat, so he didn't clean his plate? Did he habitually interrupt, so Ben was trying to teach him manners?

Her puzzled expression was all Ben needed. He set his fork down, too. "His mother had rules."

Now she understood. Although in her childhood home the Fedley children had always been allowed to talk at the dinner table, there had rarely been conversation. Grace remembered being chastised by her sister so often for her choice of subject, her tone of voice, her slang, that she had more or less given up trying. Apparently Anna had taken things a step further with her own family.

"I see." She didn't know what to say that could be said in front of the children.

Ben began to eat again.

Grace picked up her fork, an idea having occurred to her. "Well, rules are meant to be changed," she said sweetly. "You and my sister probably had so much to say to each other that there was no time for Charlie to talk to either of you. But that's changed now. Charlie, please tell your daddy about the fox." She narrowed her eyes when Ben started to interrupt. "Food goes down better with conversation, and in this family, Charlie is our very best chance to prevent indigestion."

Ben glared at her; then, as she continued to stare at him, the glare eased and just the hint of a smile took its place. "Go ahead, son," he said, without looking at Charlie. "I think the rule has changed, and besides, listening to you is a heap better than listening to your aunt Grace."

Grace looked away, afraid that she might smile, too.

Half an hour later, Adam was happily playing in his pen, and Charlie was upstairs looking for the checkers, which he had been using to build a fort for his tin soldiers yesterday. Ben lingered at the kitchen table with another cup of coffee, while Grace cleared and scraped plates.

"Anna didn't much like noise," he said, as if the conversation at the table had never ended.

"Yes, I remember that."

"You seem not to mind it."

"I like children who sound like children. Charlie's a wonderful little boy, but he's a little boy. Shouldn't he sound and act like one?"

"We took over your life. You had a lot of plans that didn't include the snuffling and snorting of kids."

Once again she was so surprised for a moment that she couldn't speak. Surprise was becoming habitual. She managed to recover this time.

"Yes, well, that's the way things happen, huh?"

"What were you going to do, Grace? You had something planned. You had savings." He gestured to the kitchen, as if to say she had not found the money for the changes she had made here or elsewhere in the small household allowance he gave her.

He was right. She had taken the money for paint and fabric from her own private store. She had also splurged on a new radio from the *Lafayette Radio Catalog,* a six-tube AC-DC Super, to replace the broken one in the living room, then installed it in the kitchen, where she spent most of her time. Her savings were now sadly depleted, much like her life.

"I was going to travel." She stacked dishes in a tin pan filled with soapy water. She had been pleased to discover that, some years ago, Ben had installed a kerosene hot-water heater to make this chore simpler.

"Where? When?"

"Oh, soon. And everywhere. I saved enough money to set

myself up somewhere else. As soon as Mama and Papa headed to Delaware, I was going to head west, work as I went, see the world. I've never been anywhere. There are oceans, mountains that make ours look tiny, people of all colors and kinds." She glanced over at him. "I wanted to see it all."

"We ruined that, the boys and me."

Just the fact he would recognize and address this warmed her heart. From his tone, she wasn't sure he was sorry. Even if he was, she didn't think he would say so. But the recognition was something.

"Mama told me once that all she ever really wanted was to open a little café in town, cook up breakfasts and lunches and talk to people when they came in every day. Instead, she cooked for us and nobody talked. That's probably where Anna got used to silence."

"You talk."

She laughed. "I guess I do. When there's somebody to talk to."

"You talk to the boys all the time. Charlie picks up new words every day. From you, from that radio of yours. He's a regular chatterbox now."

"Good for him, don't you think? A man with words is a man who can talk his way out of trouble."

"Not if he grows apples."

She was aware that she and Ben were having their first real conversation. She imagined wives all over the country pouring coffee for their men as they sat at the table and watched them clear away the remains of Sunday dinner. Rich men, men like Ben who had land but little cash to show for it, poor men who had nothing but the coffee they sipped. They were part of a chain that stretched from one ocean she hadn't seen to the other. The thought warmed her.

"I guess growing apples can be difficult," she said. "Hard to talk your way out of spots and bruises."

"I wish that's all it was. But the apple industry's been on a steady decline for years now. Every year is harder than the last."

"Why? What's changing?"

"Just a lot of hooey."

She glanced at him. "What kind of hooey?"

He seemed surprised she wanted to know. "After the war, my dad got as much as eighteen dollars for a barrel, shipping them over to England. Those were the days. Labor didn't cost much, fewer diseases, fewer government restrictions. A man could grow apples and ship them away, fill the bank with money, and that was that. Or nearly."

"It's changed now?"

"All for the worse. Now it costs so much and takes so much time to bring a tree into production that the only orchards still managing are like this one, lots of land, lots of trees, lots of headaches."

"That's why you work all the time."

"I wish there were ten more of me."

She straightened and smiled. "Well, I'm glad there's not. Having one pretend husband is bad enough."

For a moment he looked as if he wasn't sure how to take that; then he smiled at her. "You do know exactly how to say the wrong thing the right way, don't you?"

She laughed. "I'm sorry. But you asked for it."

"I guess I did."

"So what do you get for a barrel of apples now?"

"Better than we did ten years ago. It dropped as low as two dollars a barrel during the worst of the Depression. It's up from that now, but labor costs a lot more, too, and so does spray. And we use a lot more of both."

"If we go to war, that will change, won't it?"

He sobered. "Everything will change. There'll be a good market for apples, but no one will be around to grow them. We'll all be off fighting."

"Surely not *you*, Ben? The country will need its farmers. And you have two small boys. So far the draft's left you alone."

"You been listening to the news on that radio of yours? We've got a peacetime draft now, which is why the fathers get a break, but if we fight, it's going to take all of us to win it, and even then, it won't be a sure thing."

She sobered, too. She had never liked the news, people killing other people, bombs and torture and hatred. But avoiding it these days was hard. She'd heard Walter Winchell exhorting his country to go to war, Edward R. Murrow doing on-the-scene commentary from Europe. Even the farm-and-home shows devoted more and more time to news coverage. Then, just a little more than a month ago, the U.S. destroyer *Reuben James* had been sunk by a German submarine. Even an ostrich with his head buried in the sand probably knew things were changing too fast and in the wrong direction.

"A year ago, Anna said we'd be at war by now," she reminded him.

"Anna wasn't always right, but she wasn't far wrong on that. It's coming."

Charlie appeared, lugging the latched leather case filled with checkers. Ben finished the last sips of his coffee; then he hoisted the little boy up on his lap, and together they began to set up the board. Charlie was so excited that his little fingers would hardly work in tandem.

Grace tried to find the warm feeling she'd had earlier, the one that had connected her to families across the country. When

Adam began to fuss, she took him out of the playpen and brought him in to sit on the floor with Charlie's blocks. Then she turned on the radio to fill the kitchen with music.

Sammy Kaye's "Sunday Serenade" was just ending, and the announcer was saying that next up was a University of Chicago Round Table discussion of the Canadian role in the war in Europe. Grace wiped her hands on her apron and reached to turn the dial, hoping she could find something more promising to listen to. So far from a city center, reception here was dependent on the whim of the winds, but she was optimistic.

She was stopped by a new voice over the airwaves.

"From the NBC newsroom in New York. President Roosevelt said in a statement today that the Japanese…"

She turned up the volume and listened to the rest of the short announcement, eyes widening. She turned to the table and saw that Ben had heard it, too.

"Pearl Harbor?" she asked.

"That's where our Pacific fleet is based."

"What does this mean?"

Ben didn't look at her. Instead, he looked down at his son, who was setting up the red and black checkers on the same side of the board. He kissed Charlie's head before he spoke.

"It means war, Grace. It means the war is finally at our front door."

23

1941

Charlie had his family afternoon, even though his father's attention focused on the radio every time a new bulletin about the attack on Pearl Harbor was broadcast. The kitchen, still deliciously scented from the afternoon dinner and warm from the stove, became their haven. They were still there when it was time for supper, and Grace heated what remained of the earlier meal, and served the cake and peaches with it.

Ben volunteered to put the boys to bed while she washed dishes, and she accepted gratefully. Only when Charlie lifted his little arms to say good-night before he was taken upstairs did the peace in Virginia shatter, too.

"'Night, Mommy," he said sleepily.

"'Night, Charlie boy." She hugged him and kissed his cheek. "You sleep tight. Don't let the bedbugs bite." She set him on the floor and happened to glance at Ben. A moment passed before she realized why he looked so angry.

"She is not your mother," Ben said. "She is your aunt Grace."

Charlie, tired from the unusual day, stuck out his lower lip. "No, she is my mommy!"

Grace tousled his hair. "We have a tired boy here, Ben. Please let this go."

Ben stuck out his hand. "Charlie, you come with me right now."

Charlie shrank away from his father's touch. "No, I want Mommy."

Grace edged in front of him, so she was standing between the little boy and his father. "I'll bring him up in a minute. Why don't you start with Adam?" She lowered her voice, hoping Charlie wouldn't hear. "You look furious. He's afraid of you."

His expression changed instantly. He looked as if she had struck him. "He has no call to be."

When Grace had first taken over the children's care, Charlie had been so subdued, so careful not to offend, she had wondered what might be wrong with him. Was he simply sad about his mother's death? Or was physical punishment the standard at home, so Charlie was simply afraid to make a mistake?

Since then, she had seen Ben turn Charlie over his knee for a quick swat on the fanny, but only after a serious infraction. She hadn't objected, having been raised that way herself. But until tonight, Ben had never looked so angry with his son.

Now she felt embarrassed because she had interfered. She had no real evidence that Ben might hurt the little boy tonight or any night, and she shouldn't let Charlie think so, either.

"I'm sorry." She stepped out of Ben's way so that he could continue to corral his son. In a moment a mutinous Charlie placed his small hand in Ben's, and they started out of the room.

"She *is* my mommy," Charlie said, as he left the kitchen. "Is!"

She supposed courage was a good trait for a little boy in a land preparing to go to war.

By the time Ben returned, she had finished the dishes and prepared herself for the argument to come.

"Just so you know," she said, when she heard his footsteps, "I've tried to tell Charlie I'm not his mother. He knows it, but a little boy needs a mother, and since I'm right here taking care of him, I'm first choice. I hope you're not going to blame me for that, too."

"Too?"

"I've made a lot of changes around here, and I know you don't like them. I can't be Anna, and I know you wish I were."

"You're different, that's for sure."

She sighed and turned to face him. "Have you had enough coffee, or are you going straight to bed?"

"If there's more, I'll have some."

"I don't know how you drink it this late, Ben. I'd be doing the java jive every night."

"That would be interesting to see."

She tried to read his expression. Unfortunately, he was a magnificent example of that primary American male virtue: self-restraint.

"Sit," she said. "I'll make a fresh pot. This has been around too long."

He reached for the pot himself. "Don't bother. I'll eat the grounds if I have to."

"I was afraid you were going to slap him for defying you. He's such a wonderful little boy. He doesn't need slapping."

"You don't think I know that?"

"Honestly? I wasn't sure. I'm glad you do." She wondered if she should say more, but before she could, he went on.

"You've never lifted your hand to him?"

"Not on your life. That's no way to raise a child."

"Your sister thought different."

She had wondered if Anna was the reason for Charlie's initial shyness, his fear of doing something wrong. She phrased her answer carefully, reminding herself that anger at a dead woman was unproductive.

"I'm trying to do my best here, but I won't stoop to violence to subdue a normal, inquisitive little boy. I hope you don't expect it."

"Violence is overstating it. Anna just believed that sparing the rod spoiled the child."

"If letting a child have opinions and thoughts of his own and showing him how much you love him, spoils him, then I guess I'm all for it."

"So tell me how this love and spoiling is going to affect him when you walk out of here, *Mommy?*"

Instinctively, she could feel that the conversation had turned in a completely new direction. They were no longer discussing Charlie and child rearing. They were discussing something else entirely—her relationship to this family.

"You know, if there's enough coffee, pour me a cup, too," she said. "We're still picking up stations. Maybe we ought to listen a while longer."

"I can't sit at this table another minute. I'll take the coffee in the living room. We can move the radio in there."

She finished up the last of the kitchen chores, then followed him to the next room. On the few evenings they had shared here, she had always taken the overstuffed chair wedged into the farthest corner, and Ben had sat all the way across the room. Unfortunately, as part of her plan to make the house more comfortable and cheerful, she had rearranged the furniture. Now she saw her mistake. There was nowhere to sit where she wouldn't be within reach for a conversation.

With that a fact, she chose the most central spot on the sofa, while Ben set up the radio and tried to find a station, daring him to sit beside her. When he was finished, he accepted the dare, stretching his long legs in front of himself but keeping a safe distance between them.

Music was playing on the radio, the reception crackly and uneven, but audible. Outside, one of the German shepherds was barking at shadows. Something pattered against the porch roof, most likely sleet or even snow, and she didn't envy Ben, who would have to rise early tomorrow morning and see to the outdoor chores.

Grace lifted her cup. "I think a lot of people must have died today. One minute they were living their lives, going about their business, and the next…" She shook her head.

"We should have been in this war a long time ago. Roosevelt knew it was coming right to our door, too. That's why he started up the draft last year. Preparation."

"You really think you'll be called?"

"I have to go."

From his tone, she knew that even if he wasn't drafted, Ben felt he had to fight. He believed the time had come.

"When, do you think?" she asked.

"We won't have much time to plan."

She had kept herself so busy, worked so hard, spent most of her waking hours with the children. Planning hadn't been part of that. She had been too busy just moving from one hour to the next.

Now the possibilities seemed endless, her future a flood of maybes.

Maybe there would be plenty of jobs, good ones, for women

now, jobs men had done in the past. And since many women would be in her situation, maybe child care would be available while she worked. She would have to move to a town or city, find accommodations, of course, but she had family spread around Virginia and as far north as Delaware now. It was possible they might help her find a job and a place to live. They might even help with the boys.

For the brief period they were at war, she would have some freedom again, an income of her own, interesting people around her, a life of sorts.

One thing was for certain. She wouldn't have Ben to contend with. He would be far away, fighting for his country, and his wishes wouldn't matter. By the time he came home again, the boys would be a little older and less dependent on her. If he wanted to, Ben would be able to handle their care with some hired help. Or perhaps by then he would feel so estranged from his children that he would allow her to continue to raise them with a little help from her family.

If Ben came home.

At that thought and the shudder that came with it, she put down her cup and turned to him. "What did you mean when you said we have to plan?"

"If I can find somebody to pay even a portion of what it's worth, I may have to sell the orchard." He suddenly looked very tired. "It's possible there'll be no other way. I don't expect you to stay here with the boys and look after things. It's enough you gave up your dreams when your sister demanded it. I'd be a fool to expect you to work even harder."

"This land's been in your family for generations."

"It's the boys who trouble me most." He rose and began to pace. "What's going to happen to them?"

She wasn't sure what he was asking. "They'll be distraught, of course. Both of them think you're the snake's toenails. They'll miss you, that's for sure."

"I mean who's going to take care of them?"

She frowned. "Can you possibly think I'm going to abandon them the minute you put on a uniform?"

"This was temporary, you said so yourself. But this war won't be temporary, Grace. I don't know how long I'll be gone. It could be years."

"Of course you won't be gone that long. We'll win fast. It'll be over before it begins. Months at most. You won't need to sell so much as a tree."

"That's not the way it'll happen. We'll declare war on Japan, then on Germany. Probably in the next few days. Winning both? Years. And I might not come back at all."

There it was again, the obvious. Ben was strong. Ben was quick. But no man could outrun a bullet or bomb with his name on it. That freedom she had yearned for could be closer than she'd imagined.

That thought gave her no pleasure.

"You'll just have to be careful, then." She got up and stood in his path to stop his pacing. "You'll have two boys in Virginia expecting you to return. You'll just have to make sure you do."

He gave a humorless laugh. "Have you considered how much easier your life might be if I don't?"

"As a matter of fact, I just did. And you know what? I didn't like it. So I would appreciate it if you would try not to kick the bucket somewhere in Europe or the Pacific. Charlie and Adam lost one parent. Let's do our level best to make sure they don't lose the second one, okay?"

"We have to make plans for them."

"No, we don't. Wherever I go, they'll come with me. You might not approve when Charlie calls me Mommy, but that's how he thinks of me. Adam doesn't know a thing different. I'm not going to abandon them to strangers or distant relatives."

"There'll be jobs for women all over the country. You could go almost anywhere, do almost anything."

For a moment she imagined those distant peaks in Colorado, the amber cliffs of New Mexico, the sinuous rivers of wheat in the Midwest. And California? That was a dream too precious to pull out and savor now.

Then she looked into Ben's eyes, saw that his dream of the orchard he loved, the heritage he had treasured and the sons he had wanted to raise on this land was being stolen from him, as well.

"Not with the boys in tow," she said. "I won't go far afield. No matter what happens here, with the orchard, we'll stay near our family." She smiled a little. "Such as it is."

"You won't change your mind? I'll be too far away to consult."

"You think maybe I'll drop them off by the side of the road somewhere because I'm tired of them?"

He ran his hand through his hair, combing it distractedly off his forehead. "This was temporary. We made a bargain."

"Oh, I see." There it was again. Ben was hammering home his message. He had not intended their lives to stay meshed. And the longer they were, the harder it would be to untangle them.

She tried to turn away, but he put a hand on her shoulder to stop her.

"Those were *your* words, Grace. The day you married me. You made sure I knew. I haven't forgotten."

"Anna said them first. Remember? The night she died, she told me I only had to stay until you and the boys didn't need me anymore."

"Things have a way of changing." He turned her to face him, gripping both shoulders now. "I just have to know for sure you're willing to let them."

Surely he was talking about his sons, about caring for them while he was overseas, perhaps about continuing to care for them until adulthood, if he died in some foreign field. She waited and wondered, and when he didn't go on, she sighed. In relief?

She wasn't sure.

None of that could be put into words. But some things could. "I also told you the day we married that I'm not the woman Anna led you to believe I was. You want me to say this out loud? Then I will. I love those little boys. There. Like a mother, I'm afraid. And I'm not so selfish that I'd thrust them aside just to get on with my life. If you still think I would, then you haven't learned much about me."

"I've only learned what I can from a distance."

"And who made sure it was at a distance? You've looked down your nose at everything I've done here. You've worked until dark so you wouldn't have to be in the same house with me. You've told me in a hundred small ways that I don't measure up to my sister."

"I've said you're different, not that you don't measure up."

"And isn't that the same thing?"

For a moment he looked as if he wanted to answer; then he shook his head, and his hands dropped to his sides.

Immediately she missed their warmth, the wide, strong fingers holding her gently in place.

"I'll tell you what I see," he said. "A woman I as much as kidnapped for my own convenience."

She was astonished. "No. No, it's just not true. Sure, I feel that way sometimes. Like I'm some kind of slave taking care of your house and your sons. But I had choices, Ben. I chose the one Anna demanded of me, but to be honest, not out of pity or love for her. Because when it came right down to it, there was no other way. If you kidnapped me, then I was a willing enough victim."

"I don't think of you as a slave. I haven't, not for one moment."

"How *do* you think of me, then?"

He was silent for so long that she thought he wasn't going to answer. Oddly enough, she felt tears rising in her eyes.

"I try not to," he said softly.

Then he turned and left the room, the radio crackling as another announcer explained the events of the day in far-off Honolulu. She listened to the sleet striking the edges of the porch and skipping along the painted surface. And she tried not to hear the words that Ben just might have been saying.

24

Jamie looked forward to Cash's visits. He arrived early every morning with a different surprise. Some of the gifts were silly: a river stone that looked like Mickey Mouse; a dictionary of Southernisms, since she was now residing in Virginia, and a huge T-shirt that asked Does This Make Me Look Fat? with an arrow pointing to what was now a considerable bump where her waistline once resided.

Some of the gifts were more traditional. He brought chocolate truffles, bouquets of wildflowers and jewelry. The last was inspired by Halloween's rapid approach, a gaudy witch to adorn her pajamas, along with crystal-ball earrings that flashed on and off when Jamie pinched them.

She would have looked forward to his visits anyway. Cash was always good company, arriving early enough to bring breakfast on a tray, sitting beside her as she ate while supervising her daughters' preparations for school. Then, when everybody was ready, he scooped up the girls and drove them down the mountain to their schools. He swore he didn't mind, that having Hannah's observations and Alison's chatter to look forward to made the trip seem half as long. But she knew that she and the girls were taking time from his beloved horses, and she appreciated the sacrifice as much as the company.

A little over two weeks from the start of her imposed bed rest, she had good news when he arrived.

"Guess what?" She sat forward, hugging the covers over her knees. "I talked to Dr. Raille. She says if I continue to be asymptomatic, I can move to partial bed rest next week. Two long rests a day and no heavy lifting, but I can be up and around the rest of the time. And if that goes well, I can drive again in another week, at least until I get too big to fit behind the wheel."

Cash was wearing his Rosslyn and Rosslyn polo shirt, and his brown hair waved lazily over his ears. She suspected he'd used the time he would have spent at the barber shop caring for her and her daughters. She was just as glad. The look suited him, as did his grin at her announcement.

"Hey, that's terrific. We ought to do something to celebrate."

"Just getting out of bed and walking around will be fabulous."

He perched on the bed beside her, a cup of Grace's coffee in his hand. "How are the quilts coming?"

That was one thing that could be said for four-poster exile. Jamie had completed the first top and was now quilting it with the help of a small hoop that rested on her substantial belly. Her stitches were nothing to rave about, but Grace had assured her they were excellent for a first-time quilter. The babies wouldn't care, and Jamie had decided to simply forge ahead. When she tired of working with the hoop, she traced shapes for the next quilt on her chosen fabric and cut them to hand-piece. She had four blocks finished and couldn't decide which quilt she liked better.

She held up the hooped quilt for him to see. "Halfway there. I won't be entering it in any contests, but I'm pleased."

He bent closer, making a show of assessing her handiwork, although she guessed he would approve even if her stitches were as long and wiggly as earthworms.

"Good job," he said. "The girls showed me theirs. Looks like they'll stay snug this winter."

"Your grandmother's a saint. If they're in the mood, she works with them in the evenings. Hannah's about to put the binding on hers, and she's helping Alison tie. I'm glad I always bought Alison shoes with real shoelaces. At least she knows how to tie a knot."

"Even if she doesn't have much of a feel about where to put them."

"Well, there are a couple of blocks in her quilt that will never fall apart, that's for sure."

"And a few that are falling apart as we speak." He stood and felt in his pocket, and pulled out an envelope. "Speaking of celebrating. Got you something."

She batted her eyelashes at him. "You know, I love all these presents. I've learned the meaning of *cattywampus* and *nearabout*, and every single person who visits me wants a witch like this one." She pointed to the front of her plaid PJs, where the witch rode her broom just above her left breast. "But coming up with something every day has to be a strain."

"Nothing to it. Are you going to take this or not?"

"Just so you know, you can take a break now and then. I don't want to be a burden."

"I'm counting how many times you say that. If I'm not mistaken, you're into five figures."

"Am not. Four, maybe." She smiled up at him. "It's really not that easy accepting all this good will without giving anything back."

"We're just racking up points in heaven, if you want the truth. I'm counting on somebody up there keeping score."

"That could be good for you, but not so good for me."

"Oh, I think those babies will give you a point or two. I wouldn't get all tore up about it."

"Tore up? Is that in my Southern dictionary?"

"It should be."

Jamie opened the envelope. "Sal's Italian Bistro. A menu?"

"Just a stone's throw from here, and it rivals anything in the big city. And your sister called your doctor. She's okayed a trip there tomorrow night, as long as we drop you off at the door and pick you up there. A test run. You, me, the girls and Granny Grace. What do you say?"

For a moment Jamie didn't know how to respond. Something as simple as a trip to a local hangout sounded like heaven. "Can I have two of everything?"

"Not only that, you can eat all my leftovers. Right there at the table."

She crooked her finger. "Come here."

He sat down again, and she put her arms around him and pulled him close for a thank-you kiss.

She was still smiling when he was already halfway down the mountain with her daughters in tow.

Sandra brought Alison home from preschool as she did every Friday. Sandra and Cissy had each claimed shifts, and Alison was delivered to her mother's bedside every afternoon right on time. Hannah usually rode the school bus home, and Martina, a woman who worked in the apple shed and helped Grace with housework, met her at the bus stop then drove her up to the house.

Today, though, Kendra and Isaac picked up Hannah at school. Since Jamie's move, Kendra had come to visit several times. Each time she'd brought gourmet takeout from D.C. area restaurants and energy to help Grace with anything that needed to be done. Wisely, Grace had let her, even though, between Sandra and Martina, the house was well cared for and so was Jamie.

This time the Taylors brought Asian food, a selection of Chinese, Thai and Vietnamese, enough to last Grace and company for a week or more.

"I couldn't decide which to get," Kendra told Jamie, as Grace found places to put the overflow in her chest freezer, with Hannah and Isaac's help. "My decision-making apparatus seems to be shutting down. On a good day, I stand in front of the closet and can't figure out what to wear. On a bad day, I'm not even sure whether to get out of bed. I'm so ineffectual. The only place I'm still functioning normally is work."

Jamie wasn't surprised Kendra was feeling stressed; she was just surprised she was admitting it so freely. "What's this about? I'm doing great. In fact, I'm sure you know I'm going out for dinner tomorrow night on a minor test run."

"No cramping? No bleeding?"

"Nope. Babies moving normally and waking me up regularly at night. I think they're either doing each other's hair or getting ready to watch the Lions beat the Bears on Sunday. If these are boys, I hate to tell them it won't be televised here." She paused. "But you stubbornly refused to find out, didn't you?"

"I couldn't decide!"

Jamie laughed.

Isaac came in to join them. He leaned over to kiss Jamie's cheek, repeated Kendra's questions and smiled at Jamie's answers.

"Hey, that's great news, and Italian food tomorrow will be a nice break from the gallons of Asian cuisine now happily at home in Grace's freezer," he said.

"I'll relish every bite."

"On the way in, I heard you talking about the sex of the babies." He settled himself in a bedside chair, while Kendra perched on the edge of the bed.

"Kendra admitted she was the hold-up. What did *you* want to do?"

"I like to be prepared. I'd like to tell people, so the babies won't be wearing yellow and green until they're heading off to preschool. I'd like to cut the name discussion in half."

"It could be a boy and a girl," Kendra said. "We'd still need names that fit both sexes."

"But only one of each."

"That just doesn't seem like enough of a reason—"

Jamie decided to break in with her two cents' worth. "Sis, I knew ahead of time with both Hannah and Alison. It didn't spoil anything. There's so much going on in the delivery room, it was nice to have that part settled. I understand the fun of the surprise factor, but you know, with twins, there's going to be a lot more hubbub, and there won't be much time to celebrate whether you had boys or girls or both. You could do that part now."

Kendra looked at her watch. "It's too late. By the time I got anybody at the doctor's office, and they looked up the records, and—"

"Not necessary." Isaac took out his wallet and pulled out a small envelope. "I figured, just in case you changed your mind, we ought to have it in writing. So the tech wrote it down and sealed it for us to look at if we ever got ready."

"You didn't!"

"I haven't peeked, if that's what you mean."

"I mean, you didn't actually go to all that trouble?"

He reached over and took Kendra's hand. "They're already real to us, K.C. Naming them at this point isn't going to make them seem more so."

Now Jamie realized where Kendra's ambivalence came from. Her sister was afraid to feel more attached than she already did. There were months to go, more obstacles to overcome, more complications that might arise. Jamie had never had a clearer sense of what this pregnancy meant to Kendra. By becoming her surrogate, Jamie had opened a door that had been permanently sealed. And some part of her sister was still afraid to walk through it.

"It's up to you," Isaac said.

"It didn't spoil anything for you?" Kendra asked Jamie.

"By the time the girls were born, I felt like I knew them better. I liked that." She realized she'd given the wrong answer. Kendra didn't want to know these babies better. Her sister was afraid she might not be able to bear it if something went wrong.

But Kendra nodded, as if she realized that it was time to move on. "Okay."

"I want you to be sure," Isaac said. "Don't just do this for me."

"No." Kendra held out her hand for the envelope. "Give it to me."

Jamie wasn't sure if Kendra was going to open the envelope or rip it into a dozen pieces. But Kendra opened it and scanned the words. Then she handed the small scrap of paper to Isaac.

"Well, I'll be." He grinned. Then he got up and scooped Kendra off the bed for a bear hug.

"Boys," he said at last. "Two Little Leaguers."

Kendra sniffed, but sniffing was a useless protection, and in a moment tears filled her eyes. "Sons."

"Well, wow!" Jamie swallowed hard, thrilled that this moment had come. "We needed some boys in this family."

Isaac rested his hand on her belly for a moment, a privilege Jamie had extended to him the moment the babies began to move. "Hear that, guys? We need you to round things out. Now we've just got to work out some names."

Kendra started to laugh, though tears were slipping down her cheeks. "It seems just as hard as it did before. Do you know how many boys' names there are? Thousands."

"The right ones will make themselves known," Jamie said. "And you still have time."

"Boys." Kendra put her hand on top of Isaac's. Jamie felt the pleasant weight against her womb and inside her heart.

In response to the news, Grace suggested cheap indoor-outdoor carpeting for the playroom in the new house—since it would have to be replaced regularly—and bars on the windows. Although she said the last with a wink.

"They will need to be taught a lot, since they are boys," Hannah said. "Boys never seem to know the things they ought to."

"Does that go for uncles, too?" Isaac asked.

"Uncles are men. By the time a boy becomes an uncle, he has learned to behave."

"It takes that long?"

Hannah nodded solemnly. "I think it does. And not all boys become uncles."

Jamie imagined an entire continent filled with grown-up boys who hadn't made the cut. She was going to have to speak to her daughter about the many ways boys were useful, even if they took a little patience.

"You're going to like having cousins," Jamie told her, since the boy lecture had to wait for a little one-on-one time.

"They are not exactly cousins." Hannah gnawed on the tip of a finger. "And they are not exactly brothers."

Jamie wished Hannah had saved this comment for a time when her aunt and uncle weren't in the room. But Kendra saved her from having to explain, once again, that the babies were indeed cousins and nothing but.

"I know what you mean," Kendra told her. "They seem more important than cousins, don't they? Since your mommy is growing them for us."

"Bruzzins," Hannah said, her eyes lighting up. "Brother-cousins. Bruzzins."

Jamie looked at her sister to see if there were any signs of distress at this little misconception and linguistic feat. But Kendra looked delighted.

"I love that, Hannah," she told her niece. "'Bruzzins' covers it exactly. And that'll make them even more special to you."

Alison sidled up and laid her copper curls against Kendra's shoulder.

"Will we be special?"

"Of course you will be. You'll always be special to me."

"But you will have babies," Hannah pointed out. "And they will keep you busy."

"Very busy." Kendra nodded, her eyes wide. "Very, very busy, I'm afraid."

"Too busy for us?" Hannah asked.

Jamie wondered if her daughter had saved even one difficult question for later.

"Never too busy for you and Alison," Kendra promised. "And let's face it, these *are* boys. And even if boys and girls are not as different as you might think, there are things boys don't always like to do."

"Like?"

"Like...like dress up and have tea parties with their dolls." She looked befuddled, as if she had just succumbed to another gender stereotype in keeping with the entire conversation. "Of course, they might like to do that, and that would be great, right Isaac?"

Isaac looked unsure, but nodded. "Sure. Boys like dolls. The dressing up part, maybe not so much."

Jamie was trying not to laugh. "I think we ought to have a tea party before the babies arrive, don't you? Just us girls? And some of Alison and Hannah's friends. We might even have a new doll or two to add to the girls' collection, right?"

Riva had bought both Kendra and Jamie dozens of dolls when they were children, usually when she was going abroad, which was most of the time. Kendra had carefully packed and saved them, and now Jamie's belonged to Hannah and Alison, although Jamie was doling them out a few at a time. Some of the excess had already gone to First Step families.

"When?" Hannah asked.

"Well, there should be invitations. Real ones. And we have to plan what to serve and what games to play."

"No mud involved, right?" Kendra asked. "No mud pies? This time we dress up?"

"You can wear your best clothes," Jamie promised Hannah. "All the girls will be little ladies, right?"

Hannah didn't nod. Jamie could tell she was considering how possible that was.

"It'll be a great contrast to the last party, even if nobody stays exactly clean," Kendra said tactfully.

Grace intervened. "If it's warm enough, I think we should have it in the orchard. We'll still have wildflowers and maybe even some apples on the trees. With apple cake and cider. I believe I have tables that will be just the right size. And plenty of shawls to wrap up in if it's chilly."

"We don't want to put you out," Jamie said. "Wouldn't you like us to have the party down at the cabin?"

"Oh, absolutely not. We haven't had a tea party here since Sandra was a little girl. I can hardly wait."

Footsteps sounded in the hallway, and Jamie's bedroom was suddenly richer by two. Cash and his father walked in, then stopped when they saw the crowd.

"Selling tickets?" Cash asked.

"Making plans for a party." Jamie smiled a greeting to Manning. "To what do we owe this honor?"

"My fault," Grace said. "I asked Manning to have one of his men come look at the roof. I'm not sure it's going to hold for another winter, even if Cash says it will."

"I love being pitted against my son and my mother-in-law," Manning said gruffly. "That'll make my day." He nodded toward Jamie. "You're doing okay? Sandra says you are."

"You can see all the help I have, right?"

"I'm surprised you ever get any rest." He started to back out. "My roofing man couldn't come today, but I'll go look at it and see what's what."

"I'll come along, if you like," Isaac said. "I worked for a roofer during the summers when I was in college."

Manning shrugged. "Cash, are you coming, too?"

"I'll see you in a bit," Cash told Jamie.

Jamie caught the know-it-all expression on her sister's face. But even if they had been alone, she wasn't at all sure what she would have told Kendra about Cash. She didn't have words to explain a relationship she really didn't understand herself.

The three men stood on Grace's roof and examined the asphalt shingles.

"Worst mistake anybody ever made was to take off the old slate and put this mess on instead." Manning shook his head. "I don't know what your grandfather was thinking, but now I guess you're right, Cash. It should make it through a year, maybe two. By the time a new one's needed, some decisions might be made about this property."

"You're thinking of selling?" Isaac asked.

"Nobody wants to, but nobody wants to do all the work that's needed just to keep the old place limping along." Manning kicked at a shingle, and when it didn't budge, he nodded. "I'll back up your opinion, son. It'll hold a while. If anything leaks, we can patch."

Cash watched Isaac start down the ladder. He didn't smile, but he knew what the other man was thinking. Manning was too old to be climbing up and down ladders like this, and Isaac was putting himself between Manning and the ground, just in case. Cash played along and let his father go next. There was no opportunity to assure Isaac that Manning did this half a dozen times a day and never faltered. Manning would only hang up his tool belt and clipboard when it was time to pick out a suit for his casket.

"You do right well on a ladder," Manning told Isaac when he got down to the ground. "You take after your mother that way. Rachel was like a mountain goat. I saw her scurry up cliffs nobody else would even think of attempting, me included. Then she'd laugh at me, like I was some kind of sissy, just because I had the good sense not to follow. Are you a daredevil, too?"

"Not so much. That was a trait my father wasn't keen on."

"Father?"

"Adopted father. An Army colonel."

"You think he'd *want* a bit of daredevil in a boy."

"A kid testing his own limits takes supervision and patience."

"I gather you're not close?"

Cash thought that was an odd question for his father to ask Isaac. Normally Manning was as reticent as most men of his generation and upbringing. But he supposed Manning felt he owed Isaac something more, since he had been close friends with Isaac's mother.

"Colonel Grant Taylor is incapable of feeling close to anybody," Isaac said matter-of-factly. "Maybe it's a job hazard, although I saw a lot of good men and good fathers in the service. Anyway, he's not in my life anymore, and neither of us regrets it."

"I'm sorry to hear that."

"Before she died, my adopted mother did what she could. Considering the limitations she worked under, she did a pretty good job convincing me I could be happy someday. And she was right."

"Sounds like you deserved better."

"It's funny, you don't think much about this stuff until you're ready to be a father yourself." Isaac gave a small laugh. "And I'll be the father of sons, it seems. Two of them."

Cash clapped him on the back. "So you found out for sure? Good for you. Congratulations."

"Man, twin boys." Manning shook his head in wonder. "And here I thought raising one was something else."

"I might need some tips from a man who's been there." Isaac kept his voice light, but his words belied his tone. "I didn't get any from my adopted father, and I don't know what kind of man my biological father was. I know he must have left my mother, maybe just waltzed through her life. So I've got two strikes working against me, I guess."

"Oh, I don't know. Your mother was wild in some ways, but she wasn't the kind of woman who let no-account men into her life in the first place. Don't make the mistake of believing that. She was as independent as they make them." He glanced at Cash, as if he wished he weren't there to hear this, then he went on. "I'd guess, knowing Rachel, that she didn't tell your real father she was pregnant."

"What makes you say so?"

"Because that's the way she was. If she didn't want to marry him or he couldn't be part of her life—for whatever reason— then she wouldn't think of telling him. She never wanted anybody's pity or help. Did things her way and nobody else's. Your dad, whoever he was, probably didn't have any idea what was going on."

"Did you ever try to trace him?" Cash asked, because like it or not, he was included in the conversation by proximity.

"Never did," Isaac said. "Never cared. I guess I thought I knew as much about him as I needed, that he was just a man who didn't stand by my mother. Maybe I was wrong."

"Just guessing again," Manning said, "but knowing Rachel—" he hesitated "—she probably never told anybody who he was. It won't be on your birth certificate, even if you could get hold of the first one."

"*You* don't have any idea, do you?" Isaac asked.

"I hadn't seen her in years before she died. We talked on the phone once. Before you were born. But not about any men in her life."

"Long shot," Isaac said with a sad smile. "I guess it doesn't really matter. Like I said, it's strange the way having sons of your own gets you thinking about things."

"You'll be a good dad," Manning said. "You got everything it takes. And hell, what would I know about it, anyway? Look what I raised." He punched Cash on the arm.

The three men walked in companionable silence back to the farmhouse.

25

Kendra took the girls to buy party dresses. Since she'd promised them free rein, they shopped at the local discount store to minimalize damage. Alison chose a brightly patterned pink sundress, something of a disaster with her hair, but since she insisted she was going to wear it over a lavender sweater and red leggings, pink was the least of it. Alison explained about "folk fabrics" and how since the dress had splashes of lavender and red, this was exactly the right thing to do.

"*Focus* fabric," Hannah explained to her aunt. "Alison may be a fiber artist one day. Granny Grace says we must encourage her."

Wisely, Kendra nodded and said not a word when Hannah chose a black jumper to be worn over a black turtleneck, black stockings and black ballerina slippers. Black *did* go well with *her* hair, even if she looked as if she was planning to attend a funeral or a Goth reunion.

The weather cooperated for an outdoor event, bringing

autumn sunshine when it could just as likely have brought sleet or even snow. Grace had four card tables set up for the girls, their chaperones and their dolls, and refused to let Jamie buy paper tablecloths and napkins. She cut down and hemmed several old linen tablecloths; then she taught the girls how to fold matching napkins and slip them into sterling-silver napkin rings with the Cashel *C* engraved on each one. With the help of a guidebook, Kendra let the girls identify and pick wildflowers that were still blooming, both blue and golden asters, and purple milkwort. They plumped out the arrangements with tall grasses, made place cards for each girl and doll, and Hannah carefully wrote out one menu per table.

"I am certain there is a *K* in cucumber," she told Kendra. "I can hear it."

"Nope," Kendra said.

Hannah looked up, clearly curious. "Then why don't you spell your name with a *C?*"

"Because that's not the way it's spelled."

Hannah continued listing the fare. "Cucumber sandwiches with a *C*. Egg salad…" She looked up again. "How can it be salad if there is no lettuce in it?"

"I think you'd better just write out the menus, dear," Grace said from the next table over, where she was anchoring tablecloths by pinning fishing sinkers to each corner. "Time's a'wasting."

"Can we really waste time? Every minute we're breathing and our hearts keep beating, so we're doing something and not really wasting anything." Hannah chewed her lip, but she kept writing. "Fruit salad." She shook her head. "Again, no lettuce. There should be a new word. We should make one up."

Trying not to laugh, Kendra ruffled Hannah's hair—tied with a black ribbon, of course—and went to help Grace.

"That child will enrage a teacher or two along the way," Grace murmured when Kendra was in earshot. "I think we might need to start a legal-defense fund while we still have time."

"I'm assuming her father will leap right in if anything happens. From what I understand, Larry Clousell lives to keep criminals out of jail. Hannah has a safety net."

Hannah took off to ask her mother a question, and the two women spoke louder, freed from listening ears.

"That's what parents are for, I suppose," Grace said. "My boys, Charlie and Adam, always knew that if things got too bad, either Ben or I would bail them out. Of course, Ben always let them go to the brink, just to scare them to death. Most of the time that worked. My daughter, on the other hand, never got remotely near the edge. She's an organized, completely sane creature, my Sandra. I wouldn't be certain they gave me the right baby, you know, only I gave birth to her here in the farmhouse, and there were no other babies to confuse her with."

Kendra laughed. "I like your daughter. You two are so good for each other. I hope…" She stopped. She wasn't sure how they had gotten into this.

"What do you hope?" Grace asked kindly. "That you and your sons will be good for each other, too? Let me reassure you. Of course you will."

Kendra bent down and began to pin a sinker in place. "I'm not particularly talented that way. They're bound to suspect eventually."

"I won't lie and say talent's not part of parenting. Some people just seem to come into the world with untold stores of patience. Perhaps you're not one of them?"

"No, I think I'm patient."

"Good, because I think so, too. I've seen you with the girls."

"Anyone could be patient with them. They're exceptionally easy to be around."

"Oh, my goodness, they aren't, you know. Of course *we* think so, because we love them. But Hannah will drive people crazy with all her questions and observations. And Alison shows signs of being equally willful, although quite different about it. No, you're patient because you're patient."

"Well, that's a mark in my favor." Kendra reached for another sinker and moved to the next corner.

Grace refused to let go of the subject. "So you're patient. We've agreed on that. Perhaps you're not generous? Children do take a lot of time and money and energy. And perhaps you're worried you won't have enough?"

"Money's not a problem. Energy?" Kendra considered. "Maybe not as much as I'd like for twins. I'm older than I should be, going into this. But no, I probably have enough if I use it intelligently. Time? I love my job, but I can still do what I love without doing it so intensely. So I can make the time."

"Patient and generous, then."

Kendra gazed up at her. "I see what you're trying to do here."

"Me?"

"I've had a go at the parenting thing, you know. I was a miserable failure."

"You've already had a child? I'm so sorry, I didn't know."

"No, I'm talking about Jamie."

"Surely you don't judge yourself harshly because as a child yourself you weren't able to raise a younger child with an adult's insight?"

"In my defense, I was woefully short on role models."

"Your sister's told me a little about your family."

"It's strange, but I came to terms with Riva—our mother—a

long time ago. And now it's all right there again. I know I'm nothing like her. That's not it...." Kendra got up and stretched. "Why am I telling you all this? I'm boring you silly."

"No, you're not. But I'll confess, if I were younger, I'd go after your mother with a shotgun."

"It's hard to separate the woman from the illness."

Grace was quiet for a moment; then she asked gently, "Are you afraid you might be prone to the same sort of thing?"

"No. I'm really not. That would be pretty clear by now."

"Jamie turned out quite well, I think. In fact, if my grandson doesn't marry her, I'm considering adoption. Do you think she'd let me?"

Kendra felt the weight of the conversation lift from her shoulders. She managed a smile. "Only if you adopt me, as well. And two's a lot to handle. We come with baggage."

"You did better than you think, Kendra dear. I know you and Jamie had a rough go of things for a while. But you gave her the strength to pull her life back together. Not everyone's able to do that, you know. In fact, I'd have to say far too few who fall so far are able to make the climb back the way she has. And where did that strength come from, if not your love and, yes, your guidance?"

Kendra made a face, but her throat was suddenly thick with unshed tears.

"Don't look like that," Grace said. "I know what I'm talking about. Take any success story, and you'll find that no matter how dismal the childhood, the person who succeeded had at least one someone in her background who gave her the courage and belief in herself that she needed. You did that for Jamie when you were only a child yourself. How much better a mother will you be now that you're a grown-up?"

"She ran away. I was *that* good."

"She ran away. You were the anchor that stopped her and eventually helped her find her way back to the surface."

"I'm so afraid I'll screw up again." Kendra met Grace's gaze. "It's consuming me."

"You should talk to Jamie about this. For perspective."

"I can't believe I talked to *you.*"

"Oh, I can. People just do. I don't know why, but I do know I'm glad it's true." She covered the few feet between them and wrapped her arms around Kendra in a quick hug.

Tea was a success. The same girls who had jumped into the mud—plus a few additions—came arrayed in party clothes, with similarly dressed dolls and their best party manners. The clothes stayed relatively clean, although the manners disintegrated by the party's conclusion. By the time their parents were due to take them home, the girls were playing a wild game of tag among the old trees.

Jamie had been conscientious about taking a long morning rest, and now that the party was almost over, she planned an afternoon version. She'd had no recurrence of symptoms, and she felt strong and healthy. But she had to admit she also felt tired. She was glad Kendra had stayed to dismantle the tables for Grace and carry what was left of the refreshments inside.

But Kendra wasn't alone. Cash arrived just in time to witness Alison tag Bridget and Jamie announce an end to the game.

"Okay, gang, your parents are on their way to pick you up. So let's grab coats and anything else from the house, so you'll be all ready when they get here. You can have one more peek at Lucky. And let's not forget your goody bags."

Kendra stopped stacking plates. "I'll oversee that. You get off your feet and take a break."

Jamie didn't argue. Her feet and legs felt as if they were supporting several tons. She waved to Cash, then slumped into a chair and slipped off her shoes as the little girls took off for the house.

Cash came over and rested a hand casually on her shoulder. "Never having had children myself, I may need a lesson here. Are frequent parties requirements? Is there some rule about once a month?"

"This is only the second party we've had since we moved to Virginia. But I guess I'm raising party girls. I just can't wait for the sleepover stage to begin."

"The more the merrier?"

"As long as they go home eventually. I always wanted a big family, but two feels pretty big when you're single."

"And if you weren't?"

Her heart skipped a beat, but she decided the question was simply a logical extension of the conversation. "Two is still plenty. I want to have the kind of home where there's lots of room and energy, so the girls can bring their friends over and everyone feels welcome. You don't have to give birth to children to enjoy having them in your life."

"You look wiped."

She closed her eyes for a moment. "My feet just hurt. This will be the last party until the twins are born. I couldn't have done it if Kendra and Grace hadn't handled most of the work. But everybody had a great time, including them."

"Granny Grace was always giving parties here. Grandpa Ben used to call it the Greyhound Station, because so many people came in and out every day. So many of their friends have passed on or moved away, and my uncles live too far to visit as frequently as everybody would like. So you and your girls have really picked up the slack."

"I'm glad. Of course, she's done so much more for us."

Cash knelt at her feet. Jamie felt a moment of embarrassment, since she was wearing scruffy wool socks and, under them, toenails that hadn't seen a coat of polish since bending over to give them one had become more trouble than it was worth.

He picked up a foot and began to rotate his thumbs along her arch. "I generally ask a woman before I start to undress her. These socks ought to go."

"You won't like what you see."

He stripped off the sock. "I see a foot. Long, narrow and just a bit swollen."

He slid his thumbs back into place, and she closed her eyes, sighing with pleasure. "That's pretty much perfect."

"I aim to please."

"Is that what you tell all the women you undress?"

"I can't remember."

"Why, because there've been so many?"

"No, because it's been so long."

She felt warmth in places he wasn't touching, and a shiver ran up her spine. "Did you think I was asking?"

"You *were* asking. And I didn't mind answering." He stopped for just a moment. "How about you, Miss Jamie? Is there a man in your life with a right to ask personal questions?"

"No, there's not."

"So you're not pining after either of the girls' daddies?"

She laughed. "Oh, Lord, Cash, I certainly am not. I could have sworn I made that clear."

"I guess I'm the one asking the personal questions now."

She leaned down, lifted his chin and kissed him. "I'll give you that right, if you want it."

"I guess I'd consider that an honor." And this time, *he* kissed *her*.

★ ★ ★

"I think the party was quite a success, don't you?" Grace asked Jamie after the girls' guests had all gone home and Kendra had, too. Alison and Hannah were in their rooms playing Candyland, something Hannah only did when she was too tired to come up with another game to distract her little sister.

Jamie rose from the kitchen table, where she'd been finishing a glass of orange juice, and began to rummage through the cupboards. "It was perfect, and a lot of work for you. Why don't you let me make dinner tonight? I can do pasta and sauce and a salad with one hand tied behind my back."

"That sounds wonderful. I thought we'd have plenty of leftovers from tea, but those little girls rivaled any little boys that ever came through this house. I was sorry I didn't roast a pig or an ox."

Jamie shook a box of pasta shells. "We have everything we'll need. I'll start the sauce now."

"You don't feel too tired?"

"No, I'll have a good rest once it's simmering."

Grace watched as Jamie assembled ingredients. Canned tomatoes, a jar of spaghetti sauce, mushrooms and peppers, onions, garlic, oregano, basil, fennel and anise seeds. The young woman loved to cook, and Grace loved letting her.

The kitchen was warm and still smelled like the cinnamon-oatmeal cookies Jamie had made for the party. Late-afternoon sunlight filtered in through the tall windows, and pooled on the tile countertops and the pine floor. The peach walls glowed under its caress.

She wanted to hold this moment in her memory, along with the many other good memories from the years spent here. Ben coming in from a day in the orchard, cheeks nipped by frost or flushed with heat. Family meals at this table, her sons and daughter laughing or arguing, but always eating as if she had forgotten to feed them for months. The first visits of new grandchildren, who banged drum solos on the old wooden high-chair tray as they waited for their mothers or fathers to feed them.

Jamie put a large saucepan on the stove to heat and poured in a bit of olive oil; then she pulled the cutting board from its perch behind the dish rack and began to chop an onion.

"I was surprised Helen Henry didn't come up here with Cissy to get Reese," Grace said. "I thought she might want to spy on me."

"What a thing to say."

"Yes, but doesn't it sound possible?"

"As a matter of fact, Cissy told me something about Helen." Jamie pursed her lips in concentration. "I'm trying to think. There were a million things going on…" She winced and looked up. "Oh, I remember. It's sad. This is the weekend of that Houston quilt festival—"

"Well, of course it is. I can't believe I forgot that's where she'd be. What's wrong, didn't her quilt win a ribbon?"

"No, I don't think it did, but it's even worse than that. She's sick. Apparently she caught an awful cold, and they were afraid it was heading toward pneumonia. So her doctor refused to let her go."

"How terrible." Grace could just imagine what this misfortune had meant to Helen. Most of the woman's long life had been lived in Toms Brook, making do for her daughter, making do alone without a husband, making do without the rest of her family, who had been casualties, in one way or another, of the Second World War. That she had made it through those difficult years and still, somehow, continued to turn out beautiful quilts, one after another, was a testament to the woman.

Even if Grace didn't like her.

Jamie plopped the chopped onions into the pan, where they

began to sizzle as she started on the garlic. "Cissy said Helen won't even talk about it, that she says it never made sense to go all the way to Texas anyway. But I'm sure it was a real blow."

"Is she feeling any better?"

"Cissy said she was, although she's still stuck at home for a while. Nobody wants to take chances with her health. Cissy feels really bad, because she thinks Helen picked up the cold from Reese. Reese got over it right away, but Helen didn't, of course."

Grace suppressed a smile. She'd said "of course" because to someone as young as Jamie, at their age, Helen and Grace were just a few steps ahead of the Grim Reaper.

Jamie continued, unaware. "I wonder if we should take her something. I sent some cookies home with Cissy, but I could make enough pasta sauce for Helen and Cissy's family, too. Maybe I'll just double up here and take it by tomorrow."

Grace looked out the window and thought about the times she had sat right here thinking about her life. Not the good times she had imagined earlier, but the ones that hadn't been good at all, when she had been angry and filled with regret for choices foisted on her.

"I have bread in the freezer," she told Jamie, still looking out the window. "And we have plenty of things for a salad. If you make the sauce, I'll have Cash drive me down there tonight to deliver it all. He won't mind."

"*You'll* take it? Tonight?"

"Of course I'll tell her *you* made the sauce, dear."

"You know that's not what I'm referring to."

This time Grace did smile. "Maybe it's time Helen and I had a heart-to-heart. When better? She probably doesn't feel well enough to toss me out of her house. I might not have this kind of opportunity again."

"You really think a heart-to-heart is a good idea?"

"The truth is always a good idea, isn't it?"

"No way."

"This time, I think it might be. Sometimes, when you're feeling that low, the only people who can really understand you are the ones who remember you when you were a girl. The ones who know why you're the way you are and are willing to let you be that way."

"Are you willing? To let her be the way she is? Because I like her just fine, but she's awfully hard on you."

"We'll hope that part changes." Grace got to her feet. "I'll just defrost that bread. Shall I make a big salad to share with them?"

"I'd like to be a fly on the wall when you have that heart-to-heart."

Grace smiled and kissed Jamie's cheek. "I'll be sure to carry a flyswatter, then, dear. This will be one conversation no one else should hear."

26

"That's it, the farmhouse on the right. Slow down, before I'm sorry I ate Jamie's fine, fine supper."

Cash stepped on the brakes, but not so quickly that Grace had to brace herself to keep from flying through the windshield. Like most of the men raised in the area, Cash drove faster than green grass through a goose, but he was a good driver, and a safe one.

"You're sure you want to go through with this?" he asked.

"I'm absolutely sure."

"Then I'm going down to the Taylors' place to see how things are progressing on the drainage system, so I'll be close by. I've got my cell phone. Worse comes to worst, you can leave and start walking in that direction. I'll pick you up fast as I can."

"Oh, I doubt she'll come after me with her shotgun. Once she kicks me out of her house, she'll probably let me wait on the porch. She's at least that polite."

"I don't know why you're putting yourself through this. People like that don't deserve a neighbor's charity."

"Helen Henry has her version of something that happened a long time ago. It's tinder that's kept the fire burning all these years. I'm fixing to put it out tonight."

"Fixing? You're sounding like a country woman again, Granny Grace."

"Started out as one, if you recall. I suppose I'll end up that way, too."

Cash patted her knee. "Not too soon, okay? You're the glue that holds our clan together."

"That job will be yours once I'm gone. Your mother would never insist that everybody get together for holidays or vacations. There has to be time to reminisce, to make new memories. We'll need a firm hand in charge."

"You overestimate my abilities."

"At least you didn't say interest."

He pulled into a narrow drive that ran to the left of the house and stopped the pickup. "You run in and do whatever it is you think you need to. I'll be waiting for your call."

She patted his knee again; then she got out and opened the rear door to retrieve the basket she and Jamie had packed. "I'll see you in a bit, dear. You don't have to wait and see if I get in. I know she's got to be home."

"I'd tell you to take your time, only I'd like you back in one piece."

He laughed as she slammed the door shut and stepped away from the pickup. Then he saluted her, and with one arm slung lazily over the passenger seat, he backed out so fast that in what seemed like only a moment, the pickup was gone.

A light shone on the front porch, almost as if Helen was expecting company or anxious to chase away the deepening twilight.

The two maples flanking the front door had been stripped by autumn's onset, but as Grace walked toward the steps, not a single leaf crunched under her feet. Closer now, she could see that the shrubs were neatly trimmed and chrysanthemums dotted the front beds. The house looked well cared for and newly painted.

It hadn't always been so. Grace remembered trips down Fitch Crossing years ago when she had noted that the house needed some of everything: paint, landscaping, a handyman's prowess. At those times she'd always thought about Tom Stoneburner, Helen's brother, and how ashamed he would have been at the aura of disrepair. Had he or their elder brother, Obed, lived, the house would have gone to them, as houses usually did in this part of the country. Both brothers had been hard workers, although Obed had been more inclined to kick up his heels. But before he was killed in the war, Obed had married and settled down, too.

Either brother would have kept the old place in pristine condition. Helen would have, as well, had she possessed any resources besides her two work-roughened hands. As it was, the fact that she had managed to hold on to it at all was something of a miracle. Especially when she had refused all offers of help from old friends or neighbors.

The war had changed everything for so many. Grace was glad that now, after all those difficult years, Helen was finally accepting the help she needed. Old age had compensations.

She trudged up the steps, aware of the weight of the wicker basket. Years ago she wouldn't even have noticed the way it dragged her whole body lower and lower until she felt as if she were sinking by inches with each step. Helen wasn't the only one growing older.

The porch looked like a pleasant place to spend a summer afternoon: cushions on comfortable rockers, a fern still thriving on an end table, pumpkins piled beside the door. A fat tabby jumped off the railing as she approached and streaked toward the back of the house, where Grace could hear the clucking of chickens. She gratefully set the basket at her feet, opened the screen door and knocked on the one beyond.

Lights burned in the living room, just visible through sheer curtains. She thought she heard the murmur of a television set, although the door was heavy enough that she couldn't be sure. She waited, and just as she was about to knock again, the door opened slowly.

She had expected Cissy, or even Helen's daughter. But Helen herself stood across the threshold, and as Grace watched, her eyes narrowed.

"Come to gloat?" Helen demanded.

"Only *you* would think such a thing."

Helen chewed the inside of her lip; then she shrugged and stepped aside to let Grace in. "I thought maybe you was Nancy. She's on her way to spend the rest of the weekend."

Grace had forgotten Helen's daughter's name, but now she remembered the face that went with it. A pretty blond girl who had in no way resembled her mother, Nancy had been flighty, fragile, nothing like the down-to-earth woman who was ushering Grace into her house. Grace hoped the two women had eventually come to terms with their differences, the way she and Sandra had.

More or less.

"I haven't seen Nancy since she was a girl," Grace said. "How is she?"

"Happy."

"And you have grandchildren?"

"Just one." Helen paused, then added grudgingly, "And a great-grandson."

"That's wonderful. I bet you enjoy him."

"Why'd you come?"

"Because I heard you were sick." Grace lifted the basket in explanation. "Jamie and I thought you might like some of the pasta she made for our supper this evening. There's salad and homemade bread, and some of our best apples. If you've eaten already, you can save this for tomorrow. Jamie is a delightful cook."

"I'm trying to figure out why you're doing this."

"Helen, do you ever accept anything at face value?"

"Not often, I don't."

"Well, that's understandable, I suppose."

"Why?"

"You've been through some hard times. It makes one wary."

"I managed just fine."

Grace set the basket down again. "You did, but you're saying it was easy? It didn't change you?"

"Everybody changes, with an exception or two." She raised an eyebrow. "Some people don't change because they can't. That's their basic nature."

"I'll assume you mean me."

"You always did what you wanted, no matter what happened because of it."

Grace thought how far from the truth that was. In the end, despite her "basic nature," duty had ruled her life. And luckily she wasn't one bit sorry it had.

"Where would you like me to put your dinner?" she asked.

Helen looked as if she wanted to tell Grace exactly where to put it, and not in the kitchen. But at last she turned and started through the living room. Grace hefted the basket and followed her inside.

"Oh, will you look at this?" Grace stopped before she had gone far. Just ahead of her, draped in a large round hoop, was what looked to be a queen-size quilt. "Why, Helen, it's spectacular."

"Nothing much."

Grace moved closer to examine it, setting the basket down as she did. "It's perfectly lovely." She bent so that she could see the tiny little stitches. "Whig Rose?"

"No. Rose of Sharon. See the way the stems bend? Some folks claim that's the difference, but a quilt's a quilt by any name, isn't it?"

The quilt was gorgeous. Grace counted five blocks set on point so they looked like diamonds, each one with a red flower in the center, and curving stems radiating outward. Each stem was adorned with either flowers or buds, and sometimes both. The border was particularly lovely, a sinuous vine that went all the way around the quilt. It, too, was adorned with small red buds.

"This is the kind of quilt you wanted the bee to make for our Christmas quilt, isn't it?" Grace asked, lifting a corner to see it better.

"Something like this. Only once you shot me down good, I decided I'd quilt this one for myself. I made the top some time ago, and made it big enough for a bed 'cause that's where quilts ought to go, in my opinion. When I took sick, I brought it down here to work on in that hoop."

"I didn't shoot you down, dear. I just suggested something different. I like to think that's allowed. It was just that people were in the mood for something a little sillier this year. But I hope next year we'll feel like trying something this complicated and lovely."

"Not everybody could do a quilt like this." Helen made it clear by the expression in her eyes who "everybody" was.

"I'll confess it would be beyond my talents," Grace said, trying hard not to let Helen egg her on. "I've had to give up all those tiny little stitches. Not that I ever made any quite so neat."

"Those art quilts of yours don't need a lot of craftsmanship."

"No, just imagination and courage. I certainly seem to have plenty of the latter. Look where I am and what I'm doing. Against all the odds."

Helen humphed and continued through the room. With a sigh, Grace followed her into a small but attractive kitchen. With an effort she lifted the basket to the counter and reminded herself to hold her temper.

"Why don't you let me put everything in the refrigerator? I'm sure you don't feel like fussing." Grace opened the door and saw there was room if she rearranged a few things, which she did.

"I feel just fine." Helen didn't say anything for a few moments as Grace began to unpack the basket. "Now that it doesn't much matter," she added at last.

Grace spoke from behind the refrigerator door. "The timing of that cold was terrible. I'm sorry you couldn't go to see your quilt hanging at the show. Whether you believe it or not, I really do mean that. I hope you can go next year."

"Next year doesn't always come when you're as old as I am."

"Isn't that the truth?" Grace closed the refrigerator. "I wish I'd gone to more quilt shows when it was still easy enough. And more art exhibits, and traveled more to see things I can only dream about now."

"Never wanted to do all that." Helen sucked on the inside of her cheek. "Well, maybe I did once, but that was so long ago, I was a different person. I don't remember her much."

"I do. You were full of life and energy. Your eyes always sparkled, and you smiled a lot. Tom used to say you were like a candle flame that couldn't be blown out. He said no matter how dark things got, everybody counted on you to keep a light burning."

"You got no call to talk about my Tom."

"Oh, of course I do. Tom was my dearest friend."

Helen made a noise somewhere between a snort and a grumble. "Is that what you come about? To tell me how sorry you are Tom's gone, to remind me of all that?"

"Do I need to remind you? Don't you think about Tom every time you look at me?"

"Thanks for the food. But I'm feeling tired now. You'd better git."

"Helen." Grace took a risk and rested her fingers on Helen's arm. "I loved your brother. For a long time I thought Tom would be the man I married."

Helen just stared at her, eyes narrowed.

"Tom was the one who didn't want to marry *me,*" Grace said.

"That's not true! You broke his heart. There was never another girl after you went and married your brother-in-law. He carried a torch right up until the time he left here to get himself killed in Guam. There were girls aplenty who wanted him, but he wouldn't look at a one. And after he died? I had to clean out his bedroom. And I was the one found a photograph of *you* right there in the drawer by his bed."

Grace looked at her watch. She'd made a mistake coming here. There was nothing else she could say now. She'd hoped that this gesture of goodwill and a piece of the truth would soothe Helen and help her feel better about Grace's presence in the community again. But she should have known it wasn't going to turn out that way.

She looked back up at Helen. "I'll go now. I'm sorry I bothered you."

"It only bothers me you won't admit the truth. That you led my brother on, then just up and left him, high and dry. And he was so sad, so downright dejected afterward, that he didn't have any good reason to live and no good reason not to die!"

"That was a long time ago, wasn't it?"

"Not so long to me. He was my brother."

"And the man I thought I loved."

"Then why didn't you marry him? Why did you tell him goodbye? You can't say one thing and mean the other!"

So far Grace had managed to stay relatively calm, but now anger was beginning to get the better of her. "I already told you, Tom didn't want to marry me."

"Of course he did. He kept your photo, in a frame! It said 'Love from Grace' in one corner.

"Oh, I gave him the photo, all right. When I thought—" She stopped. "I'm leaving." She pivoted smartly and started back into the living room, a much lighter basket flapping against her side.

"What did you think?" Helen demanded. "That maybe Tom would leave the Valley for you? Is that what it was about? Then he told you he couldn't, that he belonged here with his family, so you threw him over so you could leave town and never look back?"

"Did I leave town?" Grace faced Helen again. "No, I didn't. I stayed here, married a man who was grieving for my sister and became a mother to my two nephews. After that, until Ben died, I never got much farther than Washington, D.C., and then only for the occasional shopping trip. So don't you try to put that on me. What happened between me and Tom had nothing to do with my desire to get out of here."

"Then what did it have to do with?"

"That was between us."

"That's all you can say, because there's nothing else *to* say. I already hit the nail on the head."

Grace exploded at last. "Really? Then while you're hammering it in a little more, let me give you something to think about. Call it a riddle. Why does a good-looking young man like Tom Stoneburner refuse to succumb to all those pretty young girls who set their caps for him? Maybe you're a country woman, but you've got at least that much sophistication, don't you? I'm telling you I loved your brother. I probably would have married him if he'd asked me. But he didn't. He loved me in his own way, but Tom used me. He wanted to show the world something, and he used me to do it."

"What? What did my brother need from the likes of you?"

"To show the world he was a real man!"

"He *was* a real man. A real man who just needed a real woman!"

"Helen, there wasn't a woman anywhere who could have made him feel more alive than I did. Don't you get it? Tom couldn't feel that way about a woman, period. You see if you can figure out the rest of it."

Helen just stared at her again. Grace knew she had gone too far. She turned and opened the door, then stepped out on the porch, letting the screen door bang behind her. She fished for her cell phone in the pocket of her bright green pants and flipped it open to call Cash. Then she felt a hand close around her arm.

"Don't you go off and run away now. Just spit it all out." Helen's voice was hoarse, and she coughed, a deep croak of a cough. "Say it out loud. What are you trying to make me believe?"

"Let go of me, Helen."

"You can't leave now. Just finish your say." She dropped her hand. Then she surprised Grace. "Please…"

Grace closed her eyes. She tried to figure out how to undo the damage anger had done, but it was past time to lie. She tried to tell the truth in the kindest way she knew.

"Times were different then. A man had to be every part a man. Didn't matter if he was brave, or hardworking, or loyal. Not if he wasn't interested in girls. So a lot of men in those days—today, too, I guess—*pretended* they were interested, Helen. Or they tried to *tell* themselves they were. Tom was one of that last kind. He wanted to love me, and he did. Only not in the way he needed to. He wanted to be like all his friends. Like Obed. He wanted to fall in love with a woman. But he finally realized that he couldn't, and he knew it wasn't fair to me to go through life pretending. Tom was in love with somebody else."

She opened her eyes. "And it wasn't somebody like *me*."

"You're lying."

"No matter what you think of me, do you think I'm the kind of woman who would make up something like this just to spite you? Why? Because we're different kinds of quilters? Or because I want to give you something to really hold a grudge for? What would be my reason?"

"Tom wasn't like that."

Grace felt all the life seeping out of her. "Like what? He was one of the best men I ever knew, the very best, next to my Ben. He died fighting for his country, even though he was a sensitive soul who hated to kill a chicken or sell off those calves he raised for beef. He used to tell me how much he hated to see anything suffer. But anybody could count on Tom to do what needed to be done, whether he liked it or not. He was a man all the way down to the bone. He was just a man who was in love with another man, and a man who despised himself because of it."

Helen felt behind her and found the arm of a chair. She lowered herself into it. Then she put her head in her hands.

Grace knew Helen was replaying all her memories of her brother, looking for proof that Grace was wrong. But she wouldn't find it. They had all been so blind in those days. Blind, careless and judgmental.

"You should have told me before," Helen said at last. "You should have told me years ago."

"Why? So you could tell yourself Tom was no good? After he was killed, I wanted to preserve his memory. He deserved that. He never deserved anything less. And people are unkind, even hateful, about homosexuality. Even today."

Helen sat up and met Grace's gaze. "You thought I wouldn't understand."

"Yes, that's what I thought. Do you?"

"Who was the man?"

"I don't know. I just know there was somebody. I had to figure out a lot of the little things on my own and confront him. It was about as awful as you can imagine." Grace sat down across from Helen. "He didn't want me to know, but he didn't want to lead me on. He told me this, he told me that, but it was only when I got a bit older that I finally understood *everything* he'd tried to say and couldn't quite get out. Then it finally all fell into place."

She waited. Helen didn't speak. Grace could see her struggling with this bombshell, trying to figure out if it was true, trying to figure out if she could admit it might be. Then Helen's shoulders slumped, and her words surprised Grace.

"Poor Tom."

Grace repressed a sigh, but for the first time that evening, she felt encouraged. "Yes, poor Tom, for living in the times and place he did. Maybe even in those days he could have found a way to be himself, if he'd lived in the big city. But there was no place like that around here."

Helen met her eyes. "Do you think that's why he went to war when he did? Why he didn't wait to be drafted? Do you think he was trying to prove something, or maybe get himself killed so he wouldn't have to face his feelings anymore?"

When it came right down to it, Grace was surprised at how quickly Helen had accepted her explanation, but perhaps there was no reason to be. Helen had grown up with Tom, and now a lot of unanswered questions and actions that she had refused to recognize were finally being resolved. On some level, buried deep inside her, perhaps she had suspected the truth all along.

"I don't think Tom wanted to die," Grace said, putting her hand over Helen's. "I think he wanted to serve his country. Just like his brother. Like the man he'd grown up to be. I think maybe if he hadn't been killed, he would have proved something to himself, maybe gone on to find a way to reconcile all the different pieces of who he was. But he *was* killed, so now we'll never know."

"I would have loved him, any way he was."

"Would you?"

Helen was silent for a while, as if she was searching deep inside her. "Maybe I wouldn't have understood, not the way I do now that I'm old, and maybe I would have tried to change him. But I would never have stopped loving him. None of us would have."

"I'm sorry he didn't know that."

Helen nodded a little. Then, as if to negate it, she shook her head. "And all these years, you've been keeping quiet about it. You never told nobody?"

"Not even Ben. I did that for Tom. He deserved the respect his sacrifice demanded, without anybody filtering it through their own prejudices."

Helen was quiet for a long time, and when she spoke, her voice was soft.

"I guess I misjudged you. You're a better woman than I thought."

Grace figured that was as much of an apology as Helen had ever given anybody in her life. She was warmed by it. She nearly smiled, but didn't, because one thing still bothered her.

"Just tell me, Helen, that you're not going to think less of *him* now. Tell me I didn't make a big mistake by letting you know the truth."

"Tom was my brother, same as Obed. They were both heroes, just like my Fate. Nobody can take that away from me. I don't think one hair less of him. I'm just sorry he died not knowing that."

Grace squeezed Helen's hand, and as the cool dusk turned to a chillier night, they sat in silence and listened to the symphony of crickets.

27

Jamie wrinkled her nose at the bowl of cereal in front of her. "With Hannah, I never craved any foods. I was too busy to worry about anything except making it through another hour of rehab. With Alison, I wanted cheeseburgers and Hershey bars. Not hard to find, but I had to go easy on both. I could have lived on them gladly, though. Nothing else appealed to me."

Grace tsked in commiseration. "When I was pregnant with Sandra, I wanted Swiss cheese. And black-eyed peas. And pickled watermelon rind."

"Ooh, watermelon rind. That sounds yummy. Is the rind crisp *and* sweet?"

"Crunchy crisp, and toe-curling sweet the way I make it. I'm sure there's a jar or two in the fruit cellar still. We'll have one with supper when you get back."

"Maybe by then I'll stop craving fresh raspberries." Jamie pushed away her breakfast cereal, oat flakes dotted with little dried bits of an assortment of berries. It was the best she'd been able to do at the local grocery store. Several weeks ago she had seen tiny flats of overripe berries that had cost the moon, and with great condescension, she had passed them by. Ever since, she'd obsessed about the way they would feel in her mouth and against her tongue, that sweet "pop" of flavor that the handpicked local berries had provided in early summer. She'd gone back to the store to humble herself and buy the overpriced, overseas, overripe substitute, and even those had disappeared.

"It's a shame you didn't want them a few months ago, when they were available," Grace said.

"A couple of months ago I wanted crisp, fresh apples."

"You certainly have plenty to choose from now."

The apple harvest was well under way, and the quiet drive up to the house was now crowded with work trucks every day. The crop was mediocre, due at least partly to drought conditions, and just good enough to keep the orchard out of bankruptcy. Jamie and the girls had spent hours watching the picking, sorting and processing. Along the way, they had completed Apples 101.

They had learned that, because of the difference in sun exposure, apples from different parts of the same tree might ripen faster, so harvest times could vary. They had watched Grace drop iodine on the cut surface of certain varieties to see if they turned blue, indicating that the proper degree of sugar had developed. For the same reason they'd learned to cut into the McIntosh variety to see if the seeds had turned brown. They'd learned about codling moths, leaf rollers and aphids, and the damage they could do. And they'd learned to fear fire blight, one of the worst diseases to hit any orchard.

They'd also tried their hands at picking apples from the lowest branches, learning to take the stem with the apple, without damaging the spur. Unfortunately, at this point, even the most loving management couldn't change the fact that the trees hadn't received the highest level of care. As they had been for several years, Cashel Orchard's apples would be "processors" targeted for juice and sauce. They would not bring the best price.

"How about a cup of hot cider to go with that cereal you're going to finish?" Grace asked.

Jamie smiled at the last part. "You don't have to wait on me. I can get anything I need."

"Why do you think I begged you to stay? I need somebody to wait on, child. Voices in the house, people who need me? That's what motivates these old bones to get out of bed in the mornings."

"You're still sure you want us to keep living here? You haven't gotten sick of us yet?"

"No chance of that, dear."

Now that Jamie was allowed out of bed for most of the day, she could manage at the cabin. But when she had tried to pack and leave, Grace had insisted she remain at the orchard, and truthfully, Jamie preferred it this way. She liked Grace's company and the help with the girls. And she had fallen in love with the old house, with its airy rooms, nooks and crannies. She felt at home here, and she loved being able to spread out.

Still, she was about to leave Grace's house anyway, although only for a little while. She had scheduled a meeting for the day after tomorrow with her faculty advisor at the university. During her weeks of enforced rest, she had worked hard on her new ideas, and she wanted to see how they would best fit into her graduate curriculum. Although they had been in touch by telephone, the time had come to visit and show him what she had on paper.

"Well, the girls will have fun at the cabin while I'm in

Michigan," she said. "And Kendra and Isaac will get a taste of full-time parenting."

"You're certain you feel well enough for the trip?"

"It's not as grueling as it sounds. It's not a long flight to Detroit, and my friend Tara will pick me up at the airport tonight. I'll stay at First Step, and they'll take good care of me. And seeing everybody will do me good."

"I'm just glad you have a doctor there you trust, just in case."

"I have the best doctor in the world," Jamie assured her. "Suz won't let anything happen to me. You can count on that. In fact, we're getting together for breakfast while I'm there."

"Well, I hope that will be all the traveling you do. I'll worry."

Having lived through one scare already, Jamie understood Grace's misgivings about her decision to travel now. But Dr. Raille had given the okay and warned Jamie that this was the time to make the trip if she had to. With twins, there was always the possibility of enforced bed rest near the end to prevent early labor, and the doctor had told Jamie to prepare. Once Kendra heard the plan, she'd wanted to drive Jamie to Michigan, taking the trip in easy stages, but Jamie had asked her sister to take care of the girls instead. Kendra and Isaac would move into the cabin while the girls continued with school.

Cash had been the only one who hadn't weighed in on Jamie's decision. When she'd explained what she intended, he had simply nodded and told her she was a big girl, and if she felt good enough to go, she ought to.

A man who trusted her to understand her own body and heart? That was a man worth knowing.

"I could make pancakes," Grace said. "I have frozen blueberries. Will that help?"

Jamie pulled the cereal bowl back toward her. "No, there's

nothing wrong with this cereal. I'm going to finish it and enjoy every bite if it kills me. I'm eating a well-balanced diet and taking vitamins. This craving is all in my head. Tomorrow I'll probably want lobster or truffles or something else not easily available."

"And something you'd need a loan to enjoy."

Jamie licked the back of her spoon, the way Hannah always did when she was trying to delay eating something that didn't appeal to her.

She decided to get something off her chest. "You know, I don't think I've ever told you, Grace, but I'm more or less an heiress."

"How can you be more or less? Either you are or you aren't."

"Well, I inherited more money than anybody has a right to, and I have less interest in having it than you might expect." She looked up. "I could afford lobster and truffles three times a day and never feel the pinch. Although I would certainly get tired of it. Wouldn't anybody?"

"I don't know, never having tried it." Grace brought Jamie the cider. "I knew your sister and brother-in-law were well off. They're not sparing any expense on the house, although it's certainly not one of those mini-mansions so many people would build there, just to show they could. But I didn't have any idea where the money came from."

"It's not something we talk about. I lived without money when I ran away. Now I'm living with it. With it is better. But that's as far as it goes."

Grace made a wise guess. "And you don't talk about it because you don't want people to treat you differently."

"It doesn't change who I am. I grew up with it. It's part of the package, and I'm used to it. Our family foundation supports so many worthwhile charities that I don't even feel particularly guilty about spending an infinitesimal share of the leftovers."

"Guilty about what leftovers?" asked a male voice in the doorway.

Jamie looked over her shoulder to see Cash coming toward her, but as lovely as it was to see him, what he carried in his hands was lovelier.

Her eyes widened. "Are those raspberries?"

"I am going to tell you exactly how hard it was to get these, so you appreciate every little bite."

"No explanation needed!" She got to her feet and put her arms around him, reaching for the carton. "You wonderful man."

He held the berries high to keep them away from her. "I have a friend in Pennsylvania. He grows them under special tunnels made out of plastic. It extends his season, so he can get top dollar for every single berry."

"And you ordered these for me?"

"Overnighted them right to me. Packed like they were diamonds, too. He probably insured them, berry by berry."

"You're a prince among men."

"Better than those leftovers you were mentioning?"

For a moment she wasn't sure what he meant; then she realized, and was wary. She wasn't sure why she hadn't mentioned the extent of her wealth to Cash or Grace before this. Part of it really was a basic belief that it didn't matter. Money hadn't made her parents happy, and conversely, some of the happiest people she had known at the university had cheerfully—as *she* had at the time—pooled pocket change for pizza and enjoyed it more for the sharing.

She was also so used to being a Dunkirk of the newspaper Dunkirks that she didn't give the sum total she had inherited that much thought. But a substantial part of not telling Cash and Grace had been fear that it would change the way they treated her. It had before, with others.

"We were talking about money," she said, pulling away. "I happen to have a lot of it, like my sister does."

He didn't seem impressed. "And you have some left over that you need to get rid of? Good. I'd suggest replacing that minivan of yours. It's not going to last forever. At least buy some better tires."

Grace looked from one of them to the other. "I believe Jamie is trying to tell you she could buy the minivan dealership if she wanted to. Or maybe the manufacturer."

Cash scratched his head, then shrugged. "You don't really want to manufacture automobiles, do you, sweetcakes? I can't see you walking down an assembly line telling folks to work faster. And I can't picture you as a used-car salesman, either. It just doesn't fit."

"Some people think I'm special because I'm rich," she said.

"Then they don't know you. You're special just because you are." He bent down to kiss her; then he handed her the carton. "Now eat your raspberries like a good girl."

Jamie and the girls arrived at the cabin at three, although Kendra and Isaac weren't due to arrive until three-thirty. Jamie had packed a carry-on with all her essentials, plus the papers she was taking to her advisor. She had a small suitcase filled with clothes, plus cans of Virginia peanuts and peanut brittle to take to the staff and clients at First Step. While she waited, she settled the girls back in their room, promised she would return by Thursday and reassured Alison at least a dozen times that Aunt Kendra and Uncle Isaac would take the absolute best care of her, such good care, in fact, that she would hardly notice Mommy was gone.

"I don't want you to go," Alison said yet again. "Good mommies don't go away."

Jamie struggled to be patient. "This one does sometimes. But she makes sure that somebody who loves you very much will be here to take care of you."

Hannah tried to help. "Uncle Isaac will take us down to the river. And Aunt Kendra will put us to bed too early, but then she will read to us as long as we want her to if we don't fall asleep."

"I want to go with you," Alison told Jamie, ignoring her sister.

Jamie knew better than to feel guilty, although she was inching in that direction. "I can't take you on this trip, sweetheart. I'll be too busy, and you wouldn't have anything to do. You need to stay and go to preschool. You're making Thanksgiving decorations, remember?"

"You don't want me 'cause you have bruzzins."

"The bruzzins aren't much company yet, are they? And they're Aunt Kendra and Uncle Isaac's babies. You're mine, remember?"

"You're giving *me* to Aunt Kendra." She puckered up.

Alison was well-adjusted and seldom clingy. Jamie saw the problem now. Family lines had become too confusing for the little girl. Jamie was giving the babies she carried to Aunt Kendra, why not give her Alison, too? When all was said and done, why not Hannah? Would Jamie really come back, or was Alison about to get a new mommy, like the babies would, once they were born?

"Alison, do you remember the story I told you about Sister Duck?"

Alison nodded, lips still pursed. Of course she remembered, because Jamie had told it at least three times a week since she first introduced it, adding details and embroidering it, until now the tale took a long time to tell. The girls asked for it repeatedly and made sure she embellished it properly.

"Well, did I explain that sometimes Sister Duck had to fly away? She had to find corn and worms—" Jamie tried to remember what ducks ate and couldn't "—and stuff to eat. You know. Duck stuff. Anyway, whenever she did, she asked Mommy Duck if she would watch *her* ducklings. And Mommy Duck, even though she had baby ducklings of her own now, was always glad to. Because Mommy Duck loved Sister Duck's ducklings, too. They were her Niece and Nephew Ducklings." Jamie realized how complex this whole situation had become and cut to the ending.

"The important thing is that the ducks took good care of each other and loved each other very much. But Sister Duck and Mommy Duck never flew far away. They always came back, and they always came back to their own ducklings. Just like I'm going to come home and take care of you as soon as I'm done in Michigan."

Alison seemed to absorb a little of this, although her bottom lip still perched against her chin. The telephone rang, which surprised Jamie. Almost everybody knew she was living at Grace's now. She hoped it wasn't Kendra announcing a flat tire or some catastrophe that would keep her from arriving in time for Jamie to get to the airport.

She left Alison to ponder her odd little family, and answered the phone.

The male voice that responded was unmistakable, Irish lilt and charm oozing across the line. "Good day to you, Jamie. How are things in Virginia?"

She glanced at Alison, who so seldom heard from Seamus Callahan that she hadn't yet learned to hope his would be the voice at the other end of the line.

"Did you get my message?" Jamie asked softly. "I left you one with the new number where you could reach us."

"Don't assume the worst. I did indeed. But I just called there, and I was told I might catch you at this number today."

She was glad to hear that Seamus had at least kept track of where to find his daughter. He was a vagabond and a thrill seeker, but like Larry, Seamus never quite forgot he was a father.

"Would you like to talk to Alison? She's right here."

"That's why I called. I'm between tournaments. I wanted to be sure we talked before things got busy again."

She chalked up a mock point in his favor and covered the receiver. "Alison, it's your daddy."

Alison looked puzzled; then her eyes brightened. She came forward and took the phone from Jamie's hand, settling it against her ear.

"Hello?"

Jamie smiled. For once Seamus's timing couldn't have been better. This was a special treat, and bound to go a long way toward cheering up her daughter. She listened as Alison answered her father's questions, even describing what she was doing in pre-school. Jamie was about to take the phone when the little girl nodded seriously, as if Seamus could see her.

"Hannah's fine."

Jamie was glad Seamus had remembered to ask. But then, Seamus had always liked Hannah. In his favor, Seamus liked everybody.

"Mommy's fine," Alison said, still nodding. "She's going to have babies."

Jamie stood very still. This was something she hadn't told Seamus, since it involved him not at all. Now she realized her mistake.

"Yes, babies. Two babies." Alison nodded at the phone again. "No, Mommy says she has too many children. She's giving some of us to Aunt Kendra."

Jamie closed her eyes. When Alison held out the telephone to her again, she took it and began to explain, before Seamus hopped on the next plane to rescue his daughter.

★ ★ ★

"Out of the mouths of babes," Kendra said, her eyes twinkling after Jamie told her the story. "What did Alison's father say?"

"I didn't give him much of a chance to say anything. He listened. Then he asked if I'd lost my bloody mind. Seamus can't imagine anybody volunteering to carry one baby, much less two, for somebody she loves. But then, Seamus pretty much just loves Seamus."

"Poor Alison."

"He's not really a bad person, and he likes her well enough. As long as she never requires any real effort."

"She'll realize that one day."

"I'm hoping by the time she does, there'll be a man in my life to give her the stability and role model she needs."

"Could that be somebody you've already met?"

Jamie felt great; she was looking forward to seeing old friends. Her life seemed complete. "Who knows?"

"Are you saying it could be Cash?"

"I don't know. Cash flew in fresh raspberries for me today. It's not hard to love a man who pays attention and follows through. And I told him I'm not poor, and he didn't care."

"If you told the story that way, you'll have to tell it again."

"He didn't ask how much. He said it didn't matter."

Kendra walked out to the porch with her. Isaac had already carried Jamie's things out to the minivan, and he was now in the yard, entertaining the girls by making Dusty, the Taylors' long-faced mutt, roll over and fetch sticks. Ten, the alley cat Isaac had rescued from certain death, was watching from the porch swing, far too snooty to perform for anyone.

"Thanksgiving's right around the corner," Kendra said. "How would you like to spend it? With us in Arlington? This'll be our first Thanksgiving together since you and I were children. You couldn't come last year because of classes. I'd really like us to make it a family tradition if we can."

"Grace wants us all up at the orchard. You and Isaac, too. All the Rosslyns, of course, and one of her sons and his family are coming, too. Would that ruin it for you?"

"No, in fact I'd like that. Extended family. And it would be lovely to have it out here in the Valley. Before long we'll be residents. Maybe next year we can have it at our new house for anybody who wants to come. The babies will be old enough to enjoy all the hubbub, won't they?"

More than she ever had been before, Jamie was struck now by the way she and Kendra had gradually blended their lives. She could count on her sister and brother-in-law to care for her girls. And, of course, Kendra and Isaac had counted on her to help give them children. Now Kendra was asking *her* for parenting advice. They were talking about their future, about establishing family traditions. The changes were happening a little at a time, but they were all so good. There were trials to come—the fine points of her relationship to the twins to work out after their birth, her possible sense of loss when the pregnancy ended—but she was sure now that everything would turn out well. After all these years, she and her sister were really going to be a family.

"They'll be at a wonderful age," she assured Kendra. "And I'd like that so much. I know Grace will let us contribute this year. Would you like to get together on Wednesday and make pies or casseroles? Just the two of us? Maybe we can figure out a few things we'll want to serve every year, so our kids will have something to carry on when they leave and start preparing dinners of their own."

"That would be great. But you're the cook. You'll come up with the recipes?"

"Gladly." Jamie slung her arm around Kendra's shoulders. "I'll be back before you know it. Thanks again for helping here."

"It's little enough in return."

They hugged awkwardly, but Jamie thought it was the most promising hug she had ever received.

28

From the street, First Step looked like many of the other homes on shabby suburban Oakleaf Avenue, northwest of metropolitan Detroit. The homes had once been the gracious abodes of upper-level managers in the automobile industry, built by the sizeable cheap pool of immigrants who had come to work in the plants. But as the city crept outward, those wealthy enough to buy more peace and tranquility had crept outward, too.

After World War II, the expansive Oakleaf homes had been converted into apartments, or partitioned and sold as multi-family residences. Some had been turned into the headquarters of charitable organizations or offices. First Step was one of two halfway houses on a four-block stretch. The other served as a home for mentally challenged adults, where First Steppers often volunteered as part of their community service requirement.

Oakleaf was the rehabilitation center's third address, but the only one Jamie had known. The program was almost twenty years old, and the last ten had been conducted here. First Step had proved to be a good neighbor, and when trouble did come calling, the staff dispensed with it quickly and effectively. The rules at First Step were clear and inflexible. They were enforced often enough that new residents learned them immediately. Clients came and went, sometimes in the same day, even though the First Step program was set up for a one-year period of residence.

Jamie had come to live here in the early months of her first pregnancy. She graduated when Hannah was just three months old, moved into a nearby apartment building and continued her job as a cook at a local restaurant while helping to mentor other First Step clients. In a year's time she went from former client to staff member, then to part-time staff member as she enrolled in college and began to pursue her bachelor's degree in architecture.

Her years here had been busy and productive, filled with hard truths and personal growth. Now, as she stood outside the floodlit French Normandy stucco, with its steeply pitched roof, multi-paned windows and gabled dormers, she felt, as she always did, that some force in the universe had been looking out for her and for Hannah when she was accepted to move to this house and pull her life together.

"It looks so good because the yard crew just did the big fall cleanup," Tara Blayne told her. "Of course, I caught our two shrub trimmers out behind the garage shooting craps. Rosario said since they found craps so fascinating that it took them away from their commitment to the program, the guys needed to teach all the residents how to play, with a special emphasis on the strategies and statistics, how much money is made and lost each year in dice games and how an addiction to gambling relates to drug addiction. He's going to make them present it as a class every Wednesday night this month, with handouts."

Jamie slung her arm over petite Tara's shoulders. Tara, an elfin blonde in her late thirties whose fascination with container gardening was in evidence on the First Step porch, had been a resident counselor with the program for several years. She and Jamie had been friends that long, too. Jamie would be spending her Michigan nights in Tara's attic apartment.

"That's our Rosario," Jamie said. "When I was a resident, I had a midnight snack attack, so I went down to the kitchen to pop corn. At that point in the treatment, I wasn't allowed out of my room at night, of course. So when Rosario caught me, he suggested that since I liked to cook at odd hours, I should be on early-morning kitchen duty. And actually, that's when I learned how much I really *did* like to cook, which led to my first restaurant job."

"Well, by the time Rosario's done with them, I doubt these guys will want to become croupiers. They won't want to see another pair of dice."

"How is funding these days? Still hand to mouth?"

"The War on Drugs isn't fighting enough battles on Oakleaf Avenue. And the private foundations have their hands full funding all those programs the government won't. Don't even get me started on insurance reimbursement. But Rosario's good at beating the bushes. We'll keep limping along."

Jamie actually knew more about First Step's financial situation than she let on. She had been able to persuade the trustees of the Dunkirk Foundation to give First Step a good-size grant, although the money was being channeled through another organization so nobody would know it had anything to do with her. The trustees had been reluctant, until she pointed out that it would be bad public relations if word ever leaked to the press that they had refused to help the very rehabilitation program that had set one of the last of the Dunkirks on the road to recovery.

"Rosario told me to pop back and see him when I got in," Jamie said. "Do you mind?"

"'Course not. I'll get one of the residents to bring your suitcases up to my apartment. You know where to find Rosario."

They parted at the front of the house, where Tara stopped to fuss with a half barrel filled with chrysanthemums that were in their final days. Jamie took the walkway around to the back. Ron Rosario and his wife lived above the garage in a two-bedroom apartment she had designed for them in her third year at the university. The neighborhood and this property still had enough magnificent old trees to shield it from the street and from the view of nearby residents. The apartment was simple and functional, but precisely because of the first, the board had been able to find the money to add it to their budget. Once it was completed, Rosario and his wife, Georgia, had moved from the attic, which was now Tara's digs. The rest of the staff lived elsewhere and went home after their shifts.

The stairs began at one side of the garage and wrapped around to the back, ending at a small deck that was just large enough for a round metal table and two café chairs. Tonight that was where she found Rosario, sitting at the table, staring into the darkness behind the house.

"Hey," she said, pulling out the other chair to join him. "This is Michigan, and it's November. Don't you know it's cold out here?"

He leaned over the table and kissed her cheek. "You look warm enough in that coat. They haven't ruined you down south. You still look like a Michigan girl."

"I'm carrying two little heaters around these days." Jamie rested her hands on her wool-covered belly.

"How are you feeling?"

"A little tired after the trip. But mostly just pregnant."

He nodded. Ron Rosario was a large man who seemed ageless to everyone who knew him. In reality, Jamie guessed he was probably in his late fifties. His only son had already left home for college by the time the program moved to Oakleaf Avenue, and these days Georgia sometimes talked about what they would do and where they would go when they retired.

Rosario still had a thick head of grizzled hair that he wore in a ponytail, and a neatly trimmed beard to match. His most arresting feature was his large dark eyes, which saw right through lies or any lesser form of pretense. If he had ever been patient or tactful, his years of working with addicts had cured him of both.

"Where's Georgia?" Jamie asked. "I brought you both some Virginia peanuts and peanut brittle." Rosario had a notorious sweet tooth.

"What, no more grants from the family foundation?"

She arched her brows and tried to look innocent. "I don't know what you mean."

"You went to a lot of trouble to hide where that money came from."

She knew better than to play games with him. "If I did, it was because I don't want anybody making a big deal out of it, including you."

"You put in your time here, paid your dues. You don't have to keep paying."

"We both know the money's there to be used, and it's not exactly coming out of my hide. Are you sorry I helped?"

"Not sorry at all. Delighted, even grateful. But just wondering when you're going to stop paying penance for the bad years."

She was a little hurt, but she was also used to this. Rosario used those big dark eyes to look beyond everything. He wasn't always right, but his miscalculations were rare enough to be notable.

"Georgia's closing up the beach house," he said, in answer to her earlier question.

The Rosarios had a cottage in the Upper Peninsula, where they retreated when they could. She had always suspected Georgia retreated the most often, not only to get away from First Step, but from the intensity of living with Ron.

"What's the difference between paying penance and just paying back a debt?" Jamie asked.

"When you pay penance, you're hoping for absolution."

"That's not happening. Not with the foundation money. I never hurt *you,* so how could you absolve me?"

"Because I'm the biggest authority figure in your life."

She smiled. "Maybe so, but I went to bat for First Step because it's important to a lot of people. Not because I needed anything from you."

"How about the pregnancy?"

The smile faded. "That's hitting below the belt."

"No pun intended?" He held out a bowl filled with rice crackers. "Did you have dinner?"

"Tara saved me a plate of whatever they made for the house tonight. I'll eat in a little while." She took a handful anyway, suddenly starving.

"We haven't had a decent meal over there since you left. I miss your lasagna."

She crunched crackers and thought about what he'd said. There was no reason to take up that particular conversation again. That was Rosario's style. Throw something out, see if anybody took the bait, leave them thinking about it until next time. He wouldn't bring up the babies again, not unless she did.

She couldn't help herself. "Don't you think that sometimes we just owe people we've hurt something extra?"

"Like risking our health, taking a year away from a promising career, moving across the country where we don't know anybody, just to prove we've changed?"

"How is it that you can make my whole life sound trivial and neurotic without half trying?"

"I'd say what you're doing is the opposite of trivial, wouldn't you?"

"It feels right."

"Lots of things feel right, Jamie. Taking drugs, for example. Stealing to buy drugs. Ask anybody in the house. Search your memory."

"I did those things for myself. I'm doing this for my sister."

"Really?"

"Of course I'm getting something out of it. The giver of a gift comes away with a sense of satisfaction. That's normal."

"Satisfaction or absolution? Is this what it'll take for your sister to forgive you? Or for you to forgive yourself?"

"I don't know if Kendra needs to forgive me. But she does need to trust me."

"And this will accomplish that?"

"I think so. But really, that's not *all* this is about. I want to do this for her. I love her. She and Isaac will be great parents. We so rarely have a chance to make this kind of difference. How could I not have helped them?"

"Easily. They didn't ask. They probably never even thought of it."

"I'm glad *I* did."

Rosario rarely gave advice. Questions were more his style. But this time he broke with tradition. "I think you need to be careful. This is a sacrifice and a gift that will resound through generations, but you have to be aware that this may not end the way you hope, with everybody happy. You have to be prepared and able to accept that."

"I know."

He nodded. "You probably do, up here." He tapped the side of his head. "But for somebody who lived on the streets for a while, you have a tender heart. And you still let it make too many of your decisions."

"I may have come away with a tender heart, but I also came away with survival skills."

"Put them to good use, then." He reached across the table to squeeze her hand. "And don't be a stranger here. Make sure you bring those girls of yours back to see us. Georgia and I think of you as family. Never forget it."

The next morning, Rosario's words played in Jamie's mind when she was in the middle of a shower. She was soaping her breasts, gazing with dismay at the large mound ballooning beneath them, when she felt a lump on the right side of her right breast.

At first she thought she had imagined it. She hung up the washcloth and began to explore with her fingers. Since the day she had begun hormones to prepare for in vitro, her breasts had felt noticeably lumpy. Of course, they had felt tender and stretched to capacity, too. Since she'd had a breast exam less than a year ago as part of the physical to determine if she could be Kendra's surrogate, she hadn't thought much about any of that, blaming the changes on the hormones, then on the pregnancy.

She turned off the water, continuing her exploration after she stepped out and dried off. She wasn't imagining this. Something that felt almost like a marble seemed to be just below the skin. Was this just a normal symptom? She wasn't sure what she felt, exactly. But she thought there was definitely something different there, something harder and more defined then the simple swelling she had more or less gotten used to.

Maybe it had *never* been simple.

She was having breakfast later with her former gynecologist, Suz Chinn. Over omelets, she could ask Suz to work her into the schedule today and check out the lump, so she could reassure Jamie there was nothing to worry about.

As soon as that occurred to her, she decided she was being silly. She was only going to be in Michigan for a few days. If the lump was still there by the time she got back to Virginia, she would make an appointment with Dr. Raille and have an examination.

The same Dr. Raille who had gotten so used to explaining every little aspect of Jamie's pregnancy to Kendra that she might feel obligated to discuss this with her, as well.

Jamie wondered what to do. Kendra was already worried enough that something was going to happen to the twins. She hadn't been happy about Jamie's trip here, although she hadn't tried to stop her. But every physical symptom Jamie experienced was like a warning bell for her sister. Jamie could not imagine what Kendra might do if Dr. Raille worried her with this.

By the time she dressed and went downstairs for the morning meeting—a requirement for anybody who stayed overnight in the house, resident, staff and guests alike—she still hadn't decided how to proceed. She greeted everyone in the airy living room where the meeting was held, listened as announcements were made and people shared their plans for the day, and then shared her own. She was meeting a friend for breakfast, then heading over to the university to see her advisor. She would be back to help with dinner that afternoon....

If she wasn't on an examination table in Suz Chinn's office.

After Tara dropped her off at the diner to wait for Suz, Jamie looked over the menu, although her mind was elsewhere. The university was only a short walk, and after her meeting with her advisor, she planned to do a little shopping for Alison and Hannah, then head back to First Step for a nap. All that seemed increasingly mundane, however. She wasn't a worrier, but she wondered now if, in this case, her previous trouble-free pregnancies had actually been a problem. A less-experienced mother or a natural worrier might have made a point of telling her physician every little symptom. Maybe then Dr. Raille would have checked her breasts more carefully. She might have ordered a mammogram, if that was safe during pregnancy, and had a radiologist she trusted check it.

But Jamie wasn't a worrier, so none of those things had happened.

She was still mulling this over when a shadow fell over the table. She stood, and she and Suz embraced, murmuring all the normal things old friends do. Then Suz took the chair across from her and signaled their server for coffee.

Suz had been born in Honolulu, to a Chinese father and native Hawaiian mother. She was beautiful and gifted, and the combination had helped assure her of confidence and success. For her younger brother, Pete, the combination of cultures had been less rewarding. A move to Detroit early in his childhood had set him adrift in an unfamiliar world where his island heritage had made him a minority and Attention Deficit Disorder had convinced him he would never succeed. He had turned to drugs and the kids who sold them for companionship. Now Pete was another of First Step's success stories, but at the time when Suz asked Jamie for help, the Chinn family had been afraid they might lose Pete to the streets.

"You're looking great," Suz told Jamie, once they were both seated again. "How do you feel?"

"I've been fine." Jamie told her about the short stint of bed rest. "Other than that though, it's been okay. Two *is* harder than one—"

"And you're that much older. But I see a lot of moms nearing menopause carrying twins. Fertility drugs, and it's just more likely at that age, anyway. So you're still a youngster."

"I'm glad to hear it. I'm not feeling so much like one."

They chatted, catching each other up on their lives. Thirty-seven-year-old Suz was engaged to a man Jamie had met and liked. They were buying a house in time for the wedding, and planning a long trip to the islands so that Suz could show him her childhood haunts. Jamie told her about Grace and the girls, and even about Cash.

Breakfast was leisurely, and they laughed a lot, but by the time they got the bill, Jamie still hadn't mentioned the lump. Suz stood to go, and Jamie felt a flutter of panic. That was enough to convince her that she needed reassurance.

"Listen," she said, standing, too. "In the shower this morning I felt what may be a lump in my breast." She gave a quick history and reminded Suz she'd had a breast exam at her pre-pregnancy physical.

"It's probably nothing," she finished. "But I wondered if you'd check it out? I hate to ask for a favor, but I'd rather *you* found bad news than my Virginia obstetrician. Then I can figure out what to do without involving my sister and her husband."

Suz didn't try to reassure her or make light of her worries. She simply nodded. "How is your afternoon shaping up? Will you have time to stop by?"

"I can come in anytime after two."

"I'll tell the receptionist to work you in whenever you get there."

"It's probably nothing."

Suz checked her watch. "If you had any idea how many times a day I hear that..."

"How often *is* it nothing?"

"Often enough that there's no real reason for you to be alarmed. Just stop by, and we'll take a quick look."

"I could wait until I got home. Now I'm feeling silly."

"Why spoil your time here with worrying? Just stop in. We'll see what's up."

Even though that sounded sensible and easy, Jamie's panic increased. By the time she was out on the sidewalk waving goodbye, she wished it was already evening and she was basking in a clean bill of health.

At four o'clock, after doing a thorough breast exam, Suz told her to sit up.

"Well, you were right," she said. "This was worth checking." She made some notes in Jamie's chart before she looked up. "There are several ways to proceed, but I'm going to suggest we get an ultrasound and probably an FNA. That's a fine needle biopsy. There's no point in doing a mammogram first. It's unnecessary radiation, and they're somewhat unreliable at this stage of a pregnancy, anyway."

Jamie shook her head. "It can't be cancer. I'm pregnant."

"I'm afraid that doesn't protect you. More pregnant women in your age bracket are diagnosed with breast cancer than those who aren't pregnant."

Jamie didn't know what to say.

Suz took her hand and warmed it between her own. "That doesn't mean it's common. It's not, not at all. Maybe one pregnant women out of every thousand gets the diagnosis. Those are excellent odds, okay? This is probably a cyst, or maybe expanded glandular tissue from all the hormones your body's producing. But hasn't your doctor been checking your breasts?"

Jamie tried to remember. "Kendra's usually in the room, and sometimes Isaac, too, so there's always a lot going on. I'm sure the doctor's checked, but certainly not every time."

"Well, I can feel it today, but maybe it hasn't been so noticeable." She checked her watch, something that seemed as much a part of her as breathing or blinking her eyes. "I have a surgeon I like. As a favor to me, he might be able to do an FNA as early as tomorrow, then a surgical biopsy while you're still in town, if necessary. Is that what you want? Or do you want to wait until you get back to Virginia?"

"I don't know what to do."

"Then let me arrange it here, as soon as I can. I know he'll do the best possible job, and the sooner you know, the better. It's probably nothing to worry about, but if it is, you'll have decisions to make."

For a moment the room seemed to be revolving slowly. Jamie blinked to make it stop. "What kind of decisions?"

"There's no reason to deal with that now, not when we don't even know there's a need to."

Jamie's gaze found Suz's. "What kind of decisions?"

"What to do about the cancer, Jamie. And what to do about the pregnancy."

29

Nearly a year had passed since the day Jamie had announced she wanted to be Kendra and Isaac's surrogate. Now, ascending the final stretch to the orchard on her way home from a "routine" appointment with Dr. Raille, she pulled over to the side of the road and looked out over Cashel Orchard, the skeletal trees stripped of the fruit that was their reason for existence.

Even denuded of leaves and apples, the sight stirred her. This orchard, in one form or another, had testified to the Valley's fertile soil and favorable climate for more than a century. She couldn't imagine that tenure ending, and she knew that when Grace, and even Grace's family, stood in this spot and looked at this site, they had to feel despair and a sense of foreboding at what the future might bring.

She understood foreboding now, better than she had ever wanted to.

Her prenatal visit hadn't really been routine, of course. She had hand carried her records from Michigan and spent the appointment informing Dr. Raille of what she had done and what she expected from her in the future.

The doctor had been appalled at Jamie's choices, and when Jamie insisted she did not want her sister and brother-in-law to learn about them until she was ready to tell them herself, Dr. Raille had threatened to remove herself from the case.

By the time Jamie left the office, she and the doctor had come to an uneasy agreement, just as she and Suz had done over her treatment. Jamie's body was her own, and it was up to her to decide how much she shared about her health with her sister and when. Nothing she had done would threaten the twins. So the doctor had no moral or professional obligation to inform the babies' biological parents about it.

Sadly, Jamie knew that the rest of her care in Front Royal would be conducted in tight-lipped silence. She just hoped Kendra didn't begin to suspect there was more to the doctor's change of attitude than professional concern about delivering healthy twins.

Kendra's suspicions were already a problem. Jamie had told her sister there was no need to accompany her to this appointment, although Kendra had come to every other. Jamie had explained that the appointment was completely routine; no ultrasound was scheduled, no tests. She had other things to do beforehand, and she couldn't spend time with Kendra afterward, because she needed to be home when Alison and Hannah arrived.

Reluctantly, Kendra had agreed. But combined with Jamie's sudden absence at Thanksgiving, her sister's decision to go to this doctor's appointment alone had surely set off alarm bells.

In truth, Kendra had every reason to feel alarmed. Thanksgiving had not been spent, as Jamie had hoped, with Kendra and Isaac and Granny Grace and her family. She hadn't sat next to Cash at the dinner table, nudging him playfully with her knee while she urged him to try the onion casserole she and Kendra had baked, or a chocolate silk pie they had added to a groaning board of desserts. Hannah and Alison had not been introduced to the idea that Thanksgiving was usually spent with family, and that in years to come, they would do it that same way again and again.

Instead, Jamie and the girls had spent the holiday as they had for so many years in the past, at First Step, with staff who hadn't been given the day off and residents who weren't yet allowed to return home or had none to return to. Jamie had cooked the turkey and made the dressing, and after the meal, she and the girls had gone upstairs to Tara's apartment and watched *Miracle on 34th Street*.

To pave the way for the trip back to Michigan, Jamie had told her sister she was needed at First Step, because so many staff were going to be absent. Even to her, the excuse had sounded lame.

Now Jamie hoped she could find a way to convince Kendra there was nothing to worry about. At least not until the day she explained that she'd been lying for these final months of the pregnancy, and there was indeed something to worry about after all.

Already she felt enmeshed in a spider's web of deceit.

Back in the minivan, she sat for a moment, head resting against the seat. She was exhausted and aching, with little she could do about either. At least in the privacy of her van she didn't have to pretend to feel better than she did. She took advantage of that and closed her eyes until the December cold spurred her to start the engine and move on. She was halfway up the driveway to Grace's house when she glanced in her rearview mirror and saw a familiar Lexus. At some point her sister had turned in behind her.

Suspicion had come directly to her doorstep.

By the time Kendra stepped out of her car and raised a hand in greeting, Jamie was waiting on the porch. Shenandoah County had yet to have its first snow, but that day seemed close at hand. A winter breeze skipped dried leaves and sticks along the ground, and despite the bright afternoon sun and a warm coat, Jamie shivered.

"What are you doing here?" she asked, trying not to sound unhappy at her sister's sudden appearance.

"They're doing more selective cutting and pruning over at the house to open up views. We were waiting until the trees lost all their leaves to make sure we had it right. We don't want them taking more than they need to, even if that means we only have certain views in the winter. I came to make the final decision."

Jamie knew that clearing trees was on the agenda. The fact that Kendra felt she had to explain it again seemed telling. Her sister was buying time while she figured out how to say what she'd really come for.

Jamie realized she was standing silently, staring at Kendra, who was pulling her jacket tighter around her. "Wow, I'm sorry. Come on in and warm up. I'll make tea. Grace is over at Helen Henry's house. They're working on some project for the bee."

Kendra followed her sister inside. "Grace and *Helen?*"

"I'm not sure what happened, but they're sort of getting along now. Helen invited her. Grace said it was an offer she couldn't refuse."

The brief rest in her van hadn't helped much. Jamie was tired from the trip to Front Royal. For the last week she had survived on Tylenol and sheer grit. Now, before the girls got home, she wanted nothing more than a chance to put her feet up.

Kendra seemed to realize she was tired, if not why. "You look beat. Let me make the tea."

In the kitchen, Jamie slipped her fleece boots off her swollen feet and sank into a chair at the table, while she directed Kendra to the stash of tea bags.

"How did the appointment go?" Kendra asked.

"Fine. Heartbeats are strong, my blood pressure's good, nothing showed up that shouldn't have." Except a visual reminder of her lies.

"How was the trip over?"

"Fine. Why?"

"Because you look wiped. And it's a long way to drive when you can hardly squeeze behind the steering wheel."

"I can squeeze behind it just fine. You don't need to worry."

"Well, I did. Worry, that is. I'd rather just go to all the appointments, even if they're completely routine. I worry too much when I'm not there, and I don't think you should be traveling that distance by yourself."

"Kendra, I just made two trips to Michigan on my own."

"I don't want to sound like your mother—"

"Then don't, okay?"

When her sister didn't answer, Jamie realized how sharp she had sounded. She closed her eyes to keep them from filling with tears. She struggled for a moment until she was sure she could speak without betraying herself.

"I'm sorry. I know you're just trying to help. And besides, our real mother wouldn't have given any of that a second thought. So you're in a league by yourself."

Kendra still didn't say anything. She waited by the stove until the tea bags had steeped long enough; then she brought the tea to the table and set one of the cups in front of Jamie. She sat down with her own cup and made a point of adding honey from the little ceramic beehive in the center of the table, even though she always drank it plain. Finally she looked up.

"You took the girls out of school and headed off for Michigan for Thanksgiving, even though we made plans to celebrate together. Then today you didn't want me at the doctor's appointment. You told me not to come."

"I never said I didn't want you, Ken. I just said I was going to be busy beforehand, and there was nothing happening that you needed to be part of."

"I know what you said. I was on the other end of the line."

"I realize you don't know much about my life in Michigan. But I owe my friends at First Step everything. So when they asked for my help over the holiday, I just didn't want to say no. I'm sure that's the last time they'll ever ask, but I was glad to do what I could."

Kendra leaned forward. "Is that all it was about, Jamie?"

For a moment Jamie wondered if Kendra had discovered the truth. "What do you mean? What else would it be?"

"The babies." Kendra pushed her tea away and folded her hands on the table. "We're getting close to the end now. You've probably got less than three months before the babies are born. It would be normal to be having some second thoughts. Wondering why you've done such a thing? Wondering if you can go through with handing the boys over to Isaac and me?"

Jamie felt a surge of relief, then realized how terrible this situation was that her sister's very realistic fears could produce such an incongruous reaction.

She played for time while she tried to think of a way out. "What would that possibly have to do with my trip to Michigan?"

"Maybe you needed some time when they were completely yours. When you and the girls and the twins were a family without anyone else laying claim? Maybe that's why you didn't want me at the doctor's office, too."

"Apparently you don't trust what I've already told you."

"It's not trust. It just seems like there has to be more to it. And there might be things you aren't comfortable telling me. Like second thoughts."

"I'm not having second thoughts."

"They would be normal."

"They might be, but I'm not having them. I love the twins. I love being pregnant with them, but I don't want to keep them."

Jamie lifted an eyebrow and sharpened her tone, because she realized that was the only way she was going to convince her sister. "But I don't love feeling like I can't have a little emotional and physical space when I need it. This is a very intense experience. I'm tired and hormonal and grouchy. If now and then I need to do something that doesn't include you, you'll just have to understand."

Kendra sat back. "I'm sorry."

"You don't need to be."

"You think I've been hovering."

"Not really. I just needed space. That's the only way I can explain it. I went back to Michigan where I had a life that didn't include tiny feet under my ribs and stretch marks. I just needed to be with people who remembered me as somebody else and celebrate Thanksgiving with them."

"Oh, Jamie, I know this has to be hard."

Jamie wanted to put her arms around her sister and reassure her, but she knew she had to be careful. Instead, she leaned across the table until their hands were almost touching. And she lied again.

"It's not as hard as you're making it sound. This was small stuff, okay? A break. Before I settle in for the long haul. I'm not upset, I'm not having second thoughts. I just needed a break and a chance to see my friends at Thanksgiving time. And today was about nothing at all. I just didn't see the point in you coming along. But if you want to come along to every single appointment in the future, I can handle it."

"I'll make a point of giving you some more space. I guess… well, I guess it's just that being with you makes this easier for me."

"You lost me there."

Kendra twisted her hands, a gesture that was at once so unusual and so evocative that Jamie couldn't watch. She looked at her own instead.

"I'm struggling, too," Kendra said at last. "I don't know how to be a mother. I don't know if I'm up to this."

"What?"

Kendra looked up as Jamie did, and their gazes locked. "That's why I waited so long to have kids. I'm not sure I would have found the courage, even when I thought I *could* have them. Then I found out I couldn't, and it was like a light went off inside me. But, Jamie, before all this, I kept putting it off and putting it off, because I was afraid."

"Of what?"

"Of failing."

Jamie understood. "Because of me?"

"Well, I never had much of a role model, and when I tried being a mommy, I wasn't all that good at it, was I?" She shook her head when Jamie started to reassure her. "I know what you're going to say. I've heard it all before. I was a child trying to raise a child. But here's what I've come to realize. That child I tried to raise?" She smiled a little. "She turned out awfully well despite everything. And she's a fantastic mother herself. So maybe I didn't do as dreadful a job as I thought."

"Oh, Ken, it was the good stuff you taught me that got me through."

"And now the good stuff you've taught *me* is going to get *me* through. Because I've finally realized that if I don't know what to do in years ahead, I've got you. In all those years to come, you'll already have gone first and eased the way for me. Toilet training, the first day of school, driver's ed? You'll be able to give me advice."

Jamie sat silently and wondered if she really would be there to help her sister. Would she still be alive in five years? Or ten? And even if she was, after Kendra realized what she had done without consulting her, would Kendra ever trust her again?

"Thank you," Kendra said, reaching for Jamie's hands and covering them with her own. "Not just for having the babies, but for being there to help me raise them."

Jamie closed her eyes and nodded. But this time she couldn't control the tears.

That night Hannah and Alison requested the Sister Duck story, and by the time Jamie finished, she was so tired that she nearly had to drag herself out of the room. But she wasn't tired enough to sleep. She knew if she got ready for bed and lay down herself, she would stare at the ceiling and think about everything Kendra had said.

Kendra rarely admitted to weakness. She had little need, since she was one of the most self-assured people Jamie had ever met. In her career, she had questioned presidents and mass murderers, ferreted out secrets despite enormous roadblocks and stood up for stories her editors had insisted she abandon. More than once she had risked her safety to find the truth.

So Kendra's courage was unquestioned. But in this new emotional realm of parenting, a realm of many potential false steps and mistakes, a realm neither she nor Jamie had been raised to inhabit, she was frightened. Jamie knew how much it had cost her sister to tell her that and to admit she would need Jamie's help. And the fact that she *had* told her was the final proof that she viewed Jamie as an equal, someone to be trusted completely.

With that last thought playing in her mind, Jamie moved quietly into the kitchen to make herself a cup of warm cider.

She was sitting at the table with only a night-light and the cider for company when Grace came in. Jamie didn't say anything, assuming Grace would speak first. But Grace said nothing and passed right by the table.

"Grace?" Jamie asked.

Grace whirled and narrowed her eyes. "Oh, I didn't see you, dear. I guess I was so busy thinking about what I was going to drink."

Jamie almost let it go, but she couldn't. Grace hadn't missed seeing her because she was thinking. She hadn't seen Jamie because the light in the kitchen was low. Grace hadn't been able to make out Jamie's outline in the darkness.

"How bad are your eyes?" Jamie asked.

Grace sighed. "Really quite bad, I'm afraid."

Jamie got to her feet. "Why don't you sit and I'll get you something to drink?"

"Oh, you don't have to worry. This didn't happen yesterday. It's been a gradual process. I know where everything is. That's one reason I came back here, you know. Everything in this house is an old friend. What I can't see clearly, I can remember. If I lose my sight entirely, I won't be at a complete loss here. I'll still be able to get around."

Jamie remembered the spills, the stumbles, and wondered how she could have missed the signs. She had been so wrapped up in her own life that she had failed to note the obvious.

"Are you keeping this a secret?"

Grace opened the refrigerator and her hand went to the milk.

Jamie realized now that Grace's refrigerator and the chest freezer were superbly organized. There was a place for everything, and whatever the item was, it was returned to exactly the same place. Milk on the right, beside the half-gallon jug of cider, exactly where Grace's hand was resting now.

Grace shut the door and took the carton of milk to the stove. She reached for one of the pans hanging on a Peg-board to the right. Always on the same peg.

"Sandra suspects my sight is failing. Cash does, too, I imagine. I'm not sure they realize quite how badly or rapidly, though. But they will soon enough."

"I'm so sorry."

"Don't be. There's hope that a new treatment I'm trying will stop the downward progress. Right now, I can still see quite a bit when the light's good. I can see bright colors especially, and with a strong magnifier, I can still see well enough to work on my quilts."

Jamie remembered the magnifier Grace always wore around her neck when she was sewing. She had simply assumed it made the tiny detail work easier, but now she realized Grace didn't work with tiny details. She worked with bold colors, three-dimensional objects that she could feel and place on her art quilts accordingly and large patterns. And when she embroidered words on a quilt top, she called the topsy-turvy alphabet "folk art."

"I manage quite well," Grace said, "although there have been a few spectacularly strange meals in this house when spices or herbs were moved around by mistake. Since then I've learned to sniff everything and cook by taste. I highly recommend it."

"I don't know how you've managed so well that nobody's really caught on. You're a marvel."

"I intend to be a marvel until the day I die."

"Did your quilts begin to change as your eyesight got worse?"

As the milk heated, Grace leaned against the stove. "Yes, and that was a bonus. Before that, I tried to do what everyone else was doing. When I no longer could, I had to improvise. And only then did I begin to find myself as an artist." She laughed a little. "Although maybe if I could see my quilts more clearly I would be appalled."

"You would be proud. They're beautiful."

"Even Helen Henry told me the sunflower isn't as bad as she expected and might have a redeeming feature or two."

Jamie laughed, but the sound felt odd in her throat, as if she had just laughed at the most serious point in a sermon.

"Don't go all sentimental on me. I highly recommend adversity, dear. It's underrated."

Jamie's breath caught, and the sound that emerged was too much like a moan. "Oh, Grace."

Grace might be losing her sight, but there was nothing wrong with her hearing. She turned off the burner and came over to the table, taking the seat closest to Jamie's.

"It's probably time to tell me what's going on." Grace felt for and took Jamie's hand. If Jamie hadn't known what she now did about Grace's sight, she wouldn't even have noticed the way Grace's hand glided across the table to find hers.

"I'm okay," Jamie said. "Things are okay."

"No, they aren't. And don't tell me I'm imagining this. Something happened in Michigan. You're a beautiful, grown-up woman, and you don't have to tell me anything you don't want to. But I do need to be sure you aren't hiding something you need to talk about. And I'm afraid my mind has gone to all sorts of dark possibilities."

Maybe if Grace hadn't shared the truth about her failing eyesight, Jamie could have lied again and repeated her reassurances. But Grace had been honest with her, and she knew she owed her the same.

"I have breast cancer. I found the lump while I was in Michigan the first time and went to see my gynecologist. She's a good friend. She was able to make things happen quickly. They did the appropriate tests and discovered it was malignant. So Suz gave me the options. Of course she skipped right over my favorite, pretending that nothing was happening and the tests were a mistake."

"And you didn't tell anybody here?"

"I couldn't! Kendra worried about everything remotely connected to me or the babies right from the moment we did the transfer. I thought she would get over it, but she hasn't. Everything concerns her. She wants these babies so much, she's sure they're going to be taken from her."

Grace didn't argue. "I know. She and I have talked. It wasn't an easy decision to let you go ahead. But that must mean you've made decisions about your health alone?" She paused. "You *have* made decisions?"

"If I wasn't pregnant, lumpectomy would have been the preferred treatment of choice. They would remove the tumor, then begin a regimen of radiation. But radiation is out of the question during pregnancy, and ending this pregnancy was never an option."

"I would have expected them to recommend it."

"No, at least in that, Suz—my doctor—and the statistics agreed with me. Instead she consulted with an oncologist, a surgeon and a radiologist, and they proposed I have a modified radical mastectomy followed—if needed—by a type of chemotherapy that would most likely not harm the babies." Jamie paused. "Grace, 'most likely' were not words I wanted associated with this pregnancy."

"Would they have made that suggestion if it wasn't wise?"

"What information they have about the drugs is promising. Based on everything that's known so far, they seem safe during pregnancy. But there are no long-term studies yet. Suz had to warn me about that. And I had to decide if I was willing to gamble the future health of Kendra's children on phrases like 'most likely' and 'seem safe.'"

There was no point in explaining every step in her decision-making now. After the diagnosis, she had gone back to First Step to consider her options and do her own research on Tara's computer. And what she had learned about chemotherapy had frightened her, not the side effects or the effect on her body, but that its stated purpose was to inhibit the growth of cells. And what was pregnancy other than one body nurturing the growth of another tiny body's cells?

She'd found and devoured stories of women like herself who had been diagnosed during pregnancy, had chemo and gone on to have healthy babies and a remission of their cancer. Each one was different. None of the situations exactly mirrored her own. They were good mothers, good women, who had done the research, spoken at length to specialists and made the right decision based on their personal situation. They had gambled that having the chemo and improving the chance that they would live to raise their own children was the answer for them.

But what was the answer for her?

"So I was left with these choices," she told Grace. "I could have a mastectomy, a surgery I would never be able to keep from Kendra and Isaac. Then I could either have the chemo—if the results from the surgery suggested I needed it—and hope the twins wouldn't be harmed, or delay it until after the twins are born."

"Apparently that's not what you chose?"

"No. My second choice? I could have a lumpectomy, with a shorter time under anesthesia, which was better for the babies, delay radiation until after the birth, then submit to whatever further treatment the doctors feel is warranted at that stage. And I could do that surgery in Michigan, without telling anybody here what's going on, and continue with the pregnancy as if nothing had happened. So that's what I did. Later, if the cancer returns, I can have a mastectomy."

"What about your doctor here?"

"I swore her to silence today."

Grace tilted her head in question. "Something tells me your decision wasn't the one your doctor favored."

"No, she didn't. They sometimes delay radiation after a lumpectomy for as long as six weeks, but that means I should be starting it just after the beginning of the new year. I'll be pushing two months beyond that. Suz is afraid the potential of upstaging—that's the cancer moving to the next stage—will be greater. Stray cells could metastasize while I wait."

"She knows that for certain? They have studies that prove if you wait until after the delivery, you'll be at a much greater risk?"

"No, it depends on the length of the delay, the changes in my breasts during pregnancy, the size of the tumor, what if any lymph nodes are involved. Suz said all those things could affect the outcome. But it's still a guessing game. She just believed I was gambling with my future."

Jamie rested her hands over her belly and glanced down. The babies were moving inside her. "But she was asking me to gamble with theirs."

Now she cut straight to the ending. "Having the lumpectomy wasn't the best option for *me*. I know that. I'm not kidding myself. Waiting for further treatment's not the best way to go. But with everything else, it was the only way I was willing to do it."

"And you didn't feel you could consult your family?"

"What if they wanted me to do whatever it took to safeguard

my own health?" She paused, then held up her hand as Grace started to speak. "And what if they didn't?"

Grace shook her head.

Jamie had hardly slept after she learned the diagnosis and the alternatives. And the more fatigued she'd grown, the more certain she had become that she could not involve Kendra and Isaac in this decision.

"There's nothing Kendra or Isaac can say that will be right. Whatever they say will stand between us forever. I don't want them to know what's going on. We're just starting to become a real family. But it's all so…so fragile. I just can't take a chance now, and I *won't* take a chance with the health of these babies."

"Have you thought about Hannah and Alison? What if the delay in radiation and maybe chemo means the cancer metastasizes?"

"I asked Suz that question. She said she couldn't tell me what might happen. But she wants me to ask Dr. Raille to induce labor the moment she feels the twins are viable. That could make a difference. I could start treatment right away—weeks earlier, maybe, than if I waited. But these are *twins.* Their birth weight is going to be lower as is. I'm not willing to take risks with their health."

"And to that she said?"

Jamie, what cross are you trying to die on?

The words still rang in Jamie's ears. She looked down at the table and shook her head.

Grace touched her hand. "Such an awful burden for someone so young."

"It could be a lot worse. The surgery went as well as could be expected. The tumor was almost two centimeters, meaning it was still a stage one. The margins were clear, and the cancer itself isn't among the most aggressive types. That's a piece of luck, since most often cancers in women my age are. A sampling of the axillary lymph nodes didn't show any indication it had spread. If I had been able to undergo radiation as required, my prognosis would be excellent. As it is, I'm hopeful my decision to wait is only going to make it slightly less favorable."

Grace was quiet for a long time. Then she squeezed Jamie's hand. "I might have done the same thing."

"Do you mean that?"

"Faced with what you've been faced with? Yes, I think I might well have."

Having someone understand and even commiserate was more than Jamie had hoped for. "I can't tell you what that means to me," she said, gripping Grace's hand so Grace wouldn't remove it. "I thought you would tell me I was wrong, just like the doctors did."

"Right and wrong are words nobody should use in this situation. With so many unknowns, you did what you thought was best. I only wish you had told your sister and let her help you decide."

"I couldn't."

"I know. You didn't want to hear what choices she would make for you."

Jamie wasn't surprised Grace understood so well. Grace knew what it was like to wonder if she was making the right decisions about her life, and to wonder if she would ever know for certain. Grace knew how hard it was to trust the people who were supposed to love you.

"Adversity may be underrated," Jamie said, "but I could cheerfully live without this."

"If it weren't for the hard times in my own life, I never would have realized a number of things," Grace said. "But this isn't the time for lessons learned. I'll only say this. Never assume you know what the people who love you are thinking or feeling. I venture to say more lives have been ruined by bad guesses than harsh truths."

"You have the bonus of being able to look back and analyze the decisions you made. I just have to falter along and hope I've done my best."

"And the people who really love you will understand that's what you did."

Jamie hoped that was true. But she wasn't looking forward to the day when she found out.

30

As January's cold breath whistled over him, Cash shoved his hands deep in the pockets of his suede jacket. Standing here, gazing up toward the sinking sun, he thought the Taylors' house was going to be Rosslyn and Rosslyn's masterpiece. Everything about it was coming together the way he had hoped but never expected. He wondered if Jamie had really envisioned how perfectly this plan would suit the site, how tactfully it mimicked the cabin that had once stood here while transforming that simple, rustic dogtrot design into something remarkable.

He and his father had added their own touches, of course. Stone columns where her design had called for wood. A different style of windows for the second story. A bathroom where a closet had been anticipated, and a closet where a reading nook had been planned. She'd approved of those and other changes when the reasons were explained. She wasn't just talented, she was accommodating and sensible.

She was also concerned about something that had nothing to do with her sister's house. Cash knew that as surely as he knew Jamie liked having her neck and shoulders rubbed and that her feet were swollen and aching after she'd been on them for any length of time. Something was worrying her.

He didn't know what the problem was, why, for the past month—even through the Christmas holidays—she had spent too much time staring into space. Why, when her daughters spoke to her, she was so often preoccupied that they had taken to repeating themselves automatically. Whatever it was, he intended to get some answers.

Just as soon as he figured out why he was making Jamie Dunkirk's happiness such a major part of his own.

Although progress on the house had been steady, the inevitable weather delays this month and next probably meant that the Taylors wouldn't be taking possession of their new home until late spring, a bit earlier if they were willing to live with the noise and confusion of last-minute alterations and finishing work. But Cash doubted the Taylors would be willing, considering that by then they would have two infants. He imagined they would continue to live in Arlington until the last contractor pulled away from the site.

He wondered where Jamie would be by then.

"If you're done gawking, I could use your advice on the trim work in the great room," Manning said, walking over to stand beside Cash. "I know that finish is going to darken up with time, but it's at least six shades lighter than the Taylors asked for."

Cash didn't have to look. He had been standing beside Kendra Taylor when she saw the trim for the first time, and she had said exactly the same thing. He had already called the subcontractor and told him to get himself back here to do the job the way he was supposed to.

"It was a stab at artistic license," Cash said. "The guy he sent to do it had his own theory on what the house needed. It'll be taken care of next week."

"Good. They're on their way down. The Taylors, I mean. I guess I should say Isaac's on his way. I asked him to come and see what he thought about the fire pit and the pond. I've got Amos scheduled to do some excavating as soon as the weather cooperates."

Cash thought that was odd. He had gone over all the landscape details with both Taylors just last week. Every part of the ground was carefully marked, and all the trees that had needed to be taken out or trimmed *had* been—almost a month ago.

"Is that why you asked me to postpone my trip down to Roanoke, too? So I could go over this with him *again?* It's been all set up for a week now."

"There he is."

Cash listened, but he didn't hear a car engine, just the quieter crunching of gravel. In a minute Isaac's Prius appeared.

"That car sure does sneak up on a body," Manning said. "Like something out of a spy novel."

"More like something out of a manual on saving the environment. You ought to approve."

"I never said I didn't."

Both men waited until Isaac got out of the car and approached. He was alone, as Manning had predicted, dressed for the cold weather in jeans and boots, topped with a dark ski jacket, although his head was bare. Cash couldn't recall ever noticing the way Isaac walked, heels digging in first, the boot rolling toward the toe, but today it struck a familiar chord, although he couldn't say why.

"Sorry to get you all the way out here," Manning said, extending his hand in Isaac's direction.

After they shook, Isaac shoved his hands deep in his pockets, the way Cash had done. "Don't worry. I figure this is a good evening to let Caleb Claiborne drive my car up and down Fitch Crossing. He's been wanting to get behind the wheel for months now."

Cash knew Isaac and Kendra had befriended Cissy Claiborne's brother, Caleb, who must finally be old enough to get his license. Cissy's in-laws, who lived just down Fitch Crossing, had adopted the boy a while ago, and Caleb seemed to be thriving under their care and affection, along with the Taylors' friendship.

"So what's changed?" Isaac asked. "What do I need to look at?"

Manning didn't speak for a moment. He just stood looking up at the house; then he turned and faced the two younger men.

"This isn't really about the house," he said. "That was just my reason for getting you both out here."

Isaac looked puzzled. Cash was puzzled, too. He couldn't remember his father ever resorting to subterfuge. Like so many of his friends and cohorts, he said what needed to be said, and that was that. He spared no feelings, although he didn't make a point of hurting anybody, either.

"What *is* it about?" Isaac asked.

"About a lie I told myself when I heard about you. And about some piece of the truth, or at least what I think might be true."

Isaac apparently knew better than to question him further. He just waited, and so did Cash.

Manning began slowly. "I told you I talked to Rachel back before you were born, and that was the last time I ever heard from her. Well, I did talk to her, but the last time wasn't on the telephone, the way I said. Rachel…"

Manning looked at Isaac. "Your *mother*, Rachel. She did call right out of the blue one day, after she'd been gone for years. She said she wanted to see me. You have to know I'd never expected that. Like I said before, she took off after high school, and I'd never heard from her again until that moment. I'd already been married once in the meantime. Cash's mother is my second wife. My first wife wasn't around for long. She was a city girl, and she left me for a man with more money and more of what she called prospects. But I didn't like being alone. I met Sandra, Cash's mother, a couple of years later, and I fell in love with her. I'd just asked her to marry me a day or two before, when I got that phone call from Rachel."

Cash saw it all laid out nice and proper in front of him. He glanced at Isaac and saw that he was beginning to suspect what Manning might say, as well. But neither of them spoke. They let the older man continue.

Manning seemed to choose his words carefully. "At first...I just thought I wouldn't go. It didn't seem right. Rachel had made her choices, and I had made mine."

He ran his hand over what hair he had left. "But I did go, because all those years ago, I'd been head over heels in love with that woman. Turned out she was living outside Tupelo, Mississippi. She'd gone there with a man, but she'd sent him packing. She was waiting on tables, cleaning houses, making a life, if not a very good one. I thought maybe she wanted me to rescue her, but Rachel wasn't that kind of woman. I never met anybody so independent. Seems she had missed me, too, and somehow she had heard my wife had up and left me. So Rachel wanted to see if there was anything left between us that we could resurrect. She said—" he looked uncomfortable "—that I was the only man she'd ever known who meant anything to her."

Cash knew what had to come next. He waited.

"There *was* something left between us," Manning said. "I'd never stopped loving Rachel Spurlock, I guess. We spent that one night together, but when I woke up the next morning, I knew what a mistake it was. Rachel would never come back here with me. And if she did, she would be right miserable. I wasn't willing to leave Shenandoah County. I knew this was where I was going to live and die, and I'd already lost one woman because of it. Then there was Sandra. What I had with Rachel, well, it was young love, that kind of fire in the blood they talk about in books. But I loved Sandra, too, and I knew she was the one I wanted to spend my life with."

Isaac shifted his weight to his left foot, but it was the only movement he made.

"And so I left for good that afternoon," Manning said. "Rachel said I was right to, that she would never be the kind of wife I wanted. I think she knew there was somebody else waiting at home, too, although we didn't talk about it. She said she would stay in touch, but she didn't. We both knew it was over."

Manning looked up and into Isaac's eyes. "Only I don't think it *was* over. I think there was more, a lot more, Rachel didn't tell me. When your wife came here and moved into the cabin and I heard about you, Isaac, and the way Leah had left the old place to you because you were Rachel's son, I told myself that Rachel was a free-spirited woman who didn't live by society's standards. I knew there had been men before me, and I figured there had been men afterward. But when I started looking through all that paperwork you and your missus signed for this house, I finally took a look at your birth date. By then I'd already figured out there was a chance you'd been conceived that one night your mother and I spent together. I saw things about you that reminded me of my own father. Little things, like the way you move. Nothing anybody could put a finger on. But they weren't that easy to push aside, and finally I just sat down with those papers…"

Cash realized now why Isaac's walk seemed so familiar.

Manning saw his own father in the way Isaac moved, but Cash saw someone else. Isaac walked exactly the way that Manning did.

"You're saying you're my father." Isaac didn't make a question out of it.

"I don't know for sure, but I think I probably am."

Manning shoved his hands in his pockets, just the way both of the other men had. "I told myself that date didn't mean anything much, that there were weeks before and after Rachel and I were together that one time when she could have gotten pregnant. Then, when I got over trying to fool myself, I figured I'd better just leave it alone and stay out of your way. You're a grown man. You don't need a stranger coming forward to tell you he might be your father. I couldn't imagine you'd appreciate hearing the story I just told you."

Manning turned slightly to include Cash. "And I couldn't imagine you'd appreciate hearing that I cheated on your mother. We weren't married at the time, but we were on the way."

"You're not the first man who slipped up," Cash said, trying to put it in perspective.

"I've been faithful to Sandra ever since. Never even thought about anyone else. But you're probably trying to figure out why I involved you this way, huh? Well, I struggled with this. But I figured you might have a brother, Cash, and I wanted you to know it. So which of you did I tell first? And, Isaac..." He turned to include him. "I didn't want you telling me Cash shouldn't know what was going on. I'm sorry, but that wouldn't have been right. So I decided to tell the two of you together."

Isaac didn't say anything. Cash didn't know what to say.

"There are tests." Manning snapped his fingers. "It would be that easy to find out. I'm willing if you want."

"Why?" Isaac asked.

"I'd like to be your father."

A muscle in Isaac's jaw worked, as if he was silently chewing Manning's words. "Does blood matter that much?" he asked at last.

"What do you mean?"

"I don't think I want to take a chance that you *aren't*."

For a moment Manning didn't seem to understand; then he did. His entire body relaxed. "You mean that?"

"You're the kind of father I wanted as a boy. I don't know what we can do about all this now, but I'd like to get to know you better. I'd like you to get to know my sons." Isaac looked at Cash. "I wouldn't mind having a brother."

Cash cleared his throat. He was surprisingly affected and glad he had not been left out of the drama. "So what does that make us? Semi—possible—could be—siblings?"

"I'll tell you true," Manning said. "I don't need a test to know what's what. You ever feel like you do need proof, Isaac, you let me know. In the meantime, we'll take this a bit at a time. But I consider you mine, son, from this day forward. And I hope someday you'll really consider me yours."

Cash watched them, his father and the man he had always liked who might well be his half brother. He saw that the two of them wanted to do more, but neither of them was a demonstrative man. There were no hugs, tears or rash promises. Manning finally stuck out his hand, and Isaac took it and clasped it.

To seal the deal, Cash began to whistle the Sister Sledge standard "We Are Family" and this time, after flashing Cash a grin, Isaac whistled the harmony.

Jamie sat with her feet propped on a chintz footstool, a stack of yellowed letters on her lap. Her hands were folded over them, and her head rested against the back of a comfortable upholstered rocker in the room Grace called the breezeway. Windows lined the outside wall, looking over old trees with winter's bare branches silhouetted against a nearly dark sky. Ben had added the room for Grace after Sandra was born, so that she would have a place to sit and nurse their little girl and still look over the orchard. The breezeway efficiently connected two smaller rooms, and from an architect's point of view, it was sensible as well as sentimental.

"Granny Grace said I'd find you here."

Jamie looked up at the sound of Cash's voice. "Hey, I thought you were heading out of town. Weren't you supposed to be meeting with a cabinet maker somewhere south of here tomorrow morning?"

"Got canceled. I've just been over at the Taylor house talking to Isaac and my dad."

"Oh?" Jamie sat a little straighter. "Was Kendra there?"

"No, he came alone." Cash pulled a chair up beside hers, slapped his hands behind his head and leaned back on the rear legs. "He and my dad went off to have some dinner together."

Jamie thought that seemed odd, since Manning had wanted very little to do with the construction of Kendra and Isaac's house. "They've suddenly become friends?"

"That's probably not the best way to put it. But they had some things to talk about. I imagine Kendra will tell you about it later." He glanced at her. "Why is it these days whenever you or I say your sister's name you get that look in your eyes?"

"What look is that?"

"It's kind of hard to describe. Something like a cross between a beagle puppy that's been kicked around and an old lab trying to learn new tricks so his master won't put him down."

"Lord, sad-dog metaphors. Or is it similes? I really didn't like English all that well."

"Doesn't matter. If the shoe fits."

"That's a proverb. I know that much." She reached over and rested her hand on his knee. "I just seem to need more time alone these days, and people tire me. I'm not sure I'm up for my sister's company right now, that's all."

"Just your sister's?"

"If you're asking if you should leave, the answer is no. You're easy to be with. I like that about you."

If he heard the compliment, he passed right over it. "And Kendra isn't?"

She tried to tell what part of the truth she could. "There's a certain amount of anxiety attached to this pregnancy for Kendra and Isaac. I can understand that. I'd feel the same way, if it was me. But I don't always have the strength to cope with it. And I'm kind of wiped this evening."

"There's more going on. Just so you know, I can tell. But I'm not going to push you. So what'll we talk about? Where are the mischief makers?"

"They're out with Grace feeding Lucky." Now that the deer was so big, Grace had started leaving the barn door open, and Lucky was going farther afield every day. One day they would go out to put down hay, and she wouldn't be waiting. Jamie knew the time would be right, but they would all miss her, especially Hannah and Alison.

"By the time the weather warms again, she'll be gone for good, won't she?" she said.

"Not for good. I bet she'll hang around the general area. We'll see her now and then."

"I worry about hunters."

"That orange collar Granny Grace put on her will help, but there's no surefire cure for a man who wants to shoot anything that moves. At least the orchard is posted."

"A time to live and a time to die."

"You're getting all philosophical on me."

She patted his knee, and smiled when he took her hand and warmed it in his. The breezeway was her favorite room in the house, but it was also the chilliest. Ben Cashel had not used energy-efficient windows. If the house belonged to her, Jamie would change that right away.

"What are you reading?" Cash asked.

"Something you ought to read one day. They're your grand-father's letters to Grace when he was training at Fort Belvoir. And some of hers that he brought back with him."

"She kept them all these years?"

"If you read them, you almost wonder why. You've never seen such struggling on paper before. And you wouldn't believe these two people ever lived together in harmony."

"I guess I've never heard *that* marriage described as living in harmony. They were as much alike as a cactus and a willow. But they loved each other. That was for sure."

Jamie lifted the letters and waved them. "Grace gave me these and told me to see if I could figure out what was happening between them. I think they loved each other but neither of them was willing to admit it, if they even realized it at this point. They wasted some precious time."

"People always think they have a lot to waste. Of course, that's not always true."

She imagined he was thinking of Kary, but she was thinking of herself. She wondered if that was the lesson Grace was trying to drive home by giving her the letters.

She dropped his hand and got to her feet. "I've got something to show you. Interested?"

"If you think you can haul yourself to wherever it is. I think those babies have grown since I saw them this morning."

She glanced down. She truly was huge. Although she had felt like Mother Earth when she was pregnant with her daughters, now she felt like the old woman who lived in the shoe. Old before her time, ungainly, a blot on the landscape.

A giant blot.

"Just how far do you think skin can stretch?" She patted the bump, which was more like a mountain now. "I just keep thinking it's going to refuse to accommodate me one of these days."

"As far as it needs to."

"I feel like a creature from outer space."

"I think you're beautiful."

She saw that he meant it. For a moment, it was even harder to breathe than usual, and not because of the rearrangement of her internal organs.

"You really know what to say."

He put his arms around her and pulled her close, or as close as he could, considering.

"I think what you're doing is beautiful." He stroked her back. "I know it's not easy. It can't be as easy as you keep saying it is."

"Okay, I'll miss the little guys. That's a given. But I'm okay with handing them over. I really am."

"You're a grown-up. It's my job to believe you."

She pulled away and took his hand. "Come see what I've made for them."

The two baby quilts were folded neatly beside the living room sofa. She held them to herself for a moment, a bit embarrassed. "Now, I know you're used to seeing your grandmother's quilts.

You have to remember, these are my first attempts. But they're all done. Every last stitch, all washed and dried and ready for the big day. Kendra hasn't seen them yet. I think she'll be pleased."

"Let me see."

She set down one and opened the other, the red, black and white. "This is for Twin Number One. I think Kendra and Isaac are still fighting over names. If they finally decide, I'll embroider it on the back. But see?" She turned it over to show him the heart in the corner that said With love from Aunt Jamie.

"It's wonderful." He fingered the binding. "Of course, I'm a guy, so what would I know? But if I were a baby again, I wouldn't let it out of my sight."

It was exactly the right, silly thing to say, and she laughed. "I'm really happy with it." She folded it quickly and unfolded the second. "And here's the other."

"Wow, will he be able to sleep?"

The quilt was bright, but she knew that any baby would be entranced. Her own girls had loved sunny, cheerful colors the best.

"And there you have my entire quilting career," she said, folding the second one.

"They're both wonderful. And they'll be treasured."

"For a guy, that's pretty good. You said all the right things."

"We aim to please."

"I'm not sure what I'll do with my hands now. This was very relaxing."

"Finishing must seem like an ending of sorts."

She knew he was heading back to the subject of giving up the twins. But this time she didn't deflect him. Endings were on her mind these days. And finishing the quilts *had* saddened her.

"Kendra and Isaac will be the best possible parents." She held the second quilt against her chest, against the scar that had forever changed her world. "I know I'm turning these babies over to a good, full life with all the love they'll ever need. In fact, if anything happens to me, I've already put Kendra and Isaac in my will as guardians for Hannah and Alison."

"When did you do that?"

"Why?"

"Well, it's kind of telling, don't you think? What made you think of it now?"

She gave the speech she'd prepared. "It was just time to do it, that's all. I should have formalized something a long time ago. If anything ever does happen to me, then I want to know they'll be well taken care of. They do have fathers, but I don't think either one would take this to court. If he did, then my wishes would still be considered."

"Are you worried something's going to happen during delivery? Is that why you've been so…" He shrugged.

"No. No! I'm fine. But it does bring some things home more clearly. Like planning for the future. I want the girls to be with people who love them. In fact, I hope you'll stay in touch with them. They're crazy about you."

"Jamie…" He took her hands. "Is this what pregnant women do? They obsess about things that aren't going to happen?"

She made herself nod and smile. "It's all part of the eternal plan. Endings and beginnings go together. That's all. It's natural to think about both at a time like this."

"You need to get out more."

She was so glad he had moved beyond the maudlin that she laughed. "Maybe I do."

"Okay, here's the plan. Dinner somewhere nice. Just you and me. Music, romance, candles."

"I feel like Babe, Paul Bunyan's ox, Cash! I'm not going

anywhere romantic looking like this. And besides, there's no place like that for, what, fifty miles? And I'm not excited about driving fifty miles, even if the sentiment makes me want to cry."

"Then we'll do it somewhere close by."

"You don't have to—"

"I'll have to get down to Roanoke over the weekend, but when I come back. On Monday. Be ready for romance."

"Have you looked at me recently? Like in the last five minutes?"

He lifted her hand and kissed it. "Let me take care of you, okay? Just a little?"

She didn't know what to say. This was the sweetest moment she had ever experienced with a man. She wanted to hold on to it forever.

And there was that word again.

"What can I do?" she asked, her voice husky.

"Show up."

"Then I will."

This time he kissed more than her hand.

By the time Grace and the girls came in from the barn, Cash had gone back to his place to see to his horses. Jamie was chopping onions for a fruit salsa to go with salmon Sandra had delivered from the grocery store, along with multiple bags of goodies. Jamie suspected a conspiracy to keep her from getting behind the steering wheel, even for short trips into town. She was afraid that made sense in January on slick country roads. For the moment, her driving days were finished.

The girls grabbed slices of carrots and apples and ran outside to pretend they were deer in the forest, although they promised they would stay where Jamie could watch from the window.

"Is Cash coming back for supper?" Grace asked, flopping into a kitchen chair.

"He took last night's leftovers and said something about shoveling manure."

"Then we'll hope he stays away. After a manure day, Ben knew he had to bathe before I'd feed him. I had standards, even if they weren't anything like my sister's."

"Speaking of Ben, I read the letters you gave me."

"So, what do you think?"

"I think you've left me to stew. There's a lot more to your story than you've shared, that's for sure."

"It's all about the way we refuse to face the obvious, isn't it? I imagine you could tell from those letters that by the time Ben went to Fort Belvoir for training, he and I were still a million miles apart."

"Maybe just a continent."

"As a matter of fact, we were lucky it wasn't *really* a continent. He could have done his training so far away he wouldn't have been able to come back before he shipped out. Of course, I was also lucky his buddy Sledge was a Virginia boy."

"Sledge? Ben mentioned him in his letters to you."

"If I remember correctly, he had a perfectly normal name, something like John or Phillip. He got the nickname because he was so strong. Ben said he could knock down walls with his bare hands. Which didn't turn out to be much help with Belvoir's obstacle course. It was the first of its kind for the Army, and something every soldier who came through had to complete or die trying. Sledge was strong as an ox, but too big to be agile. He fell off the wall he was trying to scale and broke two vertebrae in his back. They sent him home to recover. He came to see me when he was up and around again."

"The girls are happy outside. I'm happy cooking. You could tell me more."

Grace made herself comfortable. "I thought you'd never ask."

31

1942

Grace stood at the kitchen window and watched two men pacing the length of the nearest cornfield, their arms waving as they gestured to each other. One, an older man named Otis Gaff who lived half a mile up the road, was dressed in dungarees and a light flannel shirt. The other man, whose name she hadn't bothered to learn, wore a suit. She was inclined to despise them both, making no distinction between rural or urban villains. The older man was planning to steal Ben's land, and the younger man was going to help finance his thievery.

"Where's my daddy?" Charlie asked for the third time that morning.

"Charlie, son, your daddy's in the Army, remember? We talked about this. You're the man of the house now while he's away, and you have to be patient and brave."

"I don't like that Army," Charlie said, his eyes glinting dangerously. "It took my daddy."

"Your daddy went because he had to. We talked about the bad people who are trying to hurt all the good people far away. You have a good daddy, and he wants to make them stop."

"Don't want to be man of the house." He stuck out his lower lip. "I am just little."

She turned away from the sight of the two men against July's nearly waist-high corn crop. "You can be the *little* man of the house, okay?"

Charlie fell quiet to sort that out. Grace didn't bother to tell the boy that soon enough, there would be no house to worry about. A stinky old farmer would own the house and all the land, and with a most unpleasant smile, he had already told Grace he expected her to move out quickly. The moment the papers were signed, he and his wife were moving in, preferring this house to the rambling wreck they called home up the mountain. She shuddered to think what a mess they would make of this one and how soon they would manage it.

She wished she had never painted the kitchen or the downstairs rooms, or the bedroom she had never shared with Ben. And the boys' room? With its cheerful wallpaper of teddy bears playing drums and trumpets? She might strip off that paper right before she left, just so she wouldn't have to think about the old man storing tools or maybe bales of hay against its friendly surface.

She had hoped it wouldn't come to selling the orchard. Ben had tried to squeeze out one more crop before the draft took him. Maybe with just one more, they would have had enough money so that, along with what the Army gave him and perhaps with what she was able to earn, she and the boys could have survived without selling the land until Ben returned.

But all his calculations, his long evenings poring over account books, his days of consulting officials about when he might reasonably expect to be called up, had been for nothing. He had been told that farmers were probably going to be eligible for deferments. Ben had gambled on buying fertilizer and spray, using his cash reserves in hopes they would be replenished and then some, when the crop came in. With only one man to help, he had made the long trips up and down the rows with his tractor and sprayer. First oil, followed by sulfur and lead arsenate, six trips throughout the spring and early summer, caring for the apples that would save them. Then the draft board hadn't been able to meet its quota of local men. Agricultural deferments were still under debate, with priority for livestock and poultry farmers expected first. Ben's letter had arrived.

Greetings.

From the very beginning, Ben had planned to serve. He had expected to go. He had just hoped that when he did, the land and his children would be protected until he returned.

Now, the two men started toward the house, and Grace knew she was going to be required to speak with them. Yesterday, they had arrived with no warning while she and the boys were out walking. She had seen them in plenty of time to take cover among the trees Otis Gaff was so anxious to own. They'd left without discovering her hiding place, but today she wasn't that lucky.

She dried her hands on a towel and removed her apron. She plucked a protesting Adam from his high chair and entrapped him in his playpen. Charlie, apparently trying hard to live up to his new title, climbed in with his brother to play, and the protests quickly died away.

Grace answered the door, making a note to tell Ben, when next she wrote him, how helpful his oldest son had been. Her letters were perfunctory and practical. News about the boys. Reports on the old farmers' plans. A description of apartments she had seen where other women with children were moving to be closer to jobs while their husbands served in the military. She hadn't told him about the overcrowded nursery schools where children like Charlie and Adam spent too many hours packed together with little to do. She was still hoping Sylvie or her other local sister-in-law, Dolly, would agree to take the boys when she went to work.

With no smile needed, she opened the door and stood on the threshold.

"What can I help you with?" she asked, striving to at least sound polite.

"Ma'am, I haven't heard back from your husband on that new proposal of mine." Otis realized he ought to remove his cap and took it off now, although he moved so slowly that his point was made. He didn't even have to be polite to Grace. The Gaffs had the Cashels over an apple barrel. Too old to go to war himself, he could harvest the crop Ben had tried so hard to bring in without a thought for anybody else.

Grace knew nothing about a proposal. "I can't help," she said. "I don't know what you're talking about."

"Mr. Samson here," Otis said, nodding, but not looking at the skeletally thin man beside him, who looked too sickly to pass a draft physical, "he's not all that keen on these apples of your'n. Thinks maybe they won't fetch near so much as that husband of your'n tried to tell me they would. Thinks I'm paying too much for trees of this quality."

Grace knew enough about Otis Gaff to realize he was simply lighting a smokescreen. By blaming the young banker—who looked as if he didn't know a Lodi from a Golden Delicious—

Otis was planning to drive a newer, harder bargain. She wondered if Otis had even contacted Ben. Or, more likely, was he hoping that Ben's young wife, alone on the land with two small children, would be so worried about her future that she would contact him herself and plead that Ben take this new offer?

For a moment she wondered if she was strong enough to throw both men down the steps. One was too old to put up much of a fuss, one was too thin. And she was furious.

Able or not, she stepped back to give herself a moment to think. She took that one and another before she spoke. "Mr. Gaff." Realizing that she was still too angry, she took a deep breath, then blew it out slowly before she finished. "We have the best apples in the county, maybe in the whole valley. So there will be no new proposals. I hope that's clear."

"Now that husband of your'n might see things different."

"If you thought Ben would see things your way, you wouldn't have come up here to stand on *my* porch and insult me. You want me to intercede."

Throwing serenity to the wind, she took two steps forward, and stuck her index finger against his flannel-covered chest. "Well, I *will* intercede, Mr. Gaff. I'll tell my husband we need *more* money for our land. Half again as much. And I'll tell him to make sure he gets every cent of that from *you,* even if he would have taken less from some patriotic, God-fearing farmer who knows what a good apple looks like. Am I clear enough? Would you like me to write that down?" She stabbed him with her finger once more. "Or do you even know how to read?"

"You've got no call to talk to me like that. I've got a mind to just tell that man of your'n to forgit it! What do you think of that?"

"I think…you're hard of hearing. I think…you don't have the brains of a newly hatched chick. Get off our land." She nodded to the other man. "You, too. Take your proposal and eat it for supper. You look like you could use a good meal."

Mr. Samson turned paler. "I think what Mr. Gaff is trying to say—"

"Shut up. Just shut up and get off my porch, in your car and off this land. There's a shotgun just inside my door, and I'm fixing to pull it out in ten seconds and see if it's loaded."

The two men looked at each other. "No sense in trying to reason with a wet hen," Otis muttered.

They left just fast enough to make her think they'd taken the shotgun threat seriously.

Grace closed the door and stood with her back to it. Both little boys were staring at her, their jaws slack, their eyes round.

"Well," she said, clearing her throat, "I think what we need around here are oatmeal cookies. What do you say to that, boys?"

Two hours later, full of cookies and lunch, both boys went upstairs for naps in the teddybear-wallpapered room. Grace had rarely seen them so well behaved. Of course, they had rarely seen her threaten to shoot a neighbor, either. She was sure there was a connection.

Downstairs, she cleaned the cookie-scented kitchen, dusted and swept, but her heart wasn't in any of her activities. She wondered how to tell Ben the latest tidings. She had no doubt Otis would come slinking, slithering back tomorrow or the next day, magnanimously offering to go back to his original terms. All Ben had to do, of course, was sign the final papers. Now that he knew where things stood, Otis would make sure it all happened quickly.

She wished she could change the days that had led up to this one.

The months before Ben had shipped out to Camp Lee for processing hadn't been easy. With the war at his back, Ben had worked even longer hours than before, hoping for a miracle.

Although he'd eaten dinners at the house every single Sunday after the Pearl Harbor bombing, there had been no more leisurely afternoons of checkers with Charlie or revealing conversations about their future. They conversed in snatches as they ran from one chore to the other. Always about practical things, such as what she needed from town, or whether he could afford to buy more gravel for the road.

Most evenings, Ben was upstairs asleep before she even finished the supper dishes. In the mornings, he didn't wait for her to get up and make breakfast. He went without until the boys were finished and she was able to bring something out to him.

Sometimes, she mulled over the odd intimacy of that one afternoon, the powerful sense she'd had that there was more to Ben than she'd ever guessed. She wondered if she had imagined the physical pull she'd felt. And if not, if she had indeed been ready to kiss him, was that only because there were no other men in her life except the one she had married?

Now, with the boys in bed and a little time left to herself, she went to the dining room cupboard and pulled out a box. In the midst of cleaning and airing one of the many extra bedrooms just after Ben's departure, she had found it tucked under a bed, and the contents had surprised her. Although her sister's only sewing supplies seemed to consist of thread in neutral colors and fabrics of dull and duller hues, the box was filled with scraps of bright prints. She had discovered the reason at the bottom. A pattern from a mail-order quilt company was neatly folded into an envelope.

The pattern was called Sister's Choice.

For the first time since Anna's death, Grace had felt her sister's presence. She didn't know why Anna had sent away for this pattern and chosen these fabrics. Perhaps the design had appealed to some hidden desire for color and complexity in her life. But whatever the reason, Grace had realized this was another—hidden—side of the woman she had known. Anna was not entirely the somber, rigid woman who had tried so hard to subdue her. Anna, too, had yearned for joy and laughter.

Looking at the box of scraps, Grace had felt closer to Anna in death than she ever had in life. She wondered if her sister would have found the courage to make the quilt. And if she did, would she have proudly showed it to Grace? Or was this a side of her that no one was allowed to see?

Grace had decided then and there that she was going to do what her sister no longer could. As a reminder that there had been more to Anna than she had realized, Grace was going to make the quilt, using the scraps Anna had so carefully saved and boxed. When the quilt was finished, she would show it to Anna's sons and tell them all about it. This part of their mother was a part Grace wanted them to know.

Now she pulled out the pieces she had cut yesterday, using a template she had carefully glued to cardboard. She made herself at home in the chair closest to the front window and threaded her needle. Minutes passed, and she was halfway through piecing the block when she heard a car coming up the drive. She got up to peer out the window, expecting to see their hired man coming back from dinner at his home down the road. Or even Otis returning with hat firmly in hand. But this car was a stranger's, and the man getting out was not one she knew.

She debated what to do. She was alone with the boys, and the shotgun she'd threatened the men with was more or less a fiction. There *was* a shotgun locked away on the back porch, and she *did* know how to fire it. But it wasn't waiting by the front door, and she had no time—even if she'd had the inclination—to fetch and load it now.

She could pretend not to be home, and might have if the man had clearly been a tramp wandering up the front drive. But he had driven up in a nice enough truck, and his clothes were clean and fit him well. He was a large man, with a squarish head resting on a thick neck, but he didn't look mean. He looked pale and a bit weary, and he walked as if each step was harder than the last.

The hired man would be back soon, and he always checked in with her before he went to work. She decided answering the door was safe enough as long as she didn't invite the man inside.

Before he reached the front steps, she walked out on the porch, closing the door behind her. He stayed on the ground, shading his eyes to look up at her; then he grinned.

"Well, you're as pretty as Ben and your picture say you are, ma'am. Good day and nice to meet you. My name's Sledge."

Only a moment passed before she realized who this had to be. But in that moment she had already begun to consider his words. *As pretty as Ben and your picture say you are.*

"Sledge, from Ben's unit? From Fort Belvoir?"

"Lately of Fort Belvoir. I'll be back there before long, I guess, unless they send me somewhere else next time. But I had something of an accident, so they sent me home to recover. Only I got tired of lying around, so I thought I'd come up here and bring you greetings from your husband."

Grace descended the steps and held out her hand. "It's very nice to meet you. But I'm sorry about the accident."

"Oh, it wasn't much. They have what they call an obstacle course over there. Real proud of it, too. A man has to finish before they'll let him out of training. I did swell on part of it, but hauling myself over a stone wall wasn't much of a success. I fell backward and broke a couple of vertebrae." His hand—a hand large enough to swat an eagle into submission—went to his back.

"You poor man. I hurt just thinking about it." She gestured to the house, because she knew instinctively that everything he'd told her was true. In his letters, as spare and short as those letters were, Ben had mentioned Sledge repeatedly. She imagined she would get another letter soon that told her about Sledge's accident.

"Oh, it hurts a lot, but it's already a little better," Sledge said, as he slowly took the steps. "They've got me wearing a brace. It's all going to heal up just fine, and I'm going to shoot anybody needs shooting in a month or two."

"Well, that's something to look forward to."

They laughed at the same moment, his deep and uninhibited, and she understood why Ben had made friends with him.

"I've got fresh oatmeal cookies and hot coffee. Can I interest you in either? Or would you like me to make you some lunch?"

"Cookies and coffee sound perfect. I ate before I left." He told her he lived farther south but still in the Valley, and that he and his family raised cattle and corn, although he also did carpentry to make ends meet.

She gave him the most comfortable chair at the kitchen table and unwrapped the cookies, setting the platter and a plate in front of him. She poured coffee, then made a fresh pot while he worked on the first cup.

"Did you tell Ben you were coming to see me?" she asked as she set the enamelware coffeepot on the stove and got a flame roaring beneath it.

"I didn't get to see him before they sent me home. That husband of yours is making a stir, you know. He'll move up the ranks as fast as a coon up a sycamore. He's already squad leader, and that's just for openers. He's the kind of man they look for— smart, strong, knows when to talk and what to say."

"That's all well and good, but will it keep him safe?"

"Nothing much can do that. We're an engineering unit, so we'll be right in the middle, building bridges and roads, clearing minefields."

"Minefields?"

"If he's lucky, Ben'll be sending others out to do it."

Grace couldn't imagine that. She might not know Ben as intimately as her title suggested, but she knew him well enough that she was sure he wouldn't enjoy sending others to do dangerous jobs while he sat back and watched. Ben never shirked his duty.

Not even when it had come to marrying his wife's sister to preserve the way of life he was about to lose anyway.

She switched the subject, because thinking about Ben in combat upset her. "Did Ben tell you about the orchard?"

"He really loves this place. Almost convinced me to put in fifty acres of apples myself, only once he mentioned all the problems, I figured corn and cows are enough of a headache."

"Did he tell you he's selling it?"

"No. You don't mean it."

"They drafted him before he could get the next crop. And he's got too much tied up in it now."

"Somebody's got to pay for what's been done to our lives." Sledge sipped his coffee; then he hit the table with his palm. Everything jumped. "A man needs something to keep him safe, something to come home for. At least he's got you and the boys."

She didn't know what to say to that. Clearly Sledge was not such a good friend that Ben had explained their situation.

"Ben loves his boys," she said. "He'll do anything to come home to Charlie and Adam. They should be up soon, so you can meet them."

"I've seen their pictures. Right next to yours."

And there was that picture again, a picture she hadn't even known Ben had.

"I'm curious, which picture did he put up of me?"

"One from your wedding. You've got flowers in your hair, and you're holding a bouquet and smiling."

She remembered now. Sylvie had taken one of her alone with an old box camera. But Grace had never seen it, although she'd seen others taken that day. Sylvie had given them to Ben when she saw him in town a month after the wedding, and he had passed them on to her. Grace had just assumed the one of her alone hadn't turned out. Had Ben intercepted the picture and kept it? She couldn't think of another explanation, unless Sylvie had sent it to him in a letter during his training, not understanding that Ben really wouldn't care if he had a snapshot of Grace or not.

Except that he must care, or why would he have it where Sledge had seen it in his barracks? Was it just so no one would ask why he didn't have a picture of his wife? A way to avoid questions?

It hardly seemed worth that much effort.

"I was going to get married," Sledge said. "But my girl wrote me a couple of weeks after I left and said she didn't want to be married to a soldier. She's going to marry some farmhand over in Page County who has a bum foot and won't get drafted. Maybe it's a good thing to lose a woman like that, but I envy your fellow. Having you home waiting for him, even if the orchard's gone, well, that will get him through, if anything can."

"Did Ben tell you how we got married?" she asked bluntly, because what other way was there to get to the heart of this?

"Not much. Just that you stepped up to help him when he really needed it after his first wife died, and he knew how lucky he was to have you."

It wasn't exactly a profession of undying love. But coming from Ben? A man who never talked about his feelings?

"A man's lucky to find two women to love in one lifetime," Sledge said. "I'll be lucky to find one."

She lifted the coffeepot off the stove and poured him another cup. She realized her hand wasn't quite steady. "Well, Charlie and Adam needed a mother."

"Ben says you're the best mother he's ever seen. That helps a man with children who's got to leave them, you know. He can be sure they're being taken care of the right way. It's just too bad about this place and all. When he loves it so much. But those are the sacrifices a soldier has to make, I guess."

"I wonder…"

"About what?"

She realized his cup was about to overflow, and the coffee she'd poured looked as pale as peppermint tea. "Look what I've done."

She set the pot to heat some more and whisked away his cup. "I didn't realize it wasn't ready."

"I guess you're worrying about things. You have a right to."

"The farmer that wants to buy this land? He's a snake in the grass."

"I'm sorry to hear that."

"He's going to just about *steal* all those apples Ben worked so hard to raise this year and turn this beautiful old house into a pigsty."

"I'm sorry for you both. The story gets worse and worse."

"You know about all the jobs women have to do now that you men are going off to fight? Jobs in defense? Jobs in offices? You ever hear about women working in orchards? Right beside men?"

"I think a woman can do anything she sets her mind to."

Grace thought about the trees beyond her windows growing heavy with fruit. A farmer's wife had to learn to do everything.

Surely other women were out clearing fields and planting crops, women who never had done so before. Somehow they were managing that and their regular chores, too, simply because they had to.

She didn't know a lot about what happened next in the orchard, but why couldn't she learn? Their hired man knew. And he knew something more important. He knew who needed a job. He was old and not up to managing much alone, but he had lived on this mountainside all his life. He knew everybody for miles, knew their life stories and their present circumstances. Ben had once joked about that.

Ben.

"Who's taking care of *your* place while you're gone, Sledge?" she asked.

"What family's left and not in the service. They're all trading around, doing what they have to. It won't be the same when I get back, but it'll still be there."

"Nothing ever stays the same, does it?"

"You can say that again."

"Nothing ever stays the same, does it?" She smiled, and he laughed at the repetition. And suddenly she was laughing, too, an easy, genuine laugh that was out of proportion to the little joke but flooded her worried heart with golden sunshine anyway.

"I sure didn't stay the same," she said when they sobered. "And you know what? I'm planning to change some more. Ben's hardly going to know me the next time he sees me."

"Don't change too much, now. He's mighty fond of you just the way you are."

For the first time she let herself believe it might just be true. Maybe Ben really did feel more for her than he let on. At the least he felt gratitude; Sledge had made that clear. And couldn't gratitude blossom into something better and more lasting? Couldn't it blossom into love?

Now she only had to figure out if she wanted it to. It was time to search her own heart and see how she really felt about the man she had married, the father of the children that were hers in every important way.

"So, Sledge," she said, with her most winning smile. "I want you to tell me every single thing Ben ever said about me. Just think of it as comforting a poor wife left behind to grieve. It's almost your patriotic duty, wouldn't you say?"

32

"I can't believe they're so big!" Kendra couldn't seem to help herself. On the way back to the orchard from what was now Jamie's weekly appointment in Front Royal, she had hardly stopped talking. She hoped her sister—who seemed more tired than usual—could forgive just one more observation.

"They could be born right now, and they would make it. They could have been born a few weeks ago even. It finally feels real, Jamie."

"It's felt real to me since the first time I nearly tossed my cookies."

Kendra felt younger, buoyant, able to leap tall buildings, as if all the good news at the obstetrician's office had peeled away years. Heartbeats were perfect. Babies had grown. All was exactly as it should be.

"Before you know it I'm going to be taking care of twins. *Me.*"

"You really don't have any intention of hiring help?"

"Nope. Isaac and I are going to do it ourselves. I don't want to miss a minute." Kendra considered something she'd been wanting to say and hadn't known how. Then she decided just to go for it.

"You know, I realize childbirth's not like having cancer or a heart attack, but there will be some recovery time involved for you. And if you have to have a cesarian—"

She glanced at Jamie, who looked as if Kendra had slapped her.

"Hey, I'm sorry," Kendra said. "I know the doctor doesn't think you will. I just wanted you to know that if you do—"

"I won't. They're both pointed in the right direction, as unlikely as that's supposed to be. And they're squeezed pretty tight in there. They aren't going anywhere."

Kendra heard Jamie's distress. "What I'm trying to say is that when you recover from your nice, normal delivery and feel like getting out and making the trip to Arlington, you'll be very welcome to come and visit. We would appreciate your help and advice. I know the girls will still be in school here—"

"I thought we'd agreed we should put some space between us? You and Isaac will need to bond with the twins, and I'll need to distance myself."

"Every decision can be renegotiated, can't it? For my part..." Kendra glanced again at Jamie, who still looked too pale. "Well, it's just been easier than I expected, that's all. We've had some tension along the way, but I feel so close to you. I don't want you or the girls to miss time with the twins. I don't want you to feel you have to stay away if you have a free weekend. We know whose children these are, but we also know who made that possible. When it comes down to it, isn't that a huge head start on figuring out everything else?"

"I'm glad you want me." Jamie didn't continue.

Kendra wasn't sure what that meant, but she had gone as far as she could. Now Jamie would have to decide if she was ready to be that intimate with her nephews, after carrying them inside her for nine long months. She might need time, and Kendra knew she had to respect that.

They were almost to the orchard when Jamie spoke again.

"Do you remember the red cocktail dress you bought me when Cash was taking me to the dinner dance?"

"The one you didn't wear?"

"Well, I'm going to wear it tonight."

"Come on! Where?"

"Cash is taking me somewhere for dinner."

"Well, that's a surprise." In truth, it wasn't, since Cash had enlisted Kendra's help a few days ago, but Kendra was enjoying this particular white lie.

Cash, who was most likely her brother-in-law.

Kendra couldn't help but smile. Once or twice she had wondered if Cash might *become* her brother-in-law by marrying her sister. She had never fathomed that he might already be her brother-in-law because he was really Isaac's half brother.

She and Jamie had talked about this new revelation in the waiting room earlier, but now she put her smile into words. "You know, if you marry Cash, what will that make him? My double brother-in-law? Is there such a thing?"

"We're going to dinner, not making a stop at the little brown church in the vale."

"I'm just working out titles in my head, along with the fact that he and Isaac are brothers. And Manning is my father-in-law."

"Manning's a good guy. Even the fact that he stepped forward when he didn't have to says a lot. And Cash said when Manning told Sandra, she was understanding."

"Maybe she'd feel differently if they'd been married at the time, but it did happen a long time ago."

"Slow down. You'll miss the turnoff."

Kendra realized she was so preoccupied thinking about her life and immediate future, she hadn't paid attention. She slowed and only spoke again after the turn into the orchard had been safely made.

"It's so strange. When I came out to the old cabin to live, I had a sister I hadn't seen in years, a mother who pretends she never had children, and a husband I wasn't sure I wanted to stay married to. I was pretty much alone in the world. Then you appeared, Isaac and I found each other again, you volunteered to carry a baby for us and threw in a bonus, and now Isaac has a father, a half brother and a very nice stepmother, not to mention Grace." She laughed, because she was brimming with good feelings. "The world is a very funny place."

"Fate has supple hands and an unpredictable sense of humor."

Kendra realized it was time to move to another subject. Jamie was keeping up her end of the conversation, but even though her responses were appropriate, they were lackluster.

Kendra switched to something less demanding. "So you're going to wear the red cocktail dress. What are you going to wear on your feet?"

"Whatever they can fit into."

"My feet are bigger than yours."

"Don't look now, but you're wearing suede boots, which aren't necessarily the best accessory for red lace."

"No, but having noticed how much your feet are swelling and how often I see you in bedroom slippers, I brought some shoes with me for you to try on. They'll be more comfortable than what you've got, that's for sure."

"You're so good to me."

Kendra heard the catch in Jamie's voice, and it disturbed her. Jamie seemed so fragile these days. As much as her sister proclaimed she was not having second thoughts about the surrogacy, Kendra still had to wonder. She glanced at Jamie and realized she was crying.

"I'm sorry," Jamie said, wiping her eyes. "I cry about everything now. I always do when I'm pregnant. It's natural. I've stopped watching television, because the commercials upset me."

"Commercials upset *me,* too, because they interrupt whatever I'm watching."

"You know the one about the dog who starts out as a puppy and ends up an old dog, barely trudging up the steps?" Jamie sniffed. "That's the one that did it."

"Sweetie, we have got to get you in shape for tonight. Cash deserves better than tears."

"What do you suggest?"

"What do you need?"

"An emergency delivery. And new feet. Mine look awful."

"I don't think that first is an option. Will a pedicure help the second?"

"Put a medicine ball in your lap, then try to bend over to give yourself a pedicure."

Kendra pulled up in front of Grace's house and turned off the engine. She was trying not to laugh. "I will do that very thing someday, but for now, how about if I give you a pedicure? Not spa quality, but close. Deal?"

Jamie opened the door and hoisted herself out of the car. "Don't you have a life? Somewhere you need to go?"

"I'm practicing taking care of people. I'm going to be doing a lot of it in the next, oh, say, twenty years."

"Then shouldn't you rest up?"

This time Kendra did laugh. She got out, too, and walked around the car. "Come on, sis. We're going to make you beautiful for Cash. Of course, I don't know why your feet need to be beautiful. I mean, I can't imagine what the two of you would do where pretty feet will matter."

"I'm hoping for a foot rub."

"Be careful, the excitement might kill you."

"I mean it, nothing more. My libido is gone with the twins."

Kendra slung her arm over her sister's shoulders and squeezed. "I hope there's a little something left over. You've got to treat the guy well. Don't forget, nowadays, Cash is family."

Cash arrived for their date in his mother's car. He wore a dark jacket and tie, with a pale yellow shirt, and his shoes were shined to such a high gloss all he had to do was glance down to see if he'd missed a spot shaving. The clothes were worn with the casual disregard of a man who was comfortable in anything, and Jamie found that particularly sexy.

According to Cash, she didn't look so bad herself. His eyes gleamed at the sight of her in the red dress. Kendra had understated taste, tending toward classic designers such as Carolina Herrera or Ralph Lauren, but even so, Jamie felt like a pumpkin masquerading as a flamenco dancer. Even though the dress was a deep, dark red and there was no ornamentation other than the subtly patterned lace bodice, she knew the color and style only emphasized her pregnancy. Of course, jeans and a T-shirt would have done the same. Camouflage wasn't an option in the final trimester, especially when you were carrying twins.

Now, out in the car, Jamie snapped her seat belt in place, chagrined that she was forced to stretch it as far as it would go. "I hope wherever we're going, the doorway is wide enough for me to get through."

Cash turned the car around and waved goodbye to Grace and

the girls, who were shivering on the front porch. "I called ahead. They've promised to have a fire truck standing by in case you get stuck."

"Good. I'll be sure to tell the firefighters you got me in this condition, then refused to marry me."

"Maybe I didn't get you there, but those babies are my nephews."

"How strange is that? They're mine, too."

He grinned at her. "Something else we have in common."

"Make me a list. What else could possibly be on it?"

"That's not *my* job. That's a mutual exercise, but I'll start."

"Wait a minute, how long do we have before we get to wherever we're going?"

"Maybe twenty minutes."

"Then take your time. I'll have to give this some thought."

He glanced at her and grinned again, warming her with it. "We're rescuers. Somebody or something needs us, and we're off and running."

"To a point."

"Is that on your list?"

"No, it's a clarification to yours. You rescue horses because they're portable. They fit your need for freedom. I rescue people, but with the idea that when I'm done, they'll go merrily on their way."

"I didn't know we were going to get all insightful here."

"You can't make a decent list without a little insight."

"Then technically it's still your turn, since that was just a qualifier."

"Do you think I'm right?"

"I don't have time to think about it. I'm busy with my list."

She got busy with hers. "Okay, we both think my daughters are special."

"So do most people who meet them."

"You never said other people had to disagree."

"Then it's going to be a boring list, but I guess I'll give you that one."

She noted he was turning toward Woodstock. She wondered exactly where he might be taking her that this dress was appropriate. They might be heading toward the River'd Inn, at the edge of town, which was supposed to have an excellent dining room and romantic ambience. She wondered if she could bear an entire evening in a straight-back chair, arm's length from the table, while courses were slowly revealed.

"We both like slow dancing," he said. "With each other."

"Neither of us wants to see the orchard turned into a trailer park."

"I wouldn't worry about that. The county would never allow it."

"You know exactly what I mean."

"Is that another item on your list? That we understand each other so well words don't *exactly* matter?"

"If that's true, you're one behind."

He was silent, and she watched scenery fly by. Before long they were nearly to Route 11, also known as the Old Valley Pike, and she was pretty sure she'd been right about where they were going. Then, as if he was reading her mind, he turned in the opposite direction.

"Two more things, then," he said, once they were heading north toward Strasburg. "One, we're attracted to each other." He paused, as if waiting for her to object. When she didn't, he continued. "Two, we're both cautious about the opposite sex, due to our pasts."

"Not fair that you get the easy ones."

"You never said this had to be hard."

She felt herself relaxing in a way she hadn't since she had gotten her diagnosis. For the first time, she almost felt young again. Maybe tonight she could pretend that no one had said the word *cancer* in her presence, and that she had no decisions to make about it.

"Okay, I'm going to show you up," she said. "Here's a zinger. We both love the Valley, only both of us are afraid to admit we might want to put down roots and call it home once and for all."

"You might want to stay around even after the babies are born?"

She tried to analyze his voice, but all she could tell was that he seemed politely surprised, as if her staying had never really occurred to him.

"I don't know for sure. But after Detroit, it's been so restful, so problem free—"

"Different problems," he pointed out.

"Okay, every place has its problems. But I'm beginning to like the problems here. Too much open space. Too little crime. Simple pleasures."

"There's a whole lot of world out there."

"I'd like to see it, too, only maybe that's what vacations are for."

Apparently she couldn't pretend she was cancer free for long, because now she wondered if there would be enough years left in her life to take the girls to Europe, to introduce them to the pleasures of swimming off Hawaii's black-sand beaches or skiing down Colorado's slopes.

"I'm not sure that one counts, since I've never said I'm secretly pining to put down roots here," Cash said. "I already have roots here. I'm not sure they've made me happy."

She pulled herself back to the list. "Do you want to have the last word? Anything else?"

"Only that we're both wondering if we know how to move on from here."

She wished she could tell him that for her, moving on had

become much more complicated. She could make all the decisions in the world about what she wanted to happen next, and fate could have an entirely different plan for her. But she couldn't. Telling Grace had been self-indulgent. She had burdened her dear friend, and she shouldn't have. Telling Cash? Not only would he be appalled and upset, he wouldn't understand. And she didn't have the inner strength to get through that particular argument unscathed.

"I don't think we *should* wonder," she told him. "I think we should just let things happen. Wondering is a step from worrying, and I don't want this relationship to be a burden for either of us. Isn't 'letting things happen' another thing we share?"

"Maybe. Or maybe we only thought we did. You've played havoc with a few things I thought about myself."

"That sounds serious. Let's not be."

"At your command, Miss Jamie." He gave an exaggerated wink. "Does that mean tonight we can just let things happen?"

The thought gave her more pleasure than she would have expected, but she certainly didn't tell him.

"In your dreams. Oh, and if I am in your dreams, lose the bump, okay? Dream about the not-so-pregnant me. Cash, where are we going?"

She realized he had turned off the road and was now taking one that shortly turned to gravel. "Can there possibly be a place to eat here? Are we going to some great-aunt's house so she can cluck over my unmarried and pregnant state and give me cod-liver-oil advice?"

"By and by you'll probably meet the Rosslyn side of the family, and although there's not a Granny Grace in the bunch, there's also nobody who would stoop to noticing the absence of a wedding ring on that left hand. They'd probably tell you not to attend any funerals, so's not to mark the unborn babies, but that's about it."

"You still haven't told me where we're going."

"That's right, I haven't."

"And you're not going to. I get it. Surprises."

"Don't you love 'em?"

"So long as I don't have to clean out somebody's henhouse or catch a mess of catfish and fry them up."

"That I'd like to see, especially in that dress. Maybe catfish first, then the henhouse."

"I'm going to sit back and rest, since I have no idea how long this will take."

"You go right ahead, just don't get too comfortable."

Cash took a circuitous route, weaving expertly over back roads, cutting through properties on narrow farm lanes that wound through this field, then that. She glimpsed the river, then she didn't. When she finally realized where they were, she was mystified.

Fitch Crossing Road.

She waited until he had slowed and turned onto the Taylors' property.

"All this to get to the cabin? That's where we're going to eat?"

"I wanted to make it a picnic and eat in the new house. I thought we'd have the electricity on by now, and the heat, but no such luck. Anyway, I thought you might want to see the house in the moonlight."

Of course she had been to the house as often as possible, watching her own design become a reality, giving advice when asked—which had been often enough to please her. But she hadn't been there on a night like this one, the air crisp and clear, the river and its banks lit by a pale winter moon and a sky filling slowly with stars.

He slowed, and the house appeared in front of them. He

turned off the engine in the clearing, and they sat staring at the structure, which really was a house now and not simply the skeleton of one.

"This is the ultimate romantic gesture," she said at last.

"You're not disappointed?"

"You wonderful man." Tears filled her eyes. *She* had created this. On paper, yes, but no matter what happened now, this house would remain as a part of the woman she had been. The architect in training. The imagination behind this reality.

"Together, we're really something, aren't we?" She turned to him. "Look what we've done."

He kept *his* gaze straight ahead. "I've built a lot of houses. Restored a fair number, too. This one's special. You have an eye for taking advantage of a site, figuring out what to emphasize and what to hide, how to use the traditions of the area in a new way, how not to sacrifice charm and class in a quest for practicality. Your sister and—" he smiled "—*my brother* will be happy living here and raising those kids of theirs. No matter where we each end up, sometimes you and I will come here on holidays to visit them. That makes it more special."

"That's a strange thought. We aren't linked by blood, but now we're linked by family. We'll run into each other in the years to come. One way or the other, you'll watch the girls grow up."

Now he looked at her. "One way or the other?"

"You know what I mean. Who knows what the future will bring?" At the moment when she'd said "years," she had been thinking of the future the way she used to before the diagnosis. As if her life stretched into eternity. As if the years ahead were a given, an unquestionable right, when in reality each day would be a gift. Whatever course her future took, there was never a guarantee of years. Now she understood that.

"Well, if I'm going to see the girls grow up anyway, I guess there's no real need to romance their mother," Cash said.

"A little romance can sweeten almost any deal. I might visit Kendra more often."

"Let's find out." He started the pickup and backed up, turning into the drive that led to the cabin.

She was surprised to see the trees outside the door adorned with strings of tiny white lights. "Somebody's a couple of weeks late taking those down. Aren't they pretty?"

"Aren't they?" He turned off the engine.

She put her hand on his shoulder to keep him there a moment. "Did you do this for me?"

"I don't see anybody else around, sweetcakes."

Her eyes filled with tears, and she sniffed.

"Hey, I didn't plan to make you cry."

"I'm not really crying. I'm just…allergic to bright lights."

"I'll remember that and forget that weekend in Manhattan after the babies get here." He got out and came to open her door, which gave her just enough time to sniff again and wipe her eyes with the sleeve of her coat.

"It's the pregnancy, you know," she said, as he helped her out. "Pregnant women cry over everything."

"Then we maybe have a problem coming up. This wasn't the only nice thing I did."

She stumbled on a root and pitched forward, and Cash grabbed her as naturally as if he'd been watching out for her forever. "This hardly seems fair. Save one body and get credit for three."

"I'm a bonus package."

"That's how I think of you. A bonus I never expected."

"I've complicated your life."

He pushed her just far enough away that she was facing him. "You know what's scary about that? I'm finding I like it."

"Cash..."

He pulled her close again, and kissed her. Quickly. Thoroughly. Then he slung his arm over her shoulders and propelled her toward the house.

She was thrilled they were here, not in a restaurant where she would have spent the evening trying to get comfortable. She was thrilled it looked like she was going to have him all to herself, too.

Closer to the porch, she could see smoke unfurling from the stone chimney, and lights inside. Once they were standing at the door, she heard the unmistakable vibrato of strings.

"You've gone to so much trouble, Cash."

"Your sister helped."

"Kendra?"

"Is there another one? Is that one married to a brother I didn't know about, too?"

"Kendra's a lot better at keeping a secret than I thought."

"I guess those Dunkirk girls can be pretty sneaky, huh?"

For a moment she froze, wondering what he meant. "Me?"

"Look how long you were pregnant before you got around to telling me."

"I *always* have good reasons when I keep a secret." Someday she hoped he would agree.

Cash opened the door and ushered her inside. The fragrance of wood smoke, of baking bread and roasting meat, drew her farther into the room. She saw that the coffee table had been set with wineglasses, a bottle of sparkling grape juice, and a platter of cheese and crackers. The room was softly lit, and she recognized the music as something by Debussy, which was the biggest surprise of all. Cash was a man of secrets, too.

"I feel so welcomed." She turned to him. "This is just too wonderful."

He reached over and wiped away a tear. "Hey, it's not a hardship being good to you."

"I guess I'm allergic to wood smoke, too."

"You'll just have to get over that, sweetcakes. I'm a big fan of fireplaces. If you want to spend winter nights in my company, you're going to have to adjust."

Cash wasn't much of a cook, but he could follow directions and reheat. Kendra, who was the mistress of frozen gourmet, had helped him stock the refrigerator. They'd had roast pork with apple stuffing, a mashed potato casserole so scrumptious that Jamie planned to travel to the ends of the earth to find the recipe, crisply tender green beans with almonds and fresh rolls.

It was definitely a guy-inspired meal, but Jamie was so hungry she ate her portion and a second besides. Along the way she made sure to leave room for a chocolate flourless torte topped with fresh raspberries. She might be a proponent of eating foods in season, but she didn't care how far these raspberries had traveled to her plate. She ate all those on the torte and finished what was left in the carton.

"I have some kindling you could gnaw," Cash said after he'd carried their dishes to the kitchen and done the cleanup. "Or I think there's an old package of peas in the freezer. You could just swallow them whole."

From the sofa, where Cash had thoughtfully served the entire meal, Jamie sighed with pleasure. "I'm full. Not sure how long that will last, but I am. That was such a wonderful meal, and you're such a wonderful man to make it for me."

He smiled at the last, then sobered and said, "You don't look comfortable."

"Trust me, this is as comfortable as it gets."

"I have a better idea." He took a couple of pillows off the sofa and propped them on top of several more that were already on the rug in front of the fireplace.

"Let's see if we can make you comfortable down here by the fire."

"How strong are you?" She cocked her head. "You look like you might be up to the task of hauling me back to my feet eventually. Are you willing?"

"If I can haul an armful of asphalt shingles up a roof, I can probably get you back to a standing position."

"It's every woman's dream to be compared to roofing materials."

"I considered comparing you to a load of pig manure, but I figured that was too down home for a city girl. Even country boys know the score." He held out his arms. "Come here and I'll help you down, too."

For a moment she hesitated. She wasn't sure what Cash had in mind, although considering her circumstances, it couldn't be anything she was opposed to. With that in mind, with just the tiniest assistance, she lowered herself to her knees and finally her bottom. She felt as graceful as Shamu.

Cash settled himself back against the pillows and held out his arms so she could recline against him. She hesitated again but settled herself in his arms anyway.

"I'm trying to figure out where to put my hands," he said.

She folded them over her bulging belly. "Can you imagine what it's like for the babies in there?"

"They sure can't be lonely."

"Single babies just float around all day and night, no place to go, but room to move. I picture these guys with their arms around each other." She rested more comfortably against him and sighed.

"Kind of like us, right here and now."

She was absolutely comfortable. Her back was supported perfectly, and the angle felt heavenly. Even her legs and feet felt better. The only problem was that his arm was brushing against the incision, which was still tender. She'd had swelling, and although the worst of the bruising was gone, the whole area was sensitive still. She'd made certain to check the dress to be sure no telltale discoloration showed above the scooped neckline.

She adjusted his arm so it fell lower.

"Hey, don't count that as me taking liberties," he said.

"Just making myself comfortable."

He relaxed his arms. "Better?"

"I can't believe how comfortable this is. I might need you to stay like that for the next couple of months."

"We'd get kind of hungry and smelly, don't you think?"

"It might be worth it."

"You're ready for this pregnancy to end?"

She had been until the breast cancer. Now she knew she would never want any day to end sooner than necessary. Once the twins were born, she would be immersed in negotiations about the next stages of her treatment. Where to have it and exactly what to do. Once the babies were born, she would ask Elisa Kinkade to help her assemble a team of physicians to assume control of her care. With Elisa looking on, she knew she would be in good hands until it was time to move back to Michigan or elsewhere.

If that time came.

"I don't want these babies born one day earlier than necessary," she said.

"Will you miss them?"

"I can't think that way. Besides, I'll have access whenever I want it. Kendra's asked me to spend as much time with her in Arlington as I'd like."

"Will you?"

"I'll visit, but I won't hover. She and Isaac need to figure out how to be parents without somebody else giving a lot of advice. And they're both good with children. They'll be better organized than I ever was. More inclined to stick to schedules if possible."

"If they're half as good as you are with your girls, they'll do fine."

"What a nice thing to say."

"I've never seen any woman enjoy her kids as much as you do. But you still manage to act like their mother, not their best friend."

"This just gets better and better."

"I'm finished. Can't let you get a big head."

"I don't know why not. It would match the rest of me." She shifted just a bit so she could see the fire better. "You're awfully good with my girls, Cash. Do you ever ask yourself if you're missing something by not having kids of your own?"

"Not often. The horses take a lot of nurturing. I guess I tell myself I get it out of my system that way."

She and the girls had enjoyed so many happy times in the evenings walking down to the stables to watch Cash working with Sanction's Folly and Lady's Choice. The mother cat was still guarding the barn, but the kittens had all been placed in good homes. Cash was great with the horses, but even better with her girls. She was afraid if they finished out the school year at Grace's house, Cash was going to come home one day with a pony.

"I know one thing I haven't gotten out of my system, though," he said, turning her so she was looking at him, not the fire. "And that's you, Miss Jamie. I don't know if you've noticed, but I'm more or less falling hard, here."

He had stripped off his tie a while earlier, and removed his coat. She touched his cheek, then trailed her fingers down his throat to the hollow. "If you are, I'm impressed. I'm as fat as Tweedledee with somebody else's babies, I haul around two little extensions everywhere I go. I end up in bed for weeks with everybody having to wait on me. I'm so not-a-prize these days."

"You forgot that you burst into tears over every little thing."

"Not over this."

He kissed her, moving his hands up to her shoulders and pulling her closer. She sighed happily and kissed him back. She had needed this. The evening away from her children. The moonlit view of the new house. The meal in which she'd had no hand at all. But most of all? *This.* The man she was falling in love with holding her in his arms and making her feel like nothing in the world except a woman again.

She snuggled against him and put her arms around his neck. "Are you really falling hard?"

"Maybe you didn't have to catch a mess of catfish, but you're still fishing."

"I just wanted to hear it again."

"Not until I hear something coming from your direction."

"I think the only thing I'd like to catch around here is you. Only we both know it's going to take more than reeling you in. Even if we decided we wanted to be together someday, there's an awful lot of settling to do first."

"Do we have to do it tonight?"

For just a moment she wondered if tonight might be exactly the right time to tell him about the latest development in her complicated life. He had supported her in everything else; why not this? But she knew if she spoke now, this magical moment would be gone forever.

"We don't have to do anything tonight except this." She kissed him again, angling her mouth over his, this way, then that. Their tongues touched. She had told Kendra her libido had deflated as her body expanded, but that had been talk. She wasn't surprised by the rush of desire, but she *was* surprised by the strength of it.

"Ground rules," he said, as he broke away to trail tiny kisses up and down her neck. "Two teenagers in the backseat of Daddy's car and curfew…ten minutes away. No time for anything else… but this."

"If you were a teenager, ten minutes would be plenty of time."

"I feel like a teenager about now."

He leaned back farther, bringing her with him. The twins were between them, in more ways than one, but she could feel the solidity of his chest, the strength of his arms, the sweet, warm pressure of his lips against hers.

His palm pressed lightly against her throat, moving lower, edging under the neckline of her dress. Moments passed before she realized his fingers had slipped under the curve of her bra. She stiffened and winced as he passed too close to the tenderest part of her breast.

"Hey, what's wrong?" He sat up, bringing her with him.

"Nothing." Self-consciously, she tried to straighten the neckline of her dress and saw he didn't believe her. "I guess it's the pregnancy. I'm tender there."

His gaze drifted down to the top of her dress, and she realized that because of the way she was sprawled against him, there was very little he couldn't see.

His eyes met hers. "Is that a bruise?"

"It's nothing. I bruise easily."

"Jamie, what's going on?" He sat up straight and helped her do the same, creating some distance between them as he did. "Who hurt you?"

"Nobody did, Cash. I told you, I bruise easily, and—"

"Why don't you just show me?"

Her hands went to the spot he had touched, as if that might protect her. She shook her head.

"This has something to do with that trip to Detroit, doesn't it? You've been different ever since. Somebody there hurt you. Is there a man? Somebody you're involved with who likes to hurt women?"

She saw the anger in his eyes, and she saw the disappointment.

She couldn't let him believe that. "I'm not involved with any man in Detroit, and I don't let men hurt me. Never have and never will. I told you I bruise easily. The pregnancy makes it..."

She heard herself lying again, and suddenly she couldn't go on. Years ago lies had been part of survival on the streets. The line between truth and lies had been as blurry as her thoughts after nights of partying with people she hardly knew. Those had been the dark days, when she hadn't cared if she lived or died. She never wanted to live them or any days like them again. She never wanted to fall back on bad habits.

"Okay, I'm not telling the truth." She moved away from him and straightened her dress, but she was careful not to meet his eyes. "But if I tell you the truth, Cash, I can almost guarantee you aren't going to like it. So we can quit while we're ahead and forget this. It might be the easier way to go."

"Was I right? *Has* somebody hurt you?"

If she'd thought he was the kind of man who was always suspicious, she would have gotten up and asked him to take her home. But Cash wasn't like that. If anything, he preferred not to be that involved, that responsible. She had given him cause to question her. She had lied, and not well. She had lost the knack for making up stories, for fooling people, because it was easier than honesty.

"No one hurt me. Absolutely not. Is that good enough?"

"Then what's going on, Jamie? We've gotten this far. I guess we need to go the distance."

The silence stretched, and he let it. Finally she knew she had to tell him.

"When I went to Michigan in early November...I found a lump in my breast." She looked at him at last. "I'm so young. I thought it was nothing, but I was smart enough to go to my gynecologist, just to be sure. And I was wrong. It was *something*. Over Thanksgiving I had it removed. And my breast is still tender and bruised from the surgery."

"Cancer?" One word, but his tone said everything else.

"I wish it weren't true, believe me."

His expression was frozen, as if he were afraid to show whatever he was feeling.

She looked away again. "I had a lot of options for what to do. The only one I could really live with was the one I chose. Lumpectomy. That's what they call the surgery I had. It leaves most of the breast intact, and most surgeons consider it just as safe as more radical surgery, as long as it's followed up by radiation. After the babies are born, I'll have the radiation, and maybe chemo to finish the treatment. But until then, there's nothing else I'm willing to do."

"Willing?"

She wished she hadn't used that word. But it was the right word, the honest word. "I told you, I had a lot of options. One was chemo now, during the pregnancy. But nobody could assure me completely that the babies wouldn't be harmed. The studies haven't extended long enough—"

"You're taking a risk, aren't you? That's why you haven't told anybody about this."

"I told your grandmother."

"And Kendra? What about Isaac? What about *me!*"

She flinched. "Cash, think about it. If I tell Kendra and Isaac,

I'm putting them in a terrible position. What can they say? This whole pregnancy and all the implications have already been so stressful. How could I ask them to make a choice between possibly harming me or harming the babies? How could I ask them to choose between us?"

"It's easy. You tell them the truth. You don't mess around with your life. For God's sake, Jamie, what have you been thinking? This isn't like deciding whether to send Alison to Happy Toddlers Preschool or the one over at First Baptist. It's your *life!*"

"Nothing comes without risks."

"Why are you trying to be a hero?"

"I'm not!"

"So the doctor told you there was no harm in waiting until after the birth to do a follow-up? He agrees with your choices? And you got second opinions, and thirds?"

"It's not that simple. There's so much they don't know about this. And it's a clinical decision for them. Statistics, formulas, add this to that and subtract for the following. It's not just clinical for me. I told Kendra I would do this for her. I made a solemn promise that I would take care of these babies until the moment they're born. And that's what I'm going to do."

"No, you need to tell her right away. She and Isaac need to know."

"I've decided I'll tell them a few days before I deliver. I want them to have a little time to get used to it before the babies come."

"What, just enough so it won't spoil their experience?"

She gave a slight nod.

"You don't think it'll be spoiled anyway? That they won't be asking themselves over and over how things came to this? How you went and did this without consulting them?"

"Don't you think I've gone over my choices? It's a bad situation, and I'm giving the best response I can."

"They need to know *now*."

"Cash, don't you tell anybody. This is *my* decision. *My* life and *my* sister. I'm in charge of my body. This is none of your business."

He got to his feet and looked down at her. "Is that right? Not my business? Well, thanks for clarifying things. I get it. You'd like me to just sit on the sidelines and cheer while you take chances with your future. What about those little girls of yours?" He ran his hand through his hair. "Oh, wait, now I remember what you said a while ago—and why. You've already worked out their futures. Kendra and Isaac get four for the price of two. And if you die, you'd like me to drop in now and then to say hello, and maybe make up for you being gone!"

"That's cruel, and I'm not going to die. I'm going to fight this with everything I have. We caught it early. It's not the most aggressive kind. I'll let the doctors do anything they need to after the twins are born."

"You know what? It's time to leave." He got up; then, with obvious reluctance, he extended his hand to help her up, too. "Since you and Granny Grace seem to have a pact going here, why don't I just take you back up to the orchard, so she can tell you what a noble thing you've done. Because I sure can't."

"I don't need you to." Without his help, she got clumsily to her feet; then she lowered herself to the sofa to slip on her shoes.

"I'm curious, Jamie. Will this pay back that debt you think you owe your sister? Will this finally take care of it?"

"I'm done explaining myself to you."

"Done. Okay. That's a word I can live with. I don't want any part of this."

She took a deep breath, but it didn't cushion the pain. She stood and walked to the door to take her coat off the peg and slip it on without his help.

He joined her at the bottom of the steps. As she watched, he bent over and pulled the plug on the twinkling lights that had adorned the trees. They made the trip to his pickup by moonlight.

33

Only five days had passed since Cash had sat with Jamie in almost this same spot, but it felt like a lifetime. Now he leaned against the passenger door of his pickup and made notes on a clipboard. He was alone, because the men at the Taylor job site were giving him a wide berth. He supposed the fact that he'd nearly fired one of them an hour ago for leaving too much space between driveway pavers had sealed that deal.

He wasn't an easy boss, but he was known to be a fair one. Normally he would have shown the guilty party his mistakes, decided whether they were due to carelessness or a misunderstanding, then acted accordingly. At worst, Cash would have asked him to do the work over on his own time. At best, he would have shrugged it off and gotten another man to help him tear out the problem section and redo. Despite how careful he and his father were about hiring, mistakes were inevitable, something a fair boss understood and watched out for.

Today he didn't feel like being fair. He knew that was what it came down to, and he was trying to surmount it. But at the moment, he was fighting an urge to make everybody else feel as bad as he did.

With an expression that said he had been chosen to test the waters, Gig finally approached the pickup. Not warily, exactly, but not as confidently as usual. Cash stood his ground and waited to hear what his old friend had to say.

"We ran into a problem moving that boulder down the side of the slope, only nobody wants to tell you 'cause they're afraid you'll go down and try to break it up with your bare hands. And at the rate you're going today, you just might succeed."

Cash bit back his first response and waited until a second came to mind. "Then leave it alone. There was some talk about working it into the landscaping, anyway."

"Not so's I ever heard." Gig, never anybody's idea of demonstrative, rested his hand on Cash's shoulder. "There's nothing going on this afternoon that you need to be here for. I'll take care of things."

"Kendra Taylor's on her way over with carpet samples."

"You need to be here for that?"

Cash shrugged, and Gig dropped his hand. "I need to talk to her about something else," Cash said. "But she's late."

"Can I help?"

"I wouldn't wish this conversation on anybody else." He nodded as a way of telling Gig they were finished. "Thanks for the offer, though."

Gig looked like he wanted to say more but knew better. "I'll be inside, you change your mind."

"Yeah. Okay."

Cash watched the other man cross what would be a yard

come spring. Now the ground was mud, splattered with the few
patches of snow that hadn't melted as temperatures warmed.
January was one of those months when the Valley might have
a couple of weeks of weather good enough for working
outdoors, or only half that. Today a bright sun warmed the
winter landscape and some of the men were in shirtsleeves,
although Cash wore a light jacket over his flannel shirt. In
sunlight the Taylor house was nearly as lovely as it had been in
moonlight.

Some things managed to stay the same, no matter what.

He heard the sound of a car approaching, and after a few
moments the Taylors' Lexus pulled into the parking area. The
last few times he had seen Kendra, the reserve he'd come to associate with her had disappeared. She reminded him of a kid on
Christmas Eve, waiting for Santa to bring her heart's desire. Only
in real life, Santa Jamie was bringing those gifts at her own peril.

"Hey, Cash." Kendra had carpet samples tucked under both
arms, and Cash walked over to intercept her and take some.

"I've just about decided on Berber carpet for the boys' room,
but I want to see how these look with the paint and the lights you
installed. And I want to check Hannah and Alison's room one more
time." She paused, then smiled. "I bet you think I'm obsessing,
don't you? You and the guys probably think I'm a taskmaster."

"No, we think you're a woman spending a whole lot of money
to get the house she wants. You deserve to get it right the first time."

"Is everything okay?" She cocked her head. "You don't look
happy."

He knew there was still time to step back from his decision. He
could plead the problems with the driveway pavers as the source
of his mood and let this go. He could stay out of something that
truly wasn't his business. Jamie had been right about that.

"Okay, what's up?" she asked when he didn't answer right away. "Problems with the roof? Problems with the foundation?"

"Problems with your sister."

"I'm sorry." She looked uncomfortable. "I probably don't have any right to ask what, but if I can do anything..."

He was committed now, and that decision having been made, all he could do was forge ahead. "You have the right to ask, Kendra. Unfortunately, nobody has more right."

And as the carpet samples were forgotten, he told her why he had waited there to talk to her.

Kendra had to search to find her sister. Although her van was parked in its usual place, Jamie wasn't at the house. Grace said she had seen her earlier, but not for the past hour. The girls had been invited to play with Adoncia Garcia's children and weren't expected home until dinnertime, and Grace was on her way upstairs to quilt. She suggested Kendra look outside, since Jamie couldn't have gone far.

Kendra walked around the porch to the back of the house and called Jamie's name. When she didn't get an answer, she called again and started along the path to the barn where Lucky made her home. Kendra really didn't expect to find Jamie there, but when she circled to the side where the pen had been built, she found Jamie leaning on the fence feeding the little deer something that looked like grain. Lucky wasn't a fawn anymore, but certainly not yet a full-grown doe. Kendra had no idea what to call the little deer except cute. And wary. Although she was used to Jamie, at Kendra's appearance she ambled back inside the barn, swishing her little bottom.

"Didn't you hear me calling you?" Kendra asked in greeting.

Jamie frowned. "Preoccupied, I guess. And not expecting you. Can you stay for dinner? Or do you have to get right back home?"

"I'm not sure you'll want me sitting across the table once I'm done here." She watched Jamie's expression change. Jamie hadn't looked particularly happy to see her sister, but she hadn't looked uneasy, either. Now, like Lucky, she was suddenly on guard. And she looked as if she would like to follow in Lucky's footsteps and leave.

"It's getting chilly," Jamie said. "And I've been on my feet a while. Let's go in the kitchen and I'll make some tea."

"I don't want tea. I want a conversation without anybody else listening to it."

"Then we can sit in the breezeway, unless you're planning to raise your voice. Grace is probably upstairs working on her latest quilt."

"We can try, but I'm not making any promises."

Jamie didn't ask what this was about. She lifted one brow as if to say she expected Kendra to behave, then started back toward the house with Kendra beside her.

"I'm going to make myself fruit tea," she said once they were inside. "I'll take it with me to steep. May I get you anything?"

Kendra gave one shake of her head. Jamie heated a cup of water with a tea bag in the microwave; then she led her sister into the breezeway, where she turned on lamps. She chose a chair instead of the sofa, as if she knew that having Kendra sitting close wouldn't be a good idea.

"So, go for it." She dunked the tea bag rhythmically as she spoke. "What's up?"

"I just talked to Cash."

The hand holding the tea bag stopped middunk. But Jamie's composure held. Kendra supposed she had learned that trick a long time ago.

"And?" Jamie asked casually.

"And he told me how you spent Thanksgiving."

When Jamie didn't speak, Kendra exploded. "How could you? How could you believe that a decision like that didn't involve *me?*"

Jamie was quiet for a long moment, as if she was forming her answer. Then she took the tea bag from her cup and laid it on the saucer. "It didn't. I hope while Cash was revealing my secrets, he also told you that in no way can breast cancer harm the twins. They're perfectly safe, and they would be even if the cancer had spread. And since I've chosen to wait for the rest of my treatment, they won't be affected by that, either. So when it comes right down to it, you *aren't* involved. My body, my decisions, my right to do what I think is best."

Kendra leaned forward. "We're not at a rally, Jamie! You're not giving a speech about women's rights. This is *me,* remember? Your sister? The person in this world who loves you the most! And how can you say I'm not involved? You're carrying my babies! And they're the reason you've chosen not to go forward with more treatment."

"Don't exaggerate. The whole situation's bad enough already. I *will* have more treatment. But I'm not going to put anything in my body right now that might harm the twins. I'm lucky I can make that choice, when a lot of women can't. I don't have to, because the chances are good I'll be fine if I wait a bit for the chemo and radiation. So I can do this for them, and that's the decision I made. What would you have preferred? That I take chances with their futures?"

"Did you think I'd want you to sacrifice yourself?"

Jamie didn't answer.

"You really thought that?" Kendra realized how loudly she was speaking and lowered her voice. "How could you, Jamie? What have I ever done to make you think that?"

"I think this is a decision only Solomon could make, but I had to make it anyway."

"What do the doctors say? What did they want you to do?"

Kendra watched as her sister considered how to answer this, and the wait only made her angrier. She wondered if Jamie was going to lie about this, too, but when she spoke, it was clear she had decided to level.

"They were divided. I'm finding there are no easy answers in the world of breast cancer. My friend and gynecologist Suz Chinn wanted me to have a mastectomy, followed immediately by chemo if I needed it. In varying degrees, the others thought Suz was right and that probably was the best solution. But doing it my way increased the risk for long-term survival in acceptable amounts. The radiologist was the most confident I'd be okay. Of course, this way he gets the pleasure of zapping my breast five days a week for at least a month. He's young and single. I think he's looking forward to it."

"How can you joke at a time like this?"

"How can I not?"

For the first time Kendra heard the plaintive note in her sister's voice. Since her conversation with Cash, she had been so angry that she hadn't allowed herself to imagine how Jamie felt about the diagnosis. She had felt so hurt, so betrayed, that Jamie had lied to her.

But her sister, not yet thirty, had breast cancer.

"Why did you lie to me?" Kendra asked. "I guess I can understand why you've decided what you have, although I hope you don't think that's what I would have asked you to do. But why did you lie? Why didn't you just let me help you face this so we could have figured out what to do together? We could have done the research, talked to specialists in this area. Have I been such an awful sister that you thought you couldn't trust me?"

"I didn't like lying. I gave that up a long time ago, along with various other despicable habits."

"Then why?"

"Because you're always sure you know what's best for me, Ken. That's been true forever. And you've tried to change, but at heart, that's still the way things are. This time I had to figure out what was best for myself *by* myself. Without putting you in the driver's seat. How could you make the right decision when, on one hand, you had my health to consider, and on the other, your children's? I knew you couldn't look at it objectively. And I knew the emotions would tear you apart. So I spared you that."

"Don't make it sound so noble! You spared yourself from finding out what my choice would be."

"I made the best choice for everybody. I'm an adult. This is my body. I'm carrying these babies. I chose for you, for me, for them. I took every little bit of information I had, consulted with four doctors, weighed all the pros and cons. I made the choice I could live with."

Kendra knew that whatever she said next would affect her relationship with her sister for the rest of their lives. She was torn between anger at and fear for Jamie. Sadly, she also had to face the fact that some part of her was relieved that her babies, the children she would nurture and protect for the rest of her life, would be born without the risk of extra complications.

As she realized that, she also realized that some smaller but guilty part of herself was relieved Jamie had spared her the necessity of confronting this decision head-on.

Inside, the silence stretched. Outside, Kendra could hear twilight bird calls, the sound of an engine as somebody traveled down one of the orchard's dirt roads. A voice calling greetings to someone in mellifluous Spanish.

"Here's what I would have done, after I'd had a chance to consider it carefully," Kendra said at last, leaning forward a little so Jamie knew how earnest she was. "This is all you *ever* had to be afraid of. I would have told you how much I love you. Then I would have told you that I understood you had to make this decision for yourself, and whatever you chose, you had my complete support. I would have said that I know you're not my little girl anymore, and never really were. That's what these months together have done for me. I know that now, and I trust you completely to do the right thing."

She sat back. "Then I would have asked if you were really sure you wanted to take even the slightest risk with your health. Because I don't know if I can live with myself if anything happens to you just because you were trying to do something so wonderful for Isaac and me."

Tears welled in Jamie's eyes, and she wiped them away. "I'm not a martyr, Ken. I promise, if the risks were any higher, this would be a very different conversation."

"When it's cancer, *any* risk is too much. What about Alison and Hannah?"

"I'm planning to sit in the front row at their college graduations."

"And if you can't?"

"I've already spoken to an attorney. If you and Isaac consent, I'd like you to take them. I don't think either Larry or Seamus will fight it."

Kendra felt a sob rising in her throat. "If you can trust me with your daughters, why couldn't you trust me with the truth? Why couldn't you trust me with your *life?*"

"Because you're a mother now, and mothers are some of the least objective people in the world. So are sisters." Jamie took Kendra's hand. "Would you really have let me make this decision on my own? Without trying hard to influence it?"

Kendra considered, and when she nodded, she knew it was the

truth. "For the very reasons you just voiced. Because I *am* a mother and a sister."

Jamie looked unsure.

"Jamie, it's not too late for you to make another choice. I'm sure if you're willing, you can start chemo immediately. Your doctors would only use the drugs they felt were safest for the babies, and I could certainly live with that. But I'm not going to tell you to do it now, just like I wouldn't have told you then. I *will* tell you that if you change your mind and schedule treatment, I'll support you one hundred percent, just the way I will if you don't."

Tears slipped down Jamie's cheeks. "I hated lying to you. I needed you. I just couldn't..." She shook her head. "I just couldn't ruin this for you. Not when you've waited so long. I just wanted to give you something once and for all to let you know how sorry I am for all those years you had to worry about me. No strings, no anxiety, no problems. Despite everything. And I couldn't—and can't—take a chance with the babies' health. I would be watching them for the rest of my life and wondering. Tell me you understand."

Kendra knelt in front of Jamie's chair and put her arms around her. She felt Jamie relax, and in a moment she wasn't sure which of them was hugging the other harder.

Jamie found Grace working on her latest quilt. It wasn't a wall hanging, and it wasn't a bed quilt. Grace called it a play quilt, and it was a bright grass green, appliquéd with a curving gray roadway lined with pop-art buildings with doors that opened. A field with grazing cows adorned one edge; a gas station sat at the widest turn in a small town with a church and city hall.

She planned to present it to Kendra once the twins were born, along with appropriate toy vehicles for two little boys to guide along the road once they were older. In her own inimitable style, Grace was making up the pattern as she went along, sticking to bright colors and large shapes she could easily see. Jamie could already imagine how many future hours of activity had been stitched into the surface. Kendra's children would love it.

"If you're going to be up a little while longer," Jamie said from the doorway, "would you mind listening out for the girls? They're asleep, and I doubt they'll wake up. I'm going for a little drive. Not far, I promise, so I'll be fine."

"I'm not ready to go to bed. You go ahead." Grace looked up. "Unless, dear, this is something that ought to wait until morning and a night of contemplation?"

Clearly Grace, who had not chided her about driving again, knew exactly where she was going. "I'm afraid not."

Grace looked sad. "It's so easy to make mistakes and think you understand how somebody else feels about you. I made my share along the way."

"There are mistakes. And mistakes."

"It's easy to make the second kind when you're trying hard not to face your feelings. That's one way to rid yourself of the problem."

"Sometimes it works."

Grace shook her head, but Jamie knew that was as much interference as her friend believed in.

Outside, the temperature had fallen into the midforties. By Sunday, the temperature would drop below freezing again, and snow was possible. Her daughters were hoping for inches, although Jamie wanted clear roads in case she had an emergency doctor's appointment.

Isaac had loaned her his largest ski jacket for the duration of the pregnancy, and now she zipped it and pulled on woolen mittens.

She considered cutting through the orchard to Cash's trailer, but she'd spent the evening thinking about this, and she didn't need time to reconsider. She wanted this conversation over with.

The drive was short, over almost before it began, which was the only kind she could really manage now. She was afraid he might have gone somewhere for the evening, but there were lights on in the trailer, shining from the windows and spilling out of the insulation-stuffed cracks in the walls. She asked herself why the trailer itself hadn't been a dead giveaway to Cash's personality. Nobody lived this way unless they had to, or unless they had given up all thoughts of real intimacy or a future. Cash might as well have installed a blinking neon sign. *No Woman Need Apply.* But maybe she wouldn't have seen that, either.

She knocked on the door, but nobody answered. Arms folded against the cold, she walked over to the riding ring, which wasn't lit, then on to the stables, which were.

Cash wasn't in the stables, either, but she saw that Sanction's Folly was missing. Apparently he was out for a ride.

The wind was picking up, and although she was protected from it here, Czar Bright and Lady's Choice were uneasy with her presence. She wasn't sure how long she could afford to wait. She didn't belong here alone this time of night, and the horses knew it.

Outside, huddled on the stoop of Cash's trailer, she debated returning to Grace's, or just sitting in her van and hoping Cash showed up soon. She was still trying to decide when she heard hoofbeats. In a few minutes Cash and Folly appeared on one of the dirt paths weaving through the orchard.

She got to her feet, dusting off the seat of her maternity jeans, and walked down to meet them.

"Have you been here long?" he asked.

"Not really."

"Let me unsaddle him. I'll be right with you. Why don't you go inside?"

She wasn't excited about the invitation. The lack of enthusiasm in his voice matched what she was feeling. But the wind was still picking up. She shrugged and headed for the trailer.

Every other time she had been here, the place had at least been tidy. Tonight it was a shambles, clothing on the floor, frozen dinner cartons overflowing from the trash can beside the counter. She moved stacks of newspapers off the sofa so she could sit, but she didn't touch the crumpled beer and soft-drink cans on the coffee table. She wasn't here to clean house.

Cash took his time, but that didn't surprise her. She'd had hours since Kendra left for Arlington to consider her response, and now he only had the time it took to unsaddle Folly.

Although surely Cash had known she wouldn't just let this go without a word.

When he finally did come through the front door, he looked cautious, as if he expected an ambush. "Sorry about the mess," he said.

"I really don't care."

"There's not much to be done with it, anyway."

"I'm curious, would you let any of the orchard workers live in this place?"

"No."

"I'd ask you what you're trying to prove, only that's not why I'm here."

"I've got a pretty good idea why you are."

"Kendra came to see me after she talked to you. Or rather, after *you* talked to *her* and told her everything I asked you not to."

He didn't answer. Instead he went to the refrigerator and got a bottle of water. He turned and held it out to her, but she shook her head.

Cash took his time opening the water and drinking half of it. Then he joined her, sitting in a stained canvas director's chair that looked as if he had rescued it from the dump.

"Somebody had to tell her," he said at last.

"And what exactly did it change? Now she knows the situation just a little sooner than she would have if I'd been allowed to do this my own way. But I'm still not going in for chemo until after the babies are born. And I'm not going to let the doctor induce labor one moment sooner. The only difference I can see is that now we know you can't be trusted with a secret. And I can't trust you to let me make my own decisions."

"I can't believe this. You're still planning to wait?"

She got to her feet. "Yep, that's what I came to tell you. Not out of some knee-jerk reaction to what you've done. Not because I'm stupid. And certainly not because I have a death wish. But because it's the right thing under these circumstances. Is it easy? No, it's not. And you haven't made it one bit easier by talking to Kendra. Luckily she and I are still okay. You didn't ruin that. But just in case you thought you'd helped matters? Don't go to bed tonight patting yourself on the back."

She started toward the door, but he was on his feet, hand gripping her arm. "What's it going to take for you to see reason?"

She faced him. "What's it going to take for you to stop filtering my decision through your past? Your life is one big reaction to Kary's death, Cash. Everything about it. This God-awful trailer, your indecision about your future, your refusal to step up to the plate and help your grandmother figure out how to save Cashel Orchard."

"Don't get all psychological on me and turn it in my direction. You could die from this. Your decision could kill you."

"Of course you're afraid I'm going to die. Trust me, in case it slipped your notice, I'm afraid of the same thing. As soon as I reasonably can, I'm going to fight this cancer with every tool medical science has. I'm not worried about losing my hair or my breast. I *am* worried about my life, and I'll do whatever it takes to protect it. But you know, I could get hit by a car on the way to my next doctor's appointment. Or I could have an allergic reaction to a beesting or spider bite and drop in my tracks. So could you. And that's the way you live your life. Like that's a given. You don't get involved, and that way you think it'll hurt a whole lot less when something finally does happen. Because tragedies that happen to strangers aren't so tragic, are they?"

"And what about you? Are you trying to tell me this pregnancy wasn't about proving something to yourself and everybody else? And now this so-called rational decision you've made to wait months before you treat a malignant tumor isn't about proving something, too?"

"First, I *have* treated it. The tumor's gone. And when I have radiation and maybe chemo, hopefully that will take care of any stray cells."

"Not soon enough, it won't!"

She continued as if he hadn't spoken. "And maybe the pregnancy *is* a way to prove to my sister I've changed, that I can be trusted and that I care enough about her to want to make her life happier. But wow, what could be wrong with that?"

"A whole lot is wrong when you start risking your life."

"No, I took a chance, a big one, that I could make all that happen. And I have. I've done something good. Really good. And nothing can ever change that, even in the unlikely case I die sooner rather than later. Now tell me, what have *you* done? What risks have *you* taken lately? You're a good man, but you dance at the edge of everybody else's lives. Well, enjoy that little tap-dancing solo, but don't try to convince me that putting myself first, no matter what, would be good for me, as well. Because you never will."

"I'm not asking you to be selfish!"

"Then what? What *are* you asking?"

His lips were drawn tight. She waited, but he didn't speak.

"I don't need a man to run my life," she said, when clearly nothing more was coming from him. "You were right about one thing. I made a mistake when I didn't trust my sister enough to tell her the truth. No, I guess I made two. I really thought I could trust you to keep silent about this, no matter how you felt, and I was wrong. But those were the only mistakes I've made. Now stop trying to interfere. You've done your worst, and it hasn't changed a thing. So just let me get on with having these babies and dealing with my treatment afterward. You've already said you were done with me. This time, make sure you mean it."

She turned and left. He didn't come after her, but she hadn't wanted him to. She got in the van and rested her forehead against the steering wheel, trying not to cry. When she was calm enough, she backed out of her parking spot and headed for the farmhouse.

Lights were on in the kitchen, and she heard the sizzle of water coming to a boil when she got inside. She debated going straight to bed. Grace would understand if she missed this chance to talk.

She started toward her room, but two halting steps later she knew she wasn't really ready to be alone. Grace wouldn't ask what had transpired. That wasn't her way. But the comfort of her presence was enough to make Jamie turn toward the lights.

Grace was just pouring water into tea cups. She didn't look up. "When Ben was alive, this was always my favorite time of day. Of course, it was coffee he drank before bed. Can you imagine that? But it was such a strong habit, he couldn't sleep without it."

Jamie took a seat at the table. "When I was a little girl, I used to imagine this."

Grace put the kettle back on the stove. "What?"

"Having a mother, or a grandmother, who poured tea—and sympathy with it—when I was lonely or sad."

"Oh, dear…you have no idea how much I wish I could have been your grandmother. You deserved tea and sympathy. You still do."

"You've been as kind to me as any of my fantasies."

Grace took Jamie's hand. "I don't know what happened tonight with my grandson, but whatever he did or does, Jamie, don't think it'll change the way I value you and your daughters."

Jamie squeezed, but she knew she had to change the subject or risk sobbing on Grace's shoulder. "Tell me something. How could you and Cash's grandfather have been any more different?"

"As different in our ways as you and Cash are in yours? In later years, I realized we simply balanced each other. Of course, we disagreed about so many things that, when we finally found things we could agree on, we knew every possibility had been covered, so we didn't have to think about it anymore."

Jamie heard Grace's message. Two people did not have to see eye to eye to be happy together. She was sorry her problems with Cash weren't that simple.

"Maybe you didn't have to agree on everything, but didn't you have to trust each other?"

"We came to that the hard way. But we came to it."

"It's tough to imagine the good times you had with Ben, when all I've heard about are the bad ones."

"Good girl. You're making an effort, when what you really want to do is go to bed and cry yourself to sleep."

Tears sprang to Jamie's eyes, something that happened far too frequently. "Exactly how did you go from distrust and anger to falling in love?"

"Do you really feel like hearing this?"

Jamie knew the alternative was lying awake reliving her conversation—perhaps the final one she would ever have—with Cash. "Maybe I could just use at least one happy ending tonight."

Grace squeezed her hand once more; then she offered Jamie the sugar. "Ben and I fell in love an inch at a time. Maybe that's the best way, because the foundation is solid and sure. But it also means it's hard to see. And that was true for us."

34

1942

Sylvie would never be thin, but in the past four weeks she had lost a considerable amount of natural padding, and now, in overalls rolled up to the knee, she looked sleek and healthy. Her face was tanned, her cheeks rosy and her curly hair was tied back in a becoming pink kerchief. Grace stood at the bottom of the extension ladder and yelled up to her sister-in-law.

"I wish Ethan could see you now. You look like Mother Earth picking those apples."

Sylvie snapped another stem between her thumb and forefinger, and carefully placed the apple in the burlap sack hanging against her chest.

"At least Ethan wouldn't tell me picking apples isn't woman's work, the way Hiram told Dolly."

Ethan, Sylvie's husband, was Grace's second brother, always the most affable of the Fedley boys. Hiram was Grace's third brother, the one closest to her age, and the tyrannical husband of Dolly. Hiram, like Anna, had always had traditional notions about the way everything should be done. Grace suspected some Puritan Fedley forefather had gravely presided over New England witch hunts, and Grace's sister and youngest brother had been the unfortunate recipients of that heritage.

"At least Dolly told Hiram what he could do with his opinion," Grace said, just loud enough for Sylvie's ears. Dolly was picking three rows away.

"Good thing she did. She's the best picker you've got. Now go and get busy. You don't have to stay nearby. I'm not falling off this ladder, and that's a promise."

Grace wasn't comfortable with the extensions that helped her work crew get into the very top branches of the apple trees. But she knew she had to *become* comfortable. Taking chances was the order of the day. A lot of the crop was waiting to be picked, although the earliest apples were already on their way to market.

And a glorious crop it was. With soldiers in need of supplies and foodstuffs already beginning to be rationed, apples were in high demand for drying and canning as sauce for the troops. Grace could sell every apple she produced, picked and somehow carried to market. Of course, now she was learning that she had to worry about gas and tires to get the apples anywhere, and eventually might need to hitch Buddy, their retired plow horse, to a wagon to do it. She also had to repair and pray over every piece of machinery the farm had in its possession, since it was growing clearer each day that no spare parts would be available until after the war. In fact, rumor had it that every cubic inch of scrap metal would soon be carted away to be melted down for the war effort.

But those were future problems. She had enough on her hands right now.

"I'm going to check on the younger children," she told Sylvie. "Then I want to see how the older ones are doing harvesting those greens."

"I hope they're about done, because there are a lot of drops to pick up out here."

Picking up fallen fruit wasn't the whole story. There was a lot to do everywhere. Work was the one thing that was not in short supply at the orchard. Work and, of course, apples, a bumper crop in a year when one had been desperately needed. Terrible things were happening all over the world, but there were little miracles here and there, as well. Cashel Orchard was one of them.

Grace carefully placed her own apples in a crate to be hauled to the apple shed before she removed her sack and hung it on the nearest fence post.

At the rim of the orchard she stopped a moment, wistfully estimating the number of steps to the house for feet already tired from a long morning of hard work. She yearned to be able to drive the old pickup to the front door to save time and strength. But that kind of indulgence was out of the question.

Instead, she set a steady, measured pace, not too fast, so she would wear out quicker, but not too slow, so that precious time would be wasted. Every move she made these days was calculated to reap the largest benefit. Sometimes the calculations—not to mention the work—exhausted her——but more of the time she felt exhilarated. She was making a difference. She was succeeding, when just months ago failure had literally knocked on her front door and leered at her predicament.

She rested for a moment on the front porch, leaning against a post and gazing back at the orchard. From somewhere in the distance she smelled the tang of burning leaves, and from much closer, the winey fragrance of cider mash fermenting in a pile behind the house, so it could be spread with manure later in the season as fertilizer.

Even from this distance, she could hear laughter, and the high, sweet shouts of women. From the back of the farmhouse she could hear a child crying, but not as if tragedy had struck. This was a child who just wanted more attention. Adam, she thought, although possibly Sylvie's littlest girl, Roly, short for Roly Poly because, quite simply, she was. Grace hoped Roly outgrew the reason for the nickname quickly, although her real name, the Germanic Ermentraude, was likely to get her into trouble these days.

What was Ben going to think when he drove up to the orchard next week and saw what she had done? For a moment, as it did several times a day, the question made her heart beat faster. Ben had no idea what was happening here. Once her decision had been made to save the orchard, she had written him, suggesting that when Otis Gaff sent signed papers to Fort Belvoir to sign, Ben mail them back to Grace. She had explained that she'd found an attorney at the bank who would look them over for free before she delivered the copies to Gaff herself. There were rumors of Otis cheating other people, she'd said, and this was simply a precaution to preserve their future. Then she'd held her breath and hoped Ben would take her suggestion.

He did. The signed contract came to her directly, where it went into the cookstove that same night to start a merry blaze. Then she wrote a letter to Otis, so he wouldn't continue to correspond with Ben, explaining that the orchard was no longer for sale and Ben would tear up any other mail he received. With utter confidence she forged Ben's name at the bottom.

The next morning Grace delivered the forgery and explained

that since Otis had gone back on his word and tried to buy the orchard for less, Ben had decided not to sell at all. She was sorry, but after all, that was what happened when one neighbor tried to cheat another. Then she'd gotten into the pickup and driven away before the old man could sic a particularly nasty-looking dog on her.

Now she was living with the consequences of that almost euphoric burst of creativity. She had convinced her two closest sisters-in-law, whose husbands had both been inducted into the Army, to live and work at the orchard while their men were away. She had hired three more women who lived nearby for seasonal labor, as well as the brother of Ben's hired man.

Grace was paying as much as her neighbors who hired help, but not as much as any of her workers might earn in a factory. Still, here at the orchard, all the women had their children at hand and well cared for. They could visit them when they took breaks, and have meals together. The school children helped out on Saturdays, like they were doing today, and the younger were well cared for as the mothers took turns in the farmhouse entertaining them. Her sisters-in-law had company and no concerns about transportation to their jobs, and the neighbor women could work whenever they were able to leave their own chores.

Next spring she would enlarge the vegetable garden by an acre so that even more fresh and canned food would be readily available, and she would add four more acres of corn—if the tractor held out long enough. No one at Cashel Orchard would ever have to save ration coupons for a can of fruit. There was fresh milk and butter, and hogs fattening on corn and fallen apples to become ham and bacon. The work was hard, but except for the occasional spat, the women got along and enjoyed each other's company. Most of the time the children were happy to have playmates.

And if all went as planned, there would be enough money at the end of the season to pay all the orchard's debts and still have enough left over to buy the supplies they would need for next year.

Cashel Orchard would never run as efficiently, as scientifically, under her control as it had under Ben's stewardship. Grace didn't have the experience or knowledge to select new varieties for planting trials, or to experiment with updated methods of pest control or fertilization. She was forced to rely on the knowledge of their hired man and other local growers willing to share their expertise. She was reading her way through Ben's small library of pamphlets and agricultural tomes, but fifteen minutes at night before she fell into an exhausted sleep was not enough time to learn everything she needed.

When Ben came back from the war, he would find the orchard changed, perhaps somewhat the worse for decisions she'd been forced to make. But she prayed he would also find that the sign at the entrance still said Cashel Orchard and that his sons still lived on the land they would someday inherit.

At least that was what he would find if he didn't sell the orchard—this time for real—the moment he got back from basic training. She was expecting that moment early next week. Ben's last typically terse letter had informed her that he'd been granted two weeks leave between training at Fort Belvoir and shipping out to whatever unknown destination was being chosen for him. As with everything else about the war, that could change. But in the meantime, Grace was to expect him.

Right now, Ben thought that Otis had decided not to move into the house until next summer, and was allowing Grace and the boys to pay rent and continue living there while they looked for a place closer to a job for her. Ben believed Grace had deposited the sale money, minus Otis's rent, in his bank account, making certain, with the help of their fictitious attorney, that all was correct. She supposed it was a good sign that he had trusted her that far, although, of course, his trust had been misplaced.

From the moment she'd decided to ignore Ben's decision and take over management of the orchard herself, she had wondered how he would react when he discovered her deception. Had she trusted *him* more, she would simply have told him her thoughts and worked out the details with his help. But theirs was not a marriage built on sharing.

Besides, what man would believe that a woman with no experience and no training in orchard management could make a success of growing and selling apples with the help of other inexperienced women? If Grace made a mess of things, the property would be devalued, and Ben would be lucky if Otis Gaff repeated his stingiest offer. If she *did* make a success of it, then Ben would be forced to treat her like a partner, perhaps even the orchard's savior, and their entire relationship would change.

She couldn't imagine how things were going to play out. Most of the time she didn't have even a moment to worry about it. But now, with Ben's leave drawing near, she knew she was going to have to find the time to think of a way to explain it all to him.

For now, she had work to do.

Inside, she followed the noise to the kitchen, where the children were having a snack. Little heads with hair of every hue were bent over plates at the table. Lulie, Sylvie's oldest girl, was babysitting today, and they were lucky to have her. In two years she would graduate from high school and seek a more lucrative and exciting job. For now, though, she was available on weekends to care for the younger children, so all the mothers could pick apples, and the children looked forward to having her there, particularly three-year-old Roly and six-year-old Hildy, her little sisters.

Adam, still a mama's boy, held out his arms the moment he saw Grace, and she lifted him from the high chair. He was the youngest, and with all the men away at war, bound to stay that way a while. Hiram and Dolly's two youngest sons were busy eating bread slathered with apple butter. Four older Fedleys and four of the neighbor women's children were outside harvesting turnip and mustard greens from the vegetable garden. As soon as snack time ended, Dolly—today's cook—would come inside and begin work on the afternoon's dinner, the largest meal of the day. Last night Dolly had cooked beans and baked corn bread in preparation. The newly picked greens would be a welcome addition, along with apples fried in butter.

Always apples. Every meal. Grace knew they were fortunate, so fortunate, to have them, when so many in Europe were starving.

"How's my little man?" she asked Adam, kissing his cheek. "Did you eat a good snack?" She carried him around the table, saying a word or two to each child, and patting them on their tiny shoulders. Lulie looked tired, which was understandable, but she had the group well in hand. The mothers had found that sticking to a schedule worked best. Once snacks were finished, the children would have a brief rest time, each clutching one small toy that wouldn't disturb the others. Lulie would need the rest most of all.

Grace saved Charlie for the end, squatting down with Adam still in her arms and kissing his cheek. "Have you had a good morning?"

"Roly hit me."

"On purpose?"

He shrugged.

"Are you hurt?"

He shrugged again. She saw Ben in the movement. No surprise that Charlie, as young as he was, had copied it. She just hoped Charlie would learn to express his feelings a bit more clearly than his father.

"Would you like to come outside with me for a little while? I'm going to check on the older children and see how many greens they've picked."

His eyes lit up, although he did a quick scan of the table first to be sure he wasn't missing something more important. So much for being mad at his cousin.

She promised Lulie that she would be back in time to keep the boys from disrupting the scheduled rest period, and guided Charlie around the table and out the kitchen door. The patch of greens was beside the barn, and she stopped for a few moments of guilty pleasure to let the boys pat Buddy's velvety nose over the pasture fence. Then they joined their cousins and friends, who had indeed harvested enough greens to show they had been working while they told stories and laughed.

Her own childhood might have been devoid of color and conversation, but to her delight, the next generation seemed to be on a different path.

She was heading around a tall hedge-lined bend in the path back to the kitchen, the boys in tow, when Charlie's shoe came untied. Although she was teaching him how to tie his shoelaces himself, there wasn't time now for another demonstration. She squatted on the ground to do it herself, setting Adam beside her to stretch his baby legs.

"Pretty soon you'll be doing this faster than me," she said, soothing the little boy's masculine pride. "You'll be the shoe-tying champion with those strong fingers of yours."

"Daddy—"

"Even better than your daddy. In fact, by the time Daddy comes home from the Army, you'll be tying all sorts of things."

"Daddy!"

She realized Charlie wasn't talking about knots. Before she could finish, he shook himself loose and took off.

Without turning, she knew who must be standing somewhere behind her. The hedge and the curve had hidden his approach.

The hour of reckoning had arrived.

Adam toddled past her, his chubby face wreathed in smiles. She got slowly to her feet, took quick stock of what she was wearing, and silently slapped herself for not putting on something more attractive today or pinning up her hair, instead of simply gathering it in a net and covering it with a scarf. She looked like a farmhand, probably smelled like one, too, and unless she was mistaken, the wet spot on her buttoned sweater was baby drool mixed with apple butter and bread crumbs.

She brushed at the stain, but improvement was hopeless. She squared her shoulders and turned to find her husband standing just ten feet away. Ben looked thin, and his hair was so short, she could hardly tell the color. He wore olive drab with a khaki-colored necktie, and he carried his hat in his hand. He looked tired. He looked worn.

He looked wonderful.

She didn't know what to say. Apparently Ben didn't, either, because even though Charlie was tugging at his father's tie, trying to make his daddy pay attention to him, Ben was silent.

"I can explain," she said at last, shrugging the way Ben so often did. "If you'll let me."

His gaze bored right through her. "There are women in the apple orchard. Some of them look surprisingly familiar. There are children in the house. They're not mine, and they sure aren't Otis Gaff's."

"That snake in the grass probably isn't capable of producing children. He and that cockamamie wife of his would produce rats. Baboons. Donkeys."

"I'm assuming he's not around to hear that?"

"Not unless he sneaked on to your property and is slinking around somewhere. But I doubt it. He thinks I have a loaded shotgun with his name on the pellets."

"And do you?"

"No, I'm a peaceful woman. The threat was good enough. Besides, now that he has a letter from you saying you refuse to sell…" She drew a circle in the dirt with her toe, paying close attention to symmetry. "Well, he doesn't have much reason to come over here, anyway."

"A letter, you say? That's odd. I don't remember writing one."

She couldn't tell anything from his tone, but that was Ben. She suspected that when she looked up from her perfect circle, she wouldn't be able to tell anything from his expression, either. So what point was there in looking up?

"Well, I may have told a teensy-weensy lie with that letter," she said.

"Teensy?"

"Maybe a little bigger than teensy. And I may, just *may*, have signed your name to it."

"Grace, what exactly did you do?"

She finally looked up. She'd been right. Nothing showed, but he had lifted Adam into his other arm, and he was clutching the boys against his uniform as if somebody was trying to steal them.

"Here it is as fast as I can say it." She took a deep breath. "I decided I could run the place myself. Otis wanted to steal it, Ben. He was going to steal our apples! Could I let him do that? Of course I couldn't. So I sort of made up a story or two. One for you, one for him. See, I thought if you didn't know what I was doing, then you couldn't refuse to let me do it. And it's working, Ben. We've already sent all the Galas and Empires to market, and we got a great price for them. I'll show you all the figures. And I hired Dolly and Sylvie and some of the neighbor women to pick this season. They're doing great. Dolly and Sylvie have moved in, the children are being well taken care of, we're putting by lots of food so we won't be hungry while you men are off fighting, and there'll probably be enough to share with the less fortunate, not to mention sell. Maybe the orchard won't look as good as it did the day you left, you know, when you come back the next time, but it'll be here, Ben. It will still belong to you and the boys."

He didn't speak. She pressed her lips together, then bit them for good measure. She was just about to start drawing another circle with her toe when he put Charlie down on the ground and followed with Adam.

He took two steps toward her; then he stopped.

The boys seemed to sense the gravity of the moment, and they moved away, Charlie to one side, Adam to the other.

"And what about you?" Ben asked.

"What do you mean?"

"You said it will still belong to me and the boys. The orchard. Cashel Orchard. What about you, Grace? Will it belong to you as well?"

She was trembling. Now, annoyingly, her eyes filled. She sniffed. "I guess that depends on you."

He shook his head. "No, it's always depended on you. Or nearly always. Maybe on that night when Adam turned six months old and started cutting teeth, and I found you rocking him, even though you'd been carrying him around all day long and any other woman would just have let him cry. Maybe it was that night. Or maybe it was the night I saw you standing on the front porch looking up at the stars and counting them, like you ever really could. Count them all, I mean. But that didn't stop you. Whenever it was? It's depended on you from that moment. It depends on you now."

She saw the future she had wished for. And she knew it would have been a fine one, filled with sights that now she might never see, people she would surely never meet. Then she saw the future she had never wanted. A future with Ben Cashel—somber, obstinate Ben, who would never leave the place where he'd been born. Ben, who would spend his future and hers, if she let him, growing apples and raising his little family.

"Well, then, if it depends on me," she said, "then I guess I'm in this until the end of the play. But you have to promise you'll teach me how to prune an apple tree, because I'm hoping to work right beside you some of the time. Once you come back, Ben, I'm not sure I'll want you out of my sight again."

He didn't move, but he seemed to dissolve, as if all the hard edges holding him together were now soft and fluid. He smiled, not a huge grin, but the sweetest smile she'd ever seen.

And the sexiest.

He held out his arms. She went into them without a thought. And kissing him felt as natural and right as she had hoped it might.

They weren't alone until that night. Between the boys, the sisters-in-law, the hired man and the neighbors who had heard—as Valley neighbors always seemed to—that Ben was home on leave, they were surrounded by family and friends. But when nighttime came, Grace made sure Ben came to the right bedroom to sleep.

He walked in to find her putting something in a dresser.

"What's that?" he asked, coming up to stand behind her.

"I hope you won't be angry."

"I've managed to keep my temper under check so far," he said, putting his arms around her waist.

She felt the excitement of his touch, and just the faintest apprehension that they were about to really become husband and wife. She fished in the drawer and pulled out the quilt top she was making from Anna's scraps. She turned in his arms.

"I found this pattern and fabric in a box of Anna's. It's called Sister's Choice. I just felt like I needed to make it."

He looked down and fingered the top. Then he nodded. "It's right you should."

"It's not like the quilts Anna usually made. I felt drawn to it. Especially, well, because of the name."

"It's not like the ones she usually made, Grace, because she was going to make that one for *you*. She told me it was going to be your wedding quilt. She knew you would like all the fabrics and colors. She said, after a lifetime of keeping you in line, for once she wanted to give you something you would really love."

For a moment she couldn't speak or breathe. She looked up at him. "She gave me you."

His lips found hers. The quilt top fell between them. There would be time in the long, lonely years of the war to finish it. But for now, Grace had something else that had to be finished first.

35

Whenever possible, Rosslyn and Rosslyn believed in historical preservation. Cash and his father were responsible for saving more than a few cabins, stores and mills that would have been demolished if not for their intervention and skills. Despite himself, Cash had always been proud of that.

This morning, though, a month after Jamie's evening visit, he was ready to swing a sledgehammer himself. Or light the first match.

The mobile home he had called his for too many years wasn't old enough to be historic, and he doubted many good memories had been made here. For the most part, it had been temporary housing, available for a few months in the autumn if an overflow of workers came to pick and process fruit. Even then, his grandparents had made certain to keep the place in good repair until the day Granny Grace had judged that impossible and put a padlock on the door. But the old trailer had never been a real home for anybody until Cash had taken it over.

For that matter, it had never been *his* real home, either.

Cash had spent a lot of the last month wondering why a man who was devoted to preserving the past, a man who was rightfully proud of restoring and building homes that would grace Shenandoah County for decades or centuries, had, at the very same time, worked so hard both to forget his own history and to live in one of the valley's least historic eyesores.

He was not a fan of complexity. He was determined to think of himself as a simple country boy. He wanted his path through life to be straightforward and uncomplicated. But a man didn't always get what he wanted.

This morning he still wasn't sure about much, but he was sure he no longer wanted this. He did not want to live in a rusted-out tin can. Never again did he want to wake up at six on a February morning, as he had today, to find icicles forming in the gap between window and wall in his living room, and an inadequate furnace struggling unsuccessfully to heat both the interior of the trailer and too much of the great outdoors.

Normally, at a moment like this one, he would have gone up to the farmhouse and bummed coffee from his grandmother while he waited for the sun to rise. But that option was no longer available. By now Jamie would be up, getting Hannah and Alison ready for school, helping Granny Grace in the kitchen or packing lunches for her daughters. He didn't want to witness her carefully blank expression or hear her polite, condensed responses to all conversational gambits.

He had seen Jamie in the weeks since that last conversation, of course. He continued to take the girls to school in the mornings, and she allowed that, since driving them herself was now virtually impossible, particularly when the roads were as icy as they appeared to be this morning. But he didn't drop by the house just to visit his grandmother unless he knew ahead of time that Jamie wouldn't be there.

So this morning, he was spending the interval before dawn plugging every gap he hadn't bothered with before. He cut and stuffed strips of insulation into cracks, covering some of it with duct tape, some with strips of paneling, to keep it in place. And as he worked, he asked himself how his life had come to this.

He still wasn't halfway to an answer when somebody knocked. Startled, he let the hammer slip from his hand, and it landed on his foot. Muttering under his breath, he limped across the room and threw open the door, expecting to find one of his crew. Instead he found Isaac.

Cash and his "new" half-brother had gotten together four or five times since their father's revelation. They usually went out for a beer when Isaac and Kendra were in town, and let the conversation wander wherever it wanted. At this point, neither of them was trying for anything except friendship, but that seemed well on the way.

Cash was embarrassed. He had never invited Isaac to the trailer. He supposed he had been ashamed of his choices even before Jamie pointed out how revealing they were. He hadn't really wanted Isaac to see where and how he lived or question him about either.

"You're not exactly dropping in, are you?" Cash asked.

"You can tell that because the sun's not up yet and you live in the middle of nowhere, right?"

"That's about it in a nutshell. Come in, but don't take off your jacket. It's freezing in here."

Isaac stepped inside and looked around; then he shoved his hands in the pockets of his jeans as if he were afraid of frostbite. "Well, you don't live this way because you have to. I happen to know for a fact you have a good job."

If he had danced around the obvious, Cash would have thought less of him. But Isaac had gone straight to the heart of the matter, and he sounded just interested enough.

Cash listed his reasons. "It's free, it was already here and it's close to my horses. That seemed like motivation enough at the time."

"You don't spend many hours here, I bet."

"I wish I hadn't spent last night. What'd it get down to? Ten degrees?"

"Not quite. But it was cold up at the house, too. Though not nearly this cold." He nodded in the general direction of the farmhouse. "Did you know we spent last night at Grace's?"

"Nobody mentioned it."

Isaac didn't seem surprised. Cash was sure Isaac knew that he and Jamie were nearly strangers these days.

"Your grandmother heard we were going to be in town, so she asked us to stay at the house instead of the cabin. Kendra's taking Jamie to the doctor this morning, so that made it easier."

"I bet you'll be glad when your house is all done and you can just move down here. You're in the county nearly as often as you're not."

"Did you know Jamie's considering moving into our place in Arlington at the end of the school year? She might look for a job with an architect in the area if she doesn't go back to Michigan to finish her degree right away. The schools are great, and she'd be close by."

"I didn't know."

"Do you need any help?" Isaac nodded toward the insulation. "Looks like a real do-it-yourself project."

"It's what we call a stop-gap measure." Cash tried for an easy grin, but it died. "I've got to get out of here. One day pretty soon I'll go to patch something and the whole place will turn to dust."

"Thoughts about where you'll go?"

"Lots of thoughts. Not a plan in the bunch."

"I bet you have a coffeepot. Mind if I find it and make some?"

"You don't have to stay. I can take care of this, then I've got to get ready to go."

"Actually, I just came down here to tell you that on the way to that doctor's appointment, Kendra's taking the girls to school, Jamie out to breakfast and Grace to the bee, so you don't have to get moving so fast. We have four-wheel drive, so they'll be fine. But now I'm intrigued. I'll go if you want me to, but I'd rather stay and help."

"Okay. Coffee would help most of all. Black and hot."

Cash heard Isaac rummaging around in the little galley kitchen. At least he had washed dishes and put food away last night. He cut another strip and tucked it in the gap between the floor and a baseboard. He was cutting one more when Isaac came back in with two steaming mugs.

Cash motioned to the sofa. Isaac sat, and in a minute Cash joined him, propping his feet on the newspaper-strewn coffee table.

Cash cupped his hands around the mug for warmth. "Things okay up at the house?"

"Jamie's about as tired of being pregnant as you'd expect. I think the girls are anxious to have her back the way she used to be, but she won't be quite that way ever again. She's got a lot ahead of her."

Cash didn't want to talk about Jamie, but unfortunately, he had opened the door himself. "She has, what, three, four weeks to go?"

"That's what they say. But it could be any day."

"Sooner would be better."

"I know you're upset about the decisions she's made."

"She's a grown-up." Cash hesitated; then he shrugged. "I put my nose where it didn't belong. I should have stayed out of things. It was her decision when to tell you and Kendra what was going on."

"Why did you?"

"Because she was making a mistake. I still think so."

"I don't know you that well yet, but I'd guess you don't go around mopping up after other people. I've seen you on the job site. You just expect the best and get it. If somebody screws up, they make good on it by themselves or they get the ax."

"This is her life."

"I've done a lot of research, talked to some friends who happen to be doctors. Nobody's as sure as *you* are that she did the wrong thing. Some of them thought her choice was commendable, maybe even correct."

"You ever watched somebody die up close? Ever been there holding their hand?"

Isaac thought about that a moment; then he held Cash's gaze. "I guess I've never been that lucky."

For a moment Cash couldn't believe what he'd said. A polite response eluded him.

Isaac took advantage of the silence. "I've never been close enough to anybody who was dying to be there at the end. My mother—my adopted mother—was living overseas, and nobody even told me she was sick until after she was gone. I've only been really close to one person in my whole life, and that's Kendra. Of course, I almost lost her because I wasn't very good at it."

"There's nothing *lucky* about watching somebody die."

"Maybe not, but there's something pretty amazing about loving somebody so much you have a right to be there. About that level of intimacy. About knowing they would be there for you if the situation were reversed."

"It's like having your flesh peeled off an inch at a time."

Isaac set his coffee on the table. "Jamie's not trying to die, you know."

"Did she send you here?"

"You're kidding, right? You think she needs an intermediary?"

Cash realized how foolish his question had been. Asking somebody else to speak for her was one of the last things Jamie would ever do.

Isaac sat quietly, as if the two of them had sat that way a million times throughout their childhoods. Cash wasn't sure he'd ever met anyone easier to be with.

Cash spoke at last. "I'm not sure anymore that this whole thing between us is really even about her."

"I'm sure it is, at least a little." Isaac hesitated. "But maybe it's a lot about your wife."

Cash wasn't surprised that Isaac knew. Jamie had probably told Kendra about Kary. That was what sisters did. And brothers, he supposed.

"Did your wife choose an option that hastened her death?" Isaac asked.

"Kary? Kary had no options. That's what makes me so angry. Jamie had options, and she didn't take them."

"I can understand that."

"Jamie says my whole life is about not feeling anything again."

"That's pretty harsh."

"Why the hell am I telling you all this?"

"You want an answer?"

Cash considered.

Isaac picked up his cup and held it out, as if in toast. "Because whether you want to or not, you *are* feeling things," he said. "And who better than your older brother to make sure you're thinking everything through very carefully?"

★ ★ ★

Grace hadn't expected to find friendship again in Shenandoah County. She most certainly hadn't expected to find it in the person of Helen Henry, or in Helen's comrades at the Shenandoah Community Church Bee. But find it she had. Perhaps if the women ever sat down together and made a list of things they believed or didn't, very few of Grace's own choices might match with theirs. But quilting cut through superficial differences, straight to the heart of what they did agree on. They were committed to beauty, to home and family—whatever form that took—to bedrock traditional values such as helping neighbors, creating something for others to enjoy, providing color and warmth in a world that always needed more.

So here she was, surrounded by women who had spent their lives in exotic places and women who had never been farther than a day's drive. To her left was Kate Brogan, a busy young mother for whom quilting was simply a much-needed diversion. To her right was Helen, who had confided she was going to enter another quilt in the Houston International Quilt Festival, just in case her entry was accepted again and she lived long enough to travel there at the end of the year. Young and old, accomplished and all-thumbs, sophisticated and plain-speaking, somehow it didn't matter. They had become her friends, her community, and she was finally at peace with her decision to live out the rest of her life in the county she had once despised.

Helen looked over her glasses at the women assembled around the bee's quilt frame and cleared her throat loudly. "Now, maybe I'm an old woman and don't know more than a thimbleful or two, but seems to me if we sewed more and talked less, we might finish this quilt this afternoon, before those babies arrive."

Most of the women nodded, then went right back to talking.

But Grace noted that they seemed to be quilting a little faster as they did.

For her part, she had finally confided to Helen that hand quilting was too difficult with her limited sight. Helen had solved that dilemma by basting several rows of straight lines using heavy perle cotton, and now Grace could feel exactly where her own stitches were supposed to go when things got blurry. She supposed if she lost her sight entirely one day, Helen would still find a way to make sure she remained useful.

"Jamie will love this," Grace said, to no one in particular. "It will mean the world to her."

"Girl's done so much for everybody else, she deserved a quilt all her own."

"Leave it to you, dear, to come up with the perfect block." Grace looked down at the quilt at her fingertips. She could still see well enough to get the total picture. Shining Hour was a traditional pattern. A nine-patch block, on point like a diamond, adorned the center of an eight-point star, with longer ribbon-like strips extending outward to connect the star to its neighbors, so that the effect was like an elaborately woven tapestry.

This was indeed Jamie's shining hour, something everyone in the bee had come to understand. She was giving the most unselfish of gifts and had become something of a heroine to the other women.

"And leave it to you to come up with colors I would never think about putting together," Helen said grudgingly. "But they work. I'll give you that."

Grace had wanted Jamie to think of spring and hope whenever she snuggled under the quilt. She thought of this as a comfort quilt, lap size and lightweight, for Jamie to carry with her during radiation treatments or later, if the doctors decided to add chemo for her breast cancer. The blocks were assembled in colors of mint-green, lavender, aqua and a peachy pink that was the color of the "ribbons" that wove throughout the pattern. The other women weren't aware of the cancer yet. They were concentrating on Jamie's generous gift to her sister, nine patient months of carrying Kendra's two little boys. They assumed the quilt was for use after the birth. Whenever and however Jamie used it, she would feel renewed.

Kate stood and stretched. "I'm sorry, but I've got to head home now. Rory will be back from school before long. But I did finish my section."

"Anybody else planning to stay and help me complete this?" Helen asked.

Dovey and Cathy said they would. Grace got to her feet reluctantly. "My grandson's coming to get me. But if you get the quilting all finished today, I can bind it this evening and get it ready to give her."

They made arrangements for Cathy to take the quilt up to Grace at the orchard if the roads were safe enough. Grace made Cathy promise to think of a good story in case Jamie was the one who greeted her at the door.

Grace went to get her coat. She couldn't remember a colder afternoon. That morning the roads had been icy slick, and she had been surprised that so many of the quilters had managed to make it in. The local roads looked fine now, but she suspected the ones going up toward the orchard might still be a problem. She was glad Cash was driving, and she hoped Jamie and the girls had made it home safely. She had called earlier, but nobody had answered. Jamie might well have been on her way out to the road to fetch Hannah from the school bus.

From a window overlooking the parking lot she watched for

her grandson's pickup, and didn't put on her hat and gloves until she saw him pull in. Cash was out of the truck and halfway to the church door by the time she got outside.

"A lot of quilting must have gone on today for you to be here this late," he said in greeting.

She gauged his mood. She had never thought of her grandson as easygoing, although he liked to project that impression. But he was a man who knew how to control his behavior, a fair man who thought through his responses, so it wasn't obvious to everyone that the high-spirited toddler and hot-tempered teenager still resided somewhere deep inside him. She supposed she loved Cash more for the way he had come to terms with both. She only wished he had also come to terms with the part that was so easily hurt—the tender, sensitive soul that had shriveled into something harder and less accessible as Kary faded away.

"We're making a quilt for Jamie, to commemorate what she's been through for the past months. But it's a surprise. It's called Shining Hour."

He was silent. She tried to interpret that and failed.

He held the pickup door and gave her a boost as she climbed in.

"Nobody knows about the cancer but me," Grace continued once he was backing out of the parking lot. "But the other quilters wanted to do something just for her. No matter what she says now, it's going to be hard when those babies go home in their mother and father's arms. We want her to remember what a gift she's given."

"Why are you talking about Jamie?"

"Because you won't. One of us has to." She expected him to refute that, but he didn't. With no other sign, she decided to call that positive.

"One of us happens to know something that the other doesn't, too," Grace continued. "Something else about Jamie. She's not going to tell you, so I guess it's up to me."

"What's up to you? More dark secrets? I'm afraid to ask."

"That's beneath you, dear. You're afraid to ask, yes, but only because you want to know everything there is to know about her, and that scares you. You love her, have for some time, and you're so frightened of it that you've shoved her out of your heart."

"That's pretty simplistic, don't you think? You've just reduced my whole life to country-music lyrics."

"I'll tell you what she's done. And I'll show you later, if you think you can look at it with any objectivity. She's drawn up a plan for the orchard."

Grace saw that she had surprised him. He glanced at her, and his expression made that clear. "What kind of plan?"

"A brilliant one, I think." Grace smiled.

"That's all you're going to say?"

"I'd like you to ask her about it. I'm sure if you worked on her, she'd show you the plans. She hasn't said so, but I know she had Rosslyn and Rosslyn in mind to do the developing."

"Developing?"

"Yes, developing."

"I might be missing something here, but aren't you against development?"

"The kind I've seen too much of, yes. Ticky-tacky houses with grandiose ideas about themselves crowded too close together. Developments with names like Mighty Oaks and not a tree in sight. But Jamie would never stoop to something like that."

"You're going to drag this out, aren't you? Because we both know I'm not in any position to ask Jamie anything."

"A position you put yourself in."

He was silent for the next mile. She hadn't gone into this

lightly and assumed his silence might continue the whole way, but finally he spoke again.

"My life is a mess, isn't it?"

Grace felt something too much like tears fill her eyes. "I wouldn't go that far. And Lord knows, you've had your reasons for not admitting what you feel."

"Tell me about the orchard."

"She's driven or tramped every bit of the land in the past months, even with the weather like it's been and those babies weighing her down. She's made so many notes, at times I wasn't sure Shenandoah County had enough paper to suit her. But she's done a rough plan that she shared with me a few nights ago. The idea is that there are places on the property that are really wasted now. Those views we've always taken for granted, terrain that doesn't lend itself to anything but trees, and many of those need to come down since they've been poorly maintained. She isolated six places where she thinks groups of seven or eight environmentally friendly houses could be clustered in such a way everyone would have views and some private space, but most of the land around them would be held in common."

"What about the apples?"

"Her plan would still leave perhaps sixty to seventy percent of the land as orchard, and it would be under a conservation easement so everyone would know up front that it could never be developed. Of course, that's just one of many selling points."

"What else?"

"She sees taking the old packing shed and turning it into a community space, something like a clubhouse with meeting rooms, a place for people to have parties, maybe a few apartments for guest overflow. One of the barns could be developed into studio space for local artisans. Some money from the sale of the homes would go into a common fund to hire skilled workers to manage and maintain the orchard. We might even get one of the universities to plant new varieties, do some small-scale experimentation, or develop strategies so we could eventually go organic. Anyway, residents would receive a share of the orchard profits, if there were any. She hasn't worked out all those details. But she wants to be certain everyone has something at stake for keeping the orchard producing and producing well. She wants residents to feel the orchard is their heritage, too. I think she wants them to feel the same kind of enthusiasm your grandfather and I always did."

It was a long speech, and still there had been more to Jamie's plan. Much more, but this was enough to give Cash both the gist and a lot to think about. She had thought of very little herself since Jamie made her presentation.

Cash's reaction was well protected. "Does she have any idea how much money it'll cost to do this? Because a development like she's imagining might make money down the road, and maybe even pay enough to maintain the orchard in the long run, but it's not going to make anybody the kind of fast, inflated profits they'd want to go ahead with so large an undertaking."

"Well, you'd be wrong there. Jamie has the money, you see. And she's already said she'd bankroll it."

"Why?"

"Because she can, dear. And because she sees it as doing her bit to save such a lovely piece of Shenandoah Valley history while giving more people access to it."

"Granny Grace, she's doing this because she wants to make *you* happy. Jamie wants to make everybody happy, no matter what."

"Yes, I suppose that's a great deal of it. But certainly not all. She's quite taken with the idea for its own sake. I know she sees it as a chance to let some of that considerable creativity of hers loose and make a name for herself. Of course, she'll need quite a lot of help. She's talented, but she's green, much the way I was when I had to assume responsibility for our land during the war."

Grace watched Cash slow considerably as he rounded a curve close to their turnoff. She felt the tires slip a bit as he hit a patch of ice, then recovered.

She waited until they were safely moving again before she finished.

"Jamie is one of those rare people who's willing to give whatever she can when the opportunity presents itself. She has her own reasons for that, of course. I believe she hit bottom at one point in her life, and from that moment on, she has felt incredibly blessed that she was one of the lucky ones who managed to climb back up. She wants forgiveness, yes, and friendship, but that's only the smallest part of it. She wants to give back. She feels so grateful that she was given a second chance, you see. The rest of her life will be about giving second chances to others, in whatever way she can, in whatever time she has. I can understand that so much generosity of spirit might be a problem for some men. But I can't believe that if you search your heart, you'll find it's really a problem for you."

"Everybody seems to understand me so well. Except me."

"I don't think this is about understanding yourself, John Cashel Rosslyn. It's about admitting what you know and moving forward again. You've been stuck in Neutral long enough."

"Jamie said we were done."

"Did you say something similar to her?"

"I did."

"Was it true?"

He sighed.

"Then I suppose we can assume that she may not have meant it, either."

Grace expected an answer. She didn't expect him to slam on the brakes. But suddenly the pickup fishtailed and nearly went into a ditch. Grace grabbed the dashboard, but before she could ask what was going on, Cash had thrust his door open and was leaping down.

She saw why. Hannah, with no coat or hat, was running down the road in their direction. The little girl barreled right into Cash's outstretched arms.

"Mommy's having the babies!"

Grace started to ask exactly what Hannah meant, but Cash had already taken charge. He hoisted Hannah into the pickup and thrust her at his grandmother. Then he jumped in, too. And in a moment, the pickup was racing toward the farmhouse.

36

Jamie had carefully thought through her afternoon. At ten she and Kendra had seen Dr. Raille, who was much more accommodating now that Kendra had been brought into the loop about Jamie's health. Her weight and blood pressure had been checked, her urine tested, the babies probed and pummeled through her abdomen. She had been asked about contractions—erratic and unreliable—the amount and quality of kicking and whether she would like to have labor induced now that the twins—at thirty-seven weeks—were more or less considered full-term for multiples. Both babies appeared to weigh at least six pounds. They were ready to be born.

With Kendra pushing to go ahead, Jamie had promised to sleep on it, but by the time her sister dropped her at home and drove down the mountain to get Alison, she had decided Kendra was right. The time had come, and scheduling the birth meant that everyone could be present, rested and prepared. She and Kendra had already gone to the two required childbirth seminars, which were old hat for Jamie but new for her sister. Nothing would be gained by delaying another week or two, and she could begin treatment for the cancer that much sooner.

When Kendra returned, Jamie called the doctor's office and received a promise that they would call tomorrow with a day and time. Then, once Hannah's bus arrived, Jamie, Kendra and the girls celebrated the impending birthday with mugs of hot cider, oatmeal cookies and a story about the day the eggs in Sister Duck's nest began to hatch.

After that, Kendra volunteered to stay until Grace returned from the Bee, but Jamie shooed her out the door. She had just seen the doctor, the girls were home, the phone was working and Grace was due back by late afternoon. She would rest, and Kendra, who was now looking shellshocked, could break the news to Isaac, who had been using the cabin for team-building meetings with some of his colleagues. Before too many more days went by, the Taylors would be holding their sons in their arms.

Jamie had been glad to see her sister's car drive away. She wanted time to herself for another reason, too. She was about to enter a new phase of her life. Nine months had passed, and in the next days, she would be handing over the fruit of those months to her sister and brother-in-law. She knew there would be an inevitable sense of loss; then, before she could even grieve, she would have to begin treatment for the cancer. Elisa Kinkade had made arrangements for her to see some of the area's most adept professionals, and she had already met with one. But there would be more appointments and decisions, and now that everything was right around the corner, she needed a chance to say a silent goodbye to the babies and to her past.

She curled up on the sofa with the girls, and while they

watched *E.T.* on video, she closed her eyes. The next thing she remembered was a sharp, all-too-familiar pain knifing through her, and a puddle forming beneath her.

Her water had broken, and she was in labor. Not gently or considerately, but with a vengeance.

At first she was sure there was no need to panic. Previous labors had taken at least half a day. She asked Hannah to bring her the telephone, only to discover the line was dead. She had used it earlier to call Dr. Raille's office and schedule the delivery. But that had been more than an hour ago. Had she thought to check it before dismissing her sister? She couldn't remember. Ice had formed at higher elevations, and not just on the roads. Trees had probably suffered, too. Had she or even Kendra been thinking clearly, they would have realized that, as the ice melted and branches and tree limbs snapped, lines that had initially worked might come down.

She explained why the sofa was damp, then left the girls to discuss this odd biological event while she went to shower quickly and change. The next few contractions were halfhearted, but closer together than she liked. The next few weren't halfhearted at all.

Dressed again, she remembered her cell phone and attempted to call out, but she knew it was a long shot. She rarely had luck with reception at the orchard. A month ago she'd spent part of one afternoon wandering the property trying various spots for coverage. She'd found one hilltop at the property's edge where she had been able to make a call. But if she went to all the trouble now of getting in the car to drive there, she might as well drive herself into town.

Except that labor seemed to be progressing at a speed that made both options sound like a bad idea.

Hannah joined her in the bedroom then, eyebrows knit in a

straight line, cheeks pale. Jamie tried to reassure her. Granny Grace would be home before long; then somebody would be here to take Mommy to the hospital. There was plenty of time. Mommy was just going to lie down for a little while. Then, if nobody came, she might drive to a neighbor's to see if their telephone was working. But Hannah wasn't to worry.

But Hannah *had* worried. After ten minutes of rest and two strong contractions, Jamie realized that she had to do something quickly. She got up, located her purse and keys and struggled into the living room to find her older daughter gone and her younger mesmerized by a bicycling E.T.

"Alison, where's your sister?" Jamie asked, trying not to gasp out the words.

"She went for Hep." Alison glanced at her mother.

"Who's Hep?"

Hannah had gone for help. For a moment Jamie felt weak, and not from the struggle inside her. Her daughter was outside, alone, on the coldest day of the year.

"We have to find her." Jamie went for Alison's coat and found Hannah's hanging on the peg beside it. Hannah was outside alone without protection. Another contraction began, and she forced herself to move through it, ignoring the all-too-familiar tightening of a womb trying to expel guests who had overstayed their welcome.

She grabbed Hannah's coat along with Alison's, and called her youngest daughter. A mutinous Alison took her time but finally came in to slip it on.

"I want to watch *E.T.!*"

"This is an emergency. The babies are coming. And we have to find Hannah."

"She's with Hep!"

"Help, Alison. She went for *help,* because the phone's not working. And she's not wearing her coat."

"Are you sick?"

Jamie felt sick. She felt weak and scared, and although she didn't have time to chart the contractions, they weren't getting any further apart. She was worried about Hannah, and at the same time, she was hoping that her daughter had managed to scare up one of the orchard employees. Unfortunately, she knew that was doubtful. January was the slowest time of the year, and she was pretty sure that the few permanent workers were off visiting their families or enjoying warmer weather farther south.

"I'm not sick, but I do have to go to the hospital." She pulled a stocking cap over Alison's untidy curls and threaded mittens through the sleeves of her coat. "We have to do it now. You have to listen and do what I say."

Alison's eyes were big as a full moon, and she nodded. Jamie grabbed Isaac's ski jacket and began to slip it on when a new contraction hit. She sucked in a breath and felt the room fade. She collapsed into the nearest chair and put her head in her hands. She had never experienced anything quite like this.

The door opened, and she looked up, afraid that Alison, like her sister, was going to take matters into her own hands. Instead, Cash strode in, Hannah bundled against his chest. He lowered her to the floor, and Hannah leaped across the room and threw her arms around her mother.

"It's okay now, Mommy. Everything is okay now. *Cash* is here. Cash can make *anything* okay."

Jamie looked up and saw the conflicting emotions in the okay-man's expression. "Can you get me to the hospital?" The words were hardly more than a whisper. "You won't have to stay. Kendra and Isaac will take it from there."

He knelt beside her; then he leaned over and kissed her gently. "Sweetcakes, not only will I get you there, nobody's going to pry me away. Not ever again. Whether you like it or not." He hesitated, then reversed himself. "Unless that's not what you want?"

She knew there were better times for reunions. She knew there was still so much to say. But she heard everything she needed in his voice and saw even more in his eyes.

"You're all I want." She took a deep breath, then another. "You and these…babies out of here."

He grinned, kissed her quickly again, then stood. "You got it, Miss Jamie. Let's go make that happen."

Happen it did. Not with the scientific intervention that had created two little embryos. Not with the fear that had dogged every step of the initial months. Not with complications, no matter how brief. Not with the emotional drama of those final weeks in utero. And not in the place where they had been scheduled to be born.

There had been no chance of making the trip to Front Royal in time. Once they'd driven down the mountain far enough to use Jamie's cell phone, Dr. Raille had ordered them to the hospital in nearby Woodstock, where she agreed to meet them as soon as she could. With Kendra and Isaac already in town, nothing could have worked out better.

Now there were just two babies—moments from being born, heart rates exactly where they should be—lined up as if they had an agreement to enter the world without fanfare.

"I told you…this was my greatest…talent!" Jamie told Kendra, in between pushes.

Kendra wiped her sister's forehead. Cash was holding one of Jamie's hands and Isaac the other. At first, she had been delighted to have so much attention—particularly Cash's—but now she wished everybody would go away and leave her alone. Experienced as she was, she knew this was a sure sign the first baby was about to make an appearance.

"I think one more push will bring some real results, Miss Dunkirk. You're doing great. Everything's going fine."

Jamie thought this was the most enthusiasm Dr. Raille had ever showed. Annoyed, she wondered if the doctor saved her skimpy personal store for these moments. Cash leaned over so she could see him.

"Are we having fun yet?" he asked.

"I am not having fun!"

"You're a brave woman. I would never, *never,* do what you're doing. I could have warned you. I've seen mares giving birth."

He was trying to make her laugh, and he almost succeeded. Then the next contraction began, and she closed her eyes and started to push, squealing at the effort.

"Head's crowning," Dr. Raille said. "Good, good, good! Now stop pushing."

"No!" Jamie puffed and panted, but managed to do as the doctor ordered as one of the delivery nurses looked on approvingly. Moments passed, and the contraction ended without a baby, but with enough pressure to make it clear one was nearly there. Now Jamie was panting from the exertion, and the sensation that she was being stretched wide enough to give birth to a colt herself. The labor had gone so quickly that she had opted to forgo drugs, the final gift she could give the twins. But now she was sorry she'd been so generous.

"I want this…done with!" she said, to nobody in particular.

Kendra wiped her forehead again. "I'm sorry, sis. I wish I could take over."

"You and me both!"

"Okay, this one will do it. Mrs. Taylor, come and watch. Don't push now, Miss Dunkirk, let the contraction do the rest of it."

"Easy for you to saaay!" Jamie gasped and closed her eyes.

Kendra sounded ecstatic. "Oh, look. Look!"

Jamie didn't look. She was concentrating too hard to pay attention to anything else.

"Open those eyes, sweetcakes," Cash said in her ear. "And watch your nephew make his appearance."

She did open them, just to shut him up, and in the mirror at her feet she saw the full miracle come to its natural conclusion. For a moment she forgot everything else.

"Well, it's a boy," Dr. Raille said, "although we're not surprised, are we?"

Jamie had seen enough. She closed her eyes, and for a moment she couldn't think of anything except how much better she felt. At least temporarily.

She heard a cry, lusty enough to make her smile weakly. At this point in her daughters' births, she had felt such a surge of maternal love that she had wanted to sit up and take the baby in her arms, even before the doctor had examined her. Now, for the most part, she felt drained. And cautious. Not simply because of the unique situation, but because she knew there was one more to go.

"Jamie, he's beautiful!" Kendra sounded far away. "I think he has curly hair."

"I had nothing…to do with that."

"Sure you did. You made it possible!"

Reluctantly, Jamie opened her eyes. Kendra and Isaac were hovering over the doctor, who had just finished cutting the cord.

"Let the nurse weigh him, but he looks great," Dr. Raille said. "I'm guessing he's at least six pounds. And his color's good. We'll let you have him in a moment."

Jamie started to respond; then she realized the doctor was addressing her sister. For a moment she felt disoriented, as if she had run a race and won first place, but somebody else was accepting the trophy.

Cash bent over her again. "I think I can steal him for a minute, if you want to hold him," he said softly.

She was touched that he had, without words between them, understood what she was feeling. "No...let Kendra and Isaac have their time with him."

He took her hand. "What can I do for *you?*"

"You said you would never...be caught dead in a delivery room."

"I said a lot of things." He smoothed back her hair with his free hand and planted a kiss on her forehead.

"You're not...just feeling sorry for me?"

He laughed. "I do feel sorry for you. I meant what I said. I don't know how the female of the species does what she does."

"Cash...I won't be doing this...ever again. You realize?"

"You don't have to. There're a couple of little girls up at Cashel Orchard who are pretty sure I walk on water. That's good enough for me."

She blinked back tears. "I'm sorry...I didn't tell you the truth right away."

"Apparently your instincts were good." He raised her hand to his lips. "I just don't want to lose you, Jamie. But from now on I'm planning to take every minute you give me."

"Plan on a lot...of those." She closed her eyes as Dr. Raille handed over the baby to his real parents and began the business of finishing one delivery so the next twin could be born.

"I'm right here," Cash told Jamie. "You rest up now. But I think the next one's going to be easier. You're all set to go."

"I'm going to hold you…to that."

"Just keep holding my hand."

The first twin was six pounds four ounces. The second was only slightly smaller. Both passed their physicals with cheers from the grandstand. They were not identical, of course, but nevertheless, everyone agreed there was a resemblance. The first did seem to have curly hair of Kendra's distinctive reddish brown, although not much of it. The second had lighter hair that might well be straight. But Jamie knew those markers could change, and quickly, as would the dark blue of their eyes.

Now, with the birth completed, Jamie was settled in a room with Cash for company, at least until the nurse came to send him home. There had been one awkward moment right after she'd settled in, when a lactation consultant had appeared to inquire if Jamie planned to nurse the babies. The woman was so determined to make Jamie understand that nursing twins was possible that it took a full minute to convince her the babies weren't really Jamie's after all.

"I had planned to pump milk for them," Jamie told Cash after she left. "Probably just for a month or two. But that's not in the cards now, not with what's coming up."

"You've done great things. Now your sister will make sure they get everything else they need."

Jamie wasn't sure what she felt. No day of her life had been filled with so many emotional moments. Cash's return. The births. The transfer of responsibility now that the twins were here.

Kendra and Isaac were with the babies in the nursery, and although that was right and proper, Jamie felt an emptiness she couldn't explain. After the second delivery, she had held each twin for a few moments, and cooed convincingly over their cute little noses and ears, but now she felt as if every part of her—except her rational mind—was demanding more.

"It's harder than you expected, isn't it?" Cash asked. He sat on the edge of the bed and handed her a tissue.

"It's hormones."

"That's what makes the world go round."

She blew her nose. "I can't imagine doing this, handing them over, then never seeing them again. At least these babies will be part of my life. My nephews."

"*Our* nephews." His laugh was low. "Let's try to explain *that* to the lactation lady and confuse her even more."

"I have my hands full with two kids."

"Yes, you do."

"They don't look one thing like me."

"If that really matters, poor little Alison is in trouble."

She laughed, but it ended on a hiccup. "Kendra and Isaac are going to be so happy."

"Already are."

"I really am a mess."

"You really are going to be fine. Which is good, because I think you're about to have visitors."

Jamie heard scurrying in the hallway. Before she could identify the sound, the door burst open, and Alison and Hannah darted in.

"We thought you might need a little company," Grace said from behind them.

"How did you get here?" Jamie asked.

"Sandra, of course. She's good for many things, including driving me anywhere I need to go. And for waiting patiently."

Jamie held out her arms, and the girls descended on her. Cash warned them to be careful, but Jamie didn't care. "*My* babies," she said. "Aren't you wonderful to come and see me?"

Alison climbed up on the bed. "We brought you a present!"

Jamie glanced up at Grace, who held out a lovely pastel quilt. "A gift from the Bee. I'm not finished binding it, since you just couldn't wait, but everyone had a hand in making and quilting it, and I wanted you to see it tonight. It needs washing to get the markings out, and some threads probably still need to be clipped, but I didn't think you'd care. It's called Shining Hour. And this evening was certainly yours."

This time Jamie couldn't choke back the tears. She clutched the unfinished quilt; she clutched the girls. She wiped her eyes. "It's so lovely. I'll treasure it."

"Of course you will."

"The babies are gone?" Alison patted her mother's abdomen, but carefully.

"The babies are with Aunt Kendra and Uncle Isaac. They're beautiful."

"Like Sister Duck's eggs!"

"Exactly."

"I planned to walk all the way down the mountain to find somebody to help," Hannah said. "All the way!"

"You're a heroine, Hannah Banana," Cash said, lifting her up in the air and depositing her carefully next to her sister.

Hannah leaned closer to Jamie and whispered in her ear, "Are you sad, Mommy?"

Jamie brushed a lock of Hannah's hair off her cheek. "A little. But I might be a lot if I didn't have you and Alison."

"We will make sure you stay happy. Although it might not always be easy."

"You don't have to do a thing. You just have to hang around. The rest will take care of itself."

"I can do that."

"I thought you could." Jamie kissed the top of her hair.

After a few minutes, Grace corralled the girls to take them to view their cousins, then home, and Cash was alone with Jamie again.

"I'll need to go in a few minutes, too," he said. "But the doctor told me, if everything goes the way she expects, you can go home tomorrow."

"I know. And the babies go home the day after."

"I'll come and get you whenever they say. And we'll take extra good care of you at home. Anything you want."

She lifted her arms, and he sat down beside her and drew her into his.

"I love you, Miss Jamie," he said softly.

Her heart was so full it was threatening to overflow. "Hey, I think you mean it."

"It's pretty darned hard to say."

"I know. It's mutual, which maybe makes it easier?"

He held her a little tighter. "That's a good thing. Because I'm not sure why you do, but I'll take that gift gladly."

After the nurse came to shoo him out, Jamie couldn't stop thinking about Cash. About the years ahead of them, and she knew there would be years. She would do everything she could to make sure of it. Years with Cash. Years with her daughters. Years with…her nephews.

She looked up as a soft rapping at her door grew louder. Then, as she watched, Kendra and Isaac came through, each carrying one of the babies. Behind them a nurse arrived, wheeling two little bassinets from the nursery.

"What's up?" Jamie asked, trying not to stare too hard or too greedily at the babies in their arms.

"We think you need some time alone with these guys," Isaac

said. "We'll be back in a while. But for now, we thought you might like a chance just to see what you've done and enjoy it. Alone."

"Oh..." She sniffed. "You're sure?"

Kendra came over to the bed and sat on the edge, placing one of the babies in her sister's arms. "This is Colin James. Colin, meet your wonderful Aunt Jamie." She smiled at her sister. "He needs to get to know the woman who's going to be so important in his future."

"Colin James." Jamie looked up. "James?"

"What better?"

Jamie loosened the receiving blanket to get a better look at her sleeping namesake. This was the baby with the curly hair, the first born. "Oh, he's so beautiful. What did you name his brother?"

"Logan John."

"John?"

"John for John Cashel Rosslyn. We think that next to us, you and Cash will be the most important people in the babies' lives."

Jamie sniffed. "I don't know what to say."

"Absolutely nothing. We'll be back in a while. When you get tired of holding Colin, Logan will be right here."

Isaac placed Logan in the bassinet; then he held out his hand to Kendra. She stood, bent down and kissed her sister's cheek, then her son's. Hand in hand, she and Isaac left the room, and neither of them looked back.

Neither of them looked back.

Jamie peeked down at the sleeping baby again and saw his tiny lips moving. She smiled, and she felt as if light had suddenly flooded all the dark places in her soul.

For the first time in a long time, she knew everything was going to be all right. All those months ago, she had made a choice. The right choice. Now these two beautiful children were starting their lives because of her.

And she *would* be part of those lives. Kendra and Isaac had walked out of the room without a backward glance, as if to say in no uncertain terms that they knew Jamie was part of their circle and always would be. They trusted her to be part of it, and they trusted her completely with their children. Together they—all of them—were a family in a way that, in the past, they had always been afraid to be.

She had accomplished exactly what she had set out to do. Finally, she could move on and forgive herself. And as she moved on, in the years that were left to her, she would never have to say goodbye. She would never have to let go of what she had accomplished or *any* of the people she loved.

"Hello, Colin James," she said, bending down to place a kiss right on top of the one his mother had given him. "Welcome to the world, little one. You and I are going to be great pals. It's a promise."

EPILOGUE

Grace was never sure which season at Cashel Orchard was her favorite. Summer was certainly a contender, with wildflowers on hillsides and apples fattening on sturdy orchard branches. So was autumn, the harvest season, with fruit in an artist's palette of deep reds and golds, heavy with juice on limbs bending gracefully with the weight. She loved the quiet of winter, with the leafless trees like snow-dusted skeletons, stark portraits against a slate-colored sky, with only the occasional cardinal providing color where apples had recently hung.

Then, of course, there was spring. Trees in blossom, their heady fragrance enlivening every inch of the land, acres of drifting blossoms carpeting orchard rows and promising a rich new season of possibilities. Spring was the season of hope, and for that reason alone, if prodded, Grace knew spring would have to be her choice.

Especially on a day like this one.

"Okay, girls. Have you said your goodbyes?" Grace asked Hannah and Alison.

"I think she will come back to visit," Hannah said. "I feel almost sure."

Grace didn't smile, although Hannah always gave her a reason. Instead she nodded solemnly. "I think she will, too. But we won't worry if she doesn't. It's time for Lucky to find a family of her own. A deer family."

Alison looked sad, her leprechaun face wrinkled in thought. "Who will feed her?"

"Lucky can feed herself. For a few weeks, though, maybe we'll put out a little hay in the woods, just in case it takes her some time to figure out what's good to eat and what's not."

Alison looked even sadder. "But now I'll be lonely."

The girls wouldn't be lonely for long. Earlier in the season one of Gig's prize bluetick hounds had sired a litter of puppies. Unfortunately, the mother was a beagle, but the puppies were adorable. Next week, after Lucky had been properly mourned, Jamie and Cash were planning to take the girls to pick out a puppy of their own. Since the girls would undoubtedly not agree on the choice, Grace suspected they would come home with two. For now, though, that was all still a surprise.

Grace dropped a hand to Alison's shoulder and squeezed. "Lucky won't be lonely. She's going to be so happy. She already has friends. Now, are you girls ready?"

"Wait! There's Mommy. And Cash." Hannah pointed toward the house.

Grace shaded her eyes and saw that Hannah was right. Jamie and Cash were coming down the hill, hand in hand. Jamie was wearing a bright Turkish scarf wrapped around her head turban style, with black pants and a royal-blue sweater. Cash was wearing a sports coat and khakis.

Nearly three months had passed since Colin and Logan's birth. Jamie and the girls were still living in the farmhouse, much to Grace's delight, and Cash was now living in the Taylors' cabin. The Taylors had finally moved into their new house, delighted to have their builder within hailing distance for whenever inevitable adjustments were needed.

After discussion with some of the area's best physicians, plus a trip to Houston for one final consultation, Jamie had begun a course of chemotherapy, followed it with thirty radiation treatments and would soon finish treatment with a final round of chemo. Surprisingly, the first time around she hadn't lost all her hair, although it had thinned considerably. She had cut it short to compensate, and this time around, she was resigned to being completely bald. Kendra and Grace had promised her a hat-and-wig party.

Jamie claimed that, after being pregnant with twins, the first round of chemotherapy had been easy. Grace knew it wasn't true, but she applauded Jamie's determination to make everybody believe it.

Jamie's prognosis was good. There were no guarantees in medicine, but all the signs were encouraging, all the statistics in her favor. She had the best care available, and had taken advantage of every bit of it, opting for the chemo as insurance. Just as soon as the second round was completed, she and Cash were going to plan a simple wedding, although Jamie insisted she wouldn't walk down the aisle without enough hair to anchor a veil.

Grace thought Jamie was really waiting for the Bee to stop fighting over what kind of wedding quilt they should make the happy couple. Helen wanted something traditional, but Grace was inclined toward abstract sprays of apple blossoms dotted with bright red crazy-quilt apples.

"I'm glad we didn't miss this," Jamie said, gathering her daughters close. "Of course, I'm sure Lucky will be back to visit."

"Want me to do the honors?" Cash asked his grandmother.

Grace nodded, and Cash opened the gate. Lucky looked around suspiciously, big brown eyes asking if this was a trick; then she ambled outside her paddock, as she had many times before. This time, though, if she came back, Lucky was going to find the gate closed. She no longer needed the sanctuary of the pen. She was ready to be on her own.

"Bye, Lucky, bye!" the girls called in unison. Unimpressed, Lucky loped off toward the woods. In a moment, the little doe was out of sight.

"Sam and Elisa are here," Jamie said, as if she knew the girls needed something else to think about. "Cash's dad and mom are here, too. Kendra and Isaac are the only ones missing."

Grace steered the girls in the direction of the house, and at the thought of what would certainly be an adoring audience, they ran off, floral skirts swirling around their legs and sandals flapping.

Jamie slipped a hand through Cash's arm, and together they followed in the girls' wake. "Kendra still doesn't have the hang of packing up two babies and getting them in the car."

"She needs a U-Haul for all the stuff she has to bring," Cash said.

"They're going to be late for their own christening. Before the twins, Kendra was never late for anything."

As if to prove Jamie wrong, a car's engine rumbled behind the crest of the hill leading down to the farmhouse.

Cash shaded his eyes to watch until the Taylors came into view. "Think they can manage on their own?"

"The boys, yes. All the stuff that comes along with them? No."

He kissed Jamie's cheek, untangled himself, then headed off to help Isaac and Kendra. Jamie tucked her arm in Grace's, and they followed at a slower pace.

"You feeling okay?" Grace asked.

"Just tired. But this is a glorious day for a glorious event."

Grace thought about everything that had transpired in the past year. Although most of the people here today weren't technically Ben's family, she thought he would have thought of them as such, just as she did, and learned to love them, too. As always, at important moments like this one, she missed him most of all.

When the path split, Grace turned toward the house. "Let's get you inside. Cash can help your sister all she needs."

Jamie didn't argue. Inside, she found a chair by the fireplace and chatted with Elisa Kinkade, who was dressed in a skirt and blouse made from Guatemalan fabrics. Grace's fingers itched to get more just like them to use in a quilt. She would call it *The Christening*.

"This place has seen lots of rites of passage, I bet," Sam Kinkade said, coming up to stand beside her.

Grace really liked her young minister, whose generous, thoughtful brand of Christianity had inspired her to begin attending the church with Manning and Sandra recently. Sundays had become a day she looked forward to.

"People have been born here. People have died." She winked. "And people have been created. I don't know that we've ever had a christening, though. Not during my sojourn."

"To everything there is a season."

"Sorry we're late." Isaac entered the house carrying one of the babies, who was dressed in a darling little denim suit, the citrus-colored Sister's Choice quilt tucked around him. Squinting, Grace thought this twin was probably Logan, although as the boys grew, their resemblance seemed to, as well.

Jamie held out her arms, and Isaac deposited his son in them without a word, heading back out to make another trip. Kendra arrived with the second twin wrapped in the other quilt, promptly pawned him off on Elisa and followed her husband back outside.

Minutes passed, more trips and commotion, and finally Isaac and Kendra came in to reclaim their sons.

Sam consulted with them; then he turned and motioned for everybody to gather around.

"While the boys seem happy..." He grinned. "Let's take advantage of it, shall we?"

Somebody applauded; somebody else laughed. Grace went to stand beside her daughter and clasped Sandra's hand. Manning looked stern, just the way he always did when he was feeling strong emotion, but when Sandra took his hand and squeezed, he leaned over and kissed her cheek. Grace had always been proud of her daughter, but never more so than now. Sandra had gracefully accepted Isaac into her little family and was outrageously fond of her new "grandchildren."

Kendra and Isaac went to stand at the front with Sam. Then, as Grace watched, Jamie and Cash, as the babies' sponsors, went to join them.

"It always gives me pleasure to welcome a child into the world," Sam began. "But I can truthfully say that I have never welcomed any that gave me more pleasure than these little boys, Colin James Taylor and Logan John Taylor, two precious and special children who were brought into this world by a miracle, the miracle of love passed from one sister to another."

Hannah moved closer and leaned against Grace's side, and Alison wormed her way to stand just in front of her. Grace felt her heart fill with emotion. She thought of the years when she had been sure she would never have the things she wanted or needed. Now, here she was, surrounded by riches beyond compare.

For a moment she felt Ben beside her, as she often did in this room. And she smiled.